her last chance

her last chance

ALISON RAGSDALE

bookouture

Published by Bookouture in 2021

An imprint of Storyfire Ltd.
Carmelite House
50 Victoria Embankment
London EC4Y 0DZ

www.bookouture.com

ISBN: 978-1-80019-366-6
eBook ISBN: 978-1-80019-365-9

For Rabs. Always and forever. You are the one.

The risk of a wrong decision is preferable to the terror of indecision.

—**Maimonides**

PROLOGUE

As I stand at the window of our new home, it's one of those rare summer days in the eastern Highlands when the sky is clear except for a wisp or two of cloud and a gentle breeze carries the brine of the North Sea up the hill to our garden. I'm watching you, Carly, my perfect girl, lying on the grass next to your father. You are like two multicoloured starfish, splayed out and trusting, open to the promise of the day, as you both hold still and wait for butterflies to land on your sun-kissed limbs.

I love you both with such force that it leaves little room for anything else inside me, and I treasure that, but that you, my angel, behind your smile, are dealing with something so dark and ominous twists me into knots. Now, as you wince and lift your palm to shield your precious eyes from the sun, I can't hold back the tears.

When I see you with your dad, so joyful and full of hope, my life feels complete, and the sense of calm that gives me eases the creep of fear, the reminder of the damaging sword that's dangling over us all.

If I let my guard down, try to believe that we are as we once were, a perfect family unit untouched by pain, and uncertainty, that's when the toxic question surfaces in the corner of my mind. I don't know where it comes from, but when it comes, it brings with it such a sense of foreboding, it stops my breath.

Today, as I watch you, I ask it of myself again, afraid to hear the answer. What if the unthinkable were to happen, and I had to choose between you, the two halves of my heart?

CHAPTER ONE

Ava Guthrie drew the car to a halt at the end of the long gravel driveway. It had been an easy drive from Aberdeen, despite the brutal rain that had followed them for much of the journey. Then, just north of Inverness, the clouds had melted away and a watery sun had emerged. It had felt like a timely welcome as they approached the outskirts of Dornoch, in the scenic eastern Highlands of Scotland.

On the final stretch of the trip, the jigsaw puzzle of fields they'd passed, separated by miles of drystone walls, and the stretches of trees edging the silvery water of the Cromarty Firth, all provided a trail of fond memories that Ava had followed as they drew closer to their destination.

Weary from three hours behind the wheel, Ava gathered her long strawberry-blonde hair into a twist and looked out of the window at the familiar place they would now call home. The March light was gently gilding the low, whitewashed croft house, somehow romanticising its sagging pitch roof and the row of poky windows flanking the peeling paint of the front door.

The fence at the perimeter of the front garden remained only in portions, and the cobbled path was moss-covered, with several stones missing. The sign that had stood proudly at the end of the drive, bearing the name Loch na brae, that Ava's father had told her meant Inland Water, was now propped up against the side of the house, the lettering faded and the post rotten, and frayed at the end.

All these timeworn elements, rather than sadden Ava, made up a picture of such beauty that she couldn't help but smile. As she took it all in, a slew of memories of childhood summers spent here visiting her grandmother, Flora, flooded back, drawing Ava's throat tight. So much love and laughter had pumped through the veins of this little home, it was hard to believe it had stood empty for almost a year now, since her beloved gran had passed away.

Bound by their shocking, mutual loss of Ava's parents eighteen years earlier, when she had just turned twenty-four, and right before her wedding, Ava and Flora's bond had gone deeper than a typical grandmother and granddaughter.

The freak boating accident had happened in the Greek islands, the first time Ava's delicate, and often fearful, mother had thrown caution to the wind and let her boat-loving husband persuade her to join him on a sailing trip. Her parents' holiday of a lifetime had ultimately ended their lives and the irony of that would never leave Ava, but losing Flora had been just as devastating a blow.

Letting the rush of memories, and an accompanying prickle of pain, settle for a few moments, Ava shook her hair loose. Her husband Rick was fast asleep next to her, a gentle snore escaping with each exhale, and, in the back seat, her ten-year-old daughter Carly was hunched over her iPad, the hood of her rainbow-patterned sweatshirt pulled low over her forehead.

'We're here.' Ava unclasped her seat belt. 'Hey.' She nudged Rick, whose chin was on his chest. 'Wake up, MacSnorey.' She laughed softly as he lifted his head and yawned.

'Sorry, love. Couldn't stay awake for that last half-hour or so.' He stretched and rubbed a palm over his dark, close-cropped head, his hazel eyes glinting in the afternoon light.

'Apparently.' Ava prodded his thigh.

'We made it, then.' He dipped his chin and peered out of the window. 'The old place doesn't look that bad.' He smiled at her. 'Home sweet home, eh?'

Ava nodded, then turned to look at her daughter. Carly's face was only inches from the iPad, its dark edges almost obscuring her cornflower-blue eyes, duplicates of Ava's own. Under her hood, her long hair fell over one cheek, like a golden curtain, while on the other side, it was tucked neatly behind her ear.

'Carly, can you please hold that thing further away from your face? You'll damage those beautiful peepers,' Ava huffed. 'And you don't need your hood up in the car.' She shook her head.

Carly set the iPad on her lap and pulled a face as she shoved her hood back. 'But I can't see it properly, otherwise.'

'Well, if you really can't see it without almost licking it, I think you need to have your eyes tested.' Ava frowned.

Carly glowered. 'I don't need glasses, Mum. I'm just tired.'

'Well, we'll see.' Ava tipped her head to the side. 'Come on. Put it away and let's go inside.' She gestured towards the house. 'You can get settled in your new room.'

Rick unfolded his long frame out of the car, and stretched his back, like a languorous cat. 'First thing on the agenda is a decent cup of tea, then we'll get cracking on the unpacking.' He winked at Carly, who had emerged from the back seat and stood in the driveway, her backpack slung over her shoulder. 'Last one inside is a nutcase.' He laughed, as Carly, seeing his face, dashed for the front door.

Ava climbed out of the car, the familiar smell of wet pasture mixed with the heady brine of the nearby Dornoch Firth, a force that made her close her eyes for a second. The land sloped gently away from the garden in front of the croft, providing an undisturbed view of Dornoch Beach below. The pristine sand formed a honey-coloured strip along the edge of the dark water of the firth, as it leaked inland from the North Sea. The moody estuary stretched between the Highland districts of Easter Ross and Sutherland, its evocative image awash with memories of summers spent walking on the sand with her gran. This whole place was alive with images of Ava's childhood, tumbling in on each other as she breathed the dewy air.

As she soaked in the scene, suddenly she was Carly's age again, picking wild strawberries with Flora until her fingertips were scarlet, then watching her gran stir the vats of jam she produced every year. The memory of the sweetness of the strawberries made Ava's mouth water.

Licking her lips, she slid the strap of her handbag across her body and watched her husband and daughter, wrestling to get nearest to the door. 'You're *both* nutcases.' She laughed, dangling the big brass key from her forefinger. 'No one gets in, without me.' She slipped in front of them and put the key into the lock.

The heavy door swung open and both Rick and Carly shoved past her, jostling each other as they burst into the beamed living area. The noise of their laughter warmed Ava as she hesitated on the stone step. 'Rick, I'm going to walk up to the barn, I'll be in in a minute,' she called after them.

'Righto,' he called back as she turned and made her way around behind the house, her feet crunching on the gravel path that linked the main dwelling with the outbuildings, such as they were.

Two small stone structures crouched low, near the side fence, one with a shabby thatched roof and the other gaping, open to the sky. Flora had used the thatched building to house her loom, and Ava had loved to sit on a rickety stool, with her back against the cold stone wall, and watch her gran deftly moving the shuttle back and forth. Flora would guide the myriad threads to her own patterns, clicking her teeth as she wove naturally dyed wools into pretty blankets and shawls that she sold to the Highland Clothing shop in town.

Reaching the old barn, Ava turned to take in the view of the distant water and slice of golden beach that she'd appreciated so many times over the years. As a pair of seagulls banked and cawed overhead, and the crisp breeze plucked at her hair, Ava let her surroundings soak in, her sense of being exactly where she was meant to be seeping into her bones.

Inheriting Loch na brae had not come as a surprise, as Flora had always said it would be hers one day. But when they'd come up to check on the property four months ago, she'd been shocked by Rick's suggestion that they uproot and move here, from Aberdeen.

'Think about it, Ava. We could renovate the barn. Turn it into a great self-catering cottage. There's room for at least three bedrooms on the upper level.' He'd held his architect's hands up, framing the forlorn building between his thumbs. 'Can you picture it?' He'd grinned at her, the puppy-like way that stopped her heart, even after fourteen years of marriage.

'Oddly, no I can't.' She'd suppressed a smile. 'And even if I could, it'd cost a fortune, and then how would we earn enough money to keep it all going, if we're here permanently?'

Rick had laughed. 'Look, the place has got such good bones.' He'd smiled at her. 'Just like you and me.' His way of describing their relationship had tugged at her heart, and she'd taken his hand and pulled him closer. 'I could take some time off from the practice, and we'll spend a few months renovating – turning this into a moneymaking enterprise, for a good part of the year at least. We'd make a killing during all the golf tournaments at Royal Dornoch, too.' He'd raised his eyebrows. 'Then, I'll set up an office here and work remotely for most of the week.' He'd eyed her. 'It's only three hours from Aberdeen, and I'm sure I can rejig my schedule to make it work.'

Ava had not realised how serious he was until he'd spoken about taking time away from his architectural firm. Aside from herself and Carly, his company was the love of his life, and the idea that he'd put that on hold, if only for a few weeks, was startling.

After several conversations, a few bottles of wine and some panicked phone calls to her best friend, Jenna, Ava had finally begun to come around. 'So, *if* we consider this, Rick, how will Carly cope? It'll be a huge upheaval. A new school, no friends to begin with, and a lot less for her to do than here.' She'd quizzed him in the kitchen of their home, in Aberdeen's West End.

'She'll adjust. And think how great it'd be to bring her up at the croft. Surrounded by all that nature, actual fresh air, and the beauty of the place her mum's people hail from.' Rick had pressed her, 'Ava, come on. You do most of your graphic design work from home anyway, and I'll do whatever I have to, to make it work.' He'd wound his fingers through hers. 'What do you say?'

She'd taken a few days to consider the idea, and each morning, as she went on her run around the streets of the city, she'd begun to look at the grey granite buildings and the murky pre-dawn light a little differently.

One particularly drizzly morning, she'd been jogging past William Wallace's statue, blowing on her frigid fingers as she dodged two passing cars. As she'd headed for the Art gallery on Schoolhill, where, until recently, one of Carly's miniature cityscapes had hung as part of the Young Artists of the North exhibition, Ava had had a revelation. The painting had shown the centre of the city, in a muted pallet of greys and browns. Even the sky had been a shade of blue that had seemed weighted with the threat of rain. Ava had suddenly longed for the unique and magical light of Dornoch, and the way it played on the peaks of the dark water of the firth, knowing that light would provide Carly with so much beauty to capture in her painting.

While Ava had been happy in Aberdeen, the knowledge that her beloved Loch na brae stood empty now, the weather eating at it, with no one to protect and love it as it deserved, weighed on her heart. As she'd pictured the little croft house and the ramshackle barn on the hillside overlooking the beach, she'd craved the salty breeze, the feel of dewy grass under her bare feet, the musty smell of leaf mulch and the fragrant lavender that Flora had always planted either side of the front door. As Ava had wiped the mist from her face and turned at the gallery, headed for home, she'd made her decision.

Having told Rick that she was on board, and him delightedly sweeping her off her feet in a rib-crushing hug, they'd sat Carly down and asked her how she'd feel about leaving Aberdeen.

'What about school, and Mandy, my painting, and horse riding?' She'd slumped back on the sofa and pouted, her chin beginning to wobble. 'My art teacher will have a fit if I leave. She says I need to think about going to serious art school,' she'd whined.

Ava had been about to console her when Rick had jumped in. 'Look, we'll find you a great school up there, and a new riding stable. We could maybe even get you some private art lessons. And there's so much beautiful scenery for you to paint.' He'd stuck his bottom lip out comically, mimicking Carly's expression. 'Mandy can come and visit all the time. She'll love the beach.' After a few moments, seeing that he hadn't won her over, he'd pulled the ace out of the pack. 'With all that space, and a proper garden, we could even talk about getting a dog.'

Ava's mouth had dropped open as she'd tried to catch his eye, dragging her hand across her throat in a cutting action. He'd gone too far offering a dog, but now, seeing Carly's newly rapt expression, Ava knew she'd been beaten before she could even object.

The following week, they'd put their house on the market and begun making plans.

Now, as Ava leaned her head back, letting the damp of the approaching mist coat her face, she heard Carly's voice.

'Mum. Where are you?'

Ava pulled the zip of her jacket up under her chin and started walking down the path towards the house. Just as she rounded the corner of the building, she saw Carly stumble over a large stone that sat at the edge of the path, lose her balance and topple onto her side in the damp grass, her scarlet tights garish against the grey-green of the lawn.

'Jeepers.' Carly, using Rick's favourite expression, looked momentarily shocked, then, to Ava's relief, began to laugh. 'Who left that there?' She pulled her legs under her and brushed some mud from her tights. 'Didn't see it.' She looked up at Ava and shrugged.

As Ava rushed over, helped Carly up and assessed her for damage, a tiny mite of worry started burrowing into Ava's middle. 'Good grief, sweetheart. You need to be more careful.' She brushed some grass from Carly's coat and then cupped her daughter's narrow chin in her palm. As she looked deep into Carly's eyes, she noticed the shadows under them, then the left eye twitched. It was only for a split second, but Ava caught it, the odd movement alarming. 'Are you OK, love?' She frowned and held Carly's chin until the child pulled away.

'I'm fine.' Carly gave a half-smile. 'Dad says to come in. He's made tea.'

Unconvinced, Ava hesitated, then putting what she'd seen down to fatigue, she smiled. 'All right. Come on then, Flopsy. Let's get inside before the rain really comes on.' She looked up at the ominous sky.

Carly took her hand. 'I hope Dad's found something to eat. I'm starving.'

Ava laughed. 'For a change.' She let Carly lead her inside and then closed the door on the approaching clouds.

The airy kitchen had a warm glow, the old kettle steaming on the Aga, and Flora's willow-pattern tea service laid out on the scrubbed wooden table. Next to the teapot lay a packet of chocolate biscuits that Rick had thrown into the car that morning as they were leaving, and he sat at the head of the table, smiling at her.

'Please sit, m'ladies. Tea is served.' He swept a hand above the offering on the table.

Carly tugged a heavy chair out and sat down. 'Pass the milk, Dad.' She flicked her hair over her shoulder as Rick's eyebrows jumped.

'It's right in front of you, kiddo.' He pointed at the little jug sitting in front of Carly's cup. 'Right there.'

Carly lowered her chin and, as Ava watched, seemed to rotate her head slightly, as if trying to find a point of focus. 'Oh, right.' She giggled and drew the jug towards her.

A chill crept through Ava as she pictured Carly, lying on the grass, just moments ago, and she tried to catch Rick's eye. When he finally looked up at her, the smile slipped from his face and his eyes were questioning. She shook her head, almost imperceptibly, but he seemed to get the hint, so sipped some tea, then pushed his cup away.

'Right, you enjoy your tea while Mum and I get the bags in from the car before the heavens open.' He pushed his chair away from the table and locked eyes with Ava.

Grateful, Ava turned her collar up. 'Back in a jiff.' She smiled at Carly, who had pulled her iPad out of her backpack, seemingly oblivious to the fact that they were leaving the room.

Out in the driveway, Rick opened the boot and began pulling their suitcases out. 'So, what's wrong?' He frowned. 'I know that face.'

Ava forced a swallow, trying to push down the inner voice that was whispering, warning her that something heavy and ominous was coming, something that matched the bank of black clouds that were now gathering on the horizon, over the firth. 'I don't know, Rick. It's just a feeling…' Her voice trailed. 'I think there might be something wrong with Carly.' A deep sense of foreboding sucked at Ava's middle as he stopped what he was doing and turned to face her.

'Wrong? What do you mean?' He squinted at her.

'I'm not sure.' Ava shook her head. 'But I think there's something going on.'

'Ava, you know how you get about this stuff.' He frowned. 'You're probably just overreacting.'

'Don't patronise me, Rick. I know what I saw,' she snapped, as her heart began to tick under her breastbone. Whenever he dismissed her concerns this way, it brought back sad memories for Ava that she had no space for right now. She needed to focus on her daughter.

CHAPTER TWO

Two days later, the moving van had just left, and Rick and Ava were knee-deep in boxes. The larger pieces of furniture they'd brought were vaguely in the right spots, including Carly's brand-new double bed. The leather sofa now separated the long living room into two sections, their dining table and chairs sitting behind it, near the opening to the kitchen, and two soft armchairs flanking the stone fireplace at the far end, above which they would install the TV. Ava's old fisherman's trunk would serve as a coffee table, and three of Flora's antique floor lamps cast light into the darker corners of the room.

Ava had suggested Carly take the smaller of the two rooms to the right of the kitchen, as it had the largest window, overlooking the side garden. She'd told Carly that it had always been her favourite room as a child, and that if she opened the window and looked to the right, she could see a strip of the beach. Carly had gladly accepted, excited to be on a different floor to her parents for the first time and to be the closest to the main bathroom.

Rick had designed and built an ingenious corner desk that sat under the window, with plenty of storage for Carly's numerous art supplies, and a special platform for her easel so she could make the most of the light as she painted.

Ava and Rick's room was the only living space on the upper level. Three years earlier, with some planning help from Rick, Flora had updated the kitchen and central heating system, installed a narrow staircase, and had the roof opened up at the back of the house. By adding two dormer windows, they'd created a spacious master bedroom, with a characterful pitched ceiling and an en-suite shower room, in what had been the attic space. Ava had questioned the wisdom of such a significant investment for her gran, undertaking a dramatic renovation at that stage of her life, but even as she'd tried to talk Flora out of it, deep inside, Ava had known that her gran was preparing Loch na brae for Ava and her family.

Now, as she walked across the wide-planked floor of their new bedroom, Ava caught the citrus scent of the cedar chest that sat in the corner, housing various woven blankets and throws that Flora had made for her over the years. As she opened the lid to add a moss-green shawl that she loved, Ava's conscience prickled. Flora had never procrastinated when it came to matters of health, perhaps as a result of having a daughter with serious issues, but in the two days since they'd been here, with all the activity around settling in, and getting some painting done before their belongings arrived, Ava hadn't registered with a doctor yet. As she'd hovered around Carly, watching her move easily around the house and garden, Ava's fears had begun to subside, until this morning.

Carly had been in her room, hanging up the last of her clothes in the narrow pine wardrobe that stood against the wall. Checking on her progress, Ava had tapped on the door. 'Can I come in, love?' She'd hovered in the doorway, admiring the freshly painted, sunny room, as the morning light filtered in the window and cast a chequered pattern on the wooden floor.

'Yep.' Three hangers with long, brightly patterned shirts on them were hooked over Carly's index finger. 'I'm nearly done.' She'd smiled at her mother. 'Just got to hang these up.' She'd moved towards the wardrobe and, before Ava could yelp a warning, Carly walked straight into the edge of the open door.

'Oh, love.' Ava had rushed over, taken the hangers from Carly's hand and eased her onto the edge of the bed. 'Let me see.' She'd dropped the shirts, brushed the hair from Carly's face and looked at the pink line already forming across the narrow, freckled forehead. 'What's going on, Carly?' Her throat had knotted, as tears had begun to well in her daughter's eyes. 'Come on, sweetheart. You can tell me.' She'd sat next to Carly, pulling her thin frame in to her side.

Carly had blinked several times, then tucked her hair behind her ears. 'I don't know Mum.' She'd taken a shaky breath. 'I can see spots. Like these weird black spots when I look at something.' She'd pointed ahead of her and drawn a circle in the air.

Ava had felt as if the walls had shifted in closer to them as she'd taken a steadying breath. 'Are the spots there all the time, or just sometimes?' She'd edged away from Carly and turned to face her.

'It was usually just in the morning, when I woke up. I thought I had sleep in my eyes, or maybe dust or something.' Carly had sniffed. 'But now it's all the time.' She'd looked up at her mother, and the fear Ava had seen in her sweet daughter's face had threatened to choke her.

Nodding, to give herself a second to compose herself, she'd slid off the bed and knelt in front of Carly. 'Let me see if I can see anything.'

She'd gently tilted Carly's chin towards the window. As the light filled her eyes, Carly had flinched slightly, but the sky-blue irises had looked clear. Aside from the film of tears, there had been nothing unusual to see. Then, it had happened again. The left eyeball had twitched, a tiny but unmistakable movement.

Her insides flip-flopping, Ava had stood up and raked the hair away from her face. 'I can't see anything, love, but I think we should get you tested. Just in case.' She'd found a smile. 'You know, Daddy had to wear glasses for a couple of years, at your age, so if you need them too, for a while, it's not the end of the world, right?'

Carly had shrugged. 'I suppose not. But if I do, maybe I can get contacts?' She'd sounded hopeful, the innocence of her statement tugging at Ava's aching heart.

'Sure, sweetheart. We'll ask the optician.' She'd beckoned to Carly. 'Come and have some lunch. We can finish this later.'

As Carly had followed her into the kitchen, she'd tugged Ava to a stop. 'Can we change the bulb in that bedside lamp in my room, Mum? It's so bright, it hurts to look at.'

Ava had nodded, deliberately keeping her voice level. 'Of course, love. We'll find you something else.'

Now, Ava folded the shawl and slipped it into the chest. She'd managed to get an appointment for Carly with an optometrist, in nearby Tain, for the following morning. All she had to do now was focus on staying calm, try not to alarm her daughter, and manage the creep of anxiety that was filling her chest like hardening cement.

Startling her, Rick came up behind her, his arms circling her waist. 'Are you OK?' His coffee-scented breath brushed her cheek.

'Yeah.' She leaned back against his broad chest. 'Just trying to stay busy.'

He turned her gently to face him, his eyes warm as he pulled her into a hug. 'It's probably nothing. Try not to worry.' He kissed her forehead. 'We'll take her in tomorrow and I'm sure it'll be the same thing as me. Glasses for a couple of years to sort out whatever is going on, then she'll be right as rain.'

His words, rather than calming, left her feeling empty. Once again frustrated at his tendency to dismiss her concerns where Carly's health was concerned, Ava gently eased out of his arms. 'I'm not so sure.' She ducked past him and lifted a pile of shirts from the bed. 'I'm trying not to freak out, but if you'd seen the way her eye moved, Rick. It was bizarre.' She avoided his gaze and stuffed the shirts into a deep chest of drawers, sitting under the window.

Rick walked over and took her hands in his. 'Look, I'm not trying to make light of this.' A slight frown creased his brow. 'But you know how you are when it comes to her health. Remember when she was three, and she tripped over that plastic car and broke her pinkie?' He eyed her. 'Or when she was five, and she twisted her ankle at the park, and you thought she'd broken it? Both times you were convinced she'd inherited your mum's brittle bone disease.' He shrugged. 'Carly turned out to be fine then, and she will now.'

'That's completely different, Rick.' Ava pulled her hands back. 'And I had every reason to be worried, until we had her tested. You know how much that illness affected Mum's life. Well, all of our lives.' She turned away from him, leaned down and smoothed the duvet, a picture of her mother forming in her mind: Helen's birdlike frame, her turquoise eyes, huge and fearful. Ava's father, Jack, a ruddy-faced oil engineer with a heart of gold, would soothe her mother as she fretted over every tiny obstacle to her progress – a small tree branch, an unseen pothole in the pavement, a camber in the path that might cause her to trip and fall.

Each time this happened, Ava would retreat, hanging back, wishing that her gran had been with them to steady Helen's nerves, like no one else could. Flora was physically robust and hearty, the antithesis of her daughter, a cruel contrast that had plagued Ava until the day her parents had died.

Snapping her out of her memories, Rick continued, 'Look, all I'm saying is that whatever it is, we'll figure it out. We always do.'

Needing them to be united more than she needed to be right, Ava let her irritation go and moved into his arms. 'I know.' Her voice hitched. 'But she's our baby, and if there's anything…'

'Trust me. I'm sure it's nothing terrible.' He lifted her chin with his forefinger. 'It'll be all right.' He leaned in and kissed her, his mouth warm and insistent.

Giving in to the comfort of his lips, she kissed him back, a surge of love for her optimistic husband wiping away some of her anxiety. 'You're a pain in the rear, Rick Guthrie. But I love the bones of you.' She burrowed her head into his neck, sensing the smile returning to his face.

'Me too.' He squeezed her waist, then lifting her chin with his forefinger, he whispered, 'Always and forever. You are the one.'

As they stood still, lost in the moment, Carly's head appeared around the door. 'Oh, yuck. Do you have to?' She pulled a face, but Ava caught the smile Carly was suppressing. 'You two are so gross.'

Releasing Ava, Rick made to chase Carly away. 'Cheeky monkey.' As Carly turned to leave, he grabbed her and lifted her off her feet. 'Now, who's turn is it to make the tea, I wonder?' He laughed as she struggled in his grip.

'Get off, you nutter.' She giggled. 'If you let me go, I'll make some.'

Rick set her down and ran a hand down his thigh, then began limping dramatically towards the stair. 'Hurry up, then. It won't fix this bum leg of mine unless it's good and strong, and there'd better be a biscuit, too.'

Behind Rick, Ava moved quickly out into the corridor. She didn't want Carly handling the steaming kettle alone, so she tugged at his sleeve. 'I think it's my turn, actually.' She gave him the look that said, *listen to me,* and after a second, her message hit home.

As Carly began to walk down the stairs, Rick moved lithely down next to his daughter and took her hand. 'Looks like you're off the hook, kiddo.' He grinned at Carly, who leaned into his arm. 'It's Mum's turn.'

'Oh, goodie.' Carly laughed. 'Saved by the bell.'

Ava closed the bedroom door behind her and, with a shadowy memory appearing of her own mother hovering behind her on the stairs, Ava followed her husband and daughter, that unsettling sense of foreboding back, prickling under her breastbone, like a thousand needles circling her heart.

CHAPTER THREE

The following morning, having forgotten about the arrangements he'd made, Rick had said he needed to stay behind to wait for the carpenter and electrician, who were due to start work on the barn. Frustrated, but too worried about being late to argue, Ava had made tea to-go and then herded Carly into the car.

Twenty minutes later, having found a handy parking space near the centre of Tain, they walked past the ornate wrought-iron gate to The Pilgrimage, a seventeenth-century schoolhouse in the churchyard of St. Duthac Collegiate Church. The sight of the pretty gate instantly took Ava back to her childhood, and her gran's rosy cheeks puffing with pride as she told Ava about this small royal borough's rich history.

Hoping to distract her obviously anxious daughter and defaulting to her habit of talking too much to fill a silence when she was nervous, Ava pointed at the handsome church, with its impressive turrets and spires. 'King James the fourth of Scotland made lots of pilgrimages to the shrine of St Duthac, in the fourteen and fifteen hundreds.'

Carly walked on, nodding silently.

'It's one of the most beautiful medieval churches in the Highlands.'

Getting no response and wanting to bring Carly back from wherever her thoughts had taken her, Ava tried a different approach.

'It's kind of like Hogwarts, but on a smaller scale.' She nudged Carly's arm, but she simply grunted, her palm at her forehead as she shielded her eyes from the morning light.

Disappointed, but knowing her daughter, and sensing that silence was best for now, Ava gently took Carly's hand, pleasantly surprised when she didn't pull away, as had become customary since she'd turned ten.

They walked along Tower Street, the light breeze bringing with it the rich smell of roasting coffee, and something sweet that Ava couldn't identify, then they turned onto the cobbled High Street. The sweep of pretty sandstone buildings on either side of them, with their gently arched windows, and glistening slate rooves, led them naturally to the optometrist's office.

Doctor Harris was a soft-spoken man with an easy manner. Approximately in his late forties, with a close-cut beard, he wore thick glasses.

Despite her mounting nerves, and wishing he would just get on with things, Ava had also been grateful that he'd taken time to talk with Carly for quite a while before beginning her eye tests.

Carly had seemed calm and comfortable, explaining what she was experiencing. The testing had taken around twenty minutes. Doctor Harris had invited Ava to sit in with them, and she'd perched on the edge of a chair in the corner of the room, the darkness allowing her to release her strained smile, as the rise of dread and failing optimism battled inside her.

Now, the doctor rolled his stool away from the examination chair, stood up and switched the light back on. 'Well, Carly, that wasn't too bad, was it?' He smiled as she shook her head. 'Top marks for patience.' He looked over at Ava and, just before he turned his attention back to Carly, Ava saw the flash of something behind his smile that made her breath hitch. 'If you'd like to wait out in reception, Carly, I'll have a wee chat with your mum, and then we'll come and join you.' He gestured towards the door.

'OK. Thanks.' Carly looked over at Ava, who pulled her shoulders back, found a smile and nodded, then Carly walked out into the brightly lit corridor. As Ava watched her go, Carly lifted a hand to her forehead, shielding her eyes as she made her way back to reception. Seeing that movement again, icy talons clawed at Ava's insides, and when she turned to face the doctor, his expression spoke volumes. She'd been so sure that, this time, Rick was wrong, and even as she wished he was here, holding her hand, a flash of anger both at his absence and his habitual dismissal of her concerns sliced through her.

'Please, have a seat, Mrs Guthrie.' He gestured towards the chair that Ava had just risen from.

Her mind catapulting between various grim scenarios, she sat down and hugged her handbag against her middle, wanting some form of shield against whatever grenade he was about to toss into her lap.

'She's a lovely girl.' Doctor Harris leaned forward on the stool and linked his fingers between his bony knees. 'I don't want to alarm you, Mrs Guthrie, but I'm going to recommend that you take Carly to a specialist – an ophthalmologist in Inverness – for further testing.' He paused, as a deadly avalanche of dread began to bury her from within. 'I'm seeing some flecks, some discoloration on the retina, that concern me.'

Ava exhaled, her heart thumping wildly. Trying to make sense of what she was hearing, and angry that she was facing whatever this was alone, she frowned.

'These kinds of flecks are sometimes called age pigments, and they can be an indication of problems with the macula.' He scanned her face, waiting for her to acknowledge what he was saying. As his words began to take root, and in danger of lunging at him and screaming 'You're wrong, there's nothing wrong with my daughter,' Ava held her breath. 'Please remind me how old Carly is again?' He sat up and lifted the chart that lay on the counter next to him.

'She's t-en.' Her voice cracked, so she cleared her throat. 'Ten.'

Doctor Harris set the chart down. 'I can't say for sure, until further tests can be carried out, but this could, and I stress *could*, be Stargardt's disease.'

At the word *disease*, Ava's anger disintegrated, and she was overcome by a wave of nausea so powerful that she scanned the room for a wastebasket. Her upper lip was instantly beaded with sweat, and her tongue felt bone-dry and stuck to her palate. Dropping her chin, she fumbled in her bag, not knowing what she was looking for until the doctor rose and handed her a tissue.

'It's too early to be completely sure, and this is a very rare condition. I've never seen a case in my twenty years of practising.' He gave a half smile. 'But I'd be remiss if I didn't let you know what I'm seeing.'

Ava put all her might into swallowing so that she could ask him the myriad questions that were now tumbling through her brain. Afraid that she might miss something crucial, or appear to be an ignorant and totally inadequate parent, she shifted forward on the chair, focusing on the eyes behind the glasses. 'So, what exactly is Stargardt's disease, and what does that mean for my daughter? Will she have to wear glasses? I mean, will it improve with treatment? What *is* the treatment?' She knotted her trembling fingers over her bag and counted the seconds until he spoke again.

He spoke kindly. 'Stargardt's causes degeneration of the macula, over time. The amount of time varies from patient to patient, but the area in the centre of the macula that handles vision straight ahead deteriorates.' He paused. 'It often presents in youngsters around Carly's age, but I'll say again, Mrs Guthrie, this is a very rare, genetic condition. One in approximately ten thousand people get it.'

Ava tried to picture ten thousand healthy children, filling a football stadium, a big red arrow perversely finding her darling Carly among the crowd. Shaking the bizarre vision away, she refocused on the doctor, as he continued.

'As far as how it could affect her, just as Carly described, she's experiencing dark spots in her central vision. She's having problems adjusting from light to dark environments, has some sensitivity to light.' He stood up and opened a drawer in the cabinet next to him. 'I used to have some literature on this type of condition.' He rifled through the chaotic contents of the drawer, coming up empty-handed. 'I'll get you the name of the specialist I recommend in Inverness. He's marvellous, and if you tell him I referred you…' As he held Ava's gaze, his face softened. 'Look, this is a shock, I know, but young people do learn to adjust and function fairly normally with the condition. There are visual aids, and technology now…'

At this, Ava's tenuous dam of control burst. She stood and began to pace behind the chair, her insides quivering. 'So, what exactly are you saying? Is Carly going to need these visual aids?' She swiped at a tear that had broken loose and was trickling down her cheek. 'And if so, what does that *mean*? How bad is it going to get?'

He pressed his lips together and hesitated. 'Mrs Guthrie, it varies from patient to patient, but, worst-case scenario, Carly could lose her central vision completely and have compromised peripheral vision, too. In some cases, especially with early onset like this, the deterioration can happen quickly, then level off, but for most, the best we can expect is twenty-two-hundred vision, which is legally blind.' He halted, as Ava's mouth fell open.

She tried to fill her lungs, but the air in the room was thick, and sticky. She felt dizzy, the light above her head burning her scalp as the room began to spin. So as not to fall, she leant forward and tried to catch her breath.

Doctor Harris came to her side and helped her sit back down, then handed her a small bottle of water. She sipped the cool liquid, all the while imagining her daughter, her beautiful, perfect daughter, with milky-white irises replacing the cornflower-blue, and a cane that she tapped ahead of her as she walked.

Legally blind. Pressing her eyes closed, Ava took several deep breaths, and as she counted to ten, Doctor Harris cleared his throat.

'You can contact me anytime with questions. I'll get you the contact information of Doctor Anderson. He's an excellent ophthalmologist, and he'll be able to give you a definitive diagnosis. He can help you get Carly whatever she needs.' He hesitated. 'We should probably go out now. She might be getting concerned.' He smiled weakly, as Ava, knowing he was right, nodded.

'Just give me a second, please.' She wiped her nose with the tissue, the realisation that she'd have to find a way to tell Carly that her life might alter in a way they couldn't begin to understand coating Ava's skin like a layer of molten lead. The thought of that conversation brought the nausea back, followed by a creep of coldness along her limbs that made her shudder. Could she keep the truth from Carly, at least until they'd seen the specialist? Would that be fair? How was she going to tell Rick? He should have been here.

The consequences of owning this white-hot information were overwhelming, and not for the first time since her death, Ava longed for Flora. She'd have known what to do. Ava pictured the wise blue eyes, bright above the tiny spider-veins scattered across the high cheekbones, and tried to conjure the lilting voice, providing the words of comfort she craved. Whenever she was in a mess that needed iron-cast determination and boundless positivity to conquer, she defaulted to Flora rather than her poor, stricken mother, and the knowledge brought a lump to Ava's throat.

CHAPTER FOUR

Ava held it together long enough to get Carly home, set her up in the kitchen with a snack and download a film she wanted to watch on her iPad. Relieved that she had asked virtually no questions about what was wrong with her, other than if she would need glasses, Ava told her they would know more soon.

Her mind reeling as she filtered through everything she'd learned, Ava told Carly to stay put and that she'd be back in a little while. She walked outside, pausing to steady herself against the corner of the house, then, as the brisk wind buffeted her back, feeling disconnected to the damp ground under her feet, she floated up the hill and hijacked Rick from the work going on in the barn.

She simply leaned in and whispered that Carly was in trouble and that they needed to talk. While he looked alarmed, Rick calmly told Cameron and Jim Cole, the two brothers who were now working alongside him, that he'd be back soon, then he took her hand and walked her out of the barn.

Seeming to understand that they needed distance from the house before they could talk freely, he led her down the driveway and then right, onto Sutherland Road. Ava let herself be led, sucking in the silence, the words she needed to impart her news not yet fully formed in her mind.

Now, he paced slightly ahead of her, his palm scrubbing the back of his head, a telltale sign of stress. As the road veered to the left, the dense green of Canmore Wood up ahead, Ava grabbed his hand and pulled him towards the Lochans, a series of small, inland lochs known for their spectacular views of Dornoch Firth.

Unable to bear the silence any longer, she pulled him closer. 'Rick, stop. Let's find somewhere to sit.'

Hand in hand, they walked along the grassy path to the edge of the first loch. The dark, kidney-shaped pool, with a miniature island at its centre, was surrounded by layers of lush shrubs, and trees, creating a natural amphitheatre beyond which the Firth glistened, like a strip of polished ebony.

Seeing an area of flat grasses, Ava tugged his arm. 'Over here.'

Settling on the ground, she took his hand as he let out a shuddering sigh. 'OK, tell me. What's going on?' His eyes were hooded, the characteristic smile gone. 'How bad is it?'

Ava gripped his fingers and told him everything Doctor Harris had said. Rick was silent, absorbing her words as he plucked at the grass with his free hand. As he continued to stare ahead, Ava's voice grew quieter until she whispered the last, most terrifying part of Carly's prognosis.

As she finally stopped speaking, he turned to face her. 'Legally blind?' She heard her own panic reflected in his voice. 'What the hell does that mean?'

Ava shook her head. 'She needs to get more tests before we know everything. I've got the card of an ophthalmologist in Inverness. He specialises in this kind of thing.' She patted her pocket. 'Until we—'

Rick cut her off. 'But what does legally blind *mean*, Ava?' His jaw was twitching, a kind of madness hovering behind his eyes. 'Blind as in total lights out, or partially blind? Or functionally blind, if there is such a thing?' He frowned. 'Are we talking special glasses, or white sticks and guide dogs?'

The gaping holes surrounding Rick's questions seemed to engulf her. *Why had she not asked Doctor Harris for more information?* 'I'm not sure exactly, but he said that she might need some visual aids.'

At this, Rick jumped up. 'We need to go and call this other guy *now*. Start researching Stargardt's disease and find out everything we can.' He paced along the edge of the loch, massaging the back of his neck. 'There must be something we can do.' He panted the words out. 'Whatever she needs, we'll do it. We'll find it.' He eyed her, his usually ruddy complexion now deathly pale.

'Yes, of course we will.' Ava stood up and brushed some grass from the back of her jeans. Her legs quivered with the effort of staying upright when all she wanted was to collapse and let her fear seep into the long grasses that tapped her calves, whipped up by the crisp breeze that now floated across the water.

Behind Rick, a flash of white drew Ava's eye. Splitting the strip of clear blue sky above the loch, two large, white birds floated into view, then landed gracefully on the water, one stunning swan behind the other. Tucking its startling white wings away, the lead swan arched its slender neck, forming the classic question mark. The simplistic beauty of it, this pure and unsullied example of nature, of life, of the world continuing to turn despite their own devastation, made Ava's eyes fill again.

Rick stopped pacing and held her gaze. 'Why, though?' His voice caught.

'Why what?' Ava blinked her tears away.

'Why did she get it? I mean, do they know how?' He held his palms up.

Ava recalled one last piece of information Doctor Harris had given her, as she'd tried to stay focused enough to hear him. Sucking in some peaty air, she whispered, 'It's genetic.'

Rick looked startled, his brow folding as he shook his head. 'Genetic? As in you or I gave it to her?'

'I suppose so.' Her chest felt heavy, weighted down by every word, every second of this agonising and surreal conversation. She felt newly inept for not having asked more questions, demanding more in-depth information from Doctor Harris, and now that the sickening facts were beginning to sink in, she was furious with herself. 'I should've asked him more. I just couldn't think straight,' she gulped. 'I should've...' Her vision blurred again as she walked towards Rick, the sharp outline of his tall form gradually melting into the background of trees, until she was in his arms.

'It's OK.' He stroked her hair as she felt his rapid pulse through his thick sweater. 'We'll find out everything we need to.' He paused. 'But as for the genetic part…' He held her slightly away from him, looking down at her. 'Presumably that means that one of us has the same thing?'

'I don't know, Rick.' Ava scanned his faced, trying to clear her mind, dredge up any memories she could from her schoolgirl biology, but it was all hazy. All she could remember was that, generally, it took two genetic elements to create a storm like this one, but until they could be tested, there was no way of knowing which of them had passed along whatever demonic chromosome had damaged their precious girl.

As Rick wiped a hand across his mouth, his wedding ring catching the light, Ava saw another question behind his eyes.

'What is it?' She blinked, unsure what was coming.

'Should we have seen this? I mean, how come we didn't notice anything was wrong, before now?' His voice was raw, and his eyes filled. 'How did we miss this, Ava?'

'Look, I…' Ava halted. While tempting, saying *I told you so* seemed cruel, in the face of his obvious pain, so she wound her arms around his neck and, pulling him close, spoke into his wool-clad shoulder. 'Doctor Harris said that it can happen really fast, especially in someone as young as Carly.' Her voice hitched. 'I don't know that we could've seen anything any sooner.'

She blinked, asking herself the same barbed questions once again. Had she missed some obvious signs? Had she let her daughter down when she needed her mother the most? Wishing she knew the answers, she stepped back and raked the hair away from her face, twisting the long ponytail around her finger and tying it in a messy knot at the base of her neck.

'We should get back. I don't want her worrying.' She gestured towards the road.

Seeming to come back into himself, Rick's face cleared, and the determined hazel pools held hers. 'How much did you tell her?' He yanked at the sleeve of his sweater. 'Does she know?'

Ava shook her head. 'Not yet. I thought we should talk to her together.' She looked up at him. 'How are we going to tell her, Rick? She's ten years old.' Her voice cracked, and Rick pulled her back into his chest.

'We'll find a way.' He rocked her gently from side to side, the woody smell of him reminding her of what he'd been doing just moments ago, before this nightmare had become their new reality. 'But I think perhaps we should wait until we see the next doctor. Get all the facts.' He stepped back. 'What do you think?'

Ava pulled a tissue from her pocket and blew her nose. 'I think you're right. I don't want to scare her, or give her the wrong information, until we're absolutely sure what we're dealing with.' She sniffed and shoved the tissue back into her pocket.

'Agreed.' Rick gave a single nod, held his hand out to her and tried to smile. 'It's going to be all right, love.' He guided her gently back towards the path. 'We'll figure it out.'

Ava followed him, as, under her coat, beneath her sweater, her ragged heart tore a little more. Rick was wrong. It wasn't going to be all right.

CHAPTER FIVE

In his late fifties and basketball-player tall, with eyes the colour of toffee and thinning sandy hair, Doctor Anderson's manner was warm and open, and Carly seemed at ease with him as he conducted the various tests. He explained everything that he was going to do, but Ava and Rick had done their research and knew what to expect.

First, he carried out a visual field test that underwrote what they already knew, that Carly's central vision was compromised. He then conducted an optical coherence tomography test that allowed him to get detailed pictures of the retina. He tested her colour vision, and then, lastly, he took a Fundus photo, using a special filter that detects the flecks, or age pigments, that Doctor Harris had told Ava about, a telltale sign of Stargardt's disease.

As soon as the tests were completed, and while Carly waited in the main office, being entertained by a sweet-natured assistant, who produced some magazines and lemonade, Ava and Rick followed Doctor Anderson into his office to hear his findings, and the bottom line was just as devastating as Doctor Harris had suggested. Carly had Stargardt's disease, and it was progressing quickly.

'So, Mr and Mrs Guthrie, from everything I've seen today, I'm afraid it's what we feared. Even in the week since she saw Doctor Harris, Carly's central vision has deteriorated.' Doctor Anderson stood near the window, his arms folded across his middle.

They sat across the wide desk from him, Rick squeezing Ava's fingers in his as her heel began to tap the floor rapidly, her thigh jumping.

'As I'm sure you now know, people with early onset of the disease tend to have more rapid vision loss, until it eventually levels off.'

Ava shifted in the seat, once again the use of the word *disease* when referring to her precious daughter like fingernails on a chalkboard.

As if playing their roles in a morbid film, she and Rick quietly asked all their questions, looking at one another to make sure they hadn't forgotten anything, until the hardest, which came last.

Rick released her hand and leaned forward, his elbows on his knees. 'What can be done for her right away and how long until Carly reaches the worst of it?'

Doctor Anderson pulled out his chair and sat down, linking his long fingers in front of him on the desk. 'Currently, there's no treatment. There is research being done all the time, but at present…' He cleared his throat. 'In terms of things you can do now, I'd suggest Carly wears sunglasses whenever she's outside, as avoiding bright light can slow the build-up of age pigments. And if either of you smoke, I'd say don't do it around her.'

Rick shook his head. 'We don't smoke.'

'Good, good.' Doctor Anderson nodded. 'If she's taking any multivitamins with A in them, it's best to stop those, as it increases the build-up of age pigments and can speed up vision loss.'

Ava's throat was knotted, her stomach tight as a vice, as trails of prickles ran up and down her arms and across her face. As the doctor continued to speak, she leant a little closer to Rick. Sensing her need, he shifted his chair next to hers and took her hand again.

'There are a number of low-vision aids that can be helpful, like handheld lenses to magnify things, electronic reading machines, or even closed-circuit video magnification systems,' Doctor Anderson added.

Ava had researched these systems and wanted to know more. Hanging on to practicalities, however insignificant in the bigger picture, seemed like the only thing that could keep her from sliding into a place of such despair that there might be no way out. 'Those are the video cameras that project magnified images onto the TV or computer screen, right?' She scanned his face.

'Exactly.' He nodded, approvingly. 'It might be early days for Carly at the moment, but down the line, that could be extremely helpful to her.'

Rick rolled his shoulders, a sign to Ava that he wanted an answer to the second part of his question, and, as if reading his mind, Doctor Anderson continued, his voice gentle.

'As far as how soon things will level off, there's really no way of knowing exactly.' He paused. 'We'll have periodic appointments with Carly, keep track of the progression and make sure we're doing all we can.' He smiled at them. 'This is not a sprint, it's a marathon, and I'm afraid we're just at the starting line.'

Rick seemed irritated by the analogy, his eyes flicking over to Ava, ever the peacekeeper. 'I believe that counselling is important, as part of a treatment plan.' She forced a swallow.

'Absolutely. I'd recommend it. Also, as things progress, some occupational therapy. A therapist can come and assess Carly in your home, make recommendations as to how you can make the environment safer, more functional.' He looked at Rick, who'd leaned back, staring at the window, his mind obviously spinning.

'Right, of course.' Ava tried to smile, her hand going to Rick's knee to draw him back from wherever he was. 'I wanted to ask you about guide dogs, too.' She summoned every molecule of willpower to keep talking, the image of Carly being led around by a service dog surreal and nauseating. 'Is that something that would be feasible for her, if…?'

'Yes. I have a patient who got her dog at around eleven, and it's been a tremendous help, not only in her ability to function, but for her confidence in general.' Doctor Anderson pushed his chair back from the desk. 'We can give you the information on the local group.' He drew a circle over his shoulder. 'They have an excellent training facility near here, and when she gets to that stage, they'll help match Carly with the right dog and handle all the training.'

Ten minutes later, they thanked the doctor and left the office with a handful of leaflets on Stargardt's, contact information for support therapists, the guide dog group and a psychologist who worked with visually impaired patients. Numb, and stunned by everything they'd just been told, Ava floated across the car park, her hand on Carly's shoulder. Ava's face was burning, despite the chill of the afternoon, and as she looked over at Rick, he was shaking his head, his eyes fixed on the tarmac.

As soon as they set off for home, Rick turned the radio on, and while Carly stared down at her iPad, the music gave Ava licence to avoid using her untrustworthy voice, delay what would be the hardest conversation of her life, and simply watch the road slip by as she leaned her head against the window and feigned sleep.

Carly lay with her head on Ava's knee, as she ran her fingers through the long, gilded strands that spread across her thigh. The evening had turned chilly, and for comfort, Rick had lit the fire in the living room. The dry logs were popping loudly, and the heady scent of woodsmoke and the toast Ava had just made them hung in the air.

The appointment with Doctor Anderson had taken a good part of the day, and as a result, the truth of Carly's condition had been impossible to hide from her. When they'd got home, they'd told her everything, and she had melted into tears, her petite frame quivering like an injured bird in Ava's arms. Each sob had wrecked Ava a little more, as she'd rocked and tried to comfort her daughter. Not being able to kiss the pain away, wrap a ladybird plaster around it or distract Carly with a song or the promise of ice cream, as she had all her life to this point, had left Ava feeling every inch the useless, inadequate parent she had in Doctor Harris's office, a week earlier.

Now, all the leaflets lay in a messy pile on the dining table, and as Rick came back in from the kitchen, Ava shifted under the weight of Carly's head, pins and needles prickling her thigh. 'Can you sit up, sweetheart?' She put her hand on Carly's shoulder. 'Dad's got some ice cream for you.'

'I'm full.' Carly hefted herself up and crossed her legs underneath her.

Rick set the bowl on the fisherman's chest. 'Sure? It's double chocolate chip.'

'No thanks.' Carly's eyes were puffy and her mouth drawn.

'OK then. I suppose the bin will have to eat it.' Rick winked at her and scraped the ice cream into his own bowl.

Carly stared ahead at the flames in the grate, and Ava caught the disappointment flooding Rick's face as he lowered himself into one of the fireside chairs.

Reluctant to belabour things after the trauma of the day, but wanting to answer every question Carly might have, and at least try to offer some comfort, albeit an Elastoplast on a severed artery, Ava slid over and took Carly's hand. 'So, is there anything else you want to ask us at the moment?'

Carly let her fingers linger in Ava's as she focused on the jumping flames. 'Will I have to go to a special school?' She sniffed, then wiped her nose with her sweater sleeve.

Ava's breath caught at the unexpected question, as this was not something they'd thought to ask Doctor Anderson. The idea of Carly being treated differently, or being ostracised because of her condition, was yet another hurdle they'd have to overcome, so her not having started school yet felt like a blessing. 'I don't think so, but we'll talk to the school and figure that out soon, love.' She looked over at Rick, whose eyes were wide. 'Don't worry about it for now.' She stroked the back of Carly's hand. 'Anything else you want to know, or don't understand?'

Carly pursed her lips, shook the hair off her forehead and turned to face Ava. 'Will I still be able to see you, and Dad? I mean, at least at the sides.' She lifted a finger and tapped her temple. 'And what about painting? Will I still be able to see enough to…' Her voice faltered.

The questions hit Ava, high up under her ribs, and she looked over at Rick, her lips pressed tightly together. In her mind's eye, she saw Carly's painting hanging in the Aberdeen gallery.

Seeing her expression, Rick got up, moved over and eased himself in on Carly's opposite side. 'The doctor said that you'll still be able to see a little, in your peripheral vision.' He gently stroked her temple with his index finger. 'It might be a bit blurry, but you'll still be able to see us, see shapes, and light and dark, and stuff.' His voice faltered, and sensing that he was near breaking point, Ava reached around Carly and laid her hand on his shoulder, taking the emotional baton.

'You'll learn to adjust as things change, Carly. It won't happen overnight, and as you lose more of the vision in the middle, you'll get used to using the side vision more. Does that make sense?' Ava met her daughter's eyes, locking on to the beautiful blue pools that had been hiding this insidious disease since the day she'd been born. The idea that her baby girl had been blissfully unaware of what was coming, for ten glorious years, made Ava's chest ache with momentary gratitude. As a mother, she should have somehow sensed the approach of this black cloud on their horizon. Had she known, perhaps she could have done something to protect, or at least prepare, Carly for what lay ahead.

Seeming to rally, Rick pulled Carly into his side. 'So, we'll be here, every step of the way. We'll find things to help you cope. You can ask us anything, anytime. Your mum and I are here for whatever you need.'

Carly stared ahead, then leaned into her father, her head on his chest. 'Why did this happen to me?' she whispered.

Ava's heart was clattering, every trusted mechanism she had for offering her daughter comfort, solace, failing her as she looked over at Rick, who nodded almost imperceptibly. He had this, so she mouthed her thanks and swiped at her eyes.

'It's because of genetics, love.' He paused, his jaw jumping as if he was calculating something in his head. 'One, or both of us, have a gene that changed, it's called a mutation, and then when we made you, those genes caused this to happen.' He looked over at Ava, his eyes full.

'That's right.' Ava squeezed Carly's warm fingers. 'We don't know yet whether it was from me, or your dad, or both of us, but we're going to get blood tests to check.' As soon as she said it, Ava felt the utter futility of knowing the origin of the altered gene, like an ugly balloon floating above their heads. What difference would it make now? How would it help Carly, or change anything?

Even as she let the questions swirl around her, an answer floated to the surface, the one she'd faced numerous times when she looked in the mirror, searching for any trace of a clue as to how this had happened to her precious daughter. Finding out might not change things for Carly, but it would provide crucial information about the likelihood of her passing Stargardt's on to her own children. That was all the reason they needed.

Carly was nodding, seeming for a moment to take in this particular information as she would being told what was for tea. Then, as Ava watched, her perfect daughter's face crumpled and she folded forward at the waist, her hair tumbling like a golden waterfall over her shins. 'It's not fair.' Her voice cracked and the words were all but lost in a sob so gut-wrenching that Ava gasped.

'Oh, my love, I know.' She was on her knees in front of Carly, gently easing her upright. 'This is the most unfair thing that could ever have happened to you.' Tears were now coursing down Ava's face, and as she looked over at Rick, his cheeks were glistening in the firelight. 'You did nothing wrong. You don't deserve this.'

Carly slid from the sofa onto Ava's lap and curled into a ball, her head under Ava's chin.

As she rocked her daughter, in time with her sobs, Ava felt her world crumbling into a million pieces. Carly's pain was agonisingly palpable, a burden that Ava would have given everything to take on for her, and feeling Rick's arms circling them both, Ava gave in to her own fear, angry, hopeless and determined, all at once.

The image of Carly as a mother filtered back, and it was both heartbreakingly beautiful and terrifying. As it filled her mind, Ava fought to keep her jagged breaths under control. If that gene came from her side, how could she possibly live with herself, knowing she'd damaged one of the two people on the planet she'd willingly give her life for?

CHAPTER SIX

Ava slid the barn door open and walked in, balancing a tray of tea and biscuits. The envelope with their blood test results was tucked in her back pocket, its presence burning her through her jeans. It had arrived an hour earlier, but rather than open it, she'd folded it away, waiting for a moment when she and Rick could be alone.

The air inside the barn was cloudy, with tiny particles of sawdust suspended in the broad beams of light streaming in from the new windows that flanked the door. The fresh-cut wood smells reminded her of the kitchen project Rick had completed on their Aberdeen house, five years ago. Despite being an architect by trade, he still loved to work with his hands, and he'd made a wonderful job of rebuilding the old oak cabinets.

'Hello?' she called at the ceiling, as the high-pitched sound of a sander and the consistent thud of a hammer sifted down from the upper level, the mesh of noise underwritten by the rumble of male voices.

Rick had become friendly with local brothers, Jim, the electrician, and Cameron, the carpenter, who were working with him daily, and together they'd made great strides. Ava had been on the upper level a few times and she'd been impressed by how much they'd achieved in a couple of weeks.

So far, Jim had almost finished rewiring the whole building, bringing it up to current safety standards. Rick and Cameron had replaced one structural beam in the ceiling and installed sister boards where needed to reinforce the upper floor. The new spiral staircase stood at the far end of the ground level, waiting to be installed, and upstairs, they were now working on the partition walls that would separate the space into three bedrooms, and two bathrooms.

Ava set the tray on the end of the trestle table that Rick was using as a workbench-cum-drafting table. The plans for the renovation were spread across it, a black-and-white mosaic of what was to be. Scanning the drawings, she tried to picture the finished space, the high-ceilinged great room with a large, open kitchen, dining and living area, and a fireplace at one end. The spiral staircase leading to a wide hall with three bedrooms off it, each with new windows and skylights to capitalise on the southern, morning light, and the two bathrooms that Rick had cleverly fit into the space, one with a bathtub and the other with a large walk-in shower.

She shifted the top drawing towards her and caught the edge of a colourful flyer poking out from underneath. Pulling it out, she looked down at the brochure for The Guide Dog Centre and caught her breath. For a few moments, she'd forgotten. She'd allowed herself to get lost in what she was looking at, the stark picture of their new reality obscured behind Rick's vision for the future of this, their new home.

The prickle of fresh tears, frustratingly regular these days, made Ava shake her head. She had cried so much in the two weeks since their trip to Inverness that she'd thought she had no tears left, and yet, they still came. As she felt her sleeve for a tissue, the sanding above her stopped, and then Rick thumped down the old wooden staircase, his jeans and sweatshirt covered in wood shavings and his hair, slightly longer now than the usual crop, lightened by a layer of sawdust.

'Hi. I didn't hear you.' He smiled. 'Oh, tea. Brilliant.' He wiped his face with an old tea towel he had stuffed in his back pocket and scrubbed his palms over his head, brushing some of the dust off. 'I thought you were going for a run?' He frowned. 'You haven't gone for ages. Ever since…' His voice faded.

Ava frowned. 'Well, I can't exactly go off running whenever I want to now, can I?' She stepped back, irritation instantly warming her cheeks.

'Why not?' He tipped his head to the side in a curious, puppy-dog way, that generally made her smile, but not today.

'Are you serious?' She gaped at him. 'I can't leave her alone in the house. What if she fell and injured herself, burned or cut herself in the kitchen or…' She caught her breath, a vivid memory of her mother, cautioning her about always holding the bannister when she walked down the stairs, flashing brightly.

'Ava, she's still all right at the moment. You need to back off a little and keep doing normal things. God knows everything's going to change soon enough, but until then, you can't become a prisoner in the house. Go and do what you need to. She needs you sane and healthy.' He gave her a half-smile. 'You always said you didn't want to become like your mum, so hovering around Carly as if she's made of glass will only stress her out more.'

'All right, Rick. I heard you.' Feeling ambushed, Ava fought the press of tears and, determined not to let them win, she swallowed hard. 'But that's unfair. I'm not my mother. And the circumstances are completely different.' She sucked in her bottom lip as she replayed the past two weeks in her mind, seeing herself doing exactly what Rick had accused her of. She was no longer running every day, taking the occasional long walk alone on the beach, or leaving Carly at home while she went to the shops. Ava had essentially put her life on hold, the flow of normal activities entering a hiatus, where her every waking thought and worry were now about Carly's safety. She had been shadowing Carly as she moved around the house, shifting potential obstacles, worrying about sharp edges and hidden hazards. As she let the knowledge sink in, she looked up at Rick, another memory flickering to life, this time of overhearing her father telling her mother to stop nagging and holding Ava back from healthy activities. Maybe Rick was right.

Her mother, Helen, had been a gentle wisp of a woman, and while she'd suffered from brittle bone disease, her case had been mercifully mild. Regardless, it had buried a fear deep inside her that had permeated all their lives, as any serious illness will. As a result, Ava had felt, for much of her childhood, that she was living on tenterhooks, as if she was waiting for her beloved mother to shatter into a million pieces before her eyes.

Made nervous by her frailty, Helen's worries for her own physical safety would manifest as limitations on Ava; Helen constantly cautioning her, calling for her to get down from the climbing frame, telling her not to clamber over the slippery rocks at the beach, or to swing too high on the old tyre hanging from the chestnut tree in the garden. While she understood her mother's motivation, Ava had resented the constant reminders of Helen's fears and it had caused tension between them. Seeing the correlation with her own actions now, she shook her head, disappointed that, despite her best efforts, history had begun repeating itself.

Pulling her shoulders back, she nodded in the direction of the door. 'I'll try to back off. Give her more freedom.' She held Rick's gaze.

'Good.' He nodded approvingly. 'How's it going down there, anyway?' He walked over and kissed her, his mouth tasting of the soft peppermints he liked to chew as he worked.

Ava dropped the guide-dog brochure onto the table. 'OK. She watched something on TV and she's on Skype now, with Mandy. She can see her pretty well, I think.' The image of Carly, twisting her head to the side as she spoke to her best friend back in Aberdeen, had almost floored Ava, but the sound of the girls' laughter had restored her spirits a little. If Carly could find laughter in anything right now, however small, then Ava could quell her sadness, at least in front of her amazing child.

'That's good.' Rick nodded, eyeing the tray. 'Is Jenna still bringing Mandy up soon?'

'I think so. In a couple of weeks. She said we'd talk about it when the girls were finished chatting.'

Ava's closest friend Jenna, Mandy's mother, worked at the same design firm as Ava, and they'd been thick as thieves since Ava's first day, eight years earlier. Jenna, a single mother, was Ava's polar opposite. A feisty, Irish brunette, with eyes the colour of moss, a forceful nature, and opinions to match, Jenna had taken to Ava immediately. They'd soon realised that their daughters were the same age, and when they'd introduced the girls, they had instantly connected. The children's friendship created the perfect situation for their mothers, providing many an excuse for them all to spend time together, in the name of playdates and in support of the various activities the girls both enjoyed.

Thinking about it now, Ava's heart sank. Another aspect of Carly's condition that they had yet to navigate was how her compromised eyesight would affect her gift for painting and her love of horse riding, things that brought her such joy that Ava couldn't imagine her not doing them.

'What're you thinking? You look miles away.' Rick lifted a mug and a biscuit from the plate, then turned towards the stairs. 'Lads. Come and get some tea,' he shouted as the hammering above them stopped.

'Just about her painting and riding.' Ava blinked. 'How much longer she'll still be able to do that kind of thing.' Her throat narrowed as she imagined Carly, hunched over and squinting at a canvas, then slamming her brushes down in frustration.

'Yeah. I know.' He frowned. 'I was thinking about that yesterday. We should talk to Doctor Anderson, see what he says.' He bit into a biscuit, sending a puff of buttery crumbs into the atmosphere. 'I'd think the riding won't be as much of a problem.' He spoke around his mouthful. 'Maybe we can find one of those special therapy places, you know, for riders with disabilities?' He looked at her over the rim of his cup.

Something snapped inside Ava and she lifted her chin sharply. 'Don't say that. She's not disabled.' She glared at him.

Rick looked startled, setting his mug down on the tray. 'Hey. I'm sorry.' He reached for her, but Ava avoided his hand. 'I didn't mean it like that.' He frowned. 'But, Ava...'

She knew what he was saying, and the reality of it was like a physical pain spiralling through her. 'I know. I just can't bear hearing it.'

He shook his head. 'I hate it too.' He looked as if he'd tasted something sour. 'But it doesn't change anything.'

'I know that. It's just so much to take in. I need some time.'

He brought the back of her hand to his lips as Jim and Cameron clattered down the stairs and made their way towards them. 'Come on, lads. Get it while it's hot.' Rick pointed at the tray as the two men circled the table.

Jim was a medium-height, rotund man in his mid-thirties, with a monk-like half-circle of red hair, some impressive tattoos and a nose so broad that, as Flora used to say, you could hammer nails in with it. He had a habit of slapping his thigh when he laughed, and his voice would boom above the noise of power tools and hammering, making Rick laugh. The older of the two brothers, Jim was a skilled electrician, with a reputation for excellent work. When Rick had met him some months ago, while looking for local tradesmen to help with the renovation, Jim had introduced him to Cameron, his younger brother, and a master carpenter.

Cameron towered over his older brother, his large frame even dwarfing Rick, who was over six feet tall. Cameron had a wide jaw, deep-set, chocolate-brown eyes and a mop of dark hair that flopped over his forehead. He spoke in a low, melodic way that caused Ava to lean in sometimes, to catch what he was saying, and he obviously adored his raucous brother, which made her warm to Cameron even more.

The Coles had quickly become Rick's wingmen, and Ava was grateful to have them around, as aside from their great work, they were providing Rick with some much-needed male companionship.

'Enjoy your tea, guys.' She smiled at the men, then turned to Rick. 'I'll get back down there.' She jabbed a thumb at the door.

He leaned over and kissed her cheek. 'Thanks, love. I'll come in in a while.'

'We're fine. You carry on here.' She traced an arc around her. 'Don't let him slack off, boys.' She caught Cameron's eye, and smiled.

'That'll be right.' Cameron laughed. 'He's the hardest worker here.'

Laughing softly, Ava nodded. 'Yes, that I know.'

Back in the house, Carly was lying on the sofa, still talking to Mandy. She held the iPad up to her left and had tilted it away from her face.

Ava gently closed the door behind her and kicked off her shoes, as Carly caught sight of her and sat up. 'Mum, Jenna's here.' She waved the iPad in the air. 'Want to talk to her?'

Ava padded over and kissed the top of Carly's head, smelling the coconut shampoo she favoured. 'Yep, thanks.'

'O.K. Bye, Mand.' Carly waved at her friend, handed the iPad to Ava, then went into her room and closed the door.

Walking into the kitchen, Ava saw Jenna's face, jolting on and off the screen.

'Mandy, for the love of...' Jenna laughed, in the rib-cracking way that always made Ava smile. 'Will you hand it me, please.' She huffed. 'Honestly.'

Ava settled herself at the table, feeling the envelope that she'd stuffed in her back pocket wrinkling. With Jim and Cameron close by in the barn, it hadn't been the moment to bring it up, so now, she pulled it out and laid it on the table. Then she propped the iPad against the fruit bowl as, finally, Jenna appeared, her face flushed and her long, glossy hair in a messy topknot.

'That child.' She grinned, revealing the tiny gap between her two front teeth. 'So, how's tricks up there in the boonies?' She lifted a glass and sipped what looked like white wine.

'You've started early.' Ava's eyebrows jumped. 'It's not even noon?'

Jenna shrugged. 'It's Saturday.' She looked defiant, then her face folded into a smile. 'It's grape juice.' She grimaced. 'Tastes bloody awful, too.'

'Funny lady.' Ava smiled at her friend, missing her effervescent presence. 'So, what's happening there?'

They talked about work, Jenna telling Ava that she was missed around the office, the couple of times a week she would pop in. They compared notes on the weather, Jenna's disastrous dating life and then Jenna's face smoothed of the trademark smile and she leaned in close to the screen.

'How are you coping?' Her eyes locked on Ava's. 'Really.'

'OK.' Ava looked down at the envelope, then lowered her voice. 'I've cried myself sick, now I'm trying to keep it together. She needs calm, and to see us strong.' She found a smile. 'So, I'm going to do that for her.' She swallowed over a gathering lump. 'Rick needs it, too.'

Jenna nodded. 'Right, that's good. But listen. You can't be strong all the time, and if you need to talk. I mean, really talk.' She patted her chest. 'Any time, day or night. My rates are pretty good, and as long as you bring your own wine.' She wiggled the now empty glass. 'We'll be grand.'

Ava pointed at the screen, buoyed by the love of her friend, the only person, aside from Rick, who she could be completely honest with, no holds barred. 'You're the best, Jenna Doyle.'

Jenna pointed back at her. 'You're absolutely right, Ava Guthrie.'

The two friends talked for a few minutes more, then, checking her watch, Ava stood up, carrying the iPad over to the window overlooking the front garden. She turned the screen to face the window, the day bright and the sky a startling blue. 'Can you see the beach?'

'No, you eejit. I can only see the window frame.' Jenna's warm laugh crackled into the room.

'Oh, sorry.' Ava chuckled, turning the iPad back to face her. 'You'll just have to wait until you get here then.' She shrugged. 'When are you arriving?'

Jenna slipped away from the screen then came back into view. 'The fourteenth, which is a Thursday. Is that OK?' She frowned. 'I thought we could do a joint birthday thing for the girls that weekend.' She looked over her shoulder, as Mandy appeared next to her.

'Hi, Aunty Ava.' Her daughter's best friend moved her face in comically close to the screen. 'Can't wait to see you.' She grinned and waved.

'Me too, love.' Ava smiled. 'We miss you both so much.' Mandy's face was open, so innocent and unsullied, that Ava's voice suddenly failed her. She widened her eyes at Jenna, who picked up on the cue.

'Right, missy. Off you go. I want to talk to Ava about something without you hanging over my shoulder.' She shooed Mandy away. 'Go on, get lost.' She stuck her tongue out at her daughter, who returned the gesture as she walked out the door.

'Thanks. The fourteenth is great and, yes, let's plan something for them.' Ava nodded in the direction of the living room. 'I'll tell Carly. She'll be chuffed.'

Jenna stood up, the camera showing the ceiling of her kitchen. 'Call me, I mean it.' She righted the camera. 'I'm worried about you.'

Ava drew a cross across her chest. 'Promise.' She smiled. 'Love you, you nutcase.'

Jenna blew her a kiss as they said goodbye.

Ava picked up the envelope, refolded and stuffed it back in her pocket. She'd find the right time to open it later, once Carly had gone to bed.

She went to check on Carly in her bedroom, but found it empty, then, going back into the living room, her anxiety climbed up a notch. Shoving her feet into her shoes, Ava pulled the front door open and walked out into the garden.

The view of the firth was undisturbed, the sky having taken on a purplish hue, warning of a change in the weather. She shivered, as the row of tall pine trees on the right side of the property bent in the wind that had picked up since she'd come down from the barn.

Gathering the mass of hair that was now flying wildly around her face, Ava rounded the house, heading for the barn, when she saw Carly, standing near the stone outbuildings. She was talking to Rick and he was showing her something that Ava couldn't make out. Carly was peering down, her head bent close to his hand. For a second, the sight of them together filled Ava with the Zen-like sense of harmony that it always did, before the bottom had fallen out of their world.

Just as she was about to walk over, the wind carried Carly's voice to her, so Ava stood still, listening.

'So, I can really get a dog?' Carly looked up at her father, her face splitting with a smile so perfect that Ava caught her breath.

'Yes, love. That's what I'm saying.' Rick pointed to the brochure. 'It'll be a great help for you, when you need that.' He drew Carly into his side. 'You know your mum and I will do everything we can, Carly. This isn't going to be easy for you, love, but you are strong, and you can do this.'

Carly swept the hair away from her face. 'I know.' She leaned into Rick's side. 'But I'm still scared.'

At this, Rick looked over and saw Ava. 'I know you are, sweetheart. We all are.'

Ava made her way over to them and Carly looked up at her, her eyes hidden behind her new, dark sunglasses. 'Carly, you know you can talk to us about whatever you're feeling, right?' Ava tucked a golden strand behind Carly's ear, taking in her daughter's incongruously cheerful, glittery jacket, the black and yellow striped skirt, and the tights covered in bumble bees.

'I know.' Carly's nose was pinking up in the cold wind. 'I don't want to upset you, though.' She tugged her jacket closer around herself.

Ava took her hand. 'We're here for whatever you need, but you can't protect us from sadness, love. Sometimes we'll all be sad, and other days braver. It's part of dealing with what's happening, and perfectly natural.' Ava managed to smile. 'We have every faith in you, Carly.'

Carly nodded, one hand finding Ava's and the other, Rick's. 'I love you two.' She looked up at them both. 'Even though you're a bit bossy, watch really naff TV, hog the crisps and get all gross with your kissy-kissy all the time.' She pulled a face.

Ava and Rick laughed in unison, Rick's arm going around Ava's back and drawing her into a hug, with Carly squashed in between them. 'Family hug,' he called into the wind as Carly squirmed.

'Dad, you're crushing me.' She giggled. 'I'll have broken ribs *and* be blind, soon.'

Rick's gasp was audible, and Ava looked up, catching his startled expression.

Oblivious, Carly wriggled out of his embrace and raked her windblown hair into a ponytail, as Rick, turning away from them both, hastily swiped at his face with his sleeve.

'Right, young lady. Inside.' Ava held Carly's shoulders and gently turned her in the direction of the house. 'You can help me with lunch.' She glanced over her shoulder at Rick, who was pacing back towards the barn. 'We've got three hungry men to feed.'

'Oh, Mum,' Carly moaned.

'Quick march.' Ava blinked her vision clear, then let her hand linger on Carly's shoulder as she followed her daughter's laughter down the path and into the house.

Carly had been in bed for an hour when Ava remembered the envelope in her pocket. She sat at one end of the sofa, scanning an old book of Flora's on weaving, while Rick was watching TV. Having been waiting for the perfect time all day, this moment felt as good as any, so she closed the book. 'Hey.'

He looked over at her.

'Can you turn that off for a bit?' She pointed at the TV.

Frowning, he lifted the remote and turned it off. 'What's up?'

She reached into her pocket and pulled out the envelope. 'Our results came.' She waved it at him. 'I wanted to wait until she'd gone to bed.'

Rick stood up and ran his hands over his head. 'Oh, right.' He eyed the envelope, a frown creasing his forehead. 'Suppose we should open it.'

'Suppose so.' She held it out to him gingerly, as if it might explode. 'You do it.'

He walked over, took it from her and weighed it on his palm, the contents heavy with information they knew they needed, but neither of them wanted.

'Ready?' He sat on the sofa beside her, and as he slid a finger under the flap and began to open it, she grabbed his hand.

'Listen, whatever this tells us makes no difference to anything, right?' She sucked in her bottom lip.

'Of course not.' He frowned. 'We just need to know.'

She pulled her hand back and let him take the single sheet out, smoothing it over his knee. As he lifted it up and read what was on the page, his eyebrows jumped, and Ava's heart simultaneously skipped a beat. 'What does it say?'

She leaned in closer, recalling what she'd researched, and what Doctor Anderson had then told them about the genetic pattern that caused Stargardt's. They'd learned that in recessive inheritance, it would take them both carrying the altered gene to bring about the disease, and in that case, there would be a one in four chance of them having a child with Stargardt's. However, it only took one dominant copy, so, if either one of them carried the dominant gene, there was a fifty per cent chance of having a child that would inherit the disease.

As Ava nervously scanned the page, looking for a clue as to what had brought this calamity about, Rick lifted his head and looked at her, his expression so full of pain that she caught her breath. 'It's me.' He swallowed. 'I have the dominant gene.' He let the paper drop to his knee. 'I gave this to her,' he whispered. 'It's my fault.'

CHAPTER SEVEN

The air grew thick as Ava edged in closer and eased the sheet of paper from Rick's hand. Her pulse was thumping at her throat as she read the results, unable to focus on what she was seeing. When she'd lain in bed at night, wondering about this moment, about which one of them had passed this on to their daughter, she'd dreaded it being her, knowing she'd never be able to forgive herself. But she'd imagined that she would, inevitably, be the culprit, her mother's failing health having conditioned Ava to expect any weaknesses to come from her side.

Her mind reeling, and sensing the tide of guilt that was coursing through him, she took Rick's face between her hands, made him look at her. 'This makes no difference, Rick. Like we said, it's irrelevant now.' She tried to hold his focus, but he dropped his chin. 'Look at me.'

He shook his head and, escaping her hands, stood up. 'It's not irrelevant to me.' His voice was ragged. 'This is *my* fault.' He turned away from her and stared into the empty fireplace.

Ava stood and moved in beside him, her hand finding his, noting that his fingers were cold. 'Think what you would say if it was me. You'd say there's no fault to be had. Right?' She leaned against his arm. 'Rick, this is simply genetics. It could have been either, or even both of us, but at this point it makes no difference to the outcome.' She heard the logic in what she was saying, but she knew Rick's deep sense of responsibility would not allow him to shake it off as a simple glitch in his make-up, just as she wouldn't herself.

He pulled his hand back and turned to face her. 'I know what you're saying is true, but it still feels hellish.' His voice cracked. 'I'm so sorry, Ava.' He wrapped his arms around her, his chin dropping to her shoulder. 'I'm so, so sorry.'

Ava held him tightly, wishing that she could soak in some of his pain. She'd willingly have shared it, but as she held him, deep inside, a flicker of relief at her innocence made her cheeks warm with shame.

Knowing that there was nothing to be gained by telling Carly about the results at the moment, she gently stepped back. 'I don't think we need to tell her right away.'

He shuffled his feet, his hands digging deep into his pockets.

'What do you think?' She moved back to the sofa and perched on the arm.

He eyed her, his mouth working on itself for what seemed like minutes, then finally he spoke. 'Perhaps not.' He blinked. 'She'll need to know eventually, though.' His pained expression told her that his mind was jumping forward to Carly as a mother, having to carry this devastating knowledge, as well as the mutant gene, that could affect her own babies.

'Of course. We'll tell her when the time is right, but I think she's dealing with enough right now.' Ava stood up and crossed the room again. 'You need to forgive yourself, my love.' She wrapped her arms around his neck, drawing his head onto her shoulder. 'I mean it, Rick. You can't take this on. We have to be one hundred per cent focused on Carly now, so you need to let it go. Please tell me you'll try.'

He stood still, his ragged breaths grazing her cheek, then he lifted his head, his eyes brimming. As she waited for an answer, a single tear oozed free and ran down his cheek, and Ava gently wiped it away.

*

The following morning, Ava slipped out of bed before daylight crept beneath the curtains. She'd had a fitful night's sleep, and while everything ached, from her eyelids to the tips of her toes, her promise to Rick the day before circled her heart.

It had been almost three weeks since she'd been for a run, and the day loomed ahead with an unknown outline, as all their days did now. But the thought of running, letting the air course through her lungs, feeling the pull in her calves until she eventually hit that golden tipping point between pain and mastering her body, was intoxicating.

Taking her running clothes with her, she tiptoed down the stairs and dressed quickly in the chilly kitchen. For a second, as she wound a scarf around her neck, she eyed the kettle, considering bagging the run for a hot cup of tea and a blanket on the sofa, but shaking off the tempting alternative, she attached her reflective straps around her upper arms and padded towards the front door.

Outside, the dark morning was crisp and damp, the mulchy smell of sodden leaves taking her back to childhood visits to her gran. As Ava waited for her eyes to adjust to the dim light, she noticed a delicate mist hanging only inches above the grass. It instantly reminded her of the stories Flora used to tell her, that this low-lying vapour was like clouds to the fairies that lived in the garden.

Her gran's absence newly sharp, Ava smiled sadly, walked down the driveway and turned onto Sutherland Road. She walked briskly to start, feeling her taut Achilles tendons pulling up into the back of her calves. The sensation was not unpleasant as she began to jog slowly, her initial sharp breaths soon coming more easily. Within a few minutes, she was running along the road, heading for the Lochans, her heart rate picking up as she paced herself, careful to watch for any approaching headlights.

Soon, her steps were the only sound, the steady thump of her shoes on the pavement drowning out the distant chirp of the birds and even her own breathing. As she approached the Lochans, rather than continue straight as she'd intended, she turned left and ran along the path where she and Rick had been a couple of weeks earlier. The long grasses were bending lithely in the breeze as she trotted to a standstill, looking for the spot where they'd sat when she'd shared the news that had changed the shape of the future, forever.

As Ava walked along the edge of the water, the sun began to rise, shards of pink and tangerine splitting the dark grey sky, stretching left and right of the glowing disc appearing to her left. Taking her by surprise, her eyes filled, and she shook her head to clear her vision. Her heart was pattering from her run, and finding a level piece of ground, she stopped, lifted her left foot and wedged it in against her right inner thigh. Lifting her arms high up above her head, she pressed her palms together and focused on the dark trees on the small island ahead of her.

Tree pose was one of her favourite yoga positions and as she tried to maintain her balance, feeling the tremor in her supporting leg, Rick's words came back to her. '*You need to keep doing normal things. God knows everything's going to change soon.*' As she replayed the conversation in her mind, something broke inside her and suddenly tears were trailing down her cheeks, pooling under her jaw.

Who was she kidding? By putting on these clothes, these worn shoes, by turning away from their home and running towards she knew not what, it was changing nothing. This was not a normal run, or day, and, in truth, they might never have a normal day again.

CHAPTER EIGHT

Two weeks later, Jenna was fast asleep in the single bedroom next to Carly's that also served as Ava's office. Through the wall, the girls were sharing Carly's double bed, and had also turned in, an hour earlier.

The visit had gone well, and Carly and Mandy's joint birthday dinner had been a great success. Ava had served Carly's favourite, lasagne, and Mandy's requested lemon drizzle cake, courtesy of Sadie's bakery in Dornoch that made the best desserts in Sutherland. The adults had lingered at the dining table and emptied two bottles of wine, while the girls watched a Harry Potter film, both of them speaking the lines, word for word, of their favourite characters. Mandy liked Hermione Granger, mimicking her speech and gestures, and brandishing a chopstick as a wand. Carly loved Luna Lovegood, the soft-spoken girl with the silvery-white hair and eyes the same blue as Carly's own. Carly's Irish-esque accent was surprisingly good, much to Jenna's amusement, and the adults had suppressed their laughter as they eavesdropped on the girls' obvious fun.

When the youngsters eventually went to bed, Rick had taken himself upstairs to let the women talk, but under an hour later, Ava had packed a yawning Jenna off to bed, too, wanting the quiet of the kitchen to herself to finish the dishes.

Now, Ava was hovering outside Carly's door. Having realised that the girls were still awake, she was about to pop her head in and tell them to settle down. Carly and Mandy were talking in hushed voices, their laughter muffled, and the occasional shushing making Ava smile. Carly had perked up considerably since her best friend had arrived, three days earlier, and now that the short visit was coming to an end, Ava wished that Jenna had been able to take longer off work and extend the stay, but it hadn't been possible.

'I wish I could, doll,' Jenna had pouted, the previous evening. 'Work is mad at the moment, and thanks to you, I've been given the Dartford Records account, all those brooding musicians to deal with.' She'd grimaced. 'This new album cover will be the death of me.'

'I know. I was so glad to get shot of them.' Ava had grinned, poking her friend's thigh with her toe as they sat at either end of the sofa. 'There's a lot to be said for going part-time.'

'Yeah, lucky you.' Jenna had rolled her eyes. 'You owe me, big time, you know.' She'd laughed. 'Leaving me your sloppy seconds.'

'It's been such a tonic having you here.' Ava had pressed her foot against Jenna's. 'You keep me sane.'

'I'm not doing a very good job, then.' Jenna had chuckled, throwing her head back, her lush hair swinging over the back of the sofa.

Now, drawn in by more whispers, Ava shifted in closer to Carly's door, a tinge of guilt at eavesdropping overshadowed by her overwhelming need to hear her daughter laugh, one more time, before she went upstairs to join Rick.

'It's really weird because at first it was dark, like a black dot in the middle of everything I was looking at.' Carly paused. 'But now, it's coloured. I mean, if you were standing in front of a green wall, and I looked straight at you, instead of seeing all of you, the middle of what I'd see would be a green smudge, like my brain is taking the background colour and filling in the blank spot. Do you get what I mean?'

Ava held her breath. This was the most detailed description of what Carly was experiencing that she'd heard so far, and afraid to move, she gently shifted her weight to the opposite hip, willing Carly to go on.

'I think so.' Mandy sounded unconvinced. 'What if you looked this way, from the side I mean?'

'That's getting blurrier too, but I can still see better from here.'

Ava pictured Carly pointing to the side of her eye.

'The right is worse than the left. I can see you fine from here, but on the other side, hardly at all.'

'Are you scared, Carly?' Mandy's candid question brought Ava's hands into fists, and her eyes closed.

'Sometimes. But the doctor said that I'll be able to see something at the sides, hopefully always. Close up will be easier, but far away things will be gone soon.' Carly went quiet, and for a second, Ava held her breath, afraid she'd been discovered. 'Sometimes I get angry, like why did this have to happen to me. But mostly I'm worried about all the things I'll miss seeing properly.'

Ava's pulse quickened, the desire to stay and hear this so strong that a tingling paralysis crept up her legs.

'What things?' Mandy asked.

'Well, like the beach, a pretty view in the woods, or standing back to look at a beautiful painting, or even watching a film without being right up at the telly.' Carly coughed. 'I know it could be worse, but even with special lenses and stuff, I'm going to miss a lot.'

The sudden press of tears made Ava blink as she backed away from the door, careful not to make a sound. The maturity of what she had heard made her immensely proud and yet created an ache inside her so profound that her limbs felt leaden as she stumbled up the stairs. Not only was her precious girl on the brink of losing much of her vision, but, along with it, her childlike innocence, and Ava wasn't sure which was more unbearable.

Rick was propped up in bed reading and looked startled when she barged into the room and sank onto the bed by his feet. He dropped his book on his lap and beckoned to her. Ava shimmied up the bed and curled into his side, the smell of sandalwood soap lingering on his neck. 'What's going on?' He kept his voice low.

'I just overheard Carly telling Mandy what it's like. What she's seeing. Oh, Rick.' She barely got his name out before a sound escaped her that startled her. A guttural, animalistic moan that came from so deep inside that it took her over, her body beginning to tremble as Rick pulled her tighter to him.

'Shhh, love.' He rocked her gently. 'She'll hear you.'

Ava tried to catch her breath, the simple action seeming impossible. The force of the pain was so overpowering that, not for the first time, she wondered if she could muster the strength she'd need to support her daughter through this.

'Ava, just breathe.' Rick stroked her arm, his fingers leaving a trail of warmth on her now-clammy skin. 'Look at me.' He lifted her chin with his fingers. There was a calmness in his face that she wanted to reach out and touch. Seeming to read her mind, he went on, 'We can do this. One day, you're the strong one, and the next, I am. As long as we stick together, we'll manage. We *are* strong enough.' He wound his fingers through hers.

They sat in silence, their hands entwined, for ten minutes or so, then Rick shifted. 'My arm's gone to sleep.' He smiled at her. 'Come on, get ready for bed.' He stood up and held a hand out to her.

Ava let him pull her up, the wood floor cool under her bare feet. She walked into the bathroom, stripped off her clothes and, shivering, stepped into the shower and let the hot, soothing needles patter her sore skin, turning around under the flow until every inch of her was soaked. Turning off the water, she flipped her head upside down and shook it, water droplets flying across the room, peppering the mirror over the sink. Then, with her head wrapped in a towel, and her bathrobe on, she tiptoed back into the bedroom to see Rick, standing by the window. His pyjama bottoms dragged on the floor and the T-shirt he slept in had ridden up his back.

'What're you doing?' She stood next to him, her hand finding his. 'What's out there?' She leant forward, looking out into the darkness of the night. A handful of stars broke up the inky sky behind the house, as a pastel moon lit the outline of the barn.

'Nothing. I was just wondering what it's like for Carly.' He paused. 'Can you tell me what she said?' He sounded tentative, as if afraid to set her off again.

Ava nodded. 'Yes, I can. Sit down.'

A few minutes later, Rick was pacing around the bed, his eyes bright and his hand working the back of his neck. 'So, those things she talked about missing, we have to make them happen for her, now.' He looked at Ava, who had slipped under the covers, the room cooling by the minute and her damp hair making her shiver. 'Don't you think?' He stared at her, a muscle in his jaw jumping as he clenched and released his teeth.

'How do you mean?' She frowned, unsure where he was going with this.

'Seeing amazing views, oceans and waterfalls, and art galleries full of beautiful paintings.' He blinked. 'What if we took her on a trip. A once-in-a-lifetime trip, where we cram as much beauty into it as we can, before…' He stopped and sat down on the bed.

'Before she can't see it properly?' Ava felt a quickening inside, a tiny pulse of excitement. 'Go on?'

Rick swung his legs onto the bed and stretched out beside her. 'Say we take her across Europe. We go to all the greats – France, Spain, Italy, Greece.' He rolled onto his side and propped his head up on his hand. 'What do you think?'

Ava's mind wandered across the map, sticking mental pins in the places he'd mentioned, and images of them taking Carly on the rides at Disneyland in Paris, or eating gelato in a piazza in Florence, making her smile. 'I think it'd be the most wonderful thing we could do for her.' Instantly, reality popped her bubble of excitement. 'But by the time we're finished with the renovations, it could be too late,' she whispered.

Rick shook his head. 'To hell with that.' He sat up again. 'I say, let's put the work on hold, take her on the trip and we'll worry about the rest when we get back.'

This felt right, the first thing that had felt right in the weeks since they'd got the news of Carly's condition. 'If you're serious, then I think it's the best idea you've ever had.' She shifted forward and took his hand, as another levelling thought made her pause. 'But, Rick, how can we afford it all?'

He squeezed her fingers. 'We'll figure it out. Maybe I can let Max buy me out of the business. He's always wanted to be the boss.'

'No, Rick. Not the business.' She shook her head. 'There must be another way.'

He stared at her, his mind obviously spinning, already planning. 'What if I sell most of my shares to him but stay a partner, work part-time?' He shifted closer to her. 'He'd jump at the chance. Then, I could stay connected to the company but have more time to be around, help with Carly.' He nodded to himself. 'As things progress, Ava, you'll need more support than I can give you now.'

She scanned his face. This was more than a theory to him; she could see that already. This amazing man, this force of good in her life, was so selfless that he'd give up his company, his second child, to make this happen for their daughter, and the beauty of that filled her with such gratitude that there were no words to express it. Instead, she held his face between her palms, silent tears trickling over her cheeks.

'So, you'd be on board?' He frowned. 'I'd only move forward if you're fully with me on this.' The hazel eyes glittered, the distant look gone as he stared at her, a smile playing at the edges of his mouth. 'Let me do this, Ava. It's the least I…' His voice faded.

'Don't, Rick. We're in this together.' Ava hesitated for only a second. 'And, I'm on board. As long as you're absolutely sure about Max, and we can work out all the finances.'

Rick had taken the girls into Dornoch to wander around the shops while Jenna packed up their things, planning to set off for home right after lunch.

Watching them all walking towards the car, Ava had smiled to herself. Mandy was in faded jeans, black trainers and a grey zip-up hoodie with an NYC logo on the back. Carly, ever the artist, wore tie-dyed leggings under an oversized shirt covered in multicoloured pansies, a pair of sky-blue Ugg boots and a tartan bandana tied around her hair. The overall effect, rather than chaotic, was mesmerising and, for a second, Ava had gripped the windowsill, the breath leaving her as she wondered how much longer Carly would be able to clearly see and enjoy these vibrant patterns.

Seeing the shirt, the one Carly called her butterfly catcher, Ava had clenched her fists so hard that her nails had bitten into her palms. Since she'd been around nine, Carly had been convinced that if she wore this shirt, and lay still for long enough, butterflies would land on her, and Ava had often watched her daughter spreadeagled for as much as an hour in the grass, until inevitably a gossamer creature would settle on her chest, or arms. Ava could almost sense the combination of excitement and peace this generated in her daughter, and more than anything, Ava wanted to sustain that innocent optimism in Carly, whatever else lay in her future.

Now, Jenna sat at the kitchen table, her coffee cup half-empty and her eyelids heavy.

'Top-up?' Ava lifted the cafetière from the table.

'How come you look so chipper this morning?' Jenna huffed. 'My head's going to burst over here.' She raked a hand through her hair, her mouth dipping.

'Dunno. I just feel a little lighter somehow.' Ava smiled, her conversation with Rick about the trip turning circles in her mind.

'What happened after I went to bed?' Jenna gave her a coy smile. 'You minx.'

Ava laughed softly. 'No, not that.' She felt her face warming as she refilled their cups, then sat at the opposite end of the table. 'I was going to bed too, when I overheard the girls talking.' She sipped some coffee, her daughter's words scrolling through her mind like a tickertape.

'Oh yes? Anything juicy?' Jenna added some milk to her cup.

'Carly was telling Mandy what it's like for her. How she sees things now.' Ava set her cup down.

'Oh, Ava.' Jenna frowned. 'Was it hard to hear?'

'It was. She talked about all the things she was going to miss seeing, but she sounded so grown-up, almost philosophical about it, I totally fell apart. Poor Rick. I've got to stop crumbling like that.' She pulled her shoulders back.

Jenna leaned forward on her elbows. 'I'm sorry, hon. I wish there was something I could do.' She shook her head.

'You're doing it.' Ava shrugged. 'Right now.'

Jenna sat back and lifted her cup. 'So, what happened after?'

'I told Rick what she'd said, and then he had this idea. An absolutely brilliant idea.' Ava felt the same lift of excitement she'd felt the previous night.

Jenna's eyebrows lifted. 'So, tell?'

Ava explained the plan, and even as she repeated it, it began to solidify in her mind, becoming less of a fantasy. 'So, what do you think?' She eyed her friend, then shoved the plate with buttered toast on it closer to Jenna. 'Carly wasn't scheduled to start school until next term anyway, so we'll home-school her while we're away, and by the time we come home it'll probably be the summer holidays, so she can just start in August.'

Jenna lifted a piece of toast and, with it dangling in front of her mouth, she grinned and then took a huge bite. 'I absolutely love it.' She spoke around her mouthful. 'One question though?'

'Yes?' Ava scanned her friend's face.

'Can I come?'

Ava laughed, genuine happiness coursing through her, like a dormant life force that had been suddenly revived. 'I think it's brilliant, and Carly will be blown away.' She picked up a triangle of toast. 'I can't wait to tell her.'

Jenna was grinning. 'Amazing, really. He's one in a million, Ava. You both are.' She widened her eyes. 'When are you going to tell her?'

Ava shrugged. 'Not sure, but soon. We can't wait, Jenna. There's no time.'

CHAPTER NINE

Waving Jenna and Mandy off was a wrench; all the while, Ava's insides were jumping. She and Rick had agreed to tell Carly about the trip, right away, and as Jenna's Volvo disappeared at the end of the driveway, they hurried back inside, out of the pelting rain.

Carly immediately headed towards her bedroom when Rick called her back. 'Hang on, we want to talk to you, love.'

She turned around, her chin trembling. 'What about?'

Ava wrapped an arm around her shoulder. 'Jenna and Mandy will be back soon, sweetheart.' She kissed the top of her head. 'Come and sit with us for a wee bit.'

Carly sighed, then sloped into the living room. She lifted a cushion from the sofa, hugged it to her front and flopped down. 'What?' She pouted. 'I'm a bit tired.'

Ava tutted. 'Well, you shouldn't have stayed up half the night talking.' She saw Carly's eyebrows jump, a hint of a smile pulling at her mouth. 'Busted, young lady.' Ava laughed softly. 'Dad and I want to tell you something. We think you're going to like it.' She looked over at Rick, who was standing in front of the fireplace, rubbing his palms together.

'So, Mum and I were talking last night, and we wondered if you'd like to go on a trip with us.' He raised his eyebrows. 'A pretty massive trip.'

Carly sat up straight, her questioning gaze flicking between them. 'What kind of massive trip?'

Rick explained their plan, the destinations and sights they wanted her to see, reeling off countries and landmarks like days of the week, until Carly was standing, hopping from foot to foot, her purple toe-socks falling into pools around her skinny ankles, the cushion dumped on the floor.

'Are you serious?' She beamed. 'All those places?' She turned to Ava. 'How long would it take?'

Ava glanced at Rick. This wasn't something they'd discussed in detail, and now, them not knowing seemed ludicrous. She shrugged. 'Not sure.'

Rick looked caught off guard, too. 'Well, I'm guessing eight weeks at least.' He looked back at Ava for approval.

The idea of being away for two months or more made her pause. *Could they feasibly do this?* Then, seeing Carly's glowing face, and the unbridled happiness on Rick's, she threw her arms wide. 'Why not?'

Carly launched herself at Rick, her arms around his neck as he lifted her off the ground.

'Woah, so I'll take that as a yes?' His laughter was so genuinely joyful that Ava's hand went up to her mouth.

'Yes, yes, yes.' Carly threw her head back, her hair a silky curtain hanging down her back. 'Disneyland Paris, here we come.'

Rick set her down and kissed her cheek, then she walked across the room and stood in front of Ava.

'Thank you.' Her eyes were glistening.

Ava wrapped her daughter in her arms, Carly's small frame feeling brittle and precious. 'You are welcome, my love.' Ava dropped her chin onto the crown of Carly's head. 'You are so welcome.'

Three weeks later, Rick had made the deal with his business partner, Max, and paperwork for the shift in ownership was being drawn up. Ava had informed her company that she needed to extend her holiday into a leave of absence and, while they had not been pleased, they'd agreed, under the circumstances, to allow it.

Each evening, Rick and Carly would clear away the dinner dishes, then they'd all sit at the kitchen table, with Rick's laptop. They'd continue to plan, locating inns and bed-and-breakfasts that worked for the itinerary, and booking the various trains and flights that would take them on the tour they'd dubbed 'Carly's European Adventure'.

Ava had asked her to write a list of the things she particularly wanted to see and do and had been surprised by some and amused by others. The Eiffel Tower and the Louvre had seemed reasoned, if somewhat mature choices, so to see a concert by Taylor Swift in Berlin, Disneyland Paris and a tropical butterfly garden in Spain was refreshing.

As they continued to tie down their plans, Rick spent as much time as he could working around the house, and in the barn, trying to move the project forward as far as possible before closing the doors on it for weeks.

When they'd told Cameron and Jim about their change of plans, Ava had been pleased, but not surprised, when both brothers were gracious and understanding.

'Just let us know when you're back so we can schedule the rest of the work in.' Jim had patted Rick's shoulder. 'We're busy over the next few months, but we'll fit you in, pal. A few dozen rounds on you, and more of those great lunches from your good lady wife, and we'll call it square.' He'd laughed raucously.

'We're planning on getting back by the end of July.' Rick had checked his calendar on his phone. 'A good time for the next phase, I'd say.'

In contrast to his older brother, Cameron had been characteristically quieter in his acceptance of the new arrangements. 'It's a great thing you're doing for her.' He'd smiled at them both. 'The barn's not going anywhere, and we'll be here when you get back.'

Rick had been touched by their understanding and had promised to let them know of any delays.

It was now just a week before their departure, and the upstairs rooms were all partitioned off. Jim had brought in a plumber, who had installed the bathroom fittings and all the pipe and drain work for the kitchen. Rick had asked him to bring along another man the following day so they could install the spiral staircase, then all that would be left for when they returned would be to lay new wood floors downstairs, build out the custom kitchen cabinets and install the appliances.

Now, Ava stood behind Rick in the dusty barn, as they looked at the plans. So much of his vision was already in place that picturing it finished was easier. 'It's going to be gorgeous.' She leaned into his shoulder. 'You're so clever.'

Rick huffed softly. 'You're just working that out now?' He grinned. 'Slow learner.'

She skirted around the table. 'It's so lovely, I'm a little jealous. Can we move in here, and rent out the house?' She laughed, clamping the tip of her tongue between her teeth.

'I wondered when that would come up.' Rick moved over and pulled her into a hug. 'Once this is all finished, we can look at what else the house needs, although it's pretty good since Flora had all that work done and I've repaired the fence and we repainted.'

Ava leaned back, taking in the warm hazel eyes that had captured her heart at a mutual friend's wedding in Aberdeen, fifteen years earlier. 'I was kidding. The house is great.' She wiped a fleck of sawdust from his cheek. 'A last lick of paint here and there, maybe. And the garden still needs some work.' She rose onto tiptoe and kissed him. 'Can you believe we're leaving in six days?'

'Yeah, I'd better get back to work.' He tipped his head back. 'No rest for the wicked.'

CHAPTER TEN

The convertible sat in the driveway in front of the house, the 1964 Datsun Fairlady's silver wings glinting in the bright May morning.

'What did you do?' Having come out at the sound of the horn, Ava circled the car, her fingertips trailing along the silky paintwork. Earlier that morning, Rick had asked Cameron to drop him in town, and Ava hadn't understood what he was up to.

'I thought we should start the trip in style.' Rick grinned. 'Not in the old rattletrap.' He jabbed a thumb at their twelve-year-old Audi, parked at the side of the house and looking the worse for wear.

Ava leaned in, smelling the plush leather of the seats, noting the clever configuration of the two up front, and a side-facing third seat behind. The sun bounced off the immaculate walnut dashboard as she opened the driver's door. 'It's absolutely gorgeous, Rick, but is it safe?' Typically, thinking of Carly, a seed of worry bloomed inside her.

'Of course. It's absolutely fine.' He widened his eyes at her. 'I rented it for two days, so we can have a bit of fun, then leave the rattletrap here when we go. We'll drop this at Inverness airport on the way out.' Rick patted the shimmering bonnet.

Pushing down the niggle of concern that threatened to make her the ultimate party pooper, Ava smiled at him. 'Well, you think of everything.'

'I try.' He took a bow. 'Shall we go for a spin?'

Ava nodded, slipping into the driver's seat. 'If I can drive.' She gave a comic grin as he closed the door with a satisfying whump.

'Fine. I'll go and get Carly.' He touched his fingertips to his forehead, then walked over to the house and disappeared inside.

Ava ran her hands over the wide steering wheel, then rested her fingers on the gearstick and leaned her head back against the rest. Having the top down provided such a sense of freedom, the sky above her bright and striped with feathery clouds that felt so close, she could reach up and touch them. The breeze brought the brine of the firth into the car beside her and she breathed it in, thankful for this perfect morning.

As she watched, a flock of birds, possibly starlings, floated overhead in a cluster, a bubble of movement that listed left, then right, hundreds of pairs of wings working in unison, moving as one fluid entity. She rolled her head from left to right and followed their dance, marvelling at nature's awe-inspiring choreography, and then she held her breath. This was exactly the kind of thing that Carly would soon be unable to see. This gentle beauty, this simple spectacle would be lost to her and the weight of the knowledge settled on Ava's chest like an anvil.

Carly's vision was deteriorating quickly, and when they'd been back to see Doctor Anderson the day before, he'd confirmed that. When they'd told him of their trip, he'd reiterated the basic instructions about sunglasses and no Vitamin A and suggested adding a hat with a brim into the mix, but otherwise, nothing that they weren't doing already.

Carly's initial anxiety at the less than positive news had faded as she'd grown excited to tell him where they were going and, to Ava's surprise, the doctor had seemed to become slightly emotional, turning to face the window and clearing his throat. Carly, seeming to pick up on it, had asked him playfully what he wanted her to bring him back. He'd turned to her and smiled broadly, and instead of a predictable, polite refusal, he'd surprised Ava.

'What I'd really like is some goat's cheese, from Avignon. There's a little shop called Fromagerie Gérard, on the Rue les Étoiles. They sell the best chèvre you'll ever eat. They have this square one that is coated in charcoal ash, then wrapped in a vine leaf. I can't remember the name of it exactly, but I'm sure you'll find it.' He'd patted his flat stomach. 'Now that would be a great souvenir.'

Carly had smiled shyly. 'Right, I'll remember that.'

All the way home, she had chatted animatedly about the first leg of their trip, flying into London, then taking the train through the Channel Tunnel to Paris. They'd spend four days in a trendy loft in Montmartre that Carly had found online, while they took in the city sights and went to Disneyland. Then, they were to take a train to Avignon, through the beautiful scenery of the Rhone region. Ava had read about the famous vineyards that meandered south of Lyons, rolling away towards the Mediterranean, and had been touched to see it as an addition to Carly's list.

Snapping her back to the moment, the front door opened, and Rick and Carly tumbled out of the house, laughing as they jostled their way along the path. Carly was dressed from head to toe in flowers, wearing a sunflower-covered, soft cotton skirt that skimmed her ankles, a long-sleeved T-shirt with a giant pink rose on the front, and white flip-flops with huge daisies tucked between her toes. Seeing the typical jumble of pattern and colour, that shouldn't have worked but somehow did, brought a smile to Ava's face even as her heart pinched.

Rick had Ava's fleece over his arm, and he lifted it up in the air as he reached the car. 'Thought you might need this.' He handed it to her as Carly paced around the car, her mouth forming a perfect O shape.

'Wow, Dad. This is brilliant.' She opened the passenger door. 'Is it ours?' She climbed in, her red padded jacket another shot of colour against the dark leather seat.

'No, it's rented, and you are going to sit back there.' He pointed at the back seat.

'But I got in first.' She looked over at Ava. 'Right, Mum?'

Ava laughed, slipping her fleece on. 'I'm Switzerland over here. You two sort it out.'

'Come on, hop it.' Rick poked Carly's shoulder repeatedly until she gave in.

'OK, you big bully,' she grumbled, then climbed awkwardly into the back seat.

Rick got in and closed the door. 'Right, sunglasses, and seat belts on.' He twisted around to watch Carly slip on her glasses and buckle the belt across her lap, then stretching out his leg, he removed the coins from his pocket, as he always did, and dropped them in a little dip in the central console. Clipping his lap-belt on, he looked over at Ava. 'Let's go.' He lassoed his hand above his head, and Ava started the engine. 'Dornoch, here we come.'

Castle Street was quiet as they drove along, passing the little Spar shop that Carly had ridden her bike to once or twice. A couple of teenagers were now leaning against the wall, smoking, so Ava looked away and tried not to tut as they passed.

Rick chuckled. 'Go on, say it.'

'Nope.' She suppressed a smile. 'They have their own parents for that.'

As they drove on, heading for Dornoch Castle, and the town square, the pretty sandstone houses set back from the road on their left, with colourful flower gardens, manicured privet hedges, and some with wrought-iron fences springing from half-height stone walls, reminded Ava of many a trip into town with Flora, on the bus.

She'd sit next to her gran, swinging her legs as she counted off the houses until they reached the bus stop, near the gardens in front of Dornoch's beautiful, medieval cathedral opposite the thirteenth-century castle. They'd climb down from the bus and walk along Castle Street, to the Highland Clothing Store, where Flora sold her woven goods, drop off whatever new items she'd made and then go on to the tiny sweet shop in The Square, that Ava adored.

A bell would tinkle as the glass-panelled door opened, and Mrs MacKay, the owner, and a good friend of Flora's, would welcome them with open arms and, usually, a little bag of something for Ava. Mrs MacKay would tease Ava, threatening that if she didn't behave, she'd take her to the castle and give her to the ghost of Andrew McCornish, who'd been hanged there for sheep stealing.

Now, as the castle came into view, Ava looked over at Rick, who was squinting into the morning light, his palm lying lightly on her thigh. She gently stroked the back of his hand, smiling when he glanced over at her. His eyes were full of light, and hope, things Ava was struggling to hang on to as she watched the dawn slide into their room each morning, before she'd go for her run. If only she could keep focused on the good, the here and now, as Rick was doing.

Looking at the road ahead of her, Ava imagined herself back inside that little sweet shop in The Square. She remembered Flora and Mrs MacKay standing at either side of the counter, putting the world to rights, as Ava would explore the shelves, running her fingers over the rows of big glass jars, filled with colourful barley sugar, liquorice, aniseed balls, pineapple cubes and all manner of wondrous, teeth-rotting fare that sounded delicious.

Flora would eventually call to her, and Ava would know that the inevitable hug was coming. Mrs MacKay would lope towards her, her ubiquitous floral apron stretched over her ample stomach, then she'd scoop Ava up in her arms and squeeze the breath out of her. Ava always said her thank yous, then she and Flora would walk to the corner shop and pick up a few groceries, which Flora would squeeze into an ancient string shopping bag that she'd darned to within an inch of its life.

If the weather was co-operating, they'd sometimes head down Church Street, then left onto Golf Road. They'd walk the half-mile to the beach, weaving between rows of tidy bungalows, and following the lengths of drystone walls that would lead them past, and sometimes across, the magnificent fairways of the Royal Dornoch Golf Course. Being back in Dornoch had made Ava miss Flora more deeply than ever. If Flora had been here, she'd have known what to say. How to help Ava stay strong, for Carly.

Lost in her memories, she jumped when Rick said her name. 'Ava, shall we get some ice cream and drive down to the beach?'

She glanced over her shoulder to see Carly leaning forward, the wind splitting her hair at the side and wrapping it around her face as she laughed, batting it away. That relaxed laughter was the best gift of the day. Each moment like this was something Ava wanted to put in one of those big, sweet-shop jars, twist a lid on and keep safe, forever. 'Absolutely. We can go to Alfie's in The Square, then head down there.'

'Sounds like a plan.' Rick patted the dashboard. 'The beach it is, then home to finish packing, because tomorrow we're off.' He turned around just as Carly threw her head back and raised both arms above her head, letting the wind take them where it would. He glanced over at Ava and their eyes said everything to each other that needed to be said.

The following morning, Rick parked the Audi between the outbuildings, then draped a tarpaulin over it. He'd already left a set of keys with their nearest neighbour, a kind man called Henry MacFarlane, who'd said he would check on things periodically while they were away. All that was left to do was switch everything off, lock up the house and barn, strap the last of their cases to the luggage rack on the narrow boot of the car and head out.

Ava had checked her case several times, adding and removing things each time. As there was room in the car for only one medium-size suitcase each, the need to pack light was paramount, but challenging, with more than two months away from home ahead of them. She'd questioned Rick's wisdom in renting the tiny roadster when she'd realised this, but now, pressing her stomach across the bulging bag as she dragged the zip around its edge, the simplicity of the concept was thrilling.

All she was taking with her was three pairs of shoes and five sets of clothes for various types of weather, a lightweight rain jacket, and the hope that whatever awaited them they'd be equipped for. Rather than concerning, it was exciting, and as she hefted the bag off the bed and onto the floor, she let the buzz of anticipation grow. They were doing this, and now that the day had finally come, she couldn't wait to leave their cosy home behind and show Carly some of the beauty in the world, images that she could lock away in her mind's eye forever.

Downstairs, Rick had done a final walk-through, checking window locks and switching off all the non-essential electrical appliances. He'd given them a ten-minute warning some time ago, and now his excitement was tangible as he bounded up the stairs and took the case from Ava's hand. 'Give me that.' He lifted it easily, then leaned in and kissed her, leaving a trace of coffee on her lips. 'Ready?'

She cupped his cheek with her palm. 'So ready.'

Carly was standing by the door, her case already in the boot. Her red jacket was tied round her waist, her navy and white polka-dot dress swung around her knees and her hair was in a neat plait, lying over her left shoulder. Her sunglasses were shoved up onto her head, and her backpack slung over her arm, giving her a stylish, continental look that made Ava smile. 'Come on, Mum. We'll miss the flight at this rate.' She rolled her eyes, grinning at the same time.

'Since when am *I* the last one ready?' Ava skipped down the last two stairs and lifted her leather jacket from the back of the sofa. 'Right. All set.' She turned and scanned the living room. 'See you in July, Loch na brae.' She gave a wave and followed Carly and Rick out the door.

As if the universe was supporting Rick's choice to leave the top down, the morning was warm for May. The sky stretched clear and blue over the firth, where a few powdery clouds gathered, more for show than any kind of threat. The salty air felt clean and enlivening as Ava breathed deeply.

'What a fantastic day.' She held her arms out wide. 'Dornoch is giving us a great send-off.' She smiled at Rick, who was securing her case to the luggage rack.

'Come on. In you get.' He walked round and opened the passenger door for her, as Carly, who had already climbed in the back, secured her seat belt.

Ava slid into the seat, put on her seat belt and draped her jacket over her knees, as Rick got in, clipped the belt low over his hips, tossed his coins in the central console and adjusted the rear-view mirror. 'Some dwarf must've been driving last time.' He chuckled, as Ava batted him playfully, and Carly snorted behind her. 'Chocks away, ladies.'

Rick steered slowly down the drive, the gravel crunching under the narrow tires, as Ava looked over her shoulder at the croft disappearing behind them. Loch na brae looked as if it was smiling at them, the newly painted front door, a ruby-red mouth set in the warm-white stone walls, and the windows reflecting the morning light like a pair of eyes, glittering their goodbye. Exhaling, she focused ahead and counted her blessings, as she had been trying to do daily since Carly's diagnosis.

Rick had rechecked the route to Inverness airport, even though he'd driven it several times before, and now he turned left onto Sutherland Road, heading for the A9.

Ava settled back in the seat, and as the car picked up speed, the air quickly chilled her, so she draped her jacket over her front.

'Want me to stop?' Rick looked over at her.

'No. It's bracing.' She shook her head. 'It feels good.'

Nodding, he reached over and put his hand on her thigh, so she laid her hand over his for a few moments, feeling the warmth of his skin under hers.

As they turned onto the A9, Rick accelerated, the wind now circling inside the car and blowing Ava's hair across her face. Laughing, she collected it in a rough ponytail and stuffed it down the back of her shirt.

Rick smiled his approval as he slipped on his sunglasses and increased their speed a little more.

Soon, they had passed Camore and were approaching the green belt of Driemastle Wood, a pretty section of road with thick stands of pine and silvery birch trees, lined up on their right. On the left, gentle green pastures rolled away from the road, separated by a patchwork of drystone walls that seemed to go on for miles. Ava liked this stretch, looking out for the pheasant that often wandered along the verge, oblivious to the danger or proximity of the passing cars. Enjoying a rare sense of abandon, she leaned her head back and let the wind tease her hair out of her collar again.

Behind them, Carly was humming something that Ava couldn't make out. 'Dad, can you put the radio on?' Carly called into the wind, her hand on the back of Rick's seat.

He reached across himself and patted her fingers. 'Yep. If I can figure it out.' He looked down at the dashboard and began twisting various knobs.

As 'Happy' by Pharrell Williams came on, Carly threw her arms up and her head back, leaning far out over the side of the car. 'I'm so happeeee,' she shouted, her hair flying wildly in the wind, and her face aglow beneath her sunglasses.

Ava swung around, 'Carly, be careful.' She reached over and touched Carly's leg. 'Sit up, love.'

Next to her, Rick was grinning. 'Leave her be, Ava. She's fine.' He glanced at Ava, his eyes reminding her of her promise to stop hovering over Carly, then he twisted around to look at his daughter, his own smile matching Carly's in its intensity.

As Ava fought the impulse to grab the steering wheel, and tell Rick to focus, a strong gust of wind all but blinded her with her hair, just as she felt the car jerk hard to the right. Time stopped moving as she dragged her head around to look at Rick, who was now staring straight ahead at the road, his mouth contorted. He was shouting something that she couldn't make out, his words strangely elongated. The air was suddenly ice cold and Ava could hear her own breathing, her heart threatening to burst out of her chest, as her gaze slid away from Rick and back to the road. Then, the flicker of a white tail on her right drew her eye, as a large doe hesitated at the edge of the wood, then darted away between two trees, followed by her faun.

And then Ava saw what Rick already had – a lorry coming towards them, its brakes screeching as the vehicle listed dangerously to its right. Having swerved to avoid the deer, it was now drifting across their lane.

As she watched, the wheels on one side of the lorry started to lift off the tarmac as Rick swerved harder to the right to avoid it. The roadster began to glide sideways, the wheels screaming against the warm road, the smell of burning rubber filling Ava's head as they mounted the rough verge, heading for a stand of trees.

Ava turned her head, as if moving through treacle, and as she tried to call Rick's name, the coins he'd deposited in the central console floated up, seeming to hang in the air between them. She willed herself to reach out and touch him, but her arms felt as if they were held down by lead weights, as she watched the driver's side of the car fold around a tree trunk, like a silk pillowcase being wrapped around a bedpost.

The impact sounded like a thunderclap, metal against wood, and then a surreal ripping sound filled her head as the little car gave way to the gnarled trunk. She could hear Carly crying, and Rick shouting her name, as her head snapped sideways, and then banged back hard against the edge of the headrest. As she watched, with no airbag to cushion him, Rick's head bounced off the side window then snapped awkwardly over his opposite shoulders, his face rippling.

As the car slowly rocked to a standstill, Ava tried to fill her lungs with the acrid air around her, then, sending all her energy into her leaden arm, she reached out and touched Rick's shoulder, his sweater soft under her fingertips. She tried to say his name, but her mouth wouldn't work, and then she felt a trickle of something cold, running down the side of her face.

At first, there was no pain, just a sense of floating as the air slid across her skin, a cold finger tracing a line down her cheek, neck, and lingering on her collarbone. Then a dull ache started to bloom across her face as she stared at Rick, willing him to move, to say something, but there was only stillness, and silence, until everything went black.

CHAPTER ELEVEN

Ava lay in the cool hospital room, a watery light seeping in from the window, and the smell, a cloying mixture of bleach and something resembling cooked cabbage, making her nauseous. She had stitches in her temple, a concussion and the mother of all headaches. The neck collar she was wearing chafed the skin under her chin as she turned to look at Carly, who was sitting, silent, in a chair next to the bed.

Carly had no visible marks on her, as with her seat facing the side of the car, away from the point of impact, her upper body had been thrown forward into the space behind Ava's seat. Her lower abdomen was slightly bruised from the seat belt cutting into her, but otherwise she had escaped unscathed. Her face was streaked with dirt, and the tracks of dried tears, as Ava held her hand tightly, their fingers woven together like basketwork.

Ava didn't know how long she'd passed out for, but when she'd come around, Rick had still not opened his eyes, or moved, despite her shouting his name over and over. She had been afraid to move him, having seen the way his neck had twisted so unnaturally, terrified of there being damage that she might compound by trying to lift his head from the steering wheel or sit him back. She'd checked his breathing every few seconds but seeing him hunched over the wheel had been terrifying. He'd still been unconscious when the ambulance arrived, twelve minutes later.

Carly had been hysterical, trying to claw her belt off, and Ava had had to focus on keeping her calm, while releasing herself from her own seat belt. By this time, the lorry driver, a ruddy-faced man in his mid-sixties, had been pacing next to the car, shouting into his phone for help.

They'd taken them to Linden Hospital, fifteen minutes away, in Golspie, and both Ava and Carly had ridden in the ambulance with Rick. The paramedics had stabilised his neck and put him on an IV drip, and by the time they'd arrived at A and E, while still unconscious, he'd had a little more colour in his face.

Ava had not been allowed to sit close to Rick's side, or hold his hand, so she'd sat on the narrow seats opposite, pressed her back against the side of the ambulance and wrapped her arm tightly around Carly's shoulders, all the while keeping her eyes fixed on Rick's immobile face. There was a significant amount of blood on his temple, a dark slash against the relative pale of his skin that, as it glistened defiantly, had made the hairs on Ava's arms stand up until the paramedic had wiped it away with gauze, and then covered the wound.

Carly had leaned into her side, sniffing and looking down at her sunglasses, which lay neatly folded in her lap, until Ava had pulled a tissue from her bag and gently handed it to her daughter.

As they had rushed from the ambulance, met in the entrance by two doctors and a nurse in scrubs, once of the paramedics had reeled off several medical terms Ava hadn't understood as they pushed the gurney through the wide front doors at a run. Then a doctor had peeled her and Carly from Rick's side as the medical team hurried him away through a set of swing doors. As she had watched him disappear, Ava had felt a physical wrench of such force that it made her stumble, so she'd leaned a little heavier on Carly, who was wedged tightly into her side, Carly's arms circling Ava's middle.

Only after much persuasion had Ava allowed a kind-faced nurse to take Carly to another examination room so that she, Ava, could be checked out and treated by a doctor. That had been over two hours ago, and now, unable to stand not knowing what was going on one second longer, Ava swung her legs over the side of the bed. 'Stay here, sweetheart. I'll be back in a minute.' She lay a hand on Carly's shoulder as the room began to spin, a tingling sensation creeping up her back, and the ambient sounds of the hospital fading, then surging loudly in her head.

'Where are you going?' Carly looked up at her, her eyes wide and darkly shadowed. 'Can I come with you?'

Ava's equilibrium returning, she shook her head. 'No, please just stay here. I promise I'll only be a minute, and I'll tell you everything I find out.' She watched as Carly's face drooped and her chin began to quiver. 'Everything will be all right, love. You'll see.' She leaned down and kissed the top of Carly's head, the long blonde plait now mostly undone, and a spray of blood spots marring the skirt of her polka-dot dress.

Out in the corridor, Ava walked slowly towards the nurses' station, the shiny floor cool under her bare feet, her left hand trailing along the wall to steady herself. As she reached the empty desk, a nurse emerged from a nearby room and frowned at her.

'What're you doing out of bed?' she said, not unkindly, as she walked over to Ava and supported her arm. 'Let's get you back into the room.' She began to turn Ava around.

'I need to know what's happening with my husband, Rick Guthrie.' She eased herself away from the nurse's hand. 'They took him away two hours ago and I've had no information since.' Her throat was narrowing with every word, so she forced a cough, a needle of pain darting up the side of her face. Wincing, she focused on the nurse's well-manicured nails.

'Come and lie down, and I'll go and find out for you.' The woman raised her eyebrows, her curly head dipping to one side. 'Deal?'

Feeling as if she might slide down the wall, Ava nodded, grateful for the strong arm that slid back under her elbow.

Back in the room, Carly was standing at the window, her sunglasses in her hand and her hair loose down her back. She turned to look at Ava as the nurse helped her back into bed. 'Where's Dad? Is he OK?' She walked towards the bed and, catching her foot on one of the wheels, stumbled forward onto the mattress. 'Hell's bells,' she hissed, righting herself as the nurse suppressed a smile.

'Oops-a-daisy. Are you all right, pet?'

Carly looked over at Ava, a darkness behind her eyes that Ava had not seen before. 'She's fine. Just tired and shaken up.' Ava held her hand out to Carly, who took it and shifted up next to her on the bed. 'Can you please find out what's happening with my husband, Rick Guthrie?'

The woman obviously caught the edge in Ava's voice. 'All right. I'll see what I can find out.' She dipped her chin. 'Just please stay put.' She pressed the air with her palms, then turned and left the room.

'Why is it taking so long?' Carly wove her fingers through Ava's, her head settling against Ava's shoulder as it had so many times, while Ava read to her, soothed her tears, explained things that had confused or upset her.

As Ava searched for the elusive words that she needed to reassure her daughter, a slender man in his sixties, wearing a crisp white coat, walked into the room. His dark eyes were deep-set under a heavy brow, and his silvery hair was thick and wavy.

'Mrs Guthrie?' He smiled, a stethoscope dangling around his neck.

'Yes.' Ava's heart lurched as she sat up, gently easing Carly back over to the chair next to the bed.

'I'm Doctor Stewart.' He held a long-fingered hand out to her. 'How's that headache?' His tone was authoritative, and somewhat condescending, as he glanced down at her.

Ava felt the last strand of patience snap inside her. 'I'm fine, but I need to know what's happening with my husband.' She leaned forward, consciously keeping her voice calm, but firm. 'Rick Guthrie.'

'Yes. I'll update you now.' He glanced at Carly whose chin was dipped to her chest as she studied her cuticles. 'Perhaps Nurse Marion can take you to get a drink in the cafeteria, young lady?'

Carly's head snapped up as he turned to the curly-haired nurse who had come in behind him.

Panic taking over where impatience had been, Ava took a couple of steadying breaths, then, sensing the need to go along with the suggestion, turned to Carly. 'Darling, can you please go with the nurse and get me a drink?' She saw Carly's chin wobble. 'I'm dying of thirst and I'd love a lemonade, or a soda water.' She pointed at the small bedside cabinet. 'My handbag's in there. Take some money and see what you can find.' She managed a smile as Carly, looking dubious, rose and opened the cabinet door.

'What if they don't have lemonade?' She dragged Ava's purse out and opened it, peering at the notes inside.

'Just get me something else. You know what I like.'

'All right.' Carly pulled a five-pound note out and dropped the purse back into Ava's bag.

'Thank you, love.' Ava nodded encouragingly. 'Get yourself a snack too, if you want.' As Carly hesitated in the doorway, Marion put a hand on her back. 'Come on, pet. We'll find something good for you and your mum to drink, and we'll be back in a jiffy.' She looked at Ava, who nodded her thanks.

Doctor Stewart waited for Carly and Marion to turn into the corridor, then he faced Ava. She scanned his face, looking for a clue of what was to come, but when he spoke, the words felt slippery and surreal.

'So, as you know, your husband took a nasty blow to the head. When we took a scan, there was some brain swelling that was concerning.' He paused, as the volume of Ava's accelerating pulse, filling her ears, threatened to drown out his voice completely.

'OK.' She choked the word out.

'Head injuries like this can cause the brain to swell, or even bleed, and swelling like Richard's has caused the fluid to push up against the skull, causing compression on the injured side of the brain.' His palm hovered over the right side of his head. 'This swelling can cause the brain to shift and put pressure on the brain stem, which can damage the area that supports awareness, and the ability to wake up from a coma.'

He paused as Ava blinked, processing the information. The words he was using were not foreign to her and yet she struggled to sift through them, to reach the essential message, as another wave of nausea made her close her eyes for a few seconds.

'Richard is on medication to decrease the swelling. We've lowered his body temperature using ice packs, and he's on oxygen.'

Instantly picturing Rick, his lush eyelashes white with ghostly frost, she frowned. 'Why are you keeping him cold?'

'It's called neuropathic hypothermia. It's a measure we take to protect the neurons from being damaged after a traumatic injury.' He scanned Ava's face as waves of panic lapped inside her chest. 'Studies have shown that it can significantly improve the patient's chances of survival.'

The walls shifted in closer and Ava's heart flipped alarmingly under her breastbone. His use of the word survival felt like he was casually handing her a grenade, with the pin coming loose. Surely this wasn't in question, for Rick?

'At this point, he's stable but comatose, with minimal brain activity, so we'll be keeping him in the ICU, where we'll continually monitor him.'

His words were perilously spiked, and yet screaming to be touched.

'Minimal brain activity?' Ava's voice cracked as she moved the blanket away and shifted to the edge of the bed, her body leaning in towards the unwanted information. 'How long will it be until he wakes up?'

'Richard is not responding to touch, sound or pain. He can't be woken while he's in this state.' Doctor Stewart's voice was low now, gentle, and less authoritative. 'There's no way to know how long he'll remain comatose, so all we can do is watch and wait.'

Ava battled the rising nausea as the seams of her life threatened to burst open, letting everything of value seep out onto the shiny floor under her feet. 'I want to see him.' The room began to swim around her. 'I need to see him.' She hoisted herself up to standing, tugging the hospital gown away from her throat.

'You can see him soon, Mrs Guthrie, but just…'

'No.' She cut him off. 'Take me to him now, please.' She steadied herself against the bedside cabinet, as he stepped forward and slid his hand under her elbow.

'I'll take you to him, but you need to take your time. You have a concussion and I think your daughter…'

Ava sucked in her breath. Carly. What would she tell Carly?

Rick lay on his back, his head bandaged, an oxygen mask covering his nose and mouth, and various tubes and wires connecting him to an IV drip and other blinking monitors behind the bed. His skin was grey, his eyelids still, and the thick hair on his forearms was oddly matted, as if it were wet. The thistle tattoo that he'd had done on their honeymoon looked incongruously lifelike against his pallid forearm, and Ava's eyes filled as she gently touched it.

They'd argued about it briefly, as she'd never been a fan of tattoos, but Rick had talked her around, saying that wherever they went, he'd always have a wee bit of Scotland with him. Those had been the days when the world had been theirs, when they'd lie in bed at night and talk about the next trip they'd take, the landmarks they'd see and the beauty they'd witness, together.

Forcing a swallow, she slid her hand under his and closed her fingers around it. 'Rick, love?' she whispered, willing his eyelids to twitch, the trademark smile to crack the edges of the sagging mouth. 'I'm here.' She leaned in, straining to hear him breathe beneath the beeps of the surrounding machinery.

'It's good to talk to him.' The voice from behind made her jump. 'The sound of your voice is a comfort.' Marion smiled, as Ava pressed her lips together, the nurse's presence, and voice, an unwelcome, if kindly meant, intrusion. 'Holding his hand, talking, singing, or even playing music he likes can all help.' Marion checked the IV, then tapped the screen of the tablet she held.

Ava silently wished her away, the gentle advice like acid spraying Ava's skin. Her husband was in a coma, her daughter was losing her sight, and right now, at this very moment, Ava was losing her battle with the fear that filled her so profoundly that simply breathing was difficult.

'Carly's in your room.' Marion noted something down from the reading on the cardiac monitor. 'I told her you were talking to the doctor and would be back in a bit.'

Ava shivered, Rick's fingers eerily cold and lifeless in hers. 'I'll go back now.' Reluctantly, she released her grip, smoothing Rick's hand flat on the blanket. 'Thanks for taking her away for a bit.' She gave a half-smile as Marion tipped her head to the side.

'Pleasure.' She blinked. 'Have you ever had her eyesight checked? It's just that I noticed…'

Ava stood up and carefully turned to face the nurse. 'She has Stargardt's disease.'

Marion's face fell. 'Oh, I'm so sorry. I didn't mean…'

'It's OK. How would you know?' Ava shook her head. 'We just found out a few weeks ago.' The hollow space that was growing inside her was suddenly filled with the need to tell this stranger everything, every personal upsetting detail about her life. 'She's amazing, really. So strong and brave. We were going to tour Europe for a couple of months, the three of us. We were on our way when…' She couldn't continue, so she gestured towards Rick. 'We wanted her to see all these beautiful things, before she can't…' Her voice caught as a look of such profound sympathy washed over Marion's face that Ava could no longer look at it. Turning away too quickly, she immediately reached for the wall, soon feeling Marion's firm hands under her arm.

'Sit down, pet. Over here.' Marion guided her back to the chair. 'Take some deep breaths for me.' She pressed her fingertips onto Ava's wrist, feeling for her pulse. 'You've certainly had your fair share of bad luck recently, haven't you?' The kind eyes held Ava's, dark curls surrounding the pleasantly round face.

Ava was suddenly struck by the simple statement, a fact that she hadn't allowed herself to fully acknowledge. 'Yes, you could say that.'

'Well, he's in good hands.' Releasing Ava's wrist, Marion nodded at the bed. 'Doctor Stewart is wonderful, and the neuro team here…' She swept a hand around herself. 'He'll get the best care.'

Ava looked down at Rick's face. More than anything, she wanted to kiss that mouth. To feel his lips warm under hers, to hear his shallow breaths as he kissed her back, taste the tang of coffee on his tongue and feel the strong arms circling her back, their message that everything would be all right.

Before she could stop herself, she let out a sob, a mournful, raw sound that shattered the relative silence of the room. Gasping to catch her breath, Ava leaned forward, her arms across her stomach, her mouth gaping silently like a suffocating fish.

Marion circled the chair and crouched down in front of her, her hands landing lightly on Ava's shoulders. 'Let it out. It's OK to cry.' She shifted closer and pulled Ava into a tentative hug. 'We're here to help you, pet.'

As Ava dropped her chin onto Marion's shoulder, the smell of fabric softener took her back to the croft and the piles of clean clothes on their bed, ready to go into the suitcases. Releasing her breath, another sob escaped her.

'All right now,' Marion crooned. 'Just breathe.'

As Ava walked back into the room, Carly dropped her iPad into her backpack and jumped up from the chair that she'd dragged over to the window. The early-evening light was gentle, casting a golden glow over the stark furniture, as Ava held her arms out to her daughter.

'You were ages.' Carly sniffed. 'Where's Dad?'

Ava held Carly tight to her front, trying to formulate a reply that would present the facts without causing Carly any more worry or fear than she was already dealing with. As myriad, placatory sentences swirled in her mind, Ava gently eased Carly onto the edge of the bed, then sat down next to her. 'Listen to me, sweetheart. You mustn't be scared about what I'm going to say, because Dad's going to be all right.'

Carly frowned. 'What's wrong with him?'

'He hit his head quite badly, and he's unconscious.' Ava controlled her voice, searching for Doctor Stewart's matter-of-fact tone. 'He's going to be like this for a while, until his brain heals.' Ava stopped. That hadn't been what she intended on saying, and she bit her lip, seeing the horrified look on Carly's face.

'What do you mean?' Carly stood up and circled the bed, stopping as she reached the window, the light behind her turning her into a ghostly silhouette.

'Come here.' Ava beckoned to her. 'Come and sit down.'

'Why does everyone keep telling me to sit down?' Carly shouted, her hands going up to her head. 'Just tell me what's going on. I'm not a baby anymore.'

Ava steeled herself. 'He's in a coma, sweetheart. The knock to his head caused some swelling, and we have to wait for that to go down before he'll wake up.'

'How long will that take?' Her eyes were flicking wildly around the room.

'I don't know exactly.' Ava's throat was tightly knotted, making her voice gravelly. 'They're taking good care of him and doing everything they can to help him get better.'

At this, Carly looked directly at her, blinking rapidly. 'He *is* going to get better, though. Right?'

Mustering every shred of remaining resolve that she could, Ava nodded. She saw the depth of fear in her daughter's eyes, mirroring her own, as a question she'd been fighting pressed to the front of her mind. What if Rick didn't wake up?

CHAPTER TWELVE

The early-morning light filtered into the room, gilding Carly's tangled mane that was spread across the pillow. The narrow bed that they'd set up for her, in Ava's room, resembled a camping cot that Ava had slept on in her youth, and now, seeing Carly's back turned towards her, her ribs moving in gentle lifts, Ava wished that her daughter would stay in blissful sleep, for a little while longer, with no fear, or encroaching darkness to worry her.

Ava had been back to Rick's chilly room twice, during the night, the ICU nurse being kind enough to let her sit by his bedside for a few minutes each time. Ava had let her hand rest on his thigh, stroked the skin on the backs of his hands, leaned in and kissed his forehead, all the while watching his eyelids, willing them to move, to show some sign of his being aware of her presence. Nothing had come, and each time she'd left him, to go back and check on Carly, another tiny sliver of her courage had splintered off, leaving her breathless and afraid.

Doctor Stewart had wanted to keep her one night for observation, and now, other than being sore, and weary from lack of sleep, she was feeling less dizzy, and her headache had subsided. The doctor had told her that she could take the neck collar off and go home today, and that he'd keep her updated on Rick's condition, but the idea of leaving him here was unbearable.

As she tried to picture calling a taxi to take her and Carly back to Loch na brae, while Rick lay in this eerily suspended state, Carly rolled over and ground her fists into her eyes.

'Morning, love.' Ava stood up and walked over to the little bed. 'Sleep OK?'

Carly nodded, yawning widely. 'Has Dad woken up?' She stretched her arms above her head as Ava gently swept some golden strands from her forehead.

'Not yet. We'll go and see him in a bit,' she said, as Carly sat up, her vest twisted awkwardly around her slender torso.

'Can I see him, too?' She looked wary.

'Yes, I checked with the doctor and he said it was fine.' Ava nodded, revisiting her conversation with Doctor Stewart the night before.

'It's fine to have Carly come in for a few minutes tomorrow, just be sure to prepare her.' Doctor Stewart had gestured towards Rick's bed. 'If you'd like me to talk to her first…'

'No, thank you,' Ava had quickly countered. 'I know Carly, and it's best coming from me.'

'If you think that's best.'

'I do.' She'd hesitated, as, despite her fear at asking it, a stubborn, stark question was pushing its way into her mouth. 'Doctor Stewart?'

'Yes.' He'd eyed her.

'Rick will recover from this, won't he?' She'd held her breath as he'd scanned Rick's still form, Doctor Stewart's tapering fingers tapping his thigh.

'We will do everything in our power to make it happen, Mrs Guthrie, but I can't give you any guarantees.' His mouth had dipped. 'The brain is complex and unpredictable, so we'll watch and wait.' He'd smiled kindly at her. 'And hope for the best outcome possible.'

Now, with the doctor's nebulous response circling her mind, Ava sat on the edge of the little bed and pulled Carly into her arms. 'Let's get some breakfast, then we'll go and see him. How does that sound?'

Carly nodded, her hand going up to shield her eyes from the stream of sunlight seeping in through the window. 'Can you please pass me my glasses?' She pointed at the bedside cabinet.

The painful reminder like a cold slap, Ava got up, lifted the glasses and handed them to her daughter. 'Here you go.'

Carly slipped them on, then leaned back against the wall.

'What kind of things did they have in the cafeteria?' Ava asked.

Carly shrugged. 'Dunno. I wasn't really looking.'

'Well, let's get dressed and go and investigate, before they show up with soggy toast and lumpy porridge.' She poked Carly's leg as Carly laughed softly, the sound like a warm breeze around Ava's frayed nerves. 'I love you, Carly Guthrie.' Her daughter's name caught in her throat as Carly lifted the sunglasses and met her gaze.

'I love you too, Mum.' She narrowed her eyes. 'Is something wrong that you're not telling me?' Carly, intuitive as ever, leaned forward and felt for Ava's hand.

'No. I'm just so proud of you. Of the way you're handling everything that's happened.' She shrugged. 'Your dad and I are incredibly proud.'

Carly smiled shyly, shoving the blanket away and swinging her legs over the edge of the bed. 'I need the loo.' She tipped her head to the side, planting her bare feet on the vinyl floor. 'Does that make you proud, too?'

Ava nodded, accepting the unexpected sliver of humour as the bright light that it was, on what promised to be an unpredictable and difficult day.

Carly had chosen some pale-looking pancakes from the buffet counter, and Ava had grabbed a yoghurt and an apple. As they'd found a table in the already busy cafeteria, Ava had done her best to prepare Carly for seeing her father in his current state. She had seemed calm, taking in the information as she chewed. 'Are you sure you don't have any questions?' Ava had put her half-eaten apple back on the plate.

'No. I understand.' Carly had lifted her fork up to her left eye, scrutinising the triangle of spongy pancake.

'If you're sure?' Ava had frowned, the ease with which Carly seemed to be absorbing the information somewhat unsettling.

Carly had just popped the pancake into her mouth, leaving Ava to wonder whether her silence was an indication of true understanding, or more likely denial. Ava knew that Carly idolised her father. To Carly, Rick was a living, breathing superhero, infallible and, more importantly, invincible, and despite the facts of his dire situation, now was not the time to shatter that naïve illusion.

With their breakfast behind them, they'd gone back to Ava's room to get their coats, and as they walked in, Marion was standing at the end of the bed with a few sheets of paper in her hand. 'There you are. I just need you to sign these discharge papers, then you're free to go.' She held the pages out to Ava.

Carly carefully skirted the bed and, turning her head to the side, lifted her backpack, and slipped her sunglasses back on. 'Is Dad awake?' The look of innocent anticipation on her face tugged at Ava's middle.

'Not yet, pet.' Marion smiled sadly. 'You and your mum need to get home and have a wee rest, and we'll take care of Dad for a while.' She glanced over at Ava, the friendly reassurance more welcome today.

Ava signed the papers and handed them back. 'Thanks, Marion.' She extended a hand, which Marion gently batted away as she moved in and put her arms around Ava's shoulders.

'Chin up. He's in the best place, for now.' She patted Ava's back.

Ava stepped away, as a rush of mixed emotions warmed her cheeks. 'Yes, thanks.' She looked over at Carly, who was frowning, and, wanting to intercept any more questions, with unsatisfactory answers, Ava purposefully lifted her jacket from the end of the bed. 'Right, let's go and see your dad.'

Carly followed her down the corridor, her index finger looping loosely through the back of Ava's belt. The unaccustomed connection made Ava halt momentarily and catch her breath. That her daughter would need to use her as a guide like this was a staggering reminder of what their lives looked like now.

The lighting in the hospital was problematic for Carly, her sunglasses being an almost permanent fixture on her face since they'd arrived, but as they entered the ICU, Ava was now aware of the softer tone, a more yellow than fluorescent light, that felt gentler than the corridor behind them.

As if reading her mind, Carly slipped her glasses off and tucked them into her pocket.

The ICU felt positively glacial and they both shivered as they passed several glass-walled rooms, some empty, with smooth bedding, others occupied, with blinking monitors and half-drawn curtains protecting the patients inside.

A tiny bubble of hope rose inside Ava that they might walk in to find Rick sitting up and smiling at them, asking when they were going home. As she guided Carly past the nurses' station, the tall, grey-haired nurse called Sylvia, whom she'd met during the night, simply nodded, as Ava pointed towards Rick's room.

They approached the fourth door on the left, where Rick's name was now written on the narrow whiteboard mounted above the handle. 'Ready, sweetheart?' She looked at Carly, who nervously chewed the inside of her cheek.

'Yes.' She slipped her hand into Ava's.

They soundlessly slid the door open and walked into the room. The air was frigid, even colder than out in the corridor, and Ava instantly shuddered. Carly's fingers tightened around hers as Ava led her slowly forward, towards the bed.

'So, here he is. Our sleeping beauty.' She eased her hand out of Carly's and lifted the lightweight plastic chair that sat near the door. As she placed it next to the bed, Carly made an odd, hiccupping sound. 'Sit down, love. You can hold his hand, if you want to.'

Carly shook her head, her fingers linked in her lap. 'Can he hear us?' she whispered.

'I think so, yes.' Ava set her bag down on the floor, by the door. 'The doctor said it was good if we talked to him, even sang to him.' Carly turned her head to the right and studied her, her mouth working on itself. Seeing Carly's apparent paralysis, Ava moved over and lifted her daughter's hand. 'You hold mine and I'll hold Dad's, so we're all linked.' Glancing over her shoulder to see if anyone was around, Ava sat gingerly on the edge of the bed, even though she'd been told not to. With her free hand, she lifted Rick's from the blanket and gripped his fingers. 'Hi, love. We're here. Carly and I are both here.' She swallowed over a knot. 'I hope you slept well.' She looked at Carly, who was blinking furiously. 'Carly slept in my room last night, so we were close by.' She massaged the back of Rick's hand with her thumb. 'We've had breakfast, and we'll be going home soon.' Once again, the thought of leaving Rick here was gut-wrenching, a kind of spiritual amputation too gruesome to take in. 'But we'll be back tomorrow to see you.' She sniffed as Carly suddenly stood up, her fingers slipping from Ava's.

'Can we go now?' The tip of Carly's nose was pink, and as she spoke, she began backing away from the bed.

Before Ava could reach her, Carly turned towards the door and caught her foot on the leg of the chair. Time slowed down as Ava watched her daughter buckle at the knees, her kneecaps slamming down hard on the vinyl floor.

Ava was instantly on her feet, and began to scoop Carly up, but Carly held her hand out like a stop sign.

'No, Mum. I can do it.' She shook her head and, as Ava watched, desperate to hug her, or rub her knees, comfort her in some small way, Carly slowly stood up. 'You can't always help me.' Her face was flushed, but there was a steely determination there that made Ava press her lips together. 'I've got to be able to do things on my own.' Carly's voice was brittle, but her face remained composed. 'See, I'm fine.' She opened her arms wide. 'Can we go home now?'

Shaken, Ava simply nodded. 'Yes, we can go. I'm just going to say goodbye to your dad.' She turned back to Rick, his body still as wood, then she leaned over him, her lips brushing his forehead. 'Bye, my love. I'll be back soon.' Her vision blurred again as she lingered, close to his face, the chill of his skin alarming and foreign to her.

She straightened up, expecting to see Carly waiting at the door, but she was gone.

CHAPTER THIRTEEN

The taxi had dropped them at the front door just thirty minutes earlier, and Loch na brae was slowly coming back to life. Despite the relatively warm morning, feeling chilled to the bone, Ava had laid a fire in the living room, stoked the Aga, made them some tea, and run a bath for Carly.

Their wounded suitcases, Rick's badly dented and hers with a section of the top scraped away, stood at the foot of the stairs and the sight of them was jarring. Just a day ago, how different life had looked, the trip of a lifetime ahead of them, with no hint of the ugly twist that had set them on a new and unknown trajectory.

As she listened to Carly moving around in her bedroom, resisting the urge to go in and help her unpack, Ava hovered at the kitchen door, stuck between the bizarre reality of their situation and a state of shadowy denial that made her shake her head.

Rick's belongings were in a clear plastic bag, lying next to the suitcases. The soft-wool sweater, jeans and boots were squeezed in with his wallet, phone and keys and, seeing the familiar items in such an impersonal and ominous state, Ava swallowed hard and slid her hand into her pocket. Her fingertips found the smooth circle of his wedding ring, and she took a ragged breath, the tang of woodsmoke filling her head.

Sylvia had handed her the bag as she'd been about to leave the ICU, saying it was policy not to leave any valuables in the room with Rick, and while Ava understood it, the sight of his bare finger had been sickening. For as long as they'd been married, he'd never taken his ring off, and now, as she pulled it out and slipped it onto her thumb, his absence loomed so large that she could hardly breathe.

She walked over, sank onto the bottom stair, and stared at the flames that were beginning to lick the sides of the logs in the grate. Rick had taught her to build a fire, forming the basketwork of kindling sticks, then logs, stacked to leave adequate air spaces, over knots of scrunched-up newspaper. It had taken her many attempts, but she'd mastered it, and more often than not, it was Ava who now took on the task, a deep sense of satisfaction accompanying the simple act of generating warmth, that would, inevitably, magnetically, pull all three of them into the same room.

Shaking off a chilling creep of sadness, Ava stood, raked her hair up and twisted it into a tight bun. She then lifted her suitcase and carried it up the stairs, careful to avoid scratching the wooden steps with the wheels. Once in the bedroom, she quickly emptied the case of the tidy piles of clothes and put everything away, spurred on by the need to banish the cascading images of a trip that would not take place.

With her frayed case stored away at the back of the linen cupboard, she went downstairs and got Rick's slightly heavier one and hefted it upstairs. His clothes, while also clean, were a jumble, tossed in with his usual abandon. As she refolded and smoothed each item, then lifted a T-shirt and breathed in the faint scent of sandalwood, the events of the previous day played back in her mind like a morbid movie reel. The glistening convertible, the road ahead of them, the sun dappling the windscreen, the wind whipping her hair around, Carly's joyous voice, Rick's smile, the deer, the faun, the lorry, the sound of screeching brakes, the ghostly noise the metal had made as the little car folded around the tree trunk, were all snatching at her until she could take it no longer.

With the last of Rick's things put away, she put his wedding ring in the top drawer of her bedside cabinet, gathered the clothes he'd been wearing and went downstairs. In the kitchen, she shoved everything into the washing machine, eager to cleanse them of their connection with what had happened. Once the water hissed in and the drum began to turn, she picked up her phone, plugged in her headset and, rather than tackling all the cancellation calls she'd have to make but that it turned her stomach to think about, she searched for Jenna's number.

'Hey, you. Where are you now? Paris?' Jenna sounded breathless.

'Hey.' Ava walked over to the fireplace, lifted Flora's old brass poker and jabbed at the logs. 'No, we're at home, actually.' She set the poker in the stand and turned her back to the curtain of warmth radiating from the grate.

'Why?' Jenna asked cautiously. 'What happened?'

Ava knelt on the fireside rug and, her voice hitching, let the events of the previous day spill out. As she said it out loud, the reality took on even more weight, their trip slipping further and further away into the mire of uncertainty that now loomed ahead.

'Oh my God, Ava. Are you and Carly OK?' Jenna's voice went up an octave.

'We're fine. Some minor cuts and bruises, but nothing serious.' Ava gently fingered the papery dressing on her temple, wincing as her nail snagged it.

'So, what's the prognosis on Rick? I mean, do they know how long he'll be out of it?'

Ava shook her head. 'No. That's the hardest part. They have no idea.' She studied the door to the bathroom, anxious that Carly might overhear. 'Jenna, I'm scared,' she whispered.

'I know, hon. But you know Rick, he's strong as an ox. It might just take time for this swelling to go down, but he'll bounce back,' Jenna soothed. 'You need to stay strong, for him and for Carly.'

Ava closed her eyes, knowing that her friend was right, but doubting that she had the ability to put a brave face on things right now, even for Carly.

As if reading her mind, Jenna continued, 'You are one of the strongest women I know. If anyone can do this, you can.'

The prickle of fresh tears made Ava lift her chin in defiance. One way or another, she'd navigate this mess until Rick woke up and they were together again, a family.

'Let me talk to the boss tomorrow. I'll see if I can come up for a few days, just to keep you company while he's in hospital.' Jenna paused. 'If you want me to, of course.'

The idea that her friend might come back was such a relief that Ava gave way to the tears she'd been holding back. 'Yes. God, yes. If you can. It'd be great for Carly to have Mandy here too, to keep her mind off things.' She sniffed. 'She reacted kind of oddly to seeing Rick today.' Ava frowned, picturing Carly's expression, her strained posture and hasty retreat from Rick's room. 'I know it was upsetting for her, but she didn't want to touch or look at him, or even stay in the room.' She glanced back at the bathroom door. 'It was as if he wasn't there, and she was just blocking it all out, not taking it in.' Ava pulled her legs under her and stood up. 'I think I should go and check on her. She's in the bath.'

'Take it easy on her. She's dealing with a lot.'

A flash of irritation made Ava bite down on her lip. Jenna was opinionated, had no filter, and most of the time, Ava loved that about her, but this situation was far from black and white. 'You think?' Ava shook her head, then sighed. 'Sorry, I…'

'Hey, it's fine. You know my foot's permanently in my mouth.' Jenna laughed softly. 'I didn't mean to teach granny to crack eggs, or is it suck eggs?'

Ava's momentary frustration faded as she gave a half-smile. 'When do you think you can you come?'

Having popped her head into the bathroom to check that Carly was all right and being told in no uncertain terms to leave the room, Ava pulled the door almost closed, then made her way into the living room. Carly's sharp tone had taken her by surprise, but even as Ava smarted at the grumpy dismissal, her promise to Rick came back to her, so she shook her hair out of her eyes and let it go.

The folder with all their reservation information was sitting on the sideboard, so she grabbed it and, feeling suddenly flushed, turned the heating down and settled on the sofa. Looking at the top page, the glittering itinerary they'd meticulously planned as a family, with so much excitement and joy, was torturous. As she slowly dialled the first airline, her fingers felt stiff, as if her body was resisting this as much as her heart was, and after a few minutes, when her call was finally answered, she found she could barely speak.

Forty minutes later, a shockingly short time compared to how long it had taken to organise, their plans were in ashes, as dull and useless as the grey powder that she shovelled out of the fireplace each winter's morning. As she tossed the folder onto the chest, Ava was overcome by bone-deep loneliness, or was it emptiness, the sense that something crucial was missing from her existence?

Shivering again, she got up and put another log on the fire, and turning to face the room, she let the growing warmth crawl up the backs of her jeans, easing the slight tremble in her core that seemed to have become part of her make-up in the past twenty-four hours.

Carly sat at the kitchen table in her pyjamas, her iPad held up to her left eye, and her hair in a messy topknot. They'd both had a fitful night, meeting in the kitchen at 2 a.m., then watching TV for a while before filtering back to their beds. Ava had lain awake ever since, checking her phone every five minutes in case the hospital called. She'd listened to the wind whistling around the roof, and then rain pelting the windows, as she'd looked at Rick's side of the bed, the smooth pillow and undisturbed duvet bringing her worry to a dangerous crescendo.

Now, as she refilled her coffee cup, for the second time since the world had tipped on its axis, she allowed herself to consider the what ifs. *What if it took Rick days, or even weeks, to regain consciousness? What if he had lingering problems, or permanent damage of some kind? What if he lost his memory? What if...?* The more she went down the rabbit hole, the faster her heart thumped under her sweatshirt, so she pulled her shoulders back and sat opposite Carly. 'We'll go in to see Dad around eleven, OK?'

Carly nodded, not looking up.

'What are you watching?' Ava leaned in, squinting at the iPad, but Carly tipped it towards her chest and looked up, her face drawn from lack of sleep.

'Nothing. Just looking for a riding school.' She yawned. 'Might as well go for a few rides while I can still see where I'm going.'

Not for the first time, the pragmatic way her daughter was dealing with her condition shocked Ava. *Was it bravery or bravado?* Either way, this removed attitude to what was happening to her was unsettling, and the last thing Ava wanted was for Carly to shut down.

'You know you can talk to me, right?' Ava reached over and covered Carly's hand with hers. 'Whatever you're scared, or worried about, you can tell me, Carly.' She took in the filmy eyes looking back at her, the left one twitching as Ava held still and tried not to react.

'I know,' Carly pouted, 'but I can't let myself be sad, because then I won't be able to stop. And you said that Dad will be OK soon, so I can't think about it for now. My head is too full of other things, and I need to wait for him, to tell him what I'm...' She halted.

'What, love?' Ava shifted her chair closer.

'What's happening with me. He made me promise.' Carly swallowed.

'Promise what?' Ava frowned.

'That I'd tell him first, as soon as anything changed.' She blinked repeatedly, as if demonstrating her eyes' malfunction. 'I'm trying not to think about it, but…' She gulped. 'But it's so annoying.' Her voice broke as a solitary tear rolled down her cheek. 'And he's not here…'

Ava's chest ached as she pulled Carly onto her lap. This was typical of Rick, wanting to shield Ava, absorb the first wave of hurt, like Superman letting bullets rain against his chest. By asking this of Carly, he'd wanted to protect Ava from the worse of it, feed the information to her in little bites, but it was unfair to the child, and Ava needed to set things straight. 'You have to tell me too, love. Dad will understand, when he gets home. You can't keep it inside or it'll feel worse, Carly.'

Carly leaned in to her side. 'Are you sure?' She sounded very young, every inch her tender years, her fingers going up to her mouth. 'I promised him.'

Ava nodded. 'One hundred per cent sure. He won't mind.'

Carly sat up and twisted her head to the right, her left eye scanning Ava's face. 'The left one is getting darker, Mum. The smudgy part is getting bigger in the middle, and now it's more like an oval.' She drew the shape in the air between them. 'The edges are like torn, and then when I look out of the right one, the middle is so blurry, soon I won't be able to see myself in the mirror.' Tears had begun to track down Carly's face and, trembling, Ava wiped them away with her thumb. If things were progressing this quickly, the idea of Carly's ability to keep up with her art and riding, the activities she loved, or even to start at the local school, seemed impossible. The occupational therapy and counselling that Doctor Anderson had recommended suddenly shot up to the top of the priority list and as all this permeated, for a split second, Ava wondered if them not actually leaving home right now was a blessing.

'All right. It's good that you told me.' She nodded encouragingly. 'We'll call Doctor Anderson today and tell him what's going on.' She swept Carly's fringe from her brow. 'He'll give us good advice.'

Carly was assessing her, the pale irises tracking up and down Ava's face like a scanner. 'But it's not going to stop, is it?' Carly frowned. 'It's just going to keep getting worse and worse and then…' She sobbed.

'It will slow down eventually, sweetheart. Remember what Doctor Anderson said? He said it will get worse, then it'll level off. You'll still see things, my love, just not completely clearly.' Ava's throat tightened, the inability to cushion this ugly truth tearing her apart.

Carly sniffed and wiped her nose on her palm. 'I know. It's just that I thought it'd take longer to happen.' Her face was flushed as she turned and looked out of the window. 'Even the sky looks different now.' She stood up and walked to the window, her palm going up to shield her eyes. 'It's like a painting where all the colours are blobs that are melting together.'

Ava tried to imagine what Carly was describing, an image of Monet's water lilies flashing behind her eyes. That her daughter was experiencing this was bad enough, but that she could do nothing to help Carly was a cruelty too hard to stomach. 'Let's remember to tell Doctor Anderson that, when we speak to him, OK?' She watched as Carly nodded. 'Come and get dressed now. We need to get ready to go.'

Carly turned to face her, her cheeks glistening. 'Maybe Dad will have woken up by now?' A flash of hope lit her face. 'Monday *is* his favourite day.' Ava knew where Carly was going with this, so joined her at the window and put an arm around her shoulders.

'Because everyone else hates it, Monday deserves some love,' they chimed together, Carly's head leaning on Ava's chest.

'Poor old Monday,' Carly finished Rick's little homage to the most dreaded day of the week, as Ava held her daughter close to her heart.

CHAPTER FOURTEEN

The idea of driving made Ava shudder, the Audi still shrouded under the tarpaulin Rick had stretched over it, so she had called a local taxi to take them to the hospital. As the forest flicked by on her right, the driver, a rotund man named Alistair, with a mess of raven-black hair and a gravelly voice, who'd also brought them home from the hospital the day before, was chatting animatedly about his dog, Walter.

'He's a giant baby, really.' He snorted.

Ava was pleased to see Carly's interest piqued, her instantly sitting upright and looking more alert than when she'd flopped moodily into the back of the car at the house.

Alistair lifted his phone and held it over his shoulder, showing Carly some photos, as, Ava's heart in her mouth, she watched him steering with one hand. 'This is Walter on the beach.' He smiled proudly at the image of a large yellow Labrador, splashing in the water. 'He loves swimming, no matter the weather. The looney.' Alistair chuckled.

Carly took the phone and held it up to her left eye. 'He's lovely. How old is he?'

'Seven. You can scroll through. There are lots more.' Alistair mimed the action with his finger, as Ava, relieved to see both his hands back on the wheel, kept her eyes glued to the road ahead. 'I've had him since he was eight weeks old.'

Carly asked where Walter slept and what he liked to eat, and Alistair, seeming to sense her interest going beyond general politeness, sought Ava's eyes in the rear-view mirror. 'Do you have a dog?'

'No, we don't.' Ava shook her head, as Carly handed him back his phone, then turned to look out of the window.

'Are you thinking of getting one, then?' He looked expectantly at Ava, and she was on the point of changing the subject, when Carly chimed, 'Yes. I'm getting one soon.'

Ava watched her daughter's face, looking for telltale signs of distress, but instead she saw something resembling calm.

'Aw, that's brilliant. What kind?' Alistair grinned over his shoulder.

Carly held her palms up. 'Not sure yet. But I want a big one, like Walter.' She smiled, first at Alistair, then over at her mother, and seeing it, a mixture of relief and pride swelled inside Ava, like a rising tide.

When they arrived at the hospital, Alistair held the car door open for them. 'I'll hang about here, so just phone me when you're ready to leave,' he said.

Touched, Ava smiled. 'If you're going to wait, please at least get yourself something to eat. I'm not sure how long we'll be.' She pulled a note from her purse and held it out to him.

Alistair's face reddened. 'Och, not at all. I've got a Mars bar, and I'll just listen to the football on the radio. That'll do me.' He gave her a thumbs up. 'Good luck in there.' He nodded towards the entrance.

Not having told him why they'd been here yesterday, or why they were back today, Ava deeply appreciated his discretion. 'Thank you, Alistair.' She took Carly's hand. 'We'll see you in a bit.'

Inside the ICU, a nurse she didn't recognise was at the station, talking on the phone. Rather than go straight to Rick's room, Ava held Carly's hand and hovered at a polite distance until the nurse hung up. Eventually, seeing her moment, Ava approached the desk. 'We're here to see Rick Guthrie, in room six.' She spoke in a hushed tone, befitting the spot she was standing in.

'Hang on.' The nurse looked at the monitor in front of her. 'Your name?' She peered at Ava over half-lensed glasses.

'Ava Guthrie, and this is Carly. Our daughter.' She lifted Carly's hand. 'How is he? Any change?' She tried to sound collected, but she held her breath as she waited for a nugget of something positive to hang her hopes on.

The nurse, whose name tag said Sylvia, smiled at them. 'No change since yesterday, but you can go in and see him. The doctor's rounds are due soon, so if you want, you can speak to him.'

'Definitely. Thank you.' Ava squeezed Carly's hand, shoving down her rising anxiety, and led her daughter along the corridor.

The room was as frigid as before and, fittingly, Rick was frozen in place, just as she had left him the previous day. His palms were on the blanket, the oxygen mask on, and the lights dimmed to a warm, golden hue. The only noticeable change was that his jaw and chin were shaded with new growth, the sight of which gave Ava a tiny lift. Whether misplaced or not, some things were still working inside his body, and she'd take any signs of life she could get.

As Ava watched, Carly walked straight past the bed, her left hand held out at her side and, not looking at her father, carefully located the chair by the window and sat down.

Choosing not to broach it, Ava slung her jacket over the back of the other chair and slid it closer to the bed. 'Hello, my love.' She lifted Rick's hand. 'How was your night?' She ran her fingers over his hair, its springiness under her fingers incongruous compared to everything else she was seeing. 'I missed you.' She kissed the back of his hand, his skin chilly against her lips. 'We're both here. Carly's over there.' She glanced at the window. 'It's almost eleven-thirty, and we're going to wait and speak to the doctor when he comes around.' She smiled at the closed eyes. 'Hopefully, we'll find out more about what's going on.'

Behind her, Doctor Stewart slid the door open. 'Good morning.' He walked in and extended a hand to Ava. 'How are we?' As he shook her hand, he scanned the monitors behind Rick's bed, and Ava wasn't sure whether he was talking to her and Carly, or to Rick's motionless form.

'We're all right, but how's Rick doing? Have there been any changes, or improvements?' She kept her voice level, as Carly continued to stare out of the window, her sunglasses on.

'He's stable. No change so far.' He looked over at the monitors again. 'A quiet night, and, honestly, at this stage, no change is not bad news.' He paused. 'Stable, by definition, means no worse.'

Ava nodded, accepting the positive offering, however small. 'Yes. True.'

'How are you two?' He looked over at Carly. 'No more headaches or dizziness?' He turned back to Ava.

'No, I'm fine, thanks.' She fingered the dressing at her temple. 'Just tired.'

'Understandable.' His tone was sympathetic. 'Did you get some sleep?'

Touched at his concern, she swallowed. 'Not really.'

'Well, don't let that get out of hand.' He frowned. 'You need the rest.'

Carly shuffled her feet, drawing his gaze back to her.

'How about you, young lady? Any aches and pains?'

She shook her head. 'No. I'm OK.'

The doctor walked back to the door and adjusted the stethoscope around his neck. 'Do you have a moment?' He eyed Ava.

'Oh, yes of course.' She released Rick's hand and stood up, her heart-rate quickening. 'I'll be back in a minute, Carly.'

Carly nodded silently as Ava followed the doctor out into the corridor.

Doctor Stewart stood at the nurses' station. His eyes were an unusual shade of brown, reminding Ava of Rick's gold-flecked, hazel irises, the image taking her by surprise. 'So, Richard's vital signs are stable. There's no increased brain activity since yesterday, but he's holding his own.' He nodded as the nurse, Sylvia, handed him an electronic tablet. He scanned the screen, and Ava's pulse thumped at her neck as she waited for something more. *Was there a but coming?* 'We'll continue to monitor him closely, and time will tell.'

Ava's mind teemed with unasked questions, one surfacing above the others. 'People come back from this kind of thing all the time, though, don't they?' She held his gaze. 'Once the swelling goes down.'

'Of course, it's possible. The medication we have him on is reducing the swelling, but it's a slow process, and we can't speed it up without putting him at risk.' His mouth dipped. 'If, after some time, we're not seeing the results we want, we might have to consider a craniectomy.'

Ava gasped. 'Open his skull?' Aside from lying in bed listening to the wild weather during the night, she'd been researching Rick's situation. This procedure had been referred to, and she knew that by removing a piece of the skull, it allowed the brain to swell, thereby reducing the chances of increased pressure on the stem, which could cause irreversible damage.

'Yes. But we're not there yet.' He scanned her face. 'We'll keep you informed of any changes, and if we find ourselves in that position, you'll need to give your consent.'

Ava pictured herself signing forms that would mean her husband's head would be opened up like a can of soup. Shuddering, she ran her hands through her hair. 'I understand.' Her fingers were cool against her scalp, and as she let them linger there, perhaps near the spot where Doctor Stewart would use a drill on Rick, she pushed the image away.

After a few more moments of polite conversation, Doctor Stewart left her, and as Ava approached Rick's room, she heard

Carly's voice. As Ava halted outside the half-open door, careful not to be seen, Carly continued to talk.

'It's getting worse, but I'm not too scared, Dad. Colours are kind of melting together, like smudgy blobs. I'm keeping up with things though, like we said. I'm going to get on with some painting, and I'm looking for a riding school, and when Mandy comes, we'll do some other stuff together.'

Ava took a careful step forward and watched as Carly patted Rick's hand. As Carly's sleeve slid up her arm, Ava's breath hitched, shocked to see a dark bruise, the shape of an egg, on the delicate skin. As she frowned, trying to figure out when that could have happened, Carly went on.

'I'm telling Mum what's happening now because things are changing quite fast, and she's worrying about me. I told her about the promise, but she said you wouldn't be angry.' Carly dipped her head to the side. 'Can you hear me, Dad?' She leaned in and spoke close to his ear. 'If you can hear me, please wake up. I'm really, really sorry.' Carly righted herself, her hair swinging back over her shoulder. 'I need you to come home,' she whispered, her last six words making Ava feel as if the sky was falling.

CHAPTER FIFTEEN

A week later, the police had concluded their investigation of the crash, and Ava now knew that the lorry driver had escaped completely unharmed. The convertible was a write-off and she had submitted all the relevant paperwork to the insurance company. The mundane task had felt almost insulting, in the face of Rick's current state, but having done what she needed to, Ava could at least close that door, in the midst of everything else she was dealing with.

After the first visit, Carly had stopped going to the hospital with Ava. While it upset her, she thought she understood the reason. The longer Rick's condition remained unchanged, disappointment was mounting, causing fear to grow inside her daughter, and Ava reasoned that forcing Carly to see her father right now might be more damaging than letting her stay at home.

Lingering in her memory was Carly's heartfelt, if confusing, apology, and Ava was waiting for the right moment to tackle that, to understand what was behind it. After their talk, the previous week, she had called Doctor Anderson and told him about Carly's developing symptoms. While he had been kind and reassuring, he'd told her that sadly, this was the nature of the disease, leaving Ava feeling marooned, and frustrated.

Rather than leave Carly alone while she visited Rick, Ava had found a friendly young woman called Stephanie, who lived a few minutes away, and worked part-time in the Highland Shop in town, to come and sit with Carly. Despite her protests that she didn't need a babysitter, Carly had soon warmed to Stephanie, them sharing a love of horses.

Ava had carefully chosen her moment to talk to Carly about starting school, one morning after breakfast, and she was about to broach the subject again when she spotted another nasty bruise on Carly's forehead. 'Carly, what happened there?' She walked around the kitchen table and made to move Carly's hair from her face.

Carly jerked away from her, her bottom lip protruding. 'Don't. It's nothing.' She fluffed her fringe, her cheeks colouring under the scattering of freckles.

'It's not nothing, I can see you've hurt yourself.' Ava worked to keep her voice level and reached for Carly's arm. 'And here.' She slipped Carly's sleeve up to reveal the bruise she'd spotted in the hospital a few days earlier, now faded but still a brownish smudge against Carly's porcelain skin.

'I just walked into the bathroom door yesterday, and that one, I banged my arm on the bedside table when I was reaching for my watch the other night. It's not a big deal, Mum.' She rolled her eyes.

Ava released Carly's arm and walked back to her chair, the planned conversation about getting her into the local school falling apart at the seams. *If Carly wasn't safe from injury inside her own house, where everything was familiar to her, how would she function in a school where, despite a kind and willing headmistress, they had scarcely any facilities to cope with her worsening condition? And, worse still, what if the teachers drew the wrong conclusions about these bruises?*

As she poured herself some more coffee, Ava made a snap decision, then leaned forward on her elbows. 'I think we should stick with our home-schooling plan, at least until after the summer holidays.' She eyed Carly, whose mouth had fallen open. 'You weren't going to start until the autumn term anyway, and I just think…'

Carly sighed dramatically. 'Why? Just because I banged my stupid head? I want to go to school. If I don't go, I'll never make any friends up here.' She swung her arm out and caught the milk jug with her hand, toppling it over and sending milk flowing across the stack of mail Ava had dumped there after her shower. 'Hell's bells.' Carly's voice caught and she jumped up from the chair as tears began to trickle down her cheeks.

Ava grabbed a cloth and began wiping up the pooling milk, as Carly walked towards the sink, her two hands sweeping ahead of her. 'It's not just that, sweetheart.' Ava wrung the cloth out over the sink, then rinsed it under the tap. 'I'm concerned that the school here doesn't have the equipment you'll need, to move around safely, to help you see the board, or the books you'll be using.' She wiped the remainder of the milk up and tossed the cloth into the sink.

'That's not the reason.' Carly hiccupped. 'It's because you're trying to protect me, because you think they'll call me a freak or something.'

As Rick's warning about overprotecting Carly flashed back to her, Ava banished the momentary self-doubt it brought with it and pulled Carly into her arms. 'You are not a freak. I would never think that, and neither would anyone else.' Ava held her daughter, pushing away images of other children pointing or giggling as Carly tripped or fell in the playground, the visual so devastating that Ava closed her eyes to shut it out.

As Carly's sobs gradually subsided, Ava sat her at the table and handed her a paper napkin to wipe her nose.

'I think we should agree to do home schooling, just for now.' Carly turned her head to the side and met Ava's gaze, the pale eyes challenging. 'We were going to do it anyway, Carly, while we were away, so…'

'But what about making friends? I don't want to be lonely.' Carly's voice hitched. 'I miss Mandy so much.'

'I know, sweetheart. And I'm so sorry. But I promise we won't let you become a hermit. We'll get you out riding again, and Mandy and Jenna are coming soon. And maybe we can research some painting classes or…' Ava grasped at the same carrots Rick had used to get Carly here, hopeful that something would resonate.

Carly blew her nose noisily and dropped the napkin on the table. 'Dad said we could maybe get a dog.' She sniffed, turning her head to the right as she focused on Ava's face.

Seeing an opportunity to take on Rick's role of fixer, Ava nodded. 'We should probably contact The Guide Dog Centre. It could take a while to get on the list, but if you had a dog, then perhaps by next term…' Ava shrugged, seeing Carly's eyes light up. 'I'm not making any promises, but we'll make some inquiries, OK?'

Carly was up and rounding the table, and before Ava could get up, Carly was behind her winding her arms round Ava's neck. 'Thanks, Mum.' She sniffed. 'I love you.'

Rick seemed suspended in time, there being no noticeable change from day to day, and Ava's visits continued to be brief, and painful. Following the recommendations of various neurological journals, and published medical studies, and with Doctor Stewart's approval, she'd set up her phone on the bedside cabinet and played music she knew Rick loved. She'd brought in fresh thyme, lavender and rosemary from the herb garden next to the house, crushing the stems in her palm and holding them under his nose. She'd tickled his face with a feather, gently run a brush over his hair, then lifted the covers and stroked the bottoms of his feet, something that would have had him climbing the walls had he been awake, but all with no response. Everything she tried would open up a new pocket of hope inside her, and every time he continued to lie, statue-like and oblivious, the pocket would snap shut, empty.

Now, it had been over two weeks since the accident, and Ava was standing inside the barn on the phone to Jenna, who was due to arrive the following day. The smell of fresh sawdust lingered in the airy space, but the stillness, the absence of hammering and sawing, was eerie. 'It'll be so good to see you.' Ava tipped her head back and looked at the vaulted ceiling, the exposed pine beams a striking contrast to the warm cream paintwork. 'Carly's got lots planned.' She walked over to the kitchen area, the only items identifying it as such the large, copper farmhouse sink, currently propped up on an empty wooden container, and the fridge and dishwasher, still in their boxes, standing against the far wall. Seeing the project, as frozen in time as Rick was, brought a lump to her throat.

'Anything you want me to bring you from the big city?' Jenna laughed.

Ava shook her head. 'No, we're fine. Just bring yourselves.' As she said her goodbyes, a noise behind her startled her, and she swung around to see the barn door sliding open. For a split second, she imagined Rick walking in, a silly grin on his face and his hands held wide as he presented himself, saying 'Surprise. Look who woke up.'

As her insides did a somersault, a flash of red hair and the glimpse of a darkly tattooed arm snapped her back to reality. 'Oh, Jim. You scared the life out of me.' She pressed a palm to her chest.

'Jings, I'm sorry.' The electrician's face coloured as he hovered in the half-open door. 'I went to the house, and Carly told me you were up here. I didnae mean to scare you.'

'It's OK, I just wasn't expecting anyone,' she said, walking towards him. 'What's going on?'

He shuffled his boots, glancing at the floor, then back at her. 'Cameron and I were in The Castle Bar the other night and, well, we heard what happened.' He ran an intricately inked hand over his hair. 'Cameron said we should drop by, see if you're OK.' Now his face was positively flushed, as, touched, Ava found a smile.

'That's really kind,' she said, sliding her phone into her pocket. 'We're doing all right, considering.' She shrugged, the chill of the afternoon suddenly penetrating her skin as if a ghostly wind had found its way under her jacket.

'Any updates on Rick?' Jim paced across the room and lifted a large screwdriver from Rick's worktable, and as he lifted it, the blueprint it was holding down curled up into a scroll.

'No change.' Ava joined him at the table and, immediately picturing Rick deliberately placing the weighty tool there, she smoothed the drawing out, sliding a container of nails over the end to keep it flat. The layout for the kitchen seemed foreign now, despite the hundreds of times she'd looked at it with Rick, debating the flow and finalising the placement of every cabinet, drawer and stretch of countertop, their fingers meeting as they traced the outlines of the design. Seeing their hands in her mind's eye was searing, so Ava shook her head. 'He's just the same. No better. No worse.'

Jim set the screwdriver down. 'Well, that's no' too bad then.'

As if from nowhere, an idea began to form, and Ava squared her shoulders. 'I don't suppose you two could come back. Get this finished.' She swept her hand around the room. 'It'd be really fantastic to have it all done, for when he gets home.' The vision of leading Rick in, blindfolded, and revealing his plans and dreams as a beautiful reality, brought a smile to her face.

Jim scrubbed his hand over his head. 'Well, I'll speak to Cam. He started a wee project over at St. Mary's last week, and I'm no' sure how long it'll take him.' He pouted. 'I've almost finished my stuff here, so I could get the rest done in a day or so.' He tipped his head to the side. 'I'll ask him th' night and tell him to give you a ring.' As he smiled, a dimple Ava hadn't noticed before puckered his left cheek.

'Thanks, Jim. I'd really appreciate it.' She raked the hair from her face. 'It'd be so good to see this moving forward.'

Jim nodded. 'Cam's got two or three weeks of work left, maybe more, to get all the cabinetry done.' He scanned the far end of the empty room. 'He'll give you a better idea himself, but that's my guess.'

The promise of any kind of progress, even if only out here in the barn, was intoxicating. 'That's fine. There's no hurry. I'll just be grateful if you can get us back on your schedule.' She smiled. 'Thank you, Jim. Really.'

'Aye. No trouble.' He eyed her. 'How's the wee girl?'

Ava saw genuine caring there, and it drew her throat tight. 'She's coping.' She gave a half-smile. 'Better than I am.' Surprised at impulsively sharing something so personal, she cleared her throat.

'Isn't that often the way, wi' kids?' he said. 'They're stronger than we think.'

Ava recognised the wisdom of his statement as a picture of Carly flashed vividly, her telling their taxi driver about getting a dog as if it were going to be a cute puppy in her stocking at Christmas, rather than getting a highly trained companion to guide her as her world lost its definition, one day at a time.

The following evening, Jenna sat at the kitchen table, a glass of wine in front of her and her hair, still tousled from the walk they'd taken down to the Lochans, loose around her shoulders.

Ava had set the girls up in her office with watercolour paper and paints and left them giggling, as they began copying the horses on the poster above Carly's bed. The sound of her daughter's laughter was a tonic that outweighed even the pleasure of having her best friend here with her again.

'Top me up, will you, Jen?' Ava folded the tea towel over the oven handle on the Aga, and then checked her phone, the action having become a reflex, every hour or so. The fear that she might miss some word from the hospital kept her permanently balanced on a nerve's edge.

Today had been the first time since the accident that she hadn't visited Rick, and while Jenna had told her that she must allow herself the occasional day to herself, Ava's guilt was hovering under the surface of her enjoyment at having some adult company.

She set her phone down and sat opposite her friend. 'They seem happy.' She nodded towards her office, the girls' voices softly lilting as they talked, giggled and shushed each other.

'Yeah. She misses Carly a lot.' Jenna sipped her wine. 'We need to make this more regular.'

'We'd love that.' Ava pulled her glass towards her. 'And when Rick's home, maybe we can leave them with him, so you and I can sneak off to a spa or something?' She eyed Jenna, whose mouth dipped. 'What? Is that too much Ava-time for you?'

Jenna's eyes darted to the bedroom door.

'What is it?' Ava whispered.

Jenna gently slid the chair away from the table and tiptoed to the door of Ava's office. She hovered for a moment or two, carefully pulled the door closed to within an inch of the frame, then made her way back to the kitchen table.

Ava's alarm bells were clanging as Jenna sat down.

'Mandy told me what Carly was saying last night, about what's changing for her, and how she feels about it.' Jenna lay her palms over the base of her glass. 'I think you should know, hon.'

'OK.' Ava pushed her glass away, her mind instantly spiralling down a shadowy corridor, lined with all the things she still didn't know about her daughter's experience. 'What did she say?'

'She said that she's scared that by the time Rick gets better, it'll be too late for her to see anything more than blurred blobs and smudges.' Jenna hesitated. 'She said she wished that she could go and see some of the things you'd talked about, but she feels bad asking you when her dad is so ill.'

Ava sucked in a breath, the sensation of falling making her press her palms down hard on the wooden tabletop.

'Are you all right?' Jenna slid her hand across the table.

'Yes. I'm fine.' Ava blinked. 'What else did she say?'

Jenna sat back. 'That she's scared to go and see Rick now, because her ability to see him properly is going and she wants to remember his face clearly, not all fuzzy and weird, as she put it.'

Ava gulped as she pictured Carly, squinting to see her father's features, leaning over his hospital bed, his eyelids stubbornly closed and his face immobile as she tried to capture his image in her mind's eye. The vision forced Ava forward, until her forehead touched her hands.

'Ava, love. Look at me.' Jenna's voice was loaded with concern. 'Ava?'

Ava sat up and swiped the hair from her face. 'It's an impossible situation, Jenna. I want to give her that, more than anything in the world, but how can we go anywhere when Rick's like this?' She kept her voice low, the thought of her and Carly leaving Rick behind, in any way, unimaginable. 'I've cancelled everything anyway.' She eyed her friend, who was refilling her wine glass. 'I'm so sick of this whole damn mess, Jenna. I'm furious, with life for being so cruel to Carly, and with Rick, too, for hiring that stupid bloody car.' She shook her head.

Jenna took a long draught of wine and set her glass back down. 'How about you change the strategy a bit? Think about places you could take her here, or within a day's drive, so she could have some of the experiences you'd talked about?' Jenna hesitated, her eyelids fluttering as if she was witnessing something exciting.

'Go on.' Ava was intrigued, a speck of light forming in the gloom of her dilemma.

'Say you took her to the National Gallery. You could go and see a ballet or something, and find a theme park, or maybe a Center Parc. Then you could go to the west coast, maybe over to Skye. You'd have to stay a night or two if you did that, but that's some of the most stunning mountain and river scenery in the world, and you could paint it, together.' Jenna shifted forward in her chair as Ava's mind began to run alongside her friend's. Jenna held her palms up. 'We live in a beautiful country, Ava. There's so much she could see right here.' She paused. 'I know it's not Paris or Florence, but…'

Ava stood up and walked to the sink, her mind reeling. Jenna's idea had taken root and, with everything else that was going on, that she had no power over, this was something she *could* do for Carly.

As her pulse quickened, she spun around, taking in Jenna's flushed cheeks, her mess of auburn hair swinging behind her as she walked over to Ava. Ava flung her arms around Jenna's shoulders, feeling her wiry frame, and the prickle of her sweater against her wrists. 'You are a genius, Jenna Doyle.' Ava let herself enjoy the rush of excitement, then, as quickly as it had come, it began to seep away. 'But can we really go anywhere? I mean, what if he woke up and we were gadding about on Skye?' Doubt began to cast a shadow where light had been. How could she risk it – even consider being somewhere else when Rick came around?

'No. Don't do that.' Jenna wagged a finger at her. 'You can tell the hospital if you're going to be away for more than a day, and they have your mobile number. If anything changes, you can be back within twenty-four hours, regardless.' She eyed her. 'Ava, this is important for Carly, and if Rick does wake up while you're not at his bedside, as soon as you tell him what's going on, he'll say, well done, girl.' Jenna shrugged. 'You know that's true.'

Ava considered what Jenna had said, knowing that if he were here, Rick would be standing behind her telling her to start planning, and not even think about hesitating. The trip had been his idea, and doing it meant more to him perhaps even than to Carly. If she gave Carly even a taste of the experiences they'd promised her, she'd be honouring Rick's wishes too. A deep sense of certainty in her centre steadied her. 'You're right, Jenna.' She smiled at her friend. 'As usual.'

Jenna laughed and pulled back from her. 'Took you long enough to realise it.' Her eyes were full as she walked over to the table, lifted both their glasses and handed one to Ava. 'To the new plan.' Jenna held her glass out, and Ava tapped hers against it. 'The new plan.'

CHAPTER SIXTEEN

This being the last day of the visit, Jenna was in the kitchen making sandwiches for the picnic they'd planned to take the girls on, to Dornoch beach.

Since arriving, Jenna had been doing all the driving, and Ava had been relieved, more than happy to leave the Audi under wraps. Now, she was out in the driveway, folding a large tartan blanket that Flora had woven, ready to put it in the back of the Volvo, when Jenna walked up behind her, making her jump.

'Why don't you drive, today?' Jenna pointedly avoided her eyes, focusing on the cool bag she was carrying.

Startled, Ava hesitated. 'Erm, no, that's OK.' She hugged the blanket to her middle, the fresh breeze coming in from the firth wrapping it more closely around her. 'We can take yours.' She nodded at the car, as Jenna set the bag on the ground.

'Ava, you need to get back behind the wheel. You can't avoid it forever.' Her voice was firm, but not unkind, and Ava felt a rush of anxiety, laced with irritation at being hijacked.

'I will.' Ava huffed. 'Just not today.' She stared at Jenna, whose eyebrows lifted.

'Listen, you can't plan your trips with Carly if you can't drive, and if you keep taking that taxi to the hospital every day, you're going to have to take out a mortgage on this place.' She swung her arm behind her. 'Ava, come on.' She dipped her chin, the hint of a smile now tugging at her mouth. 'It's a ten-minute drive into town. Why not give it a go, while I'm here with you?'

Ava dropped her gaze and shoved some gravel into a groove between her shoes. Another gust of wind brought the salt of the nearby water with it, and she breathed it in, the earthy smell delivering something more than memories. Deep inside, she knew that Jenna was right, maddeningly so, and no matter how Ava groped for an excuse, everything she could come up with sounded pitiful inside her head. Giving up, she glared at Jenna. 'You are so annoying. Has anyone ever told you that?'

Jenna laughed loudly. 'Yes, you. Many times.' She lifted the cool bag and looked at Ava expectantly. 'So, grab the keys and let's unwrap that puppy.' She pointed at the dark mound next to the larger outbuilding.

Despite herself, Ava smiled. '*So* annoying.' She shoved the blanket at Jenna and headed back into the house.

Mandy was sitting on the sofa, the TV was on and Carly was sitting close to it, on the floor.

'Are you two ready to go, in ten minutes?' Ava opened the drawer in the sideboard and raked around, looking for her key ring. Finding the metal bundle, she turned to see Carly peering at her.

'Are you driving?' She turned her head to the right, her eyes wide.

'Yes, I am.' Ava nodded. 'So, ten minutes, OK? Turn the telly off please and get your stuff together.'

Not waiting for further questioning, or for her anxiety to get the better of her, Ava hurried into the kitchen and picked up the flask of tea that Jenna had left on the counter.

As she walked out into the living room, Carly was putting on her rainbow-striped jacket, dragging the curtain of hair out from under the collar.

'It's nice out today. It's getting warmer.' Ava smiled at her daughter.

Carly fished in her pocket for her sunglasses. 'Yeah.' She sounded unsure. 'The sun's brighter.' She waggled the glasses, the dark, polaroid lenses thick with fingerprints.

'Good lord, Carly. Those are filthy.' Ava laughed softly as she reached for the glasses. 'Give them to me and I'll clean them.'

Carly stepped back, her hip banging into the sofa as the glasses dropped onto the rug. 'Damn.' She reached down, her fingers tapping around, searching for the plastic frames.

Every sinew in Ava's body was reaching for those glasses, guiding Carly's hand and folding her fingers around her daughter's, but she stood still, even though it felt like something was tearing inside. 'Go and run them under the tap and use a clean cloth to dry them.' She jabbed a thumb over her shoulder as Mandy came up behind Carly, her dark curls in a tight ponytail and her denim jacket slung over her shoulder.

'Are we going?' Mandy bumped shoulders with Carly.

'Yep, just going to clean my glasses.' She emphasised the last word, then running her hand along the back of the sofa, headed for the kitchen.

Outside, Jenna had uncovered the Audi and was waiting next to it. 'Come on you lot. Let's get this show on the road.'

Her stomach flipping over, Ava clicked the key and heard the whump of the locks opening. The sound, something she'd never put any store in before, had such enormous significance today that she inhaled slowly.

As Jenna opened the boot and slid the bag and blanket inside, Ava took another second to gather herself.

'Here, put this in the back seat, please.' She held the flask out to Mandy, who was hovering at the side of the car.

Mandy took the flask from her and opened the back door.

'Come on, Carly.' Mandy beckoned to Carly, who, with a hand tracing the door frame above her head, slipped into the back seat.

Jenna jumped into the passenger seat, and as Ava slid into the driver's side, Jenna patted Ava's leg and whispered, 'It'll be fine.'

*

After a few initial nerves, Ava had found the driving less traumatic than she'd expected. As she'd gripped the familiar steering wheel, she'd pushed away an image of Rick's hands on the narrow wheel of the convertible. She simply couldn't allow herself to go there and, with Jenna next to her, smiling encouragingly, Ava had pressed her foot on the accelerator and moved them all forward, if slowly.

The picnic had gone well, the sun greeting them as they got out of the car and paced across the white strip of beach. It being midweek, there was hardly anyone around, and soon the girls had rolled up their jeans and were paddling in the icy water, screeching at the frigid temperature.

Jenna and Ava had lain on the blanket, their jackets zipped against the fresh breeze, and watched cotton-wool clouds slide by. Clusters of seagulls banked overhead, cawing as they dived to inches above the water before righting themselves and landing gracefully on the rippling surface.

Ava planned on going in to see Rick in the afternoon so had been able to relax into the peace of the morning, the constant knot of tension under her diaphragm easing as she breathed in the salty air and Jenna's comforting presence.

Now, back at home, the Audi sat in the driveway, waiting for her once again. Jenna had set up Carly's favourite Harry Potter film, the first with Luna Lovegood joining the cast, and the two women stifled their laughter as Mandy groaned, 'Oh, not this one again.' Then, Jenna had waved Ava off, telling her to kiss Rick for her.

Ava circled the car, opened the door and got in, and as she slung her handbag onto the passenger seat, her phone rang. Pulling it out, she saw a number she didn't recognise. Her nerves jangling, she answered. 'Hello?'

'Eh, hello. Is this Ava?'

The gravelly voice was familiar, but she couldn't place it. 'Yes. Who's this?' She frowned.

'It's Cameron Cole.' He cleared his throat as Ava pictured Jim's giant younger brother, the mop of dark hair and the kind eyes.

'Oh, Cameron. Hi.' Relief flooded through her. 'How are you?' She twisted the rear-view mirror towards her and ran a hand through her hair.

'I'm fine. I was calling to see if I could pop by and talk to you about finishing the kitchen, but how's Rick? I've been wanting to ask.'

Touched, Ava adjusted the mirror. 'Oh, he's the same, Cameron. No change yet.' She hated the words as they spiralled into the car. This statement was as cumbersome and useless as she felt when she sat at Rick's bedside, her fingers covering his cold hand and his eyelids still as closed to her as they'd been since the day their lives had imploded.

'I'm sorry,' Cameron said. 'I was gutted when I heard what had happened.'

'Thanks, I appreciate that.'

'If there's anything we can do, just say. Rick's a good lad, and Jim and I are happy to help out with things, until he gets home.'

Ava closed her eyes for a second, this unexpected dose of kindness threatening to crack the veneer of bravery she was carefully cultivating. 'Thanks, Cameron. That's very kind.' She put the key in the ignition. 'When can you come over to talk about the work?' She winced, hoping she hadn't sounded too businesslike.

'How about tomorrow morning? I could be there around half-eight.'

Ava grimaced. 'We take a wee while to get going these days, and our friends are here, but they're leaving in the morning. Could we make it a bit later, maybe around ten?' She turned the key, the engine rumbling into life.

'Aye, sure. No problem.' Cameron laughed softly. 'Take care now, and I'll see you then.'

'Thanks a million. See you tomorrow.'

Relieved, Ava did a three-point turn and nosed the car down the drive towards the road.

Doctor Stewart had just left the room, so Ava slid the chair closer to Rick's bed. There had been no improvement in his condition, but despite the status quo, Doctor Stewart seemed less comfortable to report on the situation. Ava had asked if they were still considering a craniectomy and he'd shaken his head. 'No, because the swelling is coming down.' He'd cracked his knuckles, making Ava wince. 'We'll continue the current protocol and keep watching his progress.'

The last word had grated, making Ava press her lips together. Rick didn't seem to be making any progress at all, so the doctor's use of it seemed incongruous, but rather than call him on it, she'd nodded. 'Right. I understand.'

Now, Rick's hand was in hers and Ava leaned in close to his ear. Someone had shaved him and there was a tiny row of stubble they'd missed under his jaw. She touched it gently with her finger. 'Hi, love. It's May thirtieth. You've been asleep for over three weeks now, and Rick…' Suddenly overcome, she sat upright. 'I really need you to wake up.' Her vision blurred, but rather than sadness sucking her in, Ava was filled with an angry desire to straddle him, clamp her thighs around his hips, put her hands on his shoulders and shake him until his teeth rattled.

There was no music that would soften the sharp edges of her wrecked soul today, no feathers, or fresh herbs to test him with, just Ava, in a cold room, and her husband, silent, distant, and infuriatingly still. 'Rick, please. You've got to wake up. Come on, dammit. I know you're in there.' She stared at the motionless eyelids, them still blocking her out now a slight. 'For God's sake, Rick, try.' She grabbed his hand. 'You can't do this to us.' Her fingers dug into the soft flesh of his palm. 'This whole thing was your idea. Coming up here, the barn, starting a business, turning our lives upside down.' She released his hand. 'We're here because of your dreams, and now…' She stood and walked to the window, noticing that it was open a crack, the smell of fresh-cut grass wafting in from the lawn behind the building.

Turning back to look at him, the love of her life, frozen in time, her anger seeped away as quickly as it had appeared. More than anything, she missed hearing his voice, the deep rumble of his laughter, the way he talked around a kiss, or whispered to her in the dark. Unable to let herself go where her heart wanted to lead her, she focused on what her head was telling her.

'Carly's getting worse. It's happening so fast now that I need to start making some decisions.' She walked back to the chair. 'I've decided to home-school her, just for the rest of this term. She wasn't happy about it, but I'm worried she won't be safe at school.' As she said it out loud, the decision solidified itself, then, like dominoes, others that had been spinning in the back of her mind fell into place. 'I'm going to look into applying for a guide dog, and I'm going to take her on some day trips, whatever I can manage that's within a day of here, before she can't…' She rested her palm on his forearm, the thistle tattoo an incongruous snapshot of their time together, before all their lives had become suspended.

As she pictured her and Carly, standing in a gallery, in a line at Disneyland, or on the slopes of Ben Nevis, the magnificence of the Cairngorms at their feet, within each image was a gaping hole.

Ava took a deep breath and leaned back. 'I've asked Jim and Cameron to come back and finish the work on the barn.' She dragged her hair from her forehead, her fingernails leaving trails of prickles across her scalp. 'We need to move things forward.' She took in his broad shoulders, somehow less imposing now, the weight loss most evident in the slight cleft that had appeared in each cheek. 'I can do this without you, Rick, but I don't want to.' She paused. 'Can you hear me?' She leaned in and whispered, 'I don't want to.'

CHAPTER SEVENTEEN

Ava passed Cameron's old, mud-spattered Land Rover in the driveway, as she followed him up to the barn. He'd arrived a few minutes early, but she had been ready for him. She'd got up at 7 a.m., making sure to leave time for a leisurely breakfast with Jenna, before she and Mandy set off for home. They'd talked more about Ava's plans, and Jenna had assured her that she was doing the right thing and, for now, her focus must be Carly.

As soon as Jenna's car disappeared down the drive, Carly had retreated to her room, and Ava had said she could have an hour to herself before they started lessons for the day.

Now, running through the lesson plan in her mind, Ava pulled her hood up against the fat raindrops that were pattering her head and hurried to catch up with Cameron, whose giant stride had given him a lead on her.

'Thanks for coming. I mean, fitting us back in.' She spoke to his denim-clad shoulders as he paced up the hill, his long legs and heavy boots igniting images of Rick that made Ava's breath falter.

'It's no bother.' He stopped under the narrow overhang at the barn door. 'Got the key?' He smiled at her, his dark hair, a little shorter than the last time she'd seen him, glistening from the rain. He shook his head, carefree and dog-like, sending a shower of water droplets into the air. 'Summer in Dornoch, eh?' He grinned, the gentle eyes that Ava remembered glinting warmly beneath his heavy brows.

She pulled the key from her pocket and smiled as she handed it to him. 'Here you go.'

'Cheers.' He took it and opened the door, wiping his muddy boots on the doormat that, less than four weeks ago, Ava had laid on the flagstone threshold. It had four large, black paw prints on it, and said 'Welcome Home' in bold script. It had been an odd choice, but she'd grabbed it at the Superstore in Inverness, along with a few provisions for their trip. Seeing it now brought her to a standstill, an image of them all staring up at the Eiffel Tower flickering dully behind her eyes.

Cameron stood back to let Ava pass. 'After you.' He waited for her to walk in, then followed her inside, a waft of something minty coming with him.

The chill of the barn coated Ava's damp face, and she shivered.

'So, we're fine as far as the materials go,' Cameron said, as Ava lowered her hood, releasing her hair from under her collar. He stood opposite her, at the far side of Rick's worktable. 'All the wood and hardware for the cabinets is in the warehouse, we just need to get it delivered.' He looked down at the blueprints still covering the tabletop. 'The plans are clear, and as I'll finish the other job I'm on by tomorrow, I can get started here as soon as everything arrives.' He placed a palm on the drawing. 'I wanted to ask you something, though.' He lifted his eyes to hers.

Curious, Ava brushed the beads of moisture from her jacket and met his gaze. 'OK.'

'I was wondering if you might want to think about pre-made cabinetry, even just for the island. It could speed things along, if time is a problem, or if...' He frowned. 'I can still do the work, I was just thinking you might want me out of here sooner rather than later.' He straightened up. 'Having workmen around isn't always the best, especially when…' His voice trailed.

Understanding, Ava shook her head. 'It's fine, Cameron. We budgeted for this.' She paused. 'You know, even in the few weeks you've worked with Rick, you and Jim have become more than just workmen to us.' She recognised the truth as she said it. 'Rick really enjoyed your company.' The words out, her hand went up to her mouth. She'd referred to her husband in the past tense and, as time stood still, a horrified chill slid down her back. Why had she done that? If she took it back, right now, perhaps it wouldn't have happened. Her mind taking flight, she spoke deliberately. 'He considers you and Jim friends, as do I.' She shifted her weight, feeling the grind of sawdust under her shoes.

Cameron's hands dived into his pockets. 'Aye, we feel the same.' He gave a half-smile. 'Rick's an easy man to get on with.'

'He is.' Grateful that Cameron had either not noticed, or purposefully ignored what she'd done, she exhaled. 'He drives me batty sometimes, but he's pretty amazing, really.' Not trusting her voice further, she walked to the far end of the room and took her time turning back to face him. 'I think we should stick to the plan, go custom with it all.' She drew an arc around herself. 'If we don't, there will be hell to pay when he comes home.' She found a smile.

Cameron laughed, a deep, mellow sound that injected a welcome sliver of life into the stillness of the chilly barn. 'Aye, true enough. All right then. Jim will put in the last of the power outlets over there, and then that side of things is done.' He pointed at the wall behind her.

As they talked through the final configuration of the upper cabinets, discussed the positioning of the two sets of glass-fronted doors Rick had included in the design, and reconfirmed the locations of the appliances, Ava let herself be drawn into the welcome minutia. Soon, this would be a kitchen, a place where a family might sit around the island watching someone cook. Perhaps they'd play board games while the parents shared a bottle of wine, the fire crackling in the grate as laughter floated around them. As she imagined it, the sweet normality of it all, Ava missed Rick so much that she gasped, her fingertips going to the bridge of her nose.

'Are you all right?' Cameron's hand was under her arm, gently guiding her to the scruffy director's chair that Rick used.

Ava sank down, grateful for the familiar sag of the canvas as she lifted her chin and looked at the vaulted ceiling, her hair falling over the back of the chair in a silky stream. 'God, I miss him so much.' Her voice cracked and, embarrassed about blurting this to such a new acquaintance, she gave a strangled laugh. 'Sorry, Cameron. It's OK most of the time. I mean it's not *OK*.' She righted herself. 'But I can handle it. You know?' She scanned his face, seeing his eyes full of sympathy. 'Sorry,' she whispered.

'Don't apologise. I don't know how you're coping with everything.' His eyebrows jumped. 'Most folk would be useless, so you need to give yourself some credit.' He rubbed his fingers across his chin. 'I miss my partner all the time, and he's just away working on the rigs.'

As he revealed this intimate detail about himself, his cheeks took on a rosy hue, and Ava fought the desire to jump up and fling her arms around his big, vulnerable neck. And yet, even as she saw the kindness that she'd first recognised in him, floating around him like an aura, the sight of it was blinding. Rather than thank him, all she could do was nod, torn between her gratitude for his understanding, and a surge of anger that he wasn't the one person she needed to be standing there.

Their lessons done for the day, and after Cameron had popped his head in to say goodbye, knowing the coast was clear from further visitors, Ava suggested they have a pyjama evening, something Carly loved to do when Rick was home early enough from work. They'd all get ready for bed, sit in the kitchen as someone cooked dinner, talking about their days and picking out what they'd watch on TV, then they'd eat their meals on trays.

This evening, Ava wanted to talk to Carly again about starting their trips, as she had been cautious when Ava had first brought it up, after Jenna and Mandy had left. Carly had taken a while to respond, then she'd simply said, 'But what about Dad?'

Ava had pulled her into her arms and said, 'Dad would want us to go. Trust me.'

As the evening progressed, and Ava gently reintroduced the idea, Carly's enthusiasm seemed to have grown, and now, as she sat at the kitchen table, a smile pulled at her mouth. 'So, when we go to Edinburgh, we'll see the Van Gogh painting, go to the Zoo, and then can we do the haunted tour of the city that's at midnight, or something?' She peered at Ava's laptop, where an image of Van Gogh's plum trees filled the screen. The simple beauty of the painting, coupled with her daughter's tentative enthusiasm, brought a lump to Ava's throat.

'Yes, of course we can. All of the above.' She rubbed Carly's back, her fingertips tracing the birdlike ribcage, sparking an image of a fledgling about to take flight before its wings were fully formed. 'In fact, we're going to Edinburgh first.' She felt Carly tense.

'Really? When?' Carly spun around and tipped her head to the side, focusing on Ava's mouth.

'Next week.' Ava smiled as Carly's eyebrows shot up.

'Really?'

'Yep.' Ava laughed. 'We're all booked up. We just need to pack an overnight bag and we're off.'

At this, Carly's face darkened. 'We're staying the night?'

'Yes. It's a four-hour drive, sweetheart. Too far to make it there and back in a day.' She reached for Carly's hand, as a frown wrinkled her brow. 'What is it?'

Carly licked her lips nervously. 'What if…' She halted.

'What, love? Tell me.' Ava cupped her daughter's cheek in her palm.

'What if Dad wakes up and we're not home?' She flicked her eyes to the door as if Rick was likely to walk in any second. 'He'll be all alone.'

Hearing Carly mirroring her own fear, Ava took a few moments to compose herself. 'Carly, your dad will understand. You and I talked about this the other day, and we agreed that he'd want us to go and see things. Right?'

Carly's face contorted as she processed the thought, then she nodded slowly. 'Yes, but isn't it selfish? To have fun and stuff. Especially after what I did…'

Shards of incomplete information sliding into place, Carly's tender apology at her father's bedside suddenly took on a shape that Ava did not like, at all. 'What do you mean, what you *did*?'

Carly shook her head. 'Nothing.'

Ava's hand tightened around her daughter's. 'Don't do that, please. Tell me what you mean?'

Carly swiped at her eyes. 'In the car. The day of the accident.' She hiccupped, driving a tiny arrow of pain through Ava's heart.

'What about it?' Ava's pulse quickened as she replayed the traumatic scene in her head, as she had done so many times now.

'I leaned out and shouted, made Dad turn around and look at me. I didn't sit up when you told me to.' She held her palms up. 'I made him turn around, and then…' She lost the last words in a sob, but Ava got the message, loud and clear. Carly clearly blamed herself for the accident, and Rick's injuries, and now that Ava understood that heartbreaking reality, she needed to put it out of Carly's mind, once and for all.

'You absolutely are not to blame, Carly. You mustn't think that for one second.'

Carly wiped her nose on her sleeve. 'I am, though.'

Ava eased her daughter closer, Carly settling awkwardly on her knee. 'No, you are not. We were in that daft car your dad hired, not the good old rattletrap. We had the roof down, the seat belts were only lap straps, and there were no airbags. Then, the deer ran out in front of the lorry, and the lorry swerved towards us. Dad tried to avoid it, but there wasn't time. If we'd just been in the Audi…' Her voice faded as, shockingly, she realised she was angry with Rick, and with herself, for letting him placate her about the safety of the little car. The thought simmered until she shook it away. At this point, casting blame was as useless as saying *if only*. She hugged Carly tightly. 'It was not your fault, Carly.'

Carly shivered against her, sniffing softly. 'Are you sure?'

'One hundred per cent.' Ava nodded, overcome by a rush of protective love, so powerful it made her sway. 'So, we need to do these trips now, and if Dad does wake up, we can be back home in a few hours.' Ava loosened her grip on Carly and stood up. Carly needed this and, for now, Ava's only mission was to give her daughter at least a shade of the experiences that she deserved. 'Come on, let's get excited.' She threw her arms wide. 'It'll be fun.'

Carly moved to Ava's side and wrapped her arms around her middle. 'I love you, Mum.'

'I love you more, Flopsy.' Using the pet name that Rick had given Carly years ago, Ava squeezed her tight, the gentle scent of lavender soap lingering on Carly's skin.

As they talked about their trip to Edinburgh, Ava explained that she had booked them into a posh hotel for the night, overlooking Prince's Gardens. Then, to Carly's delight, Ava made dinner reservations at Bertie's on The Royal Mile, famous for its fish and chips, and booked their tickets for the haunted city tour.

They decided on boiled eggs and toast fingers for dinner, sat side by side on the sofa and, inevitably, watched the Harry Potter film where Luna was joining Dumbledore's army. Ava tried not to notice as Carly eventually set her tray on the floor and slid off the couch, onto the rug, her head tilted to the side as she focused on the TV. The sight of her sweet girl, who used to fly around the house, turning circles as she went, now bumping the old chest with her elbow as she shifted, struggling to see the screen, was gut-wrenching. The gravity of Carly's increasing struggle was painful confirmation of the timeliness of another decision Ava had made.

CHAPTER EIGHTEEN

A few days later, hopeful that their conversation about the trips had eliminated any obstacles, Ava asked Carly if she wanted to go with her to the hospital, and when Carly shook her head, Ava's disappointment must have been obvious, as Carly turned away from her and began shuffling tubes of paint around on her desk.

Leaving Carly's room, Ava walked into the hall, and on the point of calling Stephanie to come over, she stopped herself. Ava was acutely aware of how important it was for Carly to feel self-sufficient, so instead of undermining whatever shred of that her daughter was clinging to, Ava turned around and tapped on the bedroom door again. 'Would you be OK being left alone for an hour or so, if Cameron's working up in the barn?' She paused. 'We can get you set up to do some painting, until I get back.'

Carly nodded, her eyes darting to the door. 'Yes, fine. I can always call his mobile if I need anything.'

'All right then.' Glad that her intuition had not completely failed her, Ava kissed her daughter, then ran up to the barn and asked Cameron if he would mind checking on Carly in about an hour.

'Sure, no problem.' He grinned, his hair dusty with wood shavings. 'I'll tell her I need some more biscuits, or something.' He gestured towards the empty plate on Rick's table.

'Good idea.' Ava gave him a thumbs-up. 'Thank you, again.' She pressed her palms together. 'I seem to be saying that a lot to you, at the moment.'

Cameron's face coloured and he swiped at the air. 'Not at all. Away you go. She'll be fine.'

Outside, the morning was balmy, the smell of the lavender drifting up the hill on the gentle breeze, and Ava breathed it in as she paced down towards the house, picturing Flora lovingly tending the plants.

Just as Ava turned the corner onto the front path, her phone buzzed in her back pocket. A whisper deep inside told her to stop, check who it was before going back inside, and when she looked at the screen and saw the number of the hospital, her hands began to tremble as she answered the call.

'Ava, it's Doctor Stewart.' His voice was low, metred. 'There's been a change...'

Ava sucked in a breath, stepped back and pressed her hips against the wall of the house, her arm wrapping around her middle. Whatever the change was, it clearly wasn't positive. 'What's happened?' she croaked, glancing to her side to make sure the front door remained closed, keeping Carly safely protected from whatever was coming.

'Based on this morning's examination, Richard's brain function has deteriorated. There have been some alterations and we've had to...' He cleared his throat. 'Ava, can you come in? I think we need to talk in person.'

Alterations. What the hell did that mean? Ava forced a swallow. 'I was just about to come in, but what kind of alterations?' She pushed herself away from the house and paced along the path, heading back towards the barn, her heart thumping in time with her steps.

'It's probably best if we talk when you get here. And, Ava, you need to prepare yourself. He's not doing well.' He paused. 'Can you come to my office first?'

The words penetrated her heart like a dagger as she stopped her progress up the hill and pressed her eyes closed. He'd never asked this of her before, and the images his request provoked were nightmarish. 'I'll be there in twenty minutes,' she whispered, then, unable to utter another word, she hung up.

Doctor Stewart's office was stuffy despite the open window. The desk was a mess of papers, and the chair Ava usually sat on was hidden under several files that he now reached down and moved. 'Sorry, we've been doing some housekeeping.' He tossed the files onto the cabinet next to his desk, then sat down.

Unable to stand any more preamble, Ava leaned forward. 'Tell me what's happened, please.'

Doctor Stewart nodded. 'Right. As I mentioned, Richard's brain function has deteriorated, and from what we're seeing, the chances of recovery have lessened significantly, Ava.' He lifted what she assumed was Rick's chart and scanned it, his mouth pulsing.

'What exactly do you mean?' Panic gripped her, her heart clattering dangerously under her breastbone.

'Before we get into that further, how are you?'

Still rocked by his statement, and momentarily confused by the diversion, she shook her head. 'We're all right. Carly's dealing with the visual changes better than I would. I don't know where she gets the strength, honestly.' Ava swallowed, another awkward sliver of overshared personal information chipping off her protective shell.

Doctor Stewart held her gaze. 'I'm not surprised at all.' His tone switched from all business to one of gentle admiration. 'You're coping like a champion, yourself.' He nodded. 'Listen, Ava. I think it's time we considered some options.'

A film of sweat gathering on her upper lip, Ava's eyes flicked beyond him to the door, a potential escape from what he was about to say. 'What options?' She pulled her shoulders back, readying herself for a blow.

'We've had to intubate Richard this morning, to help him with his breathing. I wanted to prepare you. With this new setback, we had no choice, so the ventilator will take care of that for him now.'

Ava stood up. She knew this had been a possibility, but having it happen was like the earth giving way under her, gravity tugging her downwards towards a jagged point. 'It sounds as if you're writing him off.' Her voice shaking, she paced around behind the chair.

Doctor Stewart shook his head. 'No. It's simply the next phase of supporting his organ function. There's no hidden agenda here, Ava. I'm just letting you know what's happening.'

She exhaled, forcing out some of the knot of pain that had gathered under her ribs. 'So, is there anything else you can do at the moment?' she asked, her fierce grip on the back of the chair the only sensation she was aware of.

'No, Ava. We've covered everything.' He shook his head. 'This is just a next step in best care for Richard, in his current condition.'

Letting the information sink in, Ava blinked, picturing the tube being inserted into Rick's throat, snaking down his oesophagus, carrying waves of crisp oxygen to his tired lungs. She forced a swallow. 'Can I see him now?'

Doctor Stewart nodded. 'Yes, but I did want to speak to you about something else, first.' He eyed her. 'This is not easy, Ava, so please sit.' He pointed at the chair.

Her insides quivering, she sat and met his gaze. 'What is it?'

'Richard is listed on the national organ donor register.' He hesitated. 'It might be time for you to consider his wishes, for end-of-life care.' He dropped his gaze to the desk as Ava's middle collapsed on itself, shock tugging her mouth open. This could not be happening.

'He never said anything to me about being a donor.' She blinked, trying to dredge up any memories she could of long-past conversations when they might have discussed what they would do in the unlikely situation where one of them was being sustained by machinery, while the other sat nearby, helpless. Unable to recall any such interaction, she shook her head. 'We never talked about it.' As she considered the fact, Ava felt the magnitude of this oversight. Not only had they not discussed this unimaginable eventuality, but she didn't even know Rick's thoughts on life support, or extreme measures of medical intervention, his feelings on death, or what kind of funeral he wanted.

There had been so much time ahead of them for that, it hadn't seemed important. As everything she didn't know about her husband began to mount up, forming a wall of ignorance that made her feel utterly inadequate, and ill-prepared, Ava folded at the waist. Her forehead dropped to her knees, as silent sobs radiated from her core, rippling their way along her back and arms, and coursing down to her numbing fingertips.

As Doctor Stewart got up and hovered awkwardly at her side, Ava managed to whisper, 'I'm not ready to talk about this. Please just take me to my husband.'

Twenty minutes later, Ava lifted Rick's hand, wrapping her fingers around his, noting the new boniness, the lack of healthy flesh, and picturing his wedding ring that lay in the drawer of her bedside table.

The ventilator ticked next to the bed, an unwelcome addition to the battery of machines he was now connected to, drawing Ava's attention away from the face she adored, the gentle mouth she'd kissed countless times, hidden behind a breathing tube that was taped to his cheek, ugly and intrusive.

As she leaned forward and let her head touch the blanket, she tried to picture his eyes, the warm hazel irises, the slight wrinkles that had started to appear at the corners before he cracked that trademark smile, but all she could see was the closed lids that had greeted her for weeks now. As she forced herself to breathe, in and out, slow and steady, Doctor Stewart's words came back to her. *It's time to consider options. Richard was on the national donor register.*

Suddenly, Ava sat up, her heart racing as she stared at her husband's impassive face. What if Rick's eyes…? No, it was too much. She couldn't let herself go there. But the more she tried to divert her thoughts back to the room, the more they were drawn to Carly's face, her cornflower blue eyes, damaged and dulled to the world. What if there was something that Rick could do for Carly, and what if, God forbid, she, Ava, had to make that decision?

CHAPTER NINETEEN

The rest of Ava's visit with Rick had been soul-crushing, and having agonised over whether to tell Carly of his deterioration, as soon as she'd pulled into the driveway Ava was convinced that it would be the worst thing she could do. Carly had only just embraced the idea of going to Edinburgh and sharing this information with her would serve only to create a new obstacle, and probably fan the embers of her unfounded guilt over the accident.

Not having the luxury of dwelling on Rick's cryogenic state, or the unthinkable question that she'd asked herself at his bedside, Ava moved around in a fog. She hugged Carly tightly and told that her dad was still unconscious, distracted her by making something to eat, then took the laptop into her office and closed the door. Knowing that Rick would urge her to do so, she turned her attention to her daughter's needs, the next set of tasks she had set herself seeming to be the only thing that would keep her from losing her mind.

Within a few minutes, she found a local riding school that could cater to Carly's condition and, with one phone call, registered her for an initial session the following week. Getting her back on a horse now seemed more critical to her overall well-being than sticking to the home-school curriculum, although Ava also knew how important it was that Carly didn't fall behind.

Next, she called The Guide Dog Centre in Inverness, and the counsellor, a soft-spoken woman called Megan, gave her the pertinent information to get Carly's application underway. Not having had any idea of what the process would involve, Ava now knew that there were several steps they'd have to work through to qualify, potentially including some residential training. With her new-found knowledge, she began to plan the timing of that around a couple of the trips she wanted to take Carly on, over the next few weeks. Time was of the essence, and with so many priorities clamouring for her attention, Ava felt the passing of it like a tide lapping at her ankles.

The following morning, getting Carly out of the house was taking longer than Ava had expected. The formerly simple tasks of washing her hair, finding what she needed from the bathroom cabinet, choosing clothes and packing her bag had become protracted, and drama-ridden, as Carly, having insisted she do it all herself, then fretted about remembering everything, while bumping around her bedroom, knocking things off her dresser and tripping on a sweater she'd left on the floor.

All the while, Ava hovered out in the kitchen, intermittently checking her phone for messages as she listened to the thumps and mutters, her body straining towards her daughter's room, the compulsion to swoop in and fix everything for her overwhelming. Instead, her own bag already sitting by the door, Ava put some laundry in the washing machine, checked her email, called the hospital to remind them that she was going to be away for the night, and left a note for Cameron with the name of their hotel, which she dashed up and pinned to the barn door.

By the time she walked back into the house, Carly was standing in the living room, her backpack stuffed full and sitting at her feet. She wore a pair of black and white checked leggings under a long floral T-shirt, and a silvery Alice band held her hair back from her face. 'See, I did it.' She grinned, fanning her face with her hand.

'Well done you.' Ava smiled at the typical collage of colours and patterns. 'I knew you could.'

Carly twisted her head and squinted at the sideboard. 'Can you see my sunglasses anywhere? I can't find them.' The smile gone, she sounded suddenly anxious.

Ava spun around, scanning the room, spotting the plastic frames folded neatly on the chest by the fire. 'They're on the chest.' She hesitated, unsure whether to slip by Carly and grab them or to wait while Carly navigated her way across the room herself.

Seeming to sense her mother's uncertainty, Carly dropped her chin. 'Could you get them, please? We're already late, and I'll probably go head-first over something.' The laugh that followed was both gentle and nervous.

Relieved that Carly was letting her help, pride in her daughter's fortitude bloomed across Ava's heart. 'Of course.' She touched Carly's shoulder as she passed. 'Do you need the loo before we go?'

Carly sighed. 'I'm not three, Mum.'

Smiling to herself, Ava lifted the glasses from the chest and made her way to the front door, as Carly grimaced.

'Oh, hang on though.' She made two fists and shoved them under her chin, twisting her face comically as if she were bearing down. 'Nope, I think I'm fine.'

'Carly Guthrie.' Ava laughed, the release like a fresh breeze across her face. 'Let's go, madam.'

During the first leg of the journey, Carly was engrossed in something on her iPad and with cars flitting past them at high speeds, Ava gripped the steering wheel tightly and kept her eyes glued to the road. The distance she was creating between her and Rick was making her nervous, and it took all her strength to focus on the objective of this trip, as something essential for Carly.

As they eventually skirted the picturesque Cairngorms National Park, swaths of dense forest lining the road on either side, Ava reached over and touched Carly's hand. 'You're missing it all.' She pointed at the dramatic, purple-tinged slopes of the mountains, arching high into the moody sky beyond the trees. 'I thought maybe we could go to Loch an Eilein one day. It's not too far from here. I went there with Gran Flora, and it's really pretty. There's a lovely little castle ruin on an island in the middle, and we can take a picnic, and do some painting.'

'Sounds nice.'

Ava glanced over as Carly adjusted her sunglasses, then looked out her window.

The loch was not only picturesque, and atmospheric, but was typical of the unspoilt beauty of the Cairngorms. Plus, as Ava recalled, it had a safe path that they could follow easily, without worrying about potential hazards for Carly. The idea that she must consider things like that for her beautiful, active daughter still rocked Ava. She'd never get used to that.

They made a brief stop for lunch in Pitlochry, a quaint Perthshire town on the banks of the river Tummel, and a favourite of Ava's. Complete with a fish ladder, and a high street with storefronts crammed with colourful tartans, more malt whiskies than you could count, and dainty tea-rooms serving tantalising baked goods, it resembled every visitor's vision of a picture-perfect Highland town.

Carly was charmed. 'It's pretty here.' She turned her head, taking in the cobbled street leading to an old watermill. 'Can we walk that way and look in the shops?'

'Sure.' Ava looped Carly's hand over her arm, hoping the gesture would come across as casual, with no agenda other than to enjoy the moment they were sharing. To her relief, Carly left her hand there and moved carefully along beside Ava, absorbing her surroundings, lingering to peer in several windows.

When they came to an art gallery, Carly stopped short, jamming her nose up to the window where a display of subtle watercolours, of handsome stags and willowy does were hung in a set of triangles. 'These look sort of normal.' A smudge of steam spread across the glass as Carly spoke, her fingertips leaving a trail of smears.

Ava was overcome that her daughter could still see something so subtle, and beautiful.

Then, Carly backtracked. 'I mean, they're still fuzzy in the middle, but I can sort of see what they are, even though the colours they've used are pretty dull.' Carly turned to her, her cheeks flushed.

Ava simply nodded, her voice suddenly feeling brittle, and not to be trusted, as she took in the rich tans of the background, and notes of orange and rusty-red in the antlers. Ava had known that colour blindness was yet another blow that Stargardt's could deliver, but until now, Carly had not mentioned anything that would indicate that that had started. If Carly could no longer see colours correctly, how could she paint? What else would this damn disease rob her precious girl of? Wishing the sickening thoughts away, Ava added another mental note to her ever-growing list, to do more reading on the subject when she got home, and to call Doctor Anderson, again.

The remainder of the drive was uneventful and once they'd made it over the Firth of Forth, Ava carefully navigated her way through the labyrinth of Edinburgh's New Town, admiring the gently curved crescents of elegant, terraced homes, with their classic architecture, tall windows and private gardens. Rick loved this part of the city, and whenever they'd visited, before Carly was born, they'd linger in this area. They would park and walk the streets, imagining what it would be like to live in one of the classy homes, perhaps take a bottle of wine into the private, locked garden they'd have a key to, and read their books as the sun went down.

Ava let the memories flood in as she pictured her and Rick holding hands, leaning into one another as they shared their innocent dreams. As she visualised it, she was grateful that they'd been unaware of what was to come, as if they had, each and every moment like those that they'd relished would have been tainted, much as the future felt to her now.

As she drove on to their hotel, on Princes Street, Ava shook off the potential for gloom and concentrated on the GPS.

Tapping her fingers on her thigh, Carly hummed to herself, finishing a tube of mints that Rick had left in the central console, next to a handful of coins that rattled with every bump they encountered, a comforting reminder of his presence.

CHAPTER TWENTY

Their room was bright and high-ceilinged, with a king-size bed and a marble-floored bathroom, with a massive tub that Carly immediately climbed into, fully clothed, laughing, and saying that she could sleep in it. Two sash windows overlooked the gardens, and the majestic castle beyond, and as they stood together, looking down on the people milling around, Carly rotated her head from side to side, tipped it to the right, then slipped her sunglasses back on.

The series of movements becoming as familiar as they were heartbreaking, Ava put her arm around her daughter's narrow shoulders and pulled her close. 'What do you want to do first?' She kissed the top of Carly's silky head.

'Get an ice-cream smoothie, and then start with the gallery?' She stepped back from the window and, as Ava held her breath, Carly managed to skirt the edge of the bed, missing the corner of the bedspread that lay, artfully draped, across the carpet. These tiny manoeuvres, seemingly so inconsequential, had become monumental, and Ava was living on her nerves each time Carly either succumbed to, or conquered them, one at a time.

'Great idea. Ice cream is the best way to start any outing.' Ava diverted her gaze to the door, as, making her way to the bathroom, Carly trailed her fingertips along the wall, another new habit that, each time she witnessed it, swept the ground from under Ava.

They quickly unpacked their bags, walked to a café down the street and picked up some blended drinks, then headed towards the National Gallery. The June afternoon was mercifully mild, so they lingered in Princes Gardens. They sat on a grassy bank for a while, people-watching, and as Carly noisily sipped her drink, her head moving away from the sun as it slid in and out from behind the light covering of clouds, Ava subtly checked her phone again. Seeing nothing, she slipped it away.

Above them, Edinburgh Castle was perched high on its basalt cliff, the Castle Rock, dominating the Old Town skyline. Ava stared up at the familiar shape, using her hand as a visor as she focused on the impressive structure, the impossibly high walls springing straight out of the rock beneath them. No matter how many times she saw this sight, it never failed to impress her. Archaeologists had suggested that the rock had been occupied, in some form or another, since the Iron Age, that fact lending even more weight to Ava's innate pride in their capital city.

Despite the thick, raspberry smoothie she'd just drunk, the smell of cinnamon in the air was making Ava hungry, so she nudged Carly's arm. 'Hey, shall we get some warm doughnuts? There's a vendor over there, near the merry-go-round.' She pointed to her right, seeing Carly squinting into the watery light, tracking the course of Ava's finger.

The merry-go-round had been a fixture in the gardens for years, and Ava remembered riding on it with her parents when she'd been just eight years old. As she helped Carly up, Ava once again slipped back in time.

Her memories of her parents, and them as a family, were numerous, and all equally as sweet, but their brief stay here over one of her mother's birthdays had stuck with Ava particularly.

The deep regret that her parents hadn't lived to see her marry her soulmate, or become a mother, rarely left her, and as Ava let herself remember, she closed her eyes for a moment and rode the merry-go-round once again. Her father's hands were firm around her waist as they shared a painted horse. She could smell the hot, sugary candyfloss, hear the jangle of the canned music and the sound of her mother's laughter as she stood back and watched them go by.

'What are you thinking about?' Carly's question snapped her back to the moment, as two young men sped past them on skateboards, one wearing a kilt and a battered leather jacket, and the other, ripped jeans, and a sweatshirt with a Doctor Who logo on the back. Before Ava could grab her, Carly's foot faltered as she dodged the second skater, and she fell onto the grass beside the path.

'Oh, sweetheart.' On a reflex, Ava jumped forward and hefted Carly up, gripping her hand. Turning back in the direction the skaters had gone, before she could stop herself, Ava shouted at their backs, 'Be careful, you idiots.' Her voice shook, and she glared at a young couple across the path who were gaping at her as she battled angry tears. When she looked back at Carly, she saw crippling embarrassment on her daughter's face and, instantly flooded with shame, Ava stuttered, 'I'm sorry, love.'

Carly pulled her hand away, the break of contact like a spark.

'I didn't mean to…'

Carly shoved her hair away from her face and tugged her jacket down at the back. 'It's OK, Mum. Let's just go,' she huffed.

Ava took a deep breath, regretting that her outburst had drawn attention to them. The best course of action now was to move quickly away, leave the incident, and her mishandling of it, behind.

A few minutes later, as they walked into the National Gallery, the strained energy between them seemed to have eased. The neoclassical building had been opened in 1859 and the air inside it, while cool, held the weight of historic significance, and the mild scent of age.

Ava stopped inside the entrance and took in the light-filled central gallery with its checked marble floor, the matching rows of Palladian arches lined up along the upper balconies, and the glass-panelled ceiling soaring above the triple-storey lobby. Hushed whispers rose from the open space below as several people wandered around, passing up and down the main staircase that connected the street and lower-level display areas.

Carly stood close to her side, her hand hovering near Ava's, the proximity of the thin fingers a magnet that Ava fought to resist. 'Shall we go down?' Ava pointed at the stairs. 'The Van Gogh is down there.' She smiled at Carly, who had moved towards the bannister, her hand tracing the broad surface of the stone.

'OK.' Carly took off her sunglasses and slid them into her pocket. 'I don't need them in here.' She turned her head, and smiled, her pale eyes full of light.

Seeing the beautiful and yet damaged blue pools, so full of anticipation, Ava's mind slipped once again to Rick, the healthy tissue that lay beneath the closed lids, and she caught her breath. What if? Could she even contemplate it? Was it even possible? If Rick could do something for his daughter, wouldn't he expect Ava to make that choice?

That she'd allowed herself to think this again was sickening, a kind of self-inflicted torture, so, banishing the gruesome imagery, and dragging her thoughts back to the now, she moved over next to Carly. Rather than take her hand, Ava walked down one step and shifted in close to the bannister, ahead of her daughter. Picking up on Ava's signal, Carly lay her palm on Ava's shoulder, and as Ava blinked to clear her vision, they walked slowly down the stairs, connected by much more than the pressure of Carly's fingers on Ava's jacket.

The first room they entered was dimly lit, the walls painted a jewel-blue colour that surprised Ava. Seeing the bold backdrop was unusual in such a setting, but, as she spied Titian's *Diana and Callisto*, the brilliance of the wall behind it, rather than detract from the work, enhanced the tones in such a way that the painting appeared to leap from the wall. 'Gosh, look, Carly. Here's the Titian.' She guided Carly up to the painting, observing a respectable distance from the work.

Carly eased in next to her and looked up at the painting. 'Wow.' She turned her head back and forth, then, seeming to find her focus, she dipped her chin. 'I can see the dog.' She pointed at the base of the painting where a hound lay, its tail curled in an S shape. 'Is this the one he painted with his fingers?' She turned to Ava, her face alive with interest.

'I think so.' Ava looked at the brochure she'd picked up as they'd come in. 'It says he often did, in order to show different textures.'

'That's cool. I'd like to try that too.' She grinned. 'Could get messy, though.'

Buoyed by her daughter's reaction, Ava laughed. 'Who cares?' She draped her arm around Carly's shoulders. 'I say we give it a go. There's always washing-up liquid.'

Carly giggled and leaned into Ava's side.

The next room had a rich burgundy colour on the walls that Ava was about to comment on, when Carly tugged her arm, and whispered, 'Why did they make the walls dark grey? It's so dull.'

The kernel of worry about Carly's colour vision exploded inside Ava. Wasn't it enough that Stargardt's had delivered critical vision loss, without stripping her gifted daughter of her joy of colour, too? Fighting to control the impulse to throw her head back and scream *what the hell else* at the universe, Ava gently moved them on.

As they circled the various paintings, Carly leaned in close to some, scanning up and down until she found her focal point, while at others she eased backwards, distance seeming to help her take them in.

The second-to-last piece they came to was their main objective, Van Gogh's *Orchard in Blossom, the Plum Trees*, and Ava blinked as she spotted it. The simplicity of the piece was stunning, and yet its vibrancy mesmerising. 'What do you think?' She watched Carly, who stepped back, her head turned to the right.

'It's different than I thought.' She squinted. 'Unless I'm just not seeing it right.' She frowned.

Disappointment snatched at Ava's throat. 'What do you mean, love? What are you seeing?'

Carly stepped further back. 'It's like it's not finished.' She looked over at Ava. 'Like he didn't finish all the trees. Some of them are just outlines.' She pointed at the right side of the painting, where the spindly trees were bare of leaves, the branches soft indications of their shape rather than detailed, and the lack of blossoms giving an almost wintry feel to the section.

Relieved that she was seeing the same thing, and impressed by Carly's insightful observation, Ava stepped in close to her side. 'You know, you're absolutely right. That side is much less detailed than the trees in the middle.' She watched as Carly twisted her head again, leaning in.

'My favourite part is the grass. I can see blue and grey there. My grass is always just green.' She shrugged.

'I think there are so many more colours to things we see, if we just look hard enough.' The words out, Ava winced, the sharp edge of her thoughtless comment slicing through the calm of the moment. She scanned Carly's face, waiting for the light to go out of it, but, to her relief, Carly simply nodded.

'Yeah. I know.' She tugged at her sleeve. 'It is lovely.' She looked up at Ava.

'Peaceful.'

'Yes, it really is.' Ava's hand went up to cover her mouth. 'Come on, let's go and see more.'

The large galleries and connecting corridors were mercifully clear of crowds, making navigating their way between the various exhibits seamless. Carly's fingers were once again loosely hooked in the back of Ava's jeans as they walked into the next room, where the sign said *Painting as Spectacle*. Ava had been looking forward to this display, a series of works from Scottish artists, particularly Sir Edwin Landseer, a long-time favourite of hers since studying art at university.

This time, the walls were a startling scarlet, and no sooner had they walked in than Carly whispered, 'Mum, look.' She pointed straight ahead. '*The Monarch of the Glen*.' She moved forward, releasing her hold on Ava's jeans. 'The one we saw online.' Carly closed in on the colossal work.

Ava followed her daughter to where she'd stopped, her upper body leaning forward, her focus intent on the magnificent painting. Carly then tipped her head to the side and took several steps back, as, beside her, Ava stared at the majestic, twelve-point stag, one of the most famous pictures of the nineteenth century.

Having become iconic as representing the might, and beauty, of Scotland's Highlands, the stag stood in rough grass, its chest proud and its head turned to the right, much as Carly's was now. The handsome muzzle was lifted as the creature caught a scent, the wise eyes telling the observer that he was aware of their presence. This was the third time Ava had seen the painting in person, and it was just as impressive as the first time she'd come here, as a child.

'Gorgeous, right?' She touched Carly's shoulder. 'The light is incredible, and the way he shows the mountains.'

'Perhaps if I paint this big, I can still do it?' She turned to her mother. 'My stuff is too small, and I can't…' Her voice faded.

Ava dived in, determined to maintain the positive momentum of the day. 'I think that'd be great. You get bogged down with the detail sometimes, instead of just slapping the paint on and having fun with it.' She mimed the action as a smile tugged at Carly's mouth. 'What?' Ava mocked offence. 'I mean it.'

Carly giggled, her hand covering her mouth. 'Slap it on. Really?' She hiccupped. 'What happened to "oh, Carly, don't make such a mess. Don't mix the colours up so much. Don't waste so much paper. Don't use all that paint in one go"...' She grinned, her nose turning a rosy pink.

Knowing she was caught in a net of her own making, Ava laughed. 'I don't... I'm not...' She flapped her hands. 'Oh, shush smarty-pants.' As Carly laughed heartily, Ava took her hand. 'You can use as much paint and paper, and make as much damn mess as you like, from now on.' She smiled at her daughter's flushed face. 'In fact, if you don't make a mess, you'll have me to deal with.' She frowned theatrically. 'Your dad will be happy, too. He does love a guddle, the messy toad.' Ava smiled, picturing Rick, rummaging through his disaster of a chest of drawers looking for something she'd folded neatly and laid on his side of the bed the day before.

Suddenly, Carly's eyes filled, bringing Ava up short.

'What is it, love?' She gently moved the hair from Carly's forehead.

'He should be here too.' Carly gulped. 'I miss him so much, Mum.'

Her heart pinching, Ava drew Carly into her middle, feeling the heat of Carly's breath against her breastbone. 'Me too, darling. Every single minute.'

CHAPTER TWENTY-ONE

Two days later, Ava stood at the living-room window watching for a car. An occupational therapist was due to arrive to assess Carly's environment and suggest any changes needed in order to keep her safe as she functioned around the house.

Ava was nervous about the visit and had spent an hour tidying up, running the hoover around and making sure everything was sparkling in the kitchen, all the while her heart in her mouth as she assessed their home for potential hazards that, just a few weeks ago, they wouldn't have had to consider as such.

Carly was in her bedroom, painting on a large watercolour canvas, with a set of extra-wide paintbrushes that Ava had bought for her at the art shop in town. She'd stopped on her way home from visiting Rick and splurged on a new easel that could support larger panels than Carly usually used and seeing her face light up had made Ava's difficult day a little easier.

Carly had been painting more, starting as soon as their school lessons were done for the day, and while Ava worried about her becoming too solitary, the joy it gave her outweighed the concern. Ava had seen a distinct change in Carly's use of colour, and her call to Doctor Anderson the day after they'd returned from Edinburgh had confirmed her fears.

'I'm afraid it's not uncommon for Stargardt's patients to see a change in the red-green colour spectrum in the early stages, Mrs Guthrie. She's likely seeing reds and purples as yellows, browns and mossy greens. Pink tones can be altered too, seen as a range from a washed-out lilac to a light grey.' He'd paused. 'Blue tones may begin to be affected too, as the disease progresses. Let's bring her in and we'll retest, to be sure.'

As she'd nodded silently, listening to the shattering update, Ava stood in front of her mirror, holding her finger over her right eye and squinting, trying to imagine what Carly was seeing. The idea that she no longer had a clear picture of what the world looked like to her sweet girl was just another blow to add to the litany of hurts that twisted Ava's insides, every waking moment. To be separated from Carly's experience in this new way was crushing, another nugget of pain that Ava would have to learn to swallow.

There had been no more talk about going to school, and afraid to upset the somewhat precarious apple cart, Ava had left well alone, making sure to stay on top of the home-school curriculum as she counted the eight weeks or so until the official summer holidays began and she could leave that responsibility behind, for a while.

June was well underway, and Sutherland's weather had been kind over the past couple of weeks. Early afternoons were the best time, when the sun hovered low in the sky beyond the firth, and the front garden was bathed in a golden light. The grass smelled of clover, and groups of gulls, and terns, would swoop overhead, switching direction with the contrary wind, leaving a whisper of their calls behind as they floated off towards the water.

Twice Ava had taken a blanket out onto the grass and they'd eaten a late lunch, tasting the salty breeze as they talked about everything they'd do once Rick was home. As Carly added new, local activities and excursions, Ava tried to visualise the three of them, paddling at the beach, on some crazy, white-knuckle ride at a theme park, or watching the northern lights. The more Carly talked, the more Ava struggled to believe, but not once did she question Carly's agenda, or throw any doubt on her sweet, unsullied certainty that her father would get better.

Snapping Ava back to the moment, a silver Honda pulled up in front of the house, so she tugged her shirt down at the sides, shook the hair from her face, and made her way to the door.

The therapist was a rosy-cheeked brunette from Glasgow called Barbara, with a firm handshake and a gentle smile. She was friendly and open, and Ava had warmed to her instantly. Barbara had met Carly for a brief chat, then toured the house, and now she and Ava were standing in the living room to talk through Barbara's findings.

'You should consider putting a rail in the downstairs bathroom and adding an additional bannister on the wall side of the staircase.' Barbara scribbled in a small, spiral-bound notebook. 'I'd suggest lifting the smaller rugs, like the one in the kitchen, as they're a trip hazard, and then I think you should be fine.' She nodded to herself as Ava made more mental notes of everything she'd have to do. 'You've a lovely home, Mrs Guthrie. You don't see too many crofts this old in such good condition.' She looked around her. 'The bathroom being down here is a real bonus, too. Carly should limit her use of the stairs.' She shrugged. 'Not that she can't go up there, it's just the worst place for falling incidents.'

'Right. I understand.' Ava's throat drew tight as she remembered Carly and Rick, just the previous year, playing a hopping game on the bottom three stairs, where one of them was going up while the other went down. How quickly life had changed.

Barbara settled herself on the sofa to drink the tea that Ava had made. 'Does your husband have time to add the bannister, et cetera?' She bit into a biscuit, her green eyes scanning the room as if looking for the missing piece of a puzzle.

Ava set her mug down on the chest. 'He's not here at the moment.' She exhaled slowly, having to explain their situation to this stranger draining. 'He's ill. Well, in hospital.'

Barbara's face coloured. 'Oh, I'm sorry. Trust me to put my big foot in it.' She grimaced. 'Not too serious, I hope?' She popped the remaining piece of biscuit into her mouth, then brushed the crumbs from her lap, onto the floor.

A wave of exhaustion swelled up inside Ava, but rather than answer, absurdly, she laughed as she watched the biscuit crumbs bouncing off the wood floor, like caramel-coloured sparks.

'Sorry, did I…' Barbara looked flustered as she shifted forward on the seat.

'No, it's fine. It's a long story. Just ignore me.' Resignation replacing exhaustion, Ava explained what had happened, and as her story unfolded, so the colour drained from Barbara's face.

'God, you've had a time of it, you poor thing.' Barbara's mouth dipped. 'That's terrible.'

Ava found a smile. 'We're just about surviving. It's extra hard for Carly, with everything that's happening to her. She needs her father.' The truth of the words stung.

'And you need your man, pet.' Barbara gave a sympathetic smile. 'That must be so hard.'

'It is.' Ava nodded, guarding her voice in case it let her down. 'But he'll be OK.'

Barbara pushed herself up from the sofa. 'Right enough. I'm sure he will.' She sounded unconvinced. 'Well, I better be off,' she said, swinging her handbag onto her shoulder. 'If you have any questions, or need help getting the rails in that we talked about, just phone me and I'll get it set up for you.'

Ava shook her head. 'That's fine, I have a friend who can probably do it.' She gestured towards the barn. 'He's pretty handy.'

As she waved Barbara off, Ava took inventory of everything she had to do over the next few days, and the exhaustion seeped back into her limbs. Then, Rick's voice filled her head. *'We are strong enough. We can do this.'* But the question now hovering behind that certainty was whether she could do it alone.

*

Over the following three days, Ava had functioned on a handful of hours of sleep, her nights becoming increasingly disturbed by dreams that had her waking up bathed in sweat. She'd see Carly, walking off the edge of a cliff, as she stood by, helpless, or Rick slipping away from her as she grabbed for his hand, quicksand sucking him under as she watched his features disappearing one at a time.

The previous night, she'd dreamt that she'd been in the chilly room, at the hospital, and had gently prised his eyelids open, only to find gaping holes in place of the hazel pools she knew so well. She'd woken up shaking, her stomach churning, all the while the empty side of the bed glaring at her as she'd considered being faced with a choice that to even contemplate made her rush to the bathroom to splash water on her face. If it was an option, could she sacrifice one of the people she loved most in the world, to help the other? There was no answer to that question she could bear to imagine.

Trembling, she'd tiptoed down to the kitchen, drunk some water and sat on the sofa listening to Flora's old mantle clock ticking, until her pulse settled to match its rhythm, and then she'd gone back to bed.

The myriad practical things she needed to accomplish each day kept her from crumbling completely. Following Barbara's visit, she had researched and then ordered a closed-circuit video magnification system that would enable Carly to use the computer more easily, and she had filled out all the paperwork for The Guide Dog Centre so they could schedule their initial assessment of Carly's suitability for a dog.

Ava had taken Carly to the riding school and watched as she was introduced to a long-legged piebald pony called Peek-a-boo. The moment Carly touched the pony's forelock, there seemed to be a connection, and the instructor, a middle-aged man called

Todd, with a long grey beard and an impressive beer belly, had whispered to Ava, his breath thick with coffee, 'Aye, that's the one. He's great wi' kids, and he liked her right away.' He'd grinned. 'A match made in heaven.'

Now, Ava sat in the car as Carly rode around the outdoor paddock, her new helmet glinting in the sunlight, as Todd paced the perimeter, giving her corrections on her posture, speaking around a length of straw that was clamped between his teeth. The comical image made Ava smile as she dialled Jenna's number.

Jenna picked up after a couple of rings. 'Hey, you. How was Edinburgh?' she asked. 'Have fun?'

'We did. It was great.' She recalled Carly, sitting in the restaurant after their visit to the gallery, a huge plate of fish and chips in front of her and a smile as wide as her face could accommodate, then, that night, her nervously grabbing Ava's hand as they'd descended the dark staircase leading to the network of underground vaults and tunnels, under the city, many of which are said to be haunted.

'Oh, good. That's great, so it is,' Jenna crooned.

Ava looked out the window to see Carly releasing her feet from the stirrups and beginning a round-the-world manoeuvre, where she turned 360 degrees on the saddle as Peek-a-boo stood still, letting her move on his back. It was a lesson in trust, and Todd had assured Ava that the pony was well trained, and accustomed to standing when told. He hovered at Peek-a-boo's head, and Ava breathed away her momentary anxiety as Carly's laughter floated across the gravel path and into the car.

'So, what's happening?' Jenna sounded breathless.

Unsure whether she wanted to share her news, Ava hedged, 'Is this a bad time?' She frowned. 'I can call back later.'

'Not at all.' Jenna laughed. 'You know my life. No time is ideal.'

Ava sighed. 'Yeah, I know.'

'So, any updates on Rick?'

Ava hesitated. 'Actually, yes. But it's not good, Jen.'

'Talk to me.'

Ava spilled the news about Rick's setback, the intubation, her conversation with Doctor Stewart and his comments about Rick's wishes. All the while, Ava's pulse tapped at her temple and a shadow of her latest nightmare flickered to life, making her shift in the seat.

'God, Ava. I'm so sorry, love. I wish I knew what to say.' Jenna hesitated. 'Why didn't you call me sooner?'

Ava shook her head. 'I wasn't ready.'

'So, what are you thinking? I mean, have you…' The soft voice faded.

Ava shook her head, suddenly sure that she needed to say out loud the thing that had been torturing her ever since she'd seen Doctor Stewart, the week before. Shaking the hair from her face, she waved at Carly, who was trotting opposite the car, then Ava closed her eyes as she spoke. 'Jenna, I've been asking myself, that if it came down to it, could I give him up if it meant that Carly could…' Her voice faltered. 'I mean…'

Jenna sucked in an audible breath. 'Mother of God, Ava. Are you serious?'

Ava felt a fat tear push over her bottom eyelid. 'I don't know what the hell I am anymore, Jenna. I'm thinking all kinds of crazy stuff.' She rooted in her handbag for a tissue and blew her nose. 'I don't even know if it's a possibility.' She blinked her vision clear.

'Have you spoken to Doctor Stewart, or done any research?'

Ava shook her head. 'I'm afraid to, in case…' She coughed.

'Do you want me to… I mean, I could…' Jenna halted. 'Ava, what are you going to do?'

Ava watched as Carly once again trotted past the car, smiling as she twisted her head to the right and waved at her. 'I have no idea.' She sniffed. 'But I'm losing my mind in the meantime.' Fresh tears coursed down her face as her breaths came in hiccups.

As was Jenna's habit, she used distraction to calm Ava down, turning the conversation to Mandy.

'So, how is she?' Ava twisted the rear-view mirror around and wiped her finger under each eye to remove the smudges of mascara.

'Och, she's being a pain at the moment,' Jenna huffed. 'All she wants to do is hide in her room. Apparently, I keep embarrassing her, and it seems I've become a general annoyance.' She gave a sharp laugh. 'But one who still provides meals, shelter, transport and a telly.' She snorted. 'Oh, the joys…'

'Yeah, you're not alone there. I embarrassed Carly in Edinburgh.' Ava shook her head. 'Seems to come with the territory, now.'

Jenna made a tutting sound. 'Right enough.'

They diverted the conversation to work, Jenna bringing her up to date on some office gossip and the most recent client horror stories, as Ava listened to the familiar voice and let herself drift. She imagined herself back in the office in Aberdeen, at her desk next to the long row of windows overlooking Union Street, the smell of coffee mixed with the musk of incense, and the ubiquitous white noise, the buzz of printers and monitors humming all around, like a swarm of bees on the prowl.

She'd enjoyed going in a couple of times a week and, thinking about it now, Ava realised that with everything she was dealing with, she hadn't had time to acknowledge her crippling loneliness, which was a small mercy she was grateful for.

As she watched Carly trotting in tight circles, the wind catching her hair and lifting it up in a golden veil behind her, Ava wished that Rick could see this. He'd be so happy to know that Carly was riding, and as she pictured his face, the broad smile and twinkling eyes, his absence drove into her like a punch to her middle.

'You all right, love?' Jenna's voice snapped Ava out of her daydream.

'Oh, yes. Sorry. I'm just watching Carly. She's riding.' She tucked her hair behind her ear. 'I found a great place near home, and this is her second lesson.'

'That's brilliant. It'll be so good for her confidence to be back on a horse,' Jenna said. 'How's she doing, overall?'

A picture show of images flicked through Ava's mind: Carly dropping her sunglasses in the grass down by the Lochans and being unable to find them. Her calling Ava into the bathroom to help her tell the difference between the shampoo and conditioner bottles. Her insisting she could make them a cup of tea, then pouring boiling water all over the kitchen surface, blissfully unaware until Ava had gently taken the kettle from her and wiped up the steaming puddle with a tea towel. The changes were coming, thick and fast, and just the previous night, Carly had snuggled up to her on the sofa, a clear sign that something was on her mind.

'Mum,' she'd whispered as Ava turned the volume down on the TV.

'Yes, love.'

'Can we go and see Doctor Anderson soon?' She'd closed her eyes, the lids fluttering as Ava's nerves followed suit.

'Of course we can, but what's happening?' Ava had shifted to look at her.

'Nothing much. I'd just like to ask him some stuff.' Carly's shoulders had bounced.

Unconvinced, Ava had frowned. 'What do you want to ask him?'

Carly had shaken her head, her mouth taking on a stubborn set. 'Just stuff.'

Carly's expression making it clear that Ava couldn't push further, she'd conceded. 'OK, I'll ring him in the morning.'

Carly had nodded, lifting the remote and turning the volume back up as she pulled her knees up to her chest.

Ava had taken in the angelic profile, seeing Carly's thick lashes and gently freckled cheekbones, the flaxen folds of hair as it separated over her shoulder, and the curve of her back as she hugged her slender knees to her middle. So many elements went to make up her precious daughter, so many perfect pieces of the whole, working in harmony to form this wondrous being that she, Ava, had something to do with creating. As she'd marvelled at the concept, Rick's voice had floated back to her, from the night they'd read their blood test results, the anguish in it something she would never forget. *'You mean I gave it to her?'*

'Ava, are you there? What's going on?' Jenna's tone rose. 'You're scaring me.'

'Sorry, it's just hard.' Ava swallowed. 'Her eyes are getting worse, and it's happening so fast, Jenna. I'm totally useless to stop it, and it's killing me.' She let out an involuntary sob, then checked herself, shaking her head briskly. 'I'm all right, but it's a lot to deal with.' She halted. 'On my own.'

'Is there anyone you can talk to there? I hate being so far away.' Jenna's voice cracked.

'Oh, for goodness sake, don't you cry, or I'll fall apart completely,' Ava whined, then, as if by magic, they both laughed, sniffing, crying, and laughing again, as only best friends can.

CHAPTER TWENTY-TWO

A loud crash downstairs brought Ava bolt upright in bed, her heart clattering under the old T-shirt of Rick's that she'd taken to sleeping in. Seeing the display on her phone reading 3.29 a.m., she panted softly as she strained to hear what was happening. Then, another bang came from the kitchen, followed by the unmistakable sound of crying.

Grabbing her robe, Ava turned on the light and hurried down the stairs, no room for any thought other than to get to her daughter. As she walked into the kitchen, Carly was standing at the sink, in the dark.

Turning the light on, Ava came up beside her to see shards of porcelain on the counter top, a dusting of shiny particles on the floor at Carly's feet, and her favourite rainbow mug in pieces in the sink. Carly was sniffling, her hair in a tangle, and her pyjama bottoms sagging around her narrow hips.

'What's going on, sweetheart?' Checking that Carly was wearing her slippers, Ava eased her away from the sink.

'I wanted a drink. I didn't want to put the light on in case I woke you up,' she sobbed, her cheeks flushed. 'Now I've broken my mug.'

'That's OK.' Ava kept her voice level as she led Carly to the table and pulled out a chair. 'Just sit here for a minute while I get the brush.' She stroked Carly's back for a few seconds, then took the broom from the pantry and began pulling the shards into a pile. 'Why were you awake, love?' She eyed Carly, who had dropped her chin onto her forearms, her mouth a miserable line.

'Couldn't sleep.' She shrugged, then wiped her nose on her sleeve.

'Oh, Carly,' Ava warned, frowning at her daughter. 'That's charming.'

Carly shrugged, a look of such fear flashing behind her eyes that Ava stopped what she was doing and walked over to the table.

'Talk to me, sweetheart. What's really going on?' Ava drew out the chair next to Carly's and sat down.

Carly sat up, shoved the hair away from her damp cheeks and, turning her head to the right, focused on Ava's face. 'If I tell you, you can't freak out.' She frowned. 'Promise?'

Ava considered the flushed, earnest face in front of her, then, her pulse quickening, she carved lines across her chest. 'Promise.'

Carly sat up straight. 'Sometimes I'm scared to close my eyes at night in case…' She halted.

'Why, love?' Ava tried to sound casual, despite her thumping heart.

'In case when I open them again, I'm blind, like everything is totally black.' She gave a juddering sigh. 'I know I'm being a baby, but that's how I feel.' She set her mouth in a firm line, just as Rick did when he was digging his heels in about something. In this moment, when Ava could have easily fallen into an abyss over the crippling fear that Carly had just confided to her, seeing Rick reflected so clearly in his daughter's face made Ava feel a little less alone.

'Carly, you're not a baby. Quite the opposite, I can assure you.' Ava leaned forward on her elbows. 'There are a thousand things I could say to you to make you feel better, but the truth is best. Agreed?' She reached over and touched her fingertips to Carly's. 'We're going to see Doctor Anderson tomorrow, so we can talk to him about everything that's happening, but I'm going to remind you what he said.' Ava took a breath. 'You will not be totally blind. You will have some vision, blurred at the edges but still there.' She held Carly's gaze. 'Your central vision will stop deteriorating soon, and then you'll be left with partial sight, still seeing light, and shapes.' Ava paused. 'You'll adjust to the sight you have left, and you'll learn to function, be independent and have a good life.' At this, Ava felt her throat thicken, and with no intention of giving in to tears, she shook her head briskly. 'You will *not* be totally blind. Do you hear me, Carly Guthrie?' She eyed her daughter, whose face had taken on a more natural colour. 'Carly?'

'Yes, I hear you.' Carly nodded. 'My ears are still working.'

Ava gasped, then seeing the faint glint return to Carly's eye, she tapped the backs of Carly's hands. 'Funny girl.' She pulled a face as Carly ran a palm down each thigh and wiggled her eyebrows.

'Mum?'

'Yes, love?'

'As you're up now, can I have some hot chocolate?'

Relief washed over Ava as she smiled at her daughter's angelic expression. 'Yes, you little toad. You can.' Ava stood up. 'Then it's back to bed and to sleep. We've got a big day tomorrow.'

Carly leaned back in the chair. 'Will I meet some dogs, or just talk to the people tomorrow?'

Ava pulled the milk from the fridge and poured some into a pan. 'We're going to Doctor Anderson first thing, then we need to be back home for eleven thirty. We have an interview here, with the assessment specialist, then, if they think you're a good candidate, I think we'll have to go into the centre in Inverness a couple of times before they put you on the waiting list for a dog.' She stirred the milk. 'Once they find your dog, we'll have that first training week I told you about, and I think we might have to stay at the centre for some of it.' Ava took the chocolate powder from the shelf and stirred some into the pan.

'Why do we have to stay there?' Carly pushed her chair back and put her feet up on the table, another of Rick's habits that drove Ava mad. 'I think that's stupid.' She pouted.

'Feet, please.' Ava jabbed the spoon at Carly and frowned, as she thumped her feet back to the floor. 'Them's the rules, kid.' Ava circled the spoon above her head like a lasso.

Carly rolled her eyes. 'You're mad.'

Ava swept her hand across her middle and dipped her shoulders. 'I aim to please.' Taking two mugs from the cupboard, she poured the frothy chocolate into them, then set one in front of Carly. 'Now, drink that and then bed.' She tutted. 'Pain in the bum.'

Carly pulled her cup towards her and tilted her head, her lips pursed. 'Did you put marshmallows in it?' She scanned Ava's face.

'Oh, my God.' Ava laughed. 'You are such a prima donna.'

At this, Carly threw her head back, her laughter unbridled. 'I aim to please,' she grinned, lifting the cup to her lips, then she halted. 'Mum?'

'What now?' Ava widened her eyes.

'You're the best mum in the world.' Carly smiled at her. 'Most of the time.'

Momentarily taken aback, Ava tipped her head to the side. 'And you're the best daughter. Most of the time.' She pulled a face and pointed at Carly's mug. 'Now, drink.'

Doctor Anderson had been predictably kind and reassuring. Having repeated some tests, he'd confirmed that there had been further deterioration in the central vision in Carly's right eye, but that the left appeared stable since the last time he'd seen her. He'd sat Carly down to talk to her, and Ava now stood behind the chair, watching her daughter's body language as he took her through his findings.

'This is what we talked about when I last saw you, Carly. We knew there would be further changes, perhaps for some time, before things level off.' His flattened palm hovered in the space between them. 'I'm seeing the changes you described and, yes, it's disappointing that your right eye has slipped a little more, but we knew it probably would.' He paused. 'Do you have any questions for me?'

Carly lifted her chin, a curious look flooding her eyes. 'Why do colours look different now?' She stared at him, as Ava held her breath. She'd hoped to delay this conversation, not having yet discussed her suspicions with Carly, but Carly had pre-empted her.

'Because there has been a change in your colour vision, as your mum mentioned to me, but at the moment it's just the red-green tones. I know it's hard, Carly, but there are special glasses that we can get for you that might help with that.' He smiled kindly at her as Carly swung around and glared at Ava, who guiltily sucked in her lower lip. 'So, we'll make an appointment for you to come back in a month and we'll check where we're at then, but I suspect things will begin to slow down soon.' He looked up at Ava, who knotted her trembling fingers low in front of her hips. 'I'm going to give your mum my mobile number.' He stood up and walked around behind his desk. 'I want you to call me if you're worried, or if you experience anything that scares you.' He opened a drawer and pulled out a business card. 'I know this is very frightening, Carly, but I have to tell you, you are coping with it extremely well.' Once again, he caught Ava's eye. 'And I know your mum is very proud of you, too.'

Carly shifted in the chair, her long plait dangling between her tartan-clad shoulders as she nibbled her thumbnail. When he held the card out, she swivelled in the seat, lowered her head and found his hand in her peripheral vision. She took the card from him and let her hand drop to her thigh. 'Thanks.'

'You're welcome.' He sat at his desk, then leaned forward on his elbows. 'I'm very sorry that your dad's still not well.'

Ava was caught off guard by this. She'd confided in Doctor Anderson when she'd called to make the appointment, so his mentioning Rick wasn't altogether unexpected, but hearing the doctor talk about him was still a jolt.

'There are so many changes happening for you at the moment, I think it would be helpful to chat to someone who can help you adjust.' He looked over at Ava, seeking her approval to continue. Them having previously discussed getting Carly in to see a counsellor, she nodded her ascent. 'There's a lady who works near here, who counsels people who are visually challenged, like you.'

He paused, letting the statement hang for a few seconds. Ava took a deep breath, the idea of any kind of label being applied to Carly drawing her hands into fists.

'Her name is Serena Headley and I think you'll like her.' He linked his long fingers in front of him. 'How do you feel about talking to her?' He eyed Carly, who had dropped her gaze to her feet.

'OK.' She shrugged, her face blank.

Ava circled the chair and stood next to Carly. 'Thanks, Doctor Anderson. We'll give her a ring this week.' Ava wrapped her fingers around her daughter's, only to have Carly pull hers away, the rejection alarming.

'And you're having your guide dog assessment today, I hear,' Anderson addressed Carly. 'They're a marvellous team over there, and they'll find you the perfect partner.' He smiled encouragingly as Carly turned her head towards the window, wincing slightly as the light washed across her face.

Having left a sulking Carly hiding in her room, Ava had gone to see Rick for an hour. Her store of words depleted, she'd sat at his side in silence, letting heavy tears roll down her cheeks.

She'd twisted herself into knots over the argument she and Carly had had in the car on the way home from Doctor Anderson's office, and having her daughter accuse her of hiding things from her was as painful as it was true.

'Why didn't you tell me?' Carly's face had been flushed. 'About the colours?'

Ava had battled to find a reason that sounded anything less than cowardly. 'I'm sorry, Carly. I should have, but I wanted you to see Doctor Anderson first, just to be sure I wasn't making a mistake.'

Carly had huffed. 'You tell me all the time to talk to you. Tell you everything. It's not fair if you don't too, Mum.'

Feeling suitably ashamed, Ava had apologised again, but Carly had turned away from her, stubbornly staring out of her window until they'd arrived at the house, when she'd scuttled into her room and slammed the door.

Ava had left her for an hour before tapping on her door and reminding her that the guide dog assessor was coming, and a reluctant Carly had sloped out of her room, eaten half of the sandwich Ava had made her, then flopped on the sofa with her iPad.

Three hours later, Ava slid the barn door open, balancing two mugs of coffee and a sandwich on a plate. Cameron was using an electric sander on the finished framework of the base units and hadn't heard her come in. As she hovered behind him, Ava watched his capable back bent over his work, the strong arms and the purposeful hands moving back and forth.

She imagined his lungs pumping, his heart beating, blood coursing through his veins and arteries, every synapse firing in his brain initiating all those physical responses, just as they should, and just as Rick's were not. The contrast to what she'd just seen at the hospital was levelling, and as she stopped herself from leaning into the all-consuming darkness of that, Cameron swung around.

'Oh, I didn't hear you.' He turned off the sander, removed his mask and brushed a cloud of fine dust from his hair. 'You don't have to feed me, you know.' He set the sander on the ground and looked at the plate in her hand, a shy smile creeping over his face.

'Oh, it's no trouble.' She held it out to him. 'It's just ham and cheese. Rick always gets hungry around this time of the afternoon.' She shrugged.

'Great. You're one in a million.' He dusted the front of his shirt off and took the plate and one of the mugs from her hand. 'Going to join me?'

'If you don't mind.' Suddenly self-conscious, Ava's face coloured. 'I won't keep you, though.' As she eyed the director's chair, Cameron, seeming to read her mind, nodded at it.

'Sit for a bit. I could do with some intelligent company.'

A few minutes earlier, as she'd walked along the front path, on her way up to the barn, she'd seen Jim's van leaving, so she looked at Cameron and frowned. 'Wasn't Jim just here?' She jabbed a thumb over her shoulder.

Cameron laughed. 'I rest my case.' His eyes shone as he lifted the sandwich and took a giant bite.

Ava laughed softly, taken by his gentle humour, and yet knowing that as much as he poked fun at his older brother, they were extremely close. 'You're lucky to have a brother. I'm an only child, and so is Rick.' She sat in the chair and sipped some coffee. 'We didn't want Carly to be an only child, but…' She stopped herself, once again surprised by how easily she was opening up to this new friend, who seemed to have materialised just when she needed him.

'After Jim, my folks were hoping for a daughter. Not that they'd ever admit it.' He shrugged. 'This is what they got.' He swept a hand down his front. 'Big disappointment.' Cameron grinned and took another bite, leaning his hips against the wooden framework that would soon house the sink. 'So, you had visitors earlier.' He spoke as he chewed. 'Not that I'm spying on you.' He grimaced, putting the last piece of sandwich in his mouth.

She smiled at his awkward expression. 'No, it's fine. The guide dog guy was here. He came to do an assessment of Carly inside the house, then we went down to Dornoch to walk around for a while, so he could get a sense of her capabilities, and ability to handle a dog.' She paused. 'I think it was mostly about gauging her confidence in being out and about in general.' Ava sipped some coffee, picturing Carly walking beside her across the Square, the now familiar hand lightly gripping Ava's belt, as the assessor lingered behind, observing.

Dan had been middle-aged, with kind eyes and a head of thick salt-and-pepper hair. He'd been soft-spoken and patient, and when he'd addressed Carly, he'd talked to her as an adult, directing his questions at her and not Ava, which Ava deeply appreciated. Carly had visibly responded, sitting up straighter, her voice gaining strength and volume as she showed him around the house and the front garden, carefully navigating her way around the path, the driveway and the front lawn. Ava's heart had been in her mouth, as Carly, head turned to the right, had managed to avoid almost all obstacles, except for one large stone that she'd scuffed her foot against, taking a moment to rebalance herself before moving on.

Dan had met Ava's eyes and shaken his head almost imperceptibly as they'd continued into the garden.

'So, how did it go?' Cameron swigged some more coffee. 'Did she pass?'

Ava shrugged. 'I don't know. He said they'd have a panel meeting to discuss his report, then he'd let us know.'

'How long will it take?' He moved over and set his cup on Rick's worktable.

'Apparently, if she meets all the criteria, and they decide she is capable of handling and caring for a dog, she goes on a waiting list. Then they'll carry out her training mainly here, at home.'

'Wow, that's quite a rigmarole.' His eyebrows jumped. 'She'll qualify, though. Won't she?'

For the first time since she'd begun the application process, Ava considered the possibility that, for some reason or another,

Carly might not qualify for a dog, so a nugget of concern opened up inside her. 'I hope so. She's had her heart set on it, ever since Rick told her she'd be getting one.' She pressed her lips together. 'We probably shouldn't have said anything until we were sure.'

A flash of irritation took her by surprise. When it came to Carly, Rick would sometimes jump the gun, and take the glory for things that Ava was still doing the groundwork on, and it used to make her resentful. Now, as she remembered Carly's delight that day outside the barn, when he'd shown her The Guide Dog Centre brochure, the tiny flame of annoyance sputtered out. There was no room for her to be angry with him about anything so petty now.

She closed her eyes, pushing away an image that made her face tingle, the flash of a sleek coffin, the swish of a black dress, the smell of calla lilies, the press of hands and whispers of condolence. No, she absolutely couldn't go there.

Swallowing the bile that had risen in her throat, she opened her eyes to see Cameron staring at her.

'Where did you go?' He frowned.

'Oh, nowhere useful.' She pulled her mouth down at the corners. 'I really try to stay positive, but sometimes…'

He moved over next to her and hunkered down beside the chair. 'You're only human, Ava. You'd have to be a machine not to have bad days, considering everything you're dealing with.'

She finished her coffee and hung the mug on her forefinger as she leaned forward, her hands between her knees. 'I can't let myself, though. Carly needs me to be strong, and I can't let her see me losing it.' Feeling the prickle of tears, Ava shook her head abruptly. 'At the very least, if I fall apart, it has to be in private.' She smiled sadly.

Cameron stood up and walked back to Rick's table. 'Look, we all get lonely. I'm usually around people, but I still miss Adam every day he's away. If you need someone to talk to, I'm here.' He spread his arms wide. 'Literally and figuratively.' He gave a lopsided grin. 'I mean I am literally here, every day.'

A surge of affection pushed up into Ava's chest. 'I know what you meant, you eejit.' A single tear trickled down her cheek. She swiped it away and stood up. 'How long is Adam away?' She realised that she knew little about Cameron's partner other than that he worked on an oil rig. 'What does he do?'

'He's a rig manager. It'll be five weeks, this time, so he'll be home in the middle of July. If I'm finished here, we're hoping to go away for a wee break. Maybe to Skye.' He smiled. 'He's a big hiker.'

'My dad was an oil engineer too. Kind of came with the territory, living in Aberdeen.' She nodded to herself. 'But you two should definitely go to Skye. Whether you're finished, or not.' Realising that she was not the only lonely person in the room was liberating, and it made her feel closer to Cameron, the shared dearth of the ones they loved a commonality that seemed to allow the skipping ahead of some customary friendship qualifiers. Feeling bold, Ava took a breath. 'Cameron, can I ask you for a huge favour?'

'Of course.' He looked surprised.

'Would you think I was a weirdo if I asked you for a hug? Purely platonic, of course.' She hesitated as she watched his face, his gentle smile telling her that she hadn't overstepped. She held her hands out at her sides. 'The thing is, by virtue of our situation, and that Jenna lives in Aberdeen, you are, de facto, my new best friend.'

At this, he laughed, allowing her to release the breath she hadn't realised she'd been holding. He moved towards her and opened his arms. 'Come on then, I haven't got all day.' He grinned. 'My client is a dragon lady, and I've got to get back to work.'

Ava raked her hand through her hair, set the mug on the table and walked into his arms. As he held her, a cocktail of sawdust and fresh sweat made her close her eyes. If she kept them closed, and really focused her mind, perhaps she could conjure Rick, have it be his arms around her, if only for a second or two. If she could have that second or two, it might be enough to get her through the rest of this day.

Carly was in the bath as Ava finished tidying up the kitchen. Their dinner had been mostly silent until Ava had apologised again, and this time Carly had seemed to accept it, albeit grudgingly. Now, as Ava heard the trickle of water as Carly topped up the bath, Ava lifted Carly's striped sweatshirt and the clogs she'd left by the front door and carried them into her room.

As Ava folded the sweatshirt and laid it on the end of the bed, something caught her eye. The corner of what looked like a white book was poking out from under the bed. Frowning, she leaned down and pulled it out, recognising the small, spiral-bound journal Rick had given Carly, to write down all the things she wanted to see on their great adventure. Smiling sadly, Ava held the book in her palms, letting it fall open, and as she glanced at the page, she felt the air being sucked out of her.

Scrawled in messy ballpoint pen was a paragraph, the handwriting barely recognisable as Carly's, but it was the words that caused Ava's breath to catch, and as she forced herself to read, they seared themselves into her heart.

> *My mum is a liar. I hate her. She breaks her promises. My dad would NEVER do that. I wish he was here. I'm so scared, all the time. I'm tired of being brave. I want to cry every single day. I want to tell Dad what's happening to me, but I can't. My eyes are getting worse. The middle bits are so dark now, and the fuzziness is worse on both sides. This is so UNFAIR. And now I can't see colours either, and Mum knew that would happen and she didn't tell me. I want my dad!!!* ☹

Ava closed the book and carefully replaced it as best she could. Hurrying out of the room, she sprinted up the stairs, walked into her bedroom and closed the door, letting the sobs she'd held back rack through her. She was guilty of what she'd been accused of, but seeing the words *I hate her* was more painful than anything she'd endured so far. It also unearthed the memory of having written the exact same words in her own diary, when her mother, Helen, had repeatedly forbidden her to go rollerblading with her friends, in case she broke an ankle.

As Ava sank onto the bed, grabbing the duvet into a bunch under her chin, she sobbed into the feathery quilt, resolving never, ever to hide anything from Carly again, no matter how hard, and Ava knew that more unimaginably hard things were coming, as well as she knew her own name.

CHAPTER TWENTY-THREE

Their school lessons finished for the day, Carly was riding Peek-a-boo around the outdoor paddock. Todd was looking on, calling instructions, and his wife, Rachel, a willowy redhead who reminded Ava of Jenna, was watching at his side.

Next to Carly, another young girl was riding a pretty bay pony, its black mane flicking up in the breeze as the girls trotted around each other in circles.

Ava sat in the car, the windows rolled down and the sweet smell of hay filtering in on the warm breeze. Rachel had welcomed them when they'd arrived and explained that this lesson would be shared with Kelly, a student with multiple sclerosis who'd been coming for over a year. 'She's a lovely kid. Doing really well so far, but we've started using a lap strap to keep her safe in the saddle.' She'd mimed the action, slender hands linking across her narrow hips. 'Carly is doing marvellously. She's such a character, too. Really fun to have around.'

Ava's pride had swelled. 'Thanks. She's pretty amazing.'

Rachel had gone on to ask if Ava might consider letting Carly join them, and one other student, on a day's trek. Ava had initially been reluctant, but as Carly had approached the fence, pulling Peek-a-boo to a stop, Ava had seen the light behind her daughter's eyes. 'Do you want to go, love?' she'd called.

Carly, looking flushed, had nodded. 'Yeah, I really do.'

With the arrangements made for the trek the coming Saturday, Ava mentally juggled the remaining day trips that she wanted to fit in before the guide dog training began.

Having heard just two days before that Carly had passed the initial assessments, and had been placed on the 'awaiting training' list for as soon as a suitable dog had been identified, they'd jumped around the living room, whooping and laughing, until they'd landed in a heap on the sofa. They'd celebrated with ice cream, then Ava had made Carly go to bed, even though she'd said she was too excited to sleep.

The following day, they'd skipped lessons and gone to Loch an Eilein, taking a picnic and their paints, and they'd spent a peaceful day walking around the picturesque loch. Then, watching the sun set over the miniature island, in the middle of the primordial water, they had attempted to capture the colours, each in their own way.

Carly had produced an impressive image of the sky using her fingers, smearing the paint on thickly, straight from the tubes, as Ava laughed and handed her whatever colours she asked for. Ava had said nothing about the choices of primarily browns, greens and greys, that particular wound still stinging from the previous altercation.

The resulting painting was now at the framers in Inverness, and Ava had promised that it would hang, in pride of place, in the living room. 'It'll go up to celebrate your dad coming home.' She'd pointed at the space above the sideboard, as Carly had beamed. 'Right there.' Ava had squinted, framing the space between her thumbs. 'It'll be perfect.'

All that remained on Carly's revised list was to see a ballet, and then, lastly, to travel northwest, to Lochinver, to witness the aurora borealis.

As she considered the two remaining experiences, Ava frowned. The aurora and the ballet had both been things that Carly was specifically saving for when Rick got home, but seeing the way she now trailed a hand along the wall wherever she walked, and consistently tipped her head back to see where she was stepping, it was obvious that they could not wait much longer.

The best time to see the aurora in Scotland was between December and February, and Ava knew, sickeningly, that by that time there was a distinct possibility that Carly wouldn't be able to fully appreciate it. What Ava wouldn't allow herself to face was a scenario where Rick had not come back to them by then, because if he hadn't, she might be faced with the nightmarish decision that was now plaguing her daily, leaving her breathless and nauseated.

As Ava watched, Carly trotted around the paddock again, her voice rising above the clop of hooves on the dry ground as she called to Kelly, 'Come this way.' She beckoned to the other girl, a small figure with long dark hair, spindly legs clad in mud-spattered jodhpurs and long boots, the yin to Carly's yang. Ava revelled in seeing the girls laugh together, pure joy sparking between them as they reached out and held hands, their ponies bumping sides as they tripped along together.

Ava checked her watch. Back at home, Cameron was making progress on the kitchen cabinets, although it was slower than she'd anticipated. It had been two weeks since she'd asked him for a hug, which was now a daily practice when she delivered his morning coffee or afternoon snack, and while he'd finished framing out the base cabinets, and the island, he hadn't even started on the upper framework.

Earlier that day, when she'd gone up to let him know that they were leaving for the riding school, an unexpected ripple of irritation had kept her quiet when he'd asked her how she thought it was looking. Then, as he'd walked around, explaining the next stage of the build-out, nothing that Ava wasn't fully aware of already, a light had gone on in her head. Cameron wasn't a slow worker, he was deliberately taking his time so he could be around longer, and as the thought had taken root, she'd crossed the space between them and wrapped her arms around his neck. 'You're an eejit, Cameron Cole, but I'm really glad you're here.'

*

The next morning, Ava walked into Rick's room at the hospital and stopped short. A tall, thin young man she didn't recognise, with a shiny shaved head, and wearing dark green scrubs, was standing at Rick's bedside. His forearm was hooked under Rick's knee as he moved Rick's leg in small circles, manipulating the hip in the socket.

The hair on Rick's shin and thigh was dark against the ghostly white of his skin and an image of him, healthy, tanned and muscular, wearing his favourite cargo shorts, flashed brightly.

Rocked, Ava blinked several times, then cleared her throat. 'Um, hello.' She moved a few steps inside the room. 'I'm Ava. His wife.' She pointed at Rick, then felt ridiculous for stating what was probably obvious.

'Oh, hello.' The young man smiled shyly, revealing a deep dimple in each cheek and a row of pearly teeth. 'I'm Simon, from physiotherapy.' He continued to move Rick's hip, the effort of supporting the weight of the leg, albeit a skinnier version than Ava had ever seen, showing across Simon's narrow back as his muscles tensed beneath his scrubs. 'We're just making sure he doesn't have muscle stiffness, or a reduced range of motion, when he wakes up.' He spoke over his shoulder, the casual, assumptive statement hitting Ava in the face like a fresh breeze.

'Right, I knew that, but I've just never been here when you were.' She moved deeper into the room, deciding to leave her jacket on, despite the sunny afternoon she'd just left outside.

'We're moving him regularly, too.' Simon walked around the bed and shifted Rick's hips slightly, then slipped his arm under the other knee. 'We don't want him getting sores.'

Ava pictured her rugged husband, his skin newly paper-like and translucent, as ugly red welts appeared across his back. Shaking the image away, she set her bag on the chair nearest the door. 'I can come back later, if that's better?' She looked over at the window, which was once again open a crack, enough to allow the breeze to lift the net curtain away from the sill like a tiny white sail. The scent of the grass, and the musk from the pink rose bushes that lined the edge of the car park below, did battle with the stringent smell of bleach as she watched Simon leaning into the movement, putting his weight on Rick's shin as he manipulated the hip.

'No need. I'm almost done here.' Simon straightened Rick's leg and pushed it up towards the ceiling, the kneecap looking oddly prominent. Then, he lay the leg back down and straightened the gown, lifted the sheet and blanket and smoothed them over Rick's hips, adjusting his lifeless hands back by his sides.

Ava watched the manipulation of her husband's body with an almost morbid curiosity, like Geppetto watching someone else pulling Pinocchio's strings. Rick's lack of response or resistance to this young man, moving him around like an action figure, while distressing, was almost comical and, buoyed up by Simon's positive assertion that Rick would wake up, she let herself smile. 'That's him had his workout, then.' She slid the other chair closer to the bed as Simon lifted a tablet from the side table and tapped the screen. 'Do you take clients who are awake?' She laughed softly.

'Uh, Rick's been here how long now?' He studied the tablet again, then looked up at her, slight apprehension hovering behind his tentative smile.

As her momentary bubble of optimism popped, Ava nodded. 'Seven weeks.' As she said it out loud, she mentally replayed the endless days that had passed since Rick had slipped away from them, then she calculated that they should have been in Barcelona by now, eating tapas so fresh you could taste the sea, with the sound of guitars floating in the air. Carly should have been sketching vivid vineyards, and soaking in the tastes, sights and smells of Spain's siesta culture, the warmth of the people and their zest for life. Spain had been the second-to-last stop on their tour and, picturing it, Ava worked to control a surge of sadness so strong that it stripped her breath away.

'Sorry, I didn't mean to upset you.' Simon was next to her, his eyes full of concern.

'It's OK.' She shook her head. 'Just hearing it out loud makes it real.'

'I understand.' He hugged the tablet to his washboard stomach, his forearms coated in fair down. 'But miracles happen all the time.' He smiled, his words seeming to seep from his mouth, like smoke.

Ava froze. Was that what Rick needed? A miracle? She eyed Simon, trying to formulate a response, when, behind him, Doctor Stewart walked in, his hand in his pockets and his stethoscope around his neck.

'All done, Simon?' He spoked pointedly to the young man, his chin thrust forward and his message clear.

'Yes, doctor. That's me finished.'

'Thanks, then.' Doctor Stewart gave him a perfunctory smile.

Simon nodded silently and walked out into the corridor, carefully sliding the door closed behind him.

'Hello, Ava. How are you?' Doctor Stewart circled the bed and scrutinised one of the monitors.

'I'm OK.' She managed to choke out the words, her mind catapulting back to the word *miracle.* As she locked on his eyes, questioning but kind, the impulse to ask the question that was keeping her awake at night was overwhelming. But even as she imagined asking it, she doubted she was strong enough to handle the answer. If he told her that what she was thinking was possible, would she be strong enough to make the right decision for Rick, for Carly, for them all?

Seeming to sense her conflict, Doctor Stewart hovered by the bed, his eyes on hers. 'Any more thoughts about what we…' He stopped.

Feeling dangerously cornered, and unprepared for an answer she didn't want to hear, she blurted, 'No. I just want to spend some time with him, please.'

She stared at the doctor, waiting to be challenged. Instead, Stewart nodded silently and left the room.

Twenty minutes later, as Ava stood up, and leaned over to kiss Rick goodbye, a wave of such exhaustion overtook her that she reached out and steadied herself against the bed frame. The room began to swim around her as her palms grew clammy and her tongue felt slack in her mouth.

Drained, she lowered herself onto the edge of the bed, willing her head to stop spinning. As the hairs on her arms stood up, she looked at Rick, his eyelids still barring her, his hands like marble renditions of themselves, lifeless on the blanket. The mound he made under the covers seemed to be melting into the mattress below him, and all she wanted was to lie down, feel him next to her, the weight of his arm around her, his breath on her skin.

Scanning the corridor through the glass, she kicked off her shoes, slid her jacket off and tossed it onto the chair, then lay down, easing herself into Rick's side. 'Move over,' she whispered, as she shifted in closer to him, careful not to disturb the breathing tube. Then, lifting his new, lightweight arm, she ducked underneath it, laying her head on his shoulder and pulling his forearm tight around her side. Weaving her fingers through his, to anchor the two of them in place, she closed her eyes and waited, searching for the trace of coffee, or mint, that always hovered on his breath. 'I love you, Rick.' She sighed. 'If you can hear me, please come home. Or tell me what to do.'

Beneath her cheek, his chest rose and fell so slightly that she momentarily worried that she might suffocate him with her weight, but as she considered getting up, she let herself relax into him, her pulse gradually slowing as she matched her breaths to his. As the sounds of the room began to ebb away, the gentle beep of monitors fading to birdsong, Ava let go, and sleep took over.

CHAPTER TWENTY-FOUR

The impressive auditorium inside Inverness's Eden Court Theatre was in darkness, the hum of the surrounding audience quietening as a distant bell rang and the houselights dimmed, indicating that the performance was about to begin. The hairs on Ava's arms prickled with anticipation, as a waft of musky perfume floated across from the woman sitting on her opposite side.

Ava had talked to Carly at length about where they should sit, and they'd pored over the diagram of the auditorium online, with its rows of seats, like wave after wave of royal blue, curving towards the stage. After some deliberation, Carly had finally said that if she was close enough to see the individual dancers clearly, she'd probably miss the bigger picture. Touched by the heartbreaking maturity of the thought process, Ava had suggested they choose seats in the middle section of the stalls, halfway back.

As she looked around now, she was glad they'd settled on this row, with a perfect view of the centre of the stage, but far enough back to give Carly perspective.

Earlier that afternoon, Ava had helped Carly get ready, while reading her the synopsis of *Romeo and Juliet*, all the while Carly peppering her with questions about the tragic story.

'So, they were teenagers then?' She had lifted her chin, letting Ava drag the brush through her hair.

'Yes, that's what makes the story so poignant.' Ava had run her palm over the golden waves, images of Carly as a little girl, skipping, carefree, with a mass of white-blonde ringlets bouncing around her rosy cheeks, making Ava smile.

They'd then talked about young love and Ava had, not for the first time, considered what Carly's future might look like as regards finding that special someone, the Rick in her life. The idea that her condition might make that more difficult than it could be already had caused Ava to excuse herself for a few minutes. She'd retreated to the hall, squeezed her hands into fists and let a burst of anger at the universe course through her.

During the drive to Inverness, Ava had played the CD of *Romeo and Juliet*, and Carly had been silent, her eyes closed, soaking in the music as Ava soaked in her daughter's delicate profile.

Now, Carly was leaning forward, her hands gripping the back of the plush, blue seat in front of her, her hair a golden curtain coating her glittery jacket. As Ava shifted in her seat, feeling the slight prickle of the velvety fabric under her thighs, Carly dipped to the side and whispered over her shoulder. 'Is it starting yet?'

Ava gently eased Carly back in her seat. 'The orchestra will start to warm up soon. Listen.' Just as Ava said it, a strange, discordant melding of string and wind instruments wailed softly from the pit, violins and oboes, clarinets and cellos all mixing together like an audible painting, the colours merging to form an impressionist landscape of sound with no discernible outline.

As the sound of the straining instruments gradually faded, and the overture began, Carly settled back, shoving her folded coat down between her thigh and the empty seat next to her. 'It's starting.' She gave Ava a smile so joyful that, not trusting her voice, Ava could only nod and turn to stare at the stage.

The first half of the ballet held Carly rapt. She leaned forward, sat back, turned her head right and left, as courtiers danced in elegant circles, friends and enemies sparred with swords, and then stood back as two young lovers met, shyly danced together and gradually lost themselves in each other. Carly laughed out loud at Juliet's nurse's antics, turning to Ava and grabbing her hand, as Ava flicked her eyes between the willowy dancers on the stage and the sheer, unadulterated pleasure she saw in her daughter's expression, each sight as fulfilling as the other.

When the interval came, Ava took Carly's hand and led her to the lobby to get a cold drink. Carly chattered about what they'd seen, and Ava stood, her back to the wall, soaking in the excitement that was pulsing from her daughter.

'Did you see the nurse?' Carly turned her head and focused on Ava's face. 'She was so funny.' She sipped some lemonade. 'Juliet is so lovely.' Carly's focus shifted to her glass. 'There's so much going on at once, but I can find one dancer and follow them.' She traced a line in the air. 'And then I see others at the sides, so I get what's going on.' She frowned. 'But I think Romeo is a bit too old for her.'

Ava laughed. 'What do you mean? They're both teenagers.'

Carly shook her head. 'He looks like he's older, though.'

Ava considered the observation, and as she pictured the principal couple, she had to admit that there was a more childlike quality to the woman's interpretation of Juliet. The fact that this subtlety was not lost on Carly was like a gift she'd given to Ava. 'You know, I agree. I think it must be hard to perform those roles though, I mean the dancers are adults portraying children. I can't imagine how they do it.' She shrugged. 'It's true artistry.'

Carly shook her head, finishing her drink. 'It's not that hard. They just have to use their memories.' She patted the surface of the high table next to her and carefully set her glass down.

Ava took in her daughter's flushed face, the high colour accentuating the sprinkling of freckles across the narrow nose and cheekbones, and the clear blue eyes that held so much behind them now, and the image was so startlingly beautiful that Ava blinked several times. Her baby was becoming an insightful and mature young woman and, for an instant, Ava turned to share her pride with Rick. She wanted to squeeze his hand and whisper *look at what a magnificent creature we made*. But next to her was nothing but a hollow space.

'What is it?' Carly was staring at her, a frown folding her forehead.

Ava shook her head. 'I was just wondering when you became so damn clever.' She took Carly's hand. 'I don't know how I got so lucky.'

Carly dipped her chin, the colour rising even higher in her cheeks. 'Aww, Mum. You're making me blush.' She looked up and grinned. 'But you are pretty lucky.' She clamped the tip of her tongue between her lips, a comical expression that was another of Rick's, and that always made Ava laugh.

'Come on. Let's get back in, before everyone else.' Ava was leading Carly out from behind the table when she gently pulled Ava to a standstill. 'What is it? Do you need the loo?' Ava frowned, scanning the lobby for a sign.

'Why do you always think I need the loo?' Carly pulled a face. 'I was just going to say thank you for bringing me.' She swept her hand in an arc. 'I really wanted Dad to be here too, but this is awesome.' She gave a half-smile. 'He'd probably have been bored, anyway.'

Ava stepped closer and pulled Carly to her middle. She kissed the top of Carly's head, letting her lips linger on the silky crown, as she pictured Rick, standing behind Carly's back, pulling a ridiculous face, then slapping on an exaggerated smile as soon as she turned to face him. 'Yes, he probably would. The big oaf.'

The following day, having dropped Carly off at the stables with a packed lunch, and the surprise of a new mobile phone, set up with a dictation, scanning and reading app, and a colour identifier app, that had prompted unexpected tears of gratitude, Ava was heading home.

She had no plans for the rest of the day, and as she considered what she might do with her free time, she was struck by the fact that she couldn't think of a single thing. Time was, with an unexpected few hours to herself, she'd have gone for a long run, or bike ride, taken a leisurely bath with a glass of wine balanced on the edge, snuggled up with a book, or painted. Now, as she considered all those former indulgences, none of them felt particularly appealing.

As the road unfolded in front of her, the morning sun glinted through the leaf-laden branches on her left, as row upon row of trees flicked by the window, drawing her closer to the site of the accident. She'd passed it numerous times now, but each time, the experience was the same. As the spot approached, a clamminess formed under her palms as she gripped the steering wheel, her upper body leaning forward, her shoulders tense as wood. Her face began to tingle as she hummed tunelessly to the radio, all the while smelling noxious, burning rubber, then seeing Rick's head snapping to the side and hitting the window, him hunched over the wheel and then, her saying his name, over and over, a stripped-bare kind of sound that floated outside her body, barely audible above Carly's screams.

Shaking off her rising anxiety, Ava consciously channelled her thoughts back to Carly. It had been unsettling leaving her behind at the stables, even knowing that she was safe and happy, and that her instructors would take great care of her, Kelly and the other rider going along.

Todd had given Ava the details of the route they were taking and told her they'd call as soon as they were heading home so that she could be at the stables when they got back. As she ran over the information in her mind, Ava's phone chirped in the central console. She glanced down, catching a glimpse of Cameron's name, then refocused ahead.

He had become a regular part of her day, one that she'd come to rely on. Their snatched coffees and talks, and the hugs if she was having a particularly hard day, were keeping her feeling less isolated, in the disconcerting limbo that was her new reality. She'd forgotten to let him know that she was taking Carly to the stables that morning, so suspecting his call was just to make sure they were OK, she let herself enjoy a moment of knowing that she was cared about as she turned the car onto Sutherland Road.

Back at the house, she parked, and rather than go inside, walked up the hill and slid the barn door open. Cameron was attaching one of the lower cabinet doors, the creamy hickory that Rick had specified looking optimistic and crisp against the newly installed dark wood floor.

'Hi. I was driving when you called.' She gestured towards the driveway. 'What's up?'

Cameron slipped the screwdriver he held into his belt and ran a hand through his hair. 'Nothing. I was just checking up on you.' He grinned. 'Like the old ma' hen that I am.' He held his hands out at his sides. 'Where's Carly?'

Ava slid her jacket off and draped it over the back of the director's chair. 'Today is her trek, with Todd and Rachel.' She sank into the sagging seat. 'It felt really weird leaving her.' She eyed him as he walked behind the base unit of the island, his hands on his hips.

'Oh, right. You mentioned that she was doing that. I forgot.'

'So, how's it going?' She pointed at the island, still a basic frame with no sides or top. 'Roaring ahead with the island, I see.' She pressed her lips together, suppressing a smile.

Cameron's eyebrows jumped. 'Hey, don't question the craftsman when he's creating. I don't tell you how to design stuff, or be a mother, do I?'

She laughed softly. 'No, I don't suppose you do.' She sat back, letting her hair fall over her shoulders, the seed of an idea taking root, and as she played with it for a few moments, it grew more enticing. 'How about you skive off today?' She widened her eyes playfully. 'Play hooky with me.' She paused. 'I'm not going into the hospital until this evening so have until around four o'clock to myself, and absolutely no idea what to do.' She shrugged. 'Pretty pathetic, eh?'

Cameron shook his head. 'Not pathetic. I'd just say not surprising.' He scanned her face, a kindness glowing behind his dark eyes that warmed her to her core. 'You spend every waking moment taking care of Carly, doing all her school stuff, taking her to her appointments, then visiting Rick almost every day and running around like a blue-arsed fly managing everything else at the house.' He leaned against the cabinet behind him. 'As far as enjoying any time to yourself, you're just out of practice.'

Ava was once again touched by this gentle man's perceptiveness. 'You're quite the philosopher, Cameron Cole. I'm impressed.'

He walked over to her. 'As for skiving off, I'd consider it.' He pouted. 'If you let me take you out for a drive, or a walk, and buy you lunch for a change, rather than *you* feeding *me*. What do you say?'

The whisper of guilt that she now heard whenever she thought about doing something for herself brushed her ear, but a welling up of need followed it, so powerful that she let herself accept. 'You're on.' She jumped up and grabbed her jacket from the back of the chair. 'But I don't want anything posh. Just a nice simple lunch, perhaps a walk, and some good, adult conversation.' She rounded the chair and stopped at the door.

'Oh, well, that last part could be problematic.' He laughed. 'But I'll do my best.'

The beer garden at the Castle hotel was quiet, with only two other tables occupied, one by an elderly couple in mud-spattered walking gear, and the other by three women about Ava's age, all wearing matching pink T-shirts.

Ava sat with her back to the sun as Cameron squinted into the midday light, his sunglasses covering the soulful eyes that, after a mere two months of friendship, could hide little from her now.

Their beer glasses were sweating on the wooden-topped table, and Cameron's burger smelled wonderful as Ava looked down at her carefully chosen salad. 'I wish I'd had that.' She pointed at his plate. 'Why do I always do that?' she said. 'Rick usually orders what I actually want, then I end up lusting after his meal and stealing half of it.' She laughed softly. 'God, I miss all that small stuff.' She swallowed, as Cameron pushed his sunglasses onto the top of his head.

'You can have some of my chips.' He dipped his chin. 'But hands off the burger.' He slid his plate towards her. 'Adam always complains about me nicking his food, too.' He lifted a fat chip and bit into it. 'Other people's just tastes better, somehow.' He grinned, dipping the remainder of the chip into the puddle of ketchup he'd poured onto his plate.

Ava took a bite of the peppery rocket she'd ordered, the lemon dressing sharp on her tongue. 'I know. It's so true. Rick's food is always better than mine, even if we choose the same thing.' She laughed, a memory of their honeymoon spiralling into view.

They'd been eating at a harbourside restaurant in Sydney, and they'd both chosen grilled barramundi in a chilli sauce. When it arrived, she'd spun her plate around, looking over at Rick's identically presented meal.

'What? Is something wrong with yours?' He'd frowned, studying her plate.

'No, but why does yours look so much better?' She'd laughed, her skin warm and taut from a day spent out on a deep-sea fishing boat, as the evocative scents of saltwater and suntan lotion floated around them.

Rick had shaken his head, lifting his plate and deftly switching them. 'Happy wife...' He'd winked at her, and rather than protest, she'd gladly accepted his meal, her heart swelling a little more with love for this selfless man she could now call her husband.

'Where did you go, again?' Cameron scattered salt on his burger. 'You're miles away.'

Ava shoved the greens around her plate. 'Australia, about fifteen years ago.' Her throat drew tight, so she lifted her glass and gulped down some frothy lager. 'Our honeymoon.'

'Nice.' Cameron nodded. 'That's somewhere I'd love to see.' He took a bite of burger, his jaw pulsing as he chewed. 'With Adam gone for great chunks of time, and my work, travelling is hard.' He shrugged. 'But we get by.'

Ava broke off a sliver of grilled salmon and popped it into her mouth, just as one of the women at the table behind them burst out laughing, a weird, throaty cackle that made Ava's eyes snap to Cameron's. His comical expression brought her lips together, her nostrils flaring as she suppressed a snort. With the tiny, shared moment, Ava recalled so many of those moments she'd had with Rick, when they'd spot the same misshapen potato in the supermarket, hear that one grating voice over the rest at a party, or both catch a whiff of the pungent body odour in the crowd next to them. Their senses were fused in some cosmic way and having him gone, suspended in an altered universe, in turn altered hers. As she tried to focus on the sky behind Cameron's head, her vision blurred.

'Hey, no tears today.' He held a golden chip out to her. 'Come on, have one. You know you want to.' He waggled it as she sniffed, swiped her cheek and took it from his hand.

'Fine. I'm fine.' She reached over, dipped the chip into the ketchup, then stuffed it into her mouth, the tang of tomato a startling departure from her fragrant salmon.

Twenty minutes later, they'd parked near the beach and begun walking towards the shore. The July sun was warm, and the breeze heavy with both salt and the sweetness of freshly cut grass drifting from the golf course behind them. Ava had slipped her shoes off, letting them dangle at her side, as she savoured the cool sand sliding between her toes.

Cameron had slowed his pace to allow her to catch up and now, as a cluster of seagulls banked overhead, and the water licked the shore, retreating with gentle hissing sounds, Ava was tugged back in time, to her childhood summers.

Her walks, and picnics on the beach with Flora, had been among her favourite times spent with her grandmother, after her parents had left her for the customary week each year. Flora would pack enough food for four people and they'd wander down the beach, pick their spot and stake it out, a large tartan blanket forming their grass. Flora insisted on putting up a folding windshield, even if there was no more than a trace of a breeze, the old-fashioned wicker picnic basket set at one corner of the blanket and their towels folded neatly at the opposite one.

They'd settle themselves, Ava with a book or a sketch pad, and Flora with the newspaper, or sometimes her knitting, and they'd sit in companionable silence until one of them would get bored and suggest a paddle. Ava would occasionally swim, despite the icy temperature of the water, and Flora would stand at the edge, her sturdy calves half submerged, her hand shielding her eyes as she watched Ava.

Those summer days had seemed to last forever, the long hours of daylight stretching into perfect, languorous slices of time that left a sweet taste on the tongue and a deep sense of peace inside Ava that, now, she recognised she had not felt in many months.

Slightly ahead of her again, Cameron had stopped walking and was staring out at the water. His shirt flapped in the breeze and the bottom of his jeans, rolled up a few times at his ankles, were dark from the water that flicked up as it curled into the shore. As she approached, he turned to her and spoke quietly.

'You know, if you need to talk, or cry, it's OK. I didn't mean to bully you earlier.'

Ava moved in next to him and took his hand. 'I know,' she said, the pressure of his fingers around hers comforting. 'Sometimes I think I can take on the world, fix everything, get us all through this.' She swept her free hand in an arc. 'Then others, it all feels so overwhelming, I think I'm drowning.' She scanned the horizon, the sail of a small boat the only dot against the expanse of blue sky that stretched away on either side of them.

'Stop beating yourself up.' Cameron squeezed her hand, then let it drop. 'You're doing fine.'

She nodded, grateful for the endorsement, while at the same time craving something to talk about that wasn't hers to bear. 'Tell me more about Adam.' She tugged his arm, moving them on. 'What's he like?'

'He's a pain in the arse.' Cameron laughed. 'He's from Edinburgh, so he thinks he's posh, but he spends most of his time in oily jeans and Arran jumpers. He loves football, plays a mean round of golf, eats like a horse but can't cook to save his life.' He grimaced. 'He sings in the shower but is completely tone-deaf, and he snores like a train.' He paused. 'He adores his mum and is the one of the kindest and most caring people I know.'

'Well, that's quite a write-up.' She leaned her shoulder against his meaty arm. 'Can I see a photo?'

He pulled out his phone and scrolled through several pictures before handing it to her. 'That's us at Ben Nevis, last year.'

Ava looked at the photo of a slender man, with thick, sandy-coloured hair, almost matching Cameron in height. Adam was smiling from under a baseball hat, his eyes a startling blue against his tanned skin, and next to him, rather than look at the camera, Cameron was looking at Adam, and smiling.

'He looks lovely.' She handed the phone back. 'How did you meet?'

Cameron slid the phone away, then gently hooked Ava's arm through his as they walked on. 'Through a job I was doing in Inverness. It was a huge reno project. One of those old Black Isle mansions. The owners were restoring it, pulling out all the stops with original materials, really keeping the character intact.' He paused as they passed a glistening mound of seaweed, and Ava drew in a deep, earthy breath. 'He came to the job site looking for his cousin. Turned out the house belonged to his aunt and uncle.' Cameron leaned down and picked up a shell, rubbed it between his thumb and forefinger, then handed it to her. 'He talked to me for a while, then got in his car and drove off. I was sort of gutted, though I didn't really know why, then, about half an hour later, he came back, with some excuse about needing to leave his cousin a note.' He laughed softly. 'But I knew…'

'Aww, I love that story.' She patted his arm. 'When you know you know, right?'

'Aye, I'd say so.' He nodded. 'Did you know right away, with Rick?'

Ava blinked into the breeze. 'Yes, sort of. He was meeting with someone at the first design firm I worked at, in Aberdeen. He'd come in with a portfolio and he seemed really nervous. I was a junior designer at the time, so was on a coffee run when I saw him sitting in reception.' She smiled to herself. 'He looked like a big puppy, all fidgety and buzzing with energy, and his jacket was about two sizes too big. Looked like he'd borrowed it from his dad, or something.' She caught Cameron smiling at her. 'For some reason, I walked over to him and asked if he'd like a coffee while he was waiting. He looked so relieved that I thought he was going to jump up and hug me.' The image was as vivid now as it had been all those years ago. 'We talked for a few minutes, then he asked me if I was busy that night.'

'Didn't waste any time then?' Cameron laughed. 'Good man.'

'No. It was more like we were familiar. Like we were already friends.' She looked up at him. 'There was no awkwardness, just a sense of being at home.' The last word stuck in her throat, and Ava turned her back on Cameron, letting the breeze pick up her hair and split it down the back of her head. As she closed her eyes, willing them to stay dry, he put a big paw on her shoulder.

'Are you going in to see him today?'

She pinched her nose and swung around to face him. 'Yes, after I bring Carly home this afternoon. I'll get her settled, then pop in for an hour.'

He nodded, his hands plunging into his pockets. 'If you want me to sit with her, I can.' He shrugged. 'That way you won't feel rushed about getting back. I can even make her some dinner.'

Taken aback by the kind offer, but this being a new level of involvement for him that she was unsure how Carly would feel about, Ava just pressed her palms together. 'Thank you, really. I'm not sure if she'll feel like company, but I'll ask her when I pick her up.'

'Sure. That's fine. You can let me know later.' His cheeks had turned rosy and the generosity of spirit that was fast becoming his trademark touched her.

'You are the best, Cameron. You really are.'

He shook his head, turning to face the water. 'Not at all.' He mumbled something else that she didn't catch, then, wanting to spare him any more embarrassment, she looped her arm through his again and tugged him back towards the road.

'Come on, big man. We better get going.'

'Right enough.'

'Thanks for a lovely lunch, and morning.' She leaned in, catching a whiff of sawdust from his shirtsleeve.

'You're welcome. You owe me a portion of chips, by the way.' He nudged her playfully. 'I feel Rick's pain.'

Ava clicked her tongue. 'Hey, whose friend are you anyway?' She kicked at a lump of wet sand, sending it splattering across his bare ankles.

Cameron looked down, assessing the mess she'd made, and before she could stop him, he lifted her up in his arms as if she was no more than a twig, and began running towards the water.

'Don't you dare.' She shouted as he held her up high, dangling her precariously over the water. 'Cameron, I mean it.' Her voice shook with laughter as he made to dump her, then pulling her back in to his chest, he set her down on the sand. 'You big...' She swatted at him, catching the glint of mischief in his eyes, the exact same look Rick had when he was plotting something he knew she'd disapprove of.

Just as the sky began to darken, Ava hesitated for a second, then took a step back and dragged her hair into a ponytail, securing it with the band that had been around her wrist.

'Come on, it's going to rain.' She turned and began running across the sand, in the direction of the car. 'Last one there's a numpty,' she shouted.

He dashed past her in a flash, kicking up clouds of sand as he called over his shoulder, 'See you there, numpty.'

CHAPTER TWENTY-FIVE

Two weeks had passed since her lunch with Cameron and, with the school holidays officially underway, Ava had called her company to discuss extending her leave of absence. Her boss had been sympathetic but had made it clear that if she was unable to get back to work, at least part-time, her position might be in jeopardy. Unsurprised, but disappointed, Ava had agreed to return on a half-time basis and was due to begin the next day.

Carly was delighted to be finished with lessons for six whole weeks, and while Ava dashed about, juggling the day-to-day tasks, visiting Rick and keeping their routine as consistent as possible, her daughter's vision continued to deteriorate. While the changes seemed to be more subtle now, it still wrecked Ava to see that, with each small slip backwards, Carly's confidence faded a little more.

The previous day, Ava had had to persuade her to go to the stables. Carly's reticence was a disappointing development that Ava had tried to navigate as sensitively as she could.

Earlier that morning, Carly had called Ava in to the bathroom, unable to find the toothpaste. Ava had subtly lifted the tube from the side of the sink as she opened the glass cabinet door, pretending the paste had been inside. 'Here it is, love.' She'd pressed the tube into Carly's hand. 'I tidied it away.' She'd stepped to Carly's side, forcing a laugh. 'My bad.'

Carly had lifted her chin, her left eye twitching as she found her focus. 'Yeah, right.' She'd pouted. 'It was right there, wasn't it?' She'd tapped the edge of the sink.

Feeling, as Flora would have put it, like a currant with a bite out of it, Ava had blushed. 'Sorry. I shouldn't have done that.'

'It's OK, Mum.'

'No, it's not. We promised we'd be honest with each other, about everything.' Ava had let her shame simmer as Carly held her toothbrush up to her left eye and squeezed, the rope of sticky white paste narrowly missing the brush and landing on the edge of the sink.

'Hell's bells,' she'd hissed, slamming the brush down.

'Carly.' Ava had tutted. 'Let me help you. Just today.'

Carly had nodded, her chin beginning to wobble as Ava wiped the sticky mess from the porcelain, squeezed some paste onto the brush and handed it to Carly.

Now, Carly was sitting out on the front lawn with her sketch pad and a packet of pastel crayons. The afternoon light was fading, and the early-evening sky was streaked with a tapestry of pre-sunset colours that leaked into the clear blue dregs of the day.

While watching Carly bent over the pad on her lap, her right arm moving back and forth as she worked intently, Ava checked her phone for messages. Seeing none, she was about to set it down when it rang, startling her, but the familiar name on the screen quickly settled her heart.

'Hello, you.' Jenna sounded upbeat. 'What's going on up in the boonies?'

'Same old, same old.' Ava shrugged, leaning forward against the sink to get a better view of Carly.

'Still good for next weekend?' Jenna asked, as Ava tucked the phone under her jaw, folded a tea towel over the handle of the Aga and walked into the living room.

'Yes, of course. We're looking forward to it.'

They chatted about what they'd do with the two days together, as Ava circled the room, lifting a sweatshirt of Rick's from the sofa that Carly had taken to wearing in the evenings and her own slippers from next to the chair.

'So, how's Carly doing? Any changes?'

Holding the items of clothing against her stomach, Ava headed for the stairs. As she climbed, she felt the slight pull in her thighs that the lack of a regular running routine had brought about. 'She's getting angry about stuff now.' She walked across the hall and into the bedroom. 'It's amazing that it's taken this long, actually.' Ava dumped the sweatshirt on the bed and then tossed her slippers onto the floor. 'I'm angry most of the bloody time.'

'She's remarkable.' Jenna sighed. 'Just like her mum.'

'Not so much, these days,' Ava huffed. 'I'm beginning to fray at the edges, Jen. Every day I go and see Rick and there's no improvement, I feel like it's all slipping away. I'm losing my grip.' She caught her reflection in the mirror behind the dressing table, her tousled hair hanging around her shoulders, her pale eyes hooded and darkly shadowed. 'And that thing I told you, about Rick being a donor.' Her voice caught. 'I just can't stop thinking about it. What if I end up in that position, I mean having to decide what to do? What Rick would want me to do?'

'Ava, I think you're jumping ahead a bit. It's too soon to be going there, surely?' Jenna's voice was low. 'Just take a breath and try not to lose hope. Rick is like a bulldog when it comes to you and Carly. He'll do everything he can to come back to you.'

Nodding sadly, Ava pictured his face, cheerful, bursting with life, and she tried to lock that image in her heart, rather than the haunting one of him wasting away in a chilly hospital room.

'Are you sleeping any better?' Jenna diverted her.

Ava shook her head. 'Not well. Still having nightmares.' She flicked the hair from her forehead, and with it the memory of her dream of the night before that had left her quaking and tearful.

'Can you talk to your doctor about it? Maybe get something to help you out for a while?' Jenna's voice dropped to a whisper. 'You need to sleep, love.'

Ava's mouth dipped. 'No. I can't take anything. I mean, what if Carly woke up, or needed me, and I was out of it?' She shook her head. 'I'm fine. I'll sleep when…' She let the sentence ebb away.

'So, how's she doing with the counselling?' The screech of a distant car alarm filtered through the phone and Ava held it away from her ear slightly.

'All right. She's been to a few sessions now, and it seems to be helping.' Ava lifted the sweatshirt, folded it and pushed it into a drawer. 'I spoke to Serena, her counsellor, about the anger and she said she'd bring it up at their next session.' She flopped onto the end of the bed, the scent of the old cedar trunk floating towards her from across the room. 'She says it's part of the process and we just have to navigate it as best we can.' She sighed. 'Seemingly it will pass, and she'll move into acceptance.' The word held an odd weight as Ava considered what a huge ask this was for a young girl, to accept her world darkening around her, in frightening leaps and bounds, helpless to stop it.

'How about you? Are you thinking about getting any counselling?' Jenna's question made Ava's eyebrows jump.

'No. I'm fine.' She frowned, lying back and bringing her knees up to her chest.

'Hmm.' Jenna sounded dubious. 'We can talk about that at the weekend.'

Ava shook her head, silently. She'd keep it together, if not for herself, then for Carly.

Jenna went on to fill her in on Mandy's recent antics, having been picked for a key role in a play at school and then, to Jenna's disappointment, deciding she didn't want to do it. 'She wanted me to tell the teacher she was ill, but I said she had to deal with it herself and tell the truth.' Jenna sighed. 'Do you think that was harsh?'

Ava shook her head against the duvet. 'No, I think that's fair. They're old enough to understand that they have to take responsibility for their choices.'

'Yeah, I thought so too. Of course, she didn't speak to me for two days,' Jenna huffed. 'It was quite peaceful, actually.'

'Jenna, really.' Ava laughed.

'What? You know it's true.' Jenna chuckled. 'Anyway, some chocolate and a trip to the cinema mended fences. We're fine now.'

Ava heaved herself up and smoothed the duvet, avoiding looking at Rick's side of the bed.

'Any news on the dog yet?' Jenna asked. 'It's been ages.'

Ava made her way down the stairs, the wooden treads cool under her bare feet. 'Nothing yet. But they did say it could take a few weeks for the right match to come up.' She crossed the living room and peered out of the window, seeing Carly still sitting on the blanket. 'I'll call them on Monday though, and see if they can give me any updates. It'd be such a boost for her. She really needs something bright on the horizon right now.'

'So do you, love. That's why *I'm* coming.' Jenna laughed, the familiar sound soft as a blanket landing on Ava's weary shoulders.

Just as she was about to hang up, the phone buzzed, indicating an incoming call. 'Hang on, Jen.' She lifted it away from her and scanned the screen. Not recognising the number, she declined the call and put the phone back to her ear. 'Never mind. No idea who that was.'

'So, we'll see you soon then.' Jenna covered the microphone and shouted to Mandy to lower the volume on the TV.

'Yes, can't wait.' Ava walked into the kitchen. 'It'll be great to spend some time together.' She filled the kettle and set it on the stove.

'So it will. Now go and put your feet up for an hour. Read a book, or paint something.'

'Yeah, perhaps.' Ava rolled her shoulders back. 'The bathroom could use a fresh coat.'

'Ha ha.' Jenna tutted. 'Bye for now.'

*

With some tea and a plate of ginger biscuits on a tray, Ava went out to the front garden. 'Fancy a cuppa?' She walked around the blanket and stood in front of Carly, blocking the sun. Carly's sunglasses held Ava's outline as she knelt and set the tray on the blanket. 'Can I join you?'

'Yep.' Carly laid her pad down. 'Are those ginger snaps?' She pointed at the plate.

'Yes.' Ava lifted a mug and held it out to Carly, careful to put the handle directly into her fingers before letting go. 'Want one?'

'In a minute.' Carly crossed her legs and balanced the mug precariously on her knee.

Fighting the urge to warn her about it, Ava lifted her own mug, looked down at what Carly had been working on and caught her breath. Using the pastels, she had drawn the early-evening sky, large swaths of blue and dove-grey blending into narrow smears of lilac and yellow, the bold use of colour, all within the spectrum that Carly could still see and appreciate, startling. 'Carly, that's amazing. Those colours are incredible.'

Carly's shoulders bounced as she slipped her glasses down her nose and squinted into the dimming light. 'I thought I'd be braver. Not worry about whether it's right or not.' She blew on the surface of the hot liquid. 'Like you said, paint what I see. Slap it on and stuff.' She peered over the top of the cup.

Ava caught the gentle teasing in her daughter's voice, which had become rare recently, and the sound warmed Ava like the sun. She pursed her lips, feigning annoyance. 'Whatever the reasoning, what you've done there is magic.'

Carly sipped some tea, then balanced the mug back on her knee. 'Really? Is it worth keeping? It's not just muddy?' She frowned at her work.

'Absolutely not. We'll frame this one too, if you like.' Ava lifted a biscuit and held it out to Carly, who tilted her head from side to side, then swung her hand out, reaching for it.

'Do you think Dad will like it?' Carly bit into the biscuit, sending a puff of crumbs onto the blanket.

'Definitely.' Ava swung her legs around and stretched them out in front of her, trying to visualise Rick standing in the living room, his hands on his hips and his head tipped to the side as he assessed the two pieces of Carly's art that would soon hang over the sideboard. As she tried to picture it, Ava was startled that she couldn't conjure the image she wanted. This time, no matter how she tried, Rick's familiar form, his long back, broad shoulders and dark cowlick at the nape of his neck, wouldn't come, and the void that stared back at her was frightening. Shaken, she blinked several times, aware that Carly was staring at her.

'What is it?' Carly spoke softly. 'Are you missing him?'

A tugging in Ava's throat made her cough. 'Yes, all the time.' She nodded. 'You?'

Carly's mouth dipped. 'Same.'

Ava shifted over and draped an arm around Carly's shoulders. 'Don't suppose you'd like to come with me to see him tomorrow?'

Carly stared ahead for a few moments, giving Ava hope, then shook her head. 'Not yet.'

Ava pressed her lips tight to dam her disappointment.

'I'll come soon.' Carly was staring at Ava's profile, but rather than meet her gaze, Ava looked at the horizon, where the sunset was now painting vivid stripes of burnt umber and magenta across the sky. The colours were stunning and, once again, the haunting question that had been cowering in the back of her mind resurfaced. What if there was a way that Rick could give Carly back the colour in her life? If there were, Ava knew that he wouldn't hesitate, and the knowledge burrowed painfully into her middle.

As she blinked to clear her vision, she pointed ahead of her. 'The colours are exactly like your painting.'

Carly lifted her chin, turned her head to the right and sighed. 'It's so pretty.'

Sadness sucked at Ava's core like a receding tide as she leaned in and kissed Carly's cheek. 'It is almost as pretty as your picture of it, but not quite.'

Ava slid the casserole into the dishwasher and closed the door. Over dinner, they'd talked about how they'd structure their days now that Ava would be working in the mornings and Carly would have to occupy herself more. Ava had suggested inviting Kelly over sometime, to keep Carly company, and, to her relief, Carly had agreed.

Carly was watching TV, so Ava lifted her phone to call Kelly's mother, and as soon as she touched the screen, the voicemail icon lit up. As always happened now when she saw the symbol, an innocuous little roll of recording tape, Ava's stomach knotted, its potential to deliver some harmless news outweighed by the alternative. As she waited for the message to play, she counted her breaths.

It was from the manager of The Guide Dog Centre and was short and sweet. Ava leaned her head back, the thumping in her chest abating. Setting the phone down, she pressed her palms together, dropped her chin to her fingertips, then walked into the living room. 'Carly, love. Can you turn it off for a minute? I need to tell you something.'

Carly looked up, startled, then fumbled for the remote that lay next to her on the sofa. 'What's wrong? Is it Dad?' She turned to face Ava, her mouth already quivering.

'No, sweetheart. It's not about Dad.' Ava sat next to her. 'I had a call from the guide dog place. They've found you a dog.' Ava took Carly's hand. 'It's a Labrador. She's two years old and you'll never guess what her name is.' She held still as Carly circled her chin, searching for her focus.

'What?' Her mouth fell open.

'She's called Luna.' Ava's throat caught as she watched Carly's face open into a smile so blissful, it pulsed from behind her eyes.

'Oh, my gosh, really? Luna?' Carly dropped her head to her chest.

'Yes, and they want to schedule your first training session this week.'

Carly's head shot up. 'Tomorrow?' She shifted to the edge of the sofa, every muscle taut and her chin dipped, like a cheetah poised on a ledge above its prey.

Ava laughed, her palms landing on Carly's eager shoulders as she eased her back in the seat. 'The day after, and remember what we talked about? It's going to take a few weeks to complete all the stages of the new partnership training. First is ten days of learning what they call core skills, where you'll meet Luna and work one-on-one with a trainer.'

Ava slid in next to Carly as her daughter scanned the wall where the TV hung, nodding excitedly, a rosy veneer creeping across her downy cheek.

Just as Ava was about to continue, Carly frowned and turned to her mother.

'Hang on. Is that the one where I have to stay there?'

'Yes, it's a ten-day course where you learn to care for and work the dog, but I think you only have to stay in for a couple of nights.'

Carly shook her head. 'No. I can't.'

'We talked about this, Carly.' Ava tucked a long golden strand behind Carly's ear. 'The brochure says they prefer you to be in-house for some of it, with the dog and the other students. It's supposed to give you the best possible start to the partnership.'

Carly stood up and, with her hand sweeping the air in front of her, walked towards the fireplace. 'I'm not sleeping there.' She shook her head. 'I don't see why I have to.' A telltale quiver to the narrow chin brought Ava to her feet.

'Carly, love, come on. It'll probably be fun. You'll meet some other people going through the same process, maybe make some friends. You won't be alone. I'll be with you, of course.' She paused, taking in the panicked expression on her daughter's face. 'It'll be like one of those summer camps we've seen on TV.' Ava grappled for some positive imagery that might help quell the fear that had visibly engulfed her daughter.

Carly's head snapped up. 'We can't go, anyway, because Mand and Jenna will be here. We can't be away if they're here.' She looked triumphant, her hair swinging behind her shoulders as she put her hands on her hips, superhero style.

Ava sighed. 'Sweetheart, we can't pick and choose when this happens. If you say no to this opportunity, it could be months before they find the right dog for you again.' She circled her arms towards her middle. 'Come here.'

Carly hesitated, then, stroking the air, stepped forward, catching her shin on the seaman's chest. Stumbling, she folded at the waist and grabbed her leg. 'Ow.' She hissed. 'God, I'm so sick of this.' Her voice shook as she righted herself, and Ava jumped up and closed the gap between them.

'I know, love.' She drew Carly to her. 'It's not fair.'

Carly leaned in, her chin resting on Ava's shoulder, the point of pressure a startling reminder of how much Carly had grown over the past few months. 'You're going to be as tall as me soon,' Ava whispered, stroking Carly's back.

Feeling the angst pulsing from Carly's body like an electric current, Ava frantically ran through various potential scenarios in her mind: her driving them into Inverness as needed, going to visit Rick, then trying to fit work, housework and errands around the training schedule, each scenario becoming more complicated as she considered it.

'Carly, I need to work too, love. With all the driving, it'd probably be easier if we stayed there, just when we have to.' Ava sucked in her bottom lip as she willed a solution to materialise.

Carly stepped back from her, her eyes full of tears and her face a picture of misery. 'Please don't make me sleep there.' She scanned Ava's face. 'I just can't.'

Knowing there was more to this than simple stubbornness, Ava led Carly back to the sofa. 'What's going on, Carly? We said no more secrets, right?'

Carly nodded, swiping at her nose with her palm as she sank onto the sofa next to Ava. 'It's just that this is the only place I feel safe. I know there are seven steps from my bed to the hall, then ten more to the bathroom. I know that the sink is six steps from the fridge, and I know how to find the light switches by feeling the wall, level with my shoulder.' She held her arm out in front of her. 'If I go somewhere new, I won't be able to move around without crashing into things. Even if you're there, you can't be with me all the time, and people will stare at me.' She hiccupped, the miserable sound driving a nail straight through Ava's heart. 'Please don't make me, Mum.' She tipped sideways, her head thumping against Ava's breastbone as Carly let go, shuddering sobs coursing through her. Ava began rocking her sweet girl, and afraid that she couldn't hold herself together for another second, she clamped her hand over her mouth.

As mother and daughter clung to one another, and Carly's crying slowly subsided, Ava considered their options, a watery compromise surfacing. She eventually eased Carly upright and wiped her thumb under each swollen eye. 'OK. I'll talk to the centre and see what they say, because I might be wrong about sleeping over. And we'll ask Jenna if they can come another weekend, after training. But I think it's too important for you to pass up on this dog, Carly.'

Carly released herself from Ava's arms, sweeping her hand to her right as she made her way back to the fireplace. 'So, we'll just ask Jenna if they can come later?' Looking defeated, she flopped onto Rick's armchair.

Ava moved over and stood next to her daughter. 'I'm sure they won't mind.' She took Carly's hand in hers. 'You're going to get a dog, Carly. This is exciting.' She rubbed her thumb over the smooth palm. 'We should celebrate.' Ava dug deep and forced jollity into her voice. 'Come on. What do you want to do? Paint our nails? Watch Harry Potter? Go into town tomorrow and raid Sadie's bakery?'

Carly pulled her shoulders back, twisted her head to the side and sighed. 'All of the above.' She shrugged, then sought Ava's eyes. 'But I'm still not sleeping there.' Her determination was clear, and Ava knew that she'd won the battle, if not the war.

'I'll call them first thing tomorrow.' She tipped her head to the side. 'I'm not promising anything, but I'll try.'

Carly nodded, a look of resignation replacing the one of fixed determination that had been a duplicate of her father's. 'I'm not going to, though,' she huffed.

Ava sighed. 'Carly, I said I can't make any promises.'

CHAPTER TWENTY-SIX

Doctor Stewart was in the corridor outside Rick's room and it seemed to Ava that he'd have walked on, had she not called to him. When he turned back to her, he asked after Carly, telling Ava in his usual hushed tone that Rick was the same, no new changes to worry about. The notion of not worrying struck her as monstrous, and then ludicrous, and, to her mortification, Ava laughed.

'Well, I'll just stop doing that then,' she quipped, holding her hands out at her sides. 'I wish I'd known. I could've stopped weeks ago.'

Doctor Stewart seemed embarrassed, his collected demeanour slipping a little as he took her arm and led her to a small sitting area at the end of the ward. 'I'm sorry if I upset you, Ava. It's a reflex to tell patients not to worry, you must understand. In no way was I being reductive about Richard's situation. Quite the contrary.'

She gladly sank into the pulpy fabric of the chair. 'I know. I'm sorry. It's just been so long, and every day I come here, he's the same.' She swallowed over a nut. 'Each time I walk through those doors, I hold my breath, thinking perhaps today will be the day that you'll meet me in the hall and smile, tell me that some needle or other has moved, that there's some sign of my husband coming back to me.' She paused. 'But it never happens.'

Doctor Stewart sat opposite her and leaned forward, his elbows on his knees and his stethoscope roped between his hands. 'Ava, there is no given formula to coma.' He shrugged. 'All we can do is what we're doing.' He sat back and lassoed the stethoscope around his neck, and Ava noted the clear eyes assessing her kindly. Then, he threw down the gauntlet once more. 'It's been a few weeks since we talked about it, but have you given any more thought to Rick's wishes, or about withdrawing care?'

'No. I haven't.' She shook her head, meeting his gaze. 'No.'

Rocked by the implication of the questions, every nightmare and morbid fantasy she'd been having running rampant inside her, Ava excused herself and withdrew to the ladies' room until she gradually rallied. Then, after checking herself in the mirror, noting the deepening shadows under her pale eyes, she went in and sat next to Rick.

She played his favourite Jack Johnson song on her phone as she talked about the progress Cameron was making on the kitchen, her feelings about going back to work, and Carly's painting. All the while, Rick's hands lay motionless at his sides, the veins seeming to visibly pulse under the incongruously colourful thistle tattoo, as the ventilator ticked next to him, his chest rising in gentle heaves that Ava found she was matching her breathing to.

After a while she fell silent, as Doctor Stewart's question eased itself back into her heavy heart. Feeling light-headed, she leaned forward and moved a curl away from Rick's neck. 'Why did we never talk about stuff like this? What we'd do if one of us ended up...' She shook her head. 'Doctor Stewart keeps asking me what I want to do, and I have no idea.' She gulped. 'I'm asking myself all these awful, morbid questions, about you, the future, and Carly's future, wondering what you'd want me to do. Whether you could help... Whether *I* could...' She stopped herself, as continuing was a giant step too far.

As she stared at his translucent eyelids, stubbornly shutting her out, her sadness suddenly evaporated, and she grabbed his hand, her nails digging into his palm. 'Rick, for God's sake. If you can hear me, you need to come back. You can't leave me here to make these kinds of decisions. To deal with all of this alone. I'm telling you I need you to wake up.' Her voice shook as fat tears trickled down her cheeks. 'It's enough, now.' She tugged his arm violently. 'Rick, please.'

The following morning was bright, a band of wispy cloud hovering far out, over the firth, and a cool breeze carrying the smell of moss in the open kitchen window as Ava made coffee. She tipped four heaped teaspoons of fresh grounds into the cafetière and filled it three-quarters with boiling water. Rick always teased her about the strength of her coffee, saying the spoon could stand up in it, and as she watched the honey-coloured foam spin on the top, his face came to her, the sparkling brown eyes, the tapered nose and the wide mouth she loved to kiss, all making her ache with such emptiness that she steadied herself against the countertop.

She pushed the image away with a sigh and, coffee mug in hand, tiptoed down the hall, halting at the half-open door to Carly's bedroom. Ava peeked in, seeing that Carly's head was buried under the duvet. The curtains were tightly drawn and the room a murky grey, as Ava backed out silently and closed the door. She needed this time to switch back into work mode, and now that school lessons weren't dictating the structure of their day, that Carly had begun sleeping well into the morning was a blessing.

Ava set her coffee down and scanned the list of emails in her inbox. As she mentally prioritised them, she checked the time and them dialled The Guide Dog Centre. After a few moments she was connected to Dan, the man who'd carried out Carly's home assessment. He listened quietly, allowing her to explain the delicate nature of the situation, and Carly's reluctance to sleep away from home, and when he finally spoke, his voice was reassuring.

'There would only have been one or two nights when we'd have preferred students to stay here, but because of her age, it's fine.'

'You mean we won't have to stay overnight at all?' Ava's eyebrows jumped.

'No, Mrs Guthrie. Once she's been introduced to her dog here at the centre, and done the first, basic course, the majority of Carly's training will take place at your home and in her surrounding environment. As long as you can be with her for the duration of the course.'

A weight lifted from Ava's back and she rolled her shoulders. 'Oh, thanks a million, Dan. That's such a relief. I should've asked you this when you were here, I'm sorry, I'm just so…' She paused. 'I wouldn't ask for any special treatment, it's just with her dad being so ill.'

'It's all right. We quite understand,' he said. 'The most important thing is that Carly is in a positive mindset when she meets Luna, as that initial bonding is critical to the success of the partnership.'

Ava scrolled through the list of emails, her anxiety rising at the magnitude of what she had to achieve that day, and for the next ten. 'Right. Absolutely. I really appreciate you being so understanding.'

'You're welcome. So, we can expect her tomorrow morning?' Dan covered the microphone and mumbled something to someone nearby.

'Yes, absolutely. We'll be there, with bells on.' Ava wedged the phone under her chin as she began to type an email to her boss, explaining that while she may not be completely available during business hours over the next week or so, her work would get done. 'Thanks again, Dan. She's over the moon about Luna.'

'You're welcome. We'll see you tomorrow then, bright and early.'

'You will.'

As Ava rearranged the items on her desk, her eyes locked onto the framed photograph of her, Rick and Carly sitting in a rowboat on Loch Lomond the previous year. Carly was laughing as Rick grinned and brandished an oar above his head, and Ava was looking over her shoulder at him while a friendly woman who'd been passing had snapped the shot. It had been one of Ava's favourites, ever since that trip, and it had sat on her desk at the design firm in Aberdeen. Each time she glanced at it was a reminder of her good fortune in her perfect family.

Lifting the frame, tears welled in her eyes as she dusted the photo with her fingertips, taking in the serenity of the image, the glassy water; her own smooth profile, innocent of what was coming, before she had any inkling of where she'd be today, sitting in Loch na brae, her daughter losing her sight, and her strong, nurturing husband floating on an unreachable plane just fifteen minutes away, and yet, worlds away at the same time. That, in a matter of months, this had become her life was surreal.

Shaking off the swell of self-pity, Ava scraped her hair into a ponytail and secured it with an elastic band. Her list of clients, while shorter than before, was still healthy, and she was happy to see that her two favourites were still with her. *Bee-kind* was a group of Highland beekeepers who produced organic honey, and one hundred per cent natural beeswax products, and *Planteaux* was a grassroots company based in Fort William that made a range of vegan skincare products, many of which now sat in Ava's bathroom cabinet. She enjoyed the concept of working on products that made a difference to the planet in some way or another, and while they weren't always huge moneymakers for the firm, they were important social anchors in a world where the bottom line often overtook decisions of conscience.

As she scanned the brief for a new packaging project for *Planteaux,* her phone rang. Seeing Jenna's number, she grabbed it. 'Hey.' She smiled, looking out of the window at the flagstone path, moss-covered and undulating up the hill towards the barn. Cameron was already working, and the faint sound of the sander filtered down towards the house. 'I was going to call you today.'

'Oh, yeah? Our ESP must be in tune because I almost called last night, but then decided I'd left it too late.' Jenna snorted. 'It was after ten and I knew you'd be fast asleep already.'

Ava rolled her eyes. 'Yes, I know. I'm a boring old fart, curled up in my flannel jammies, with a cup of cocoa at nine-thirty. So shoot me.' She laughed. 'What were you calling about?' Ava skipped down her email list, deleting some obvious spam.

'Mandy's got a cold. She's pretty miserable, so I was thinking maybe we should postpone.' She sighed. 'I'd not want to bring anything with us. You've got enough on your plate without a sick kid to be dealing with.'

A rush of relief brought Ava's eyes closed briefly. 'Well, that's considerate of you, but I was actually going to ask you to postpone anyway.' She sipped some coffee and set her mug down on the coaster Carly had painted for her when she turned six, the arc of a rainbow hovering above a little black dog.

'Really?'

'Carly's got a dog. I mean they've found her a match, and they want her to start training tomorrow.'

'Oh, that's fantastic, so it is,' Jenna chimed.

'The first part of the course is ten days long, mostly here at home. Then they'll continue to come out over time and keep adding to her skills.' Ava sat back, feeling the wooden bones of the chair bite into her back. Hearing a noise behind her, she turned to see Carly padding in, yawning widely, her hair mussed behind her head and her feet bare. 'Oh, sleeping beauty has just emerged.' Ava beckoned to Carly, who moved over and then slid onto her lap, something she hadn't voluntarily done in a while. Taken aback, Ava wrapped her arm around her daughter's narrow frame and breathed in the scent of coconut, youth and sleep.

'Well that's great. We're over the moon for her,' Jenna said. 'Tell her we love her, and we'll see you both soon.'

Ava nodded, the tang of coffee still coating her tongue. 'Will do. Love you two.'

'Ditto.'

Ava set the phone on the desk and hugged Carly tightly. 'Guess what, Flopsy?'

Carly shrugged against Ava's chest.

'We don't have to stay in Inverness at all. I spoke to Dan, and he says when we go in to meet Luna, you'll do the first section of training at the centre, then they'll do the rest here.'

Carly jolted upright. 'Really? Cross your heart?'

Ava drew two lines across her front. 'Honest.'

Carly's eyes filled, and she wrapped her arms around Ava's neck and squeezed so tight that Ava began to cough.

'Woah, there.' She laughed. 'Don't choke me.'

Carly sniffed and leaned back, shoving the hair from her face. 'Sorry.' She smiled as she scanned the window, her eyelids lowering protectively.

'Right. I've got to get some work done. Can you manage your own breakfast, or do you need help?' Ava asked.

Carly slid off Ava's lap and yawned. 'I can manage.' She tugged her pyjama top down at the sides. 'I'm just having cereal anyway.'

Ava grimaced. 'Can you please have some protein, too? How about a yoghurt?'

Carly mimed vomiting. 'No way.' She turned towards the door. 'So, when you're finished, can we read the course stuff again, to see if I need to take anything with me?'

'Sure. I've got a few hours to do here, then after lunch, we'll go into town and pick up anything you might need. We'll get everything organised so we can put our feet up and have a telly dinner tonight. How does that sound?'

Carly walked out into the hall, the fingers of her left hand tracing the curve of the wall. 'Great.'

Just as Ava was about to turn back to her computer, Carly halted and swivelled around, her lips pulsing.

'What is it, love?'

'I just wanted to say thanks for being so patient with me.' Carly swept the hair away from her forehead, the light tan she'd acquired over the past couple of weeks highlighting the smattering of freckles on her nose. 'I know I'm a pain sometimes, it's just that new places scare me.' She blinked as she turned her head to the right. 'I know I'll be better when I get more used to it. Or when I have Luna, but still…' She swallowed.

Ava stood up and rounded the desk, overwhelmed by the need to make contact with her daughter. 'You are not a pain. You're brave, Carly. So incredibly brave. I don't know how you do what you do.' She lifted Carly's hand and kissed the back of it. 'You amaze me, utterly and completely, and if certain things are particularly frightening, and it all seems too much, you are entitled to feel that way.' Ava once again marvelled at this incredible creature before her, one minute a vulnerable child curled in her lap and the next a lucid, logical young woman with a mixture of understanding and fear in her heart. 'Your dad would be so proud of you, he'd literally puke, if he was here.' Ava laughed suddenly, surprised by her outburst.

Carly looked shocked for a second, then started to laugh, her face growing pink as she clamped a hand over her mouth. 'Nice one, Mum,' she sputtered. 'Very nice.'

'Oh, go and eat your breakfast, smarty-pants.' The gaps inside Ava filled with a wave of love, like the creep of molten lava, as she gave Carly a gentle shove. 'And have some protein please.'

Carly turned into the corridor and, laughing, patted her way down the hall towards the kitchen. 'Yeah, yeah. I heard you the first time.'

Cameron's back was to Ava as she walked into the barn. Having finished her work, made a quick lunch, taken Carly into Dornoch for some supplies, then dropped her at home before going to spend half an hour with Rick, Ava felt the tug of fatigue as she climbed the gentle hill.

Knowing that she wouldn't be driving again that day, two cold beers dangled between her fingers as she slid the door closed and walked over to the worktable, still strewn with Rick's drawings, and now some of Cameron's tools. 'Hello.' She set the bottles down and looked around the light-filled space. The base units were all finished, complete with doors and hardware. The back and sides of the island were fully panelled, with just the doors on the front to be finished and fitted, and then all that remained to complete the kitchen was to install the countertops and connect the appliances that still stood against the far wall, safely wrapped in plastic.

Cameron turned and slid his earphones off. 'Hi. I didn't hear you come in.'

'How's it going?' She circled the island, taking in the clean lines of the panelling, the tang of the freshly milled wood. 'These look great.' She ran a hand over the front of the largest panel, the smooth surface like glass under her fingertips.

'Yes, the hickory was a good choice. Rick knows his stuff.'

She smiled to herself as she recalled their discussion about the kitchen. She'd wanted a more contemporary look, with white cabinets, and Rick had persuaded her to go with a natural wood, and a simple varnish. She'd called him old-fashioned, but now, seeing the results, she laughed softly, reminded that, as far as interiors went, Rick was inevitably, and irritatingly, right.

'What is it?' Cameron was watching her, his eyes crinkling in amusement.

'I was just thinking how incredibly annoying Rick is.' She shrugged, then pointed at the beer bottles. 'Take a break?'

Seeming to understand her, Cameron nodded, wiped his hands on a rag that hung from his belt and lifted a bottle. Twisting the top off, he handed it to her. 'Adam's the same. We argue about stuff for ages. I give in, then, in the end, he's usually right.' He shrugged, a sheepish smile creeping across his face.

She accepted the bottle and took a long draught of the cold beer. The taste, malted, effervescent, took her back to lazy summer afternoons spent with Rick, in fragrant beer gardens, children laughing as they ran between warped tables, and wasps dive-bombing their glasses.

Cameron leaned back against the counter. 'You're miles away, again.'

Ava shrugged. 'Just reminiscing. I seem to do that a lot these days.'

A look of concern lifted his brows. 'Any changes?'

She shook her head. 'No, and I got a bit snappy with the doctor yesterday. He basically said there's nothing more we can do but wait.' She paused. 'That's so much easier said than done, and I'm just so tired, and angry, Cameron. This is all so shitty, I want to scream at the universe.' She panted the words out, tipping her head back, her desire to share her deepest fears suddenly unstoppable. 'The thing is, Rick is an organ donor.' She righted herself, the statement raw and ominous.

'OK.' Cameron sounded confused.

'I don't even know if this is a possibility, but what if Rick could… I mean, if Rick's chances of coming back from this are as remote as Doctor Stewart says…' Her voice failed her as Cameron's eyes widened.

'Oh, God.' He frowned. 'I think I get you.'

Seeing the shock in her friend's face, a mere sliver of what she'd been feeling at herself for even considering this, Ava pulled her taut shoulders down. 'Look, I'm not saying I can, or would, do anything. It's too horrible to contemplate. But what if there was a chance?' She eyed Cameron, who was pacing in front of the island, his hand raking through his hair. 'I just can't imagine being faced with that decision, but I keep asking myself, what if there's something that Rick could do for her? He'd want to, I know he would.' A tear ran down her cheek as she stared at her hands, suddenly picturing herself signing documents, paper after paper, until Rick's life was just one signature away from being over, her hand gripping the pen. Closing her eyes, she gulped down a sob. 'What would you do, Cam, if it was Adam?'

Cameron moved to the worktable and set his bottle down. 'Look, I think it's too soon to be going there. But then I don't know enough about it.' He frowned. 'What I do know is that Rick adores Carly.' He focused on Ava. 'And if she was my daughter…' He held his palm up, his eyes full of concern.

Ava nodded, knowing it was too much to expect Cameron to give her the answers she needed right now. If she only knew what those were.

He smiled at her sadly. 'Is it that time?' His long arms opened wide.

Ava nodded, walked forward and let him hug her, catching the scent of sawdust and a musky cologne as he squeezed her to his chest.

'You're the strongest person I know, Ava. You'll know what to do, and when to do it.'

Ava shook her head. 'But I don't know if I am strong enough for this.' She closed her eyes, seeing Rick's lifeless hands lying on the sterile blanket, his frozen eyelids a barrier to her that, every time she saw it, tore her to shreds.

CHAPTER TWENTY-SEVEN

Ava was walking on the beach, the sand cold and slick under her bare feet as the salty breeze lifted her hair behind her, the weight of it tugging at her scalp. Ahead of her, Rick stood with his hands on his hips, watching her progress towards him. He held a child's bucket and spade, and was willing her to move faster, though he stood perfectly still, his eyes fastened to hers, urgent, knowing.

She tried to pick up her pace as his crisp outline began to smudge against the streaky sky behind him, but the sand was sucking at her feet, making it hard to move forward. She paused to look down, just as her ankles disappeared into the gluey sand.

Panic ticking in her chest, she looked up at Rick, whose legs were fading as if a giant cosmic eraser was wiping them away from the knee down. As she focused on the space where his shins had been, his thighs and pelvis burst into thousands of shards of light, cascading down onto the glistening sand beneath him.

Her heart thumping wildly, she dragged her leaden legs, heaving herself forward as she tried to call his name, but her throat was thick as treacle. As she watched, his stomach began to disintegrate, sparkles of light dancing away from him and floating up towards the layer of cloud that hovered above the shoreline.

Ava reached out a hand, the need to touch him pulling at her core with magnets of such force she couldn't draw breath. As she sucked in cloying air, he reached out a hand, the little bucket dangling from his fingers, then the wind picked up and blew his arm away, the bucket falling to the sand then rolling towards the water's edge. She tried to scream, the distance between them now growing as she waded into the breeze and fought the pull of the sand.

Rick began to shake his head, his chest splintering into dust as his other arm lifted in the air, his palm spread wide.

Ava leaned her body into the whistling wind that was now stinging her face, willing herself to make it to him. As she stepped forward, a blinding light made her shield her eyes for a moment, then, when she squinted into the burst of sunshine, Rick was gone.

She opened her mouth to shout his name, but she was mute, no manner of force or will producing any sound at all and, as she sank to the ground, feeling the wetness of the sand gathering around her knees, the alarm shattered the dream, bringing her upright in the bed, the sound of the ocean in her ears, and tears streaming down her face.

This was the second time she'd had this dream. The first time, just a week or so earlier, the imagery had been so vivid that she'd dashed to the bathroom and vomited. Now, as she breathed shakily into her middle, she slapped the button on the alarm clock and let her eyes adjust to the darkness around her.

Knowing that they must leave Loch na brae around 7.30 a.m., she had planned to get up at 4.30 a.m. and cram a couple of hours' work in before they set off for Inverness. It had seemed like a good idea the night before, but now, her insides quivering from her nightmare, Ava slid to the edge of the bed and cursed the decision.

As the room came into focus, she looked over at the window, a dark violet light hovering around the edges of the curtains, dawn readying itself to make an appearance. Stretching her back, her arms above her head, she yawned, feeling a tiny pop in her jaw that brought her palm up to her cheek. She'd been grinding her teeth in her sleep, the dull ache that radiated from her jaw down the side of her neck evidence of the tension she held inside, day and night.

Feeling for her slippers, she slid them on and stood up, adjusting Rick's baggy T-shirt around her. She'd noticed her gradual weight loss over the past few weeks, her jeans becoming loose around her hips and thighs, and the need to pull her belts in tighter around her waist. While she was slender, she'd never been skinny, and Rick would tell her how much he loved the softness of her form as he'd stroke her side, his fingers lingering on the love handles she hated. She'd swat his hand away, make some comment about middle-age spread as he'd pull her to him, his eyes holding hers as he'd say, 'It's just more of you that I want to hold on to.'

Putting her hands on her waist, her fingertips found her hip bones, making her eyebrows lift as she padded towards the bathroom. She needed to get the day started with a blast of hot water and then some strong coffee, before she ventured into her little office and started to work down the list of emails that she knew were waiting for her.

'Carly, come on, love. We're going to be late.' Ava stood at the front door, her bag on her shoulder. They'd spent half an hour deciding what Carly should wear, this being the auspicious day that she would meet Luna for the first time. Despite Ava's amusement at the concept of the dog giving two hoots what Carly was wearing, she'd humoured her daughter, savouring her tangible excitement, and helping her in and out of various combinations of jeans, patterned leggings, floral T-shirts, including the butterfly catcher, a tartan skirt that was quickly abandoned and then finally back into the jeans and unicorn-emblazoned T-shirt she'd started with.

Just as Ava was about to call out again, Carly appeared at her bedroom door, her hair neatly plaited down her back, a few tendrils curling around her flushed cheeks, her sunglasses pushed up onto the top of her head, and her feet in her favourite leather clogs. Her backpack was slung over one shoulder and her expression was carefree, full of excitement.

Ava caught her breath, for a fleeting moment forgetting that those eyes, those incredible blue eyes, were deceiving in their clarity. 'You look great, love.' She beckoned to her daughter. 'Let's hit the road.'

Carly walked across the hall and into the living room, her fingers stroking the wall and then finding the back of the sofa as she made her way towards the door. 'I'm ready. Luna, here we come.' She stuck one arm out in front of her, Superman style, and laughed.

Smiling, Ava eased her out of the door and locked it behind them. 'Come on, you. Can't keep a good dog waiting.'

The drive seemed to go quickly as they talked about the equipment they'd bought for Luna. A fluffy dog bed, big enough for all three of them, lay by the fireside, a slightly smaller one tucked in at the far side of Carly's bed, by the window. Shiny water and food bowls were stacked on a special non-slip mat near the back door in the kitchen, and a basket full of soft toys and chewy rings sat in the living room, next to Rick's armchair. A fleecy, tartan dog-jacket hung on a coat hook, next to Rick's heavy parka, and a pile of tea towels that Ava no longer used was stacked in a basket by the back door, for wiping muddy paws.

The Guide Dog Centre had said they'd provide a collar and harness, so all Carly needed to bring was the little bag of treats. Carly had checked the treat bag numerous times, tapping it as it hung at her hip, the mild scent of barbeque now permeating the car.

'They smell quite good. Can I have one?' Ava steered around a tractor, hay bales bulging over the edges of the trailer that bumped along behind it.

'Mum, they're for Luna.' Carly giggled. 'They probably taste like poo, anyway.'

'Carly.' Ava laughed. 'Why on earth would they taste like poo?'

'I read about it. Apparently, most dogs like to eat their own poo, or other animals' poo. Something about protecting their pack from parasites or…' She hesitated. 'Or was it that they eat it if they *have* parasites?' She glanced over at Ava, her brow furrowed.

Ava reached over and patted Carly's thigh. 'Well, either way, I'm quite sure Luna will be far too polite to eat poo. She won't have parasites, and we're going to be her pack, so no need to worry there.' She squeezed the bony knee. 'It's going to be great, Carly.'

Carly studied her profile, then nodded. 'I know.' She rolled her head to the right, something that Rick did regularly to stretch out his neck but that was also a sign of stress.

'What is it, love?' Ava focused ahead, catching the flash of a deer skipping into the woods to their left, setting off a cascade of memories that made her press her lips together.

'What if she doesn't like me?' Carly was looking at her, her lips rippling as she chewed on them.

'Of course she will. Why on earth wouldn't she? You're absolutely wonderful.' Ava tutted. 'Dogs sense good people and you are good people, Carly.'

Carly nodded, her brow smoothing. 'It's about chemistry, though. The website said that is what forms the bond between a person and their dog. So, what if it doesn't work?'

The seriousness of this for Carly was keeping Ava's mind clear on her mission. 'Remember when you met Hector, Gran Flora's old dog, who hated everyone?' Ava slowed to let a car turn across the lane ahead of them. 'He would snap and growl at anyone who came near him, even me, and he'd known me for years.' She laughed softly. 'Then, when you came along, he turned to putty. He'd let you sit on the rug with him and play with his ears, touch his feet, which were off limits even for Gran, and then he'd fall asleep with his head on your leg.'

Carly nodded, a smile tugging at her mouth. 'He was really grumpy.'

'He was a little devil, but you won him over. So, there's no reason to think that it will be any different with Luna.'

'Right.' Carly nodded. 'Yes.' She sat up straight. 'Who wouldn't love me, right?' She flicked a glance over her shoulder and pursed her lips comically. 'Duh.'

'Totally.' Ava laughed. 'So, don't worry. I have a feeling in my bones that Luna is going to be a wonderful addition to the family.'

Forty minutes later, they pulled into the parking area behind The Guide Dog Centre in Inverness. A long, single-storey structure with a row of large windows, the centre was wedged between two taller, modern buildings, giving it an approachable feel. The front door was scarlet, and several rose bushes, heavy with crimson blooms, lined the path that led to it. The parking area was quiet, and as Ava turned off the engine, the front door opened, and Dan walked out. His straggly beard had been neatly trimmed and he was wearing red-framed glasses that Ava didn't recognise from their last meeting.

Seeing them, he waved. 'Morning. Good to see you.' He grinned as Carly slid out of the car and slung her backpack over her shoulder.

'Hi, Dan.' Ava crossed the car park, Carly close at her side. 'Good to see you too.'

He extended a plump hand, which Ava shook.

'Ready for the big day, Carly?' He gave a thumbs up and winked at Carly.

'Yes, ready.' Carly smiled. 'Is Luna here?' She tipped her head to the side as she searched for her focal point behind him.

'She is indeed.' He nodded. 'Come inside and we'll get the last of the paperwork done, then you can meet her and her trainer, Malcolm. She's a bonnie girl, and that's the truth.'

They followed him through the brightly lit reception. A semi-circle of comfortable-looking chairs hugged the back wall, where a young woman was sitting holding hands with her partner. Perhaps in her early twenties, the woman's toffee-coloured eyes were darting around the room, repeatedly flicking to the top right-hand corner of her visual field, as the young man next to her leaned in and whispered in her ear. Then, as Ava watched, the woman's expression melted into a secret-laden smile. The young man was handsome, in a rumpled sort of way, his big hand swamping the woman's slender fingers, protectively wrapping them within his.

As they passed the couple, Ava focused on those hands, the linked fingers, the combined strength of the tightly woven skin and bone, and imagined Carly having that deep connection one day to a man who loved her so much that he would stop breathing for her if he had to. Ava needed to believe with every fibre of her being that it would happen for Carly, as it had for her, and this young couple served as a sign that it could, and likely would. Seeing it, Ava breathed a little more easily as they made their way down a wide corridor.

Dan led them into a bright room with a wall of windows on one side and several sets of tables and chairs set in groups around the edges. In the centre was a large pen, much like the one they'd used in their kitchen in Aberdeen to contain Carly as a toddler. Around them, the walls were covered with colourful posters of various breeds of dogs in different settings: snoozing in long grass, wading in sunlit rivers or lying belly-up on fluffy rugs.

As Carly skirted the room, getting up close to each poster and twisting her head to find her focus, Dan pointed to a table over by the window. 'Have a seat. I'll grab the forms and then Malc will bring Luna in.'

'Thanks.' Ava nodded, settling herself in a short, wooden-backed chair, a memory of middle school flashing up as she laid her palms on the plastic tabletop. 'Carly, come and sit, love.' Ava fought the ever-present desire to jump up and help as she watched Carly, her head twisting back and forth, navigate her way around another table, bumping an occasional chair with her hip until she reached her mother.

'I can't wait.' She sat opposite Ava. 'What's taking so long?' She bounced in the seat.

'We just got here.' Ava laughed. 'Patience.'

Carly looked up at the ceiling and shook her head. 'Patience is for the birds.'

As another of Rick's sayings floated from her daughter, the door behind Carly opened and Ava watched Dan cross the room. 'Right, just sign here and here, Mrs Guthrie, and we'll be off to the races.'

Ava signed the form approving the centre's ability to retain Carly's contact information in their system and agreeing that she would take responsibility for the dog's welfare while Carly remained a minor, and then Dan was gone again.

Carly was tapping the tabletop with her fingernails, the ticking sound chasing the beat of Ava's quickening heart. This meeting had to go well for all their sakes, but it was critical for Carly. She really needed a positive in her life and, hopefully, this highly trained companion would open doors that even Ava couldn't for her daughter, inside her changing world.

Carly sat up abruptly as the door opened again. This time, a tall, thin man in his twenties, with a long chin, deep-set eyes and short fair hair, stepped into the room. He held the lead of a slender, butter-coloured dog, who was looking up at him adoringly as he made his way across the room. 'Forward, Luna. Come and meet Carly.'

The dog tripped happily alongside him as the young man approached their table.

Carly was on her feet, her face glowing as she circled her chin until she could focus on Luna.

'Halt, Luna.' Malcolm spoke firmly but kindly, and the dog stopped its progress towards Carly, who Ava could see was desperate to engage with the animal but was holding back, dancing from foot to foot.

Malcolm dropped the lead, and the dog looked up at him. 'OK. Go and say hello.' He swept his hand towards Carly, and the dog, its tail swinging wildly, lunged at Carly just as she sank to her knees.

Luna put her front paws on Carly's thighs and began licking her face furiously as Carly laughed, all the while tears tumbling down her cheeks. 'Hello, Luna. Hello, girl.' She stroked the silky head as the dog wriggled with joy and pawed her legs, licking her face, hands and hair.

Ava's hand went to her mouth, her daughter's palpable joy a gift that Ava had been given less and less lately, so all the more precious. 'Oh, she's gorgeous.' She spoke to Malcolm, who smiled like a proud parent would at their child.

'Aye, she's a good girl.' He extended a hand. 'Good to meet you, Mrs Guthrie.'

Ava shook his hand. 'You too.' She looked back at Carly, who was now sitting on the floor with both legs out in front of her, as Luna hunkered down on her stomach, mimicking Carly's position. Luna's tail was swishing across the floor as Carly talked quietly to her, the dog's golden head tilting to the side as if she was not only understanding Carly's words but considering their worth.

'Well, that went well.' Malcolm gestured towards the twosome. 'They're just like old pals.'

'It's miraculous.' Ava raked around in her bag for a tissue, then, finding it, wiped her nose. 'Just perfect.'

*

Six hours later, Ava drove back towards home, the sun hovering low over the water to her right and the temperature so kind that they'd wound down the windows to allow the fresh scent of the forest to seep into the car.

Carly was sitting in the back seat with Luna, chattering about how well they'd done in their first training session, as Ava nodded, and commented here and there, when she could get a word in. As Carly went over the commands they'd learned, forward, halt, sit, come and stay, all the while stroking Luna's neck, Ava pictured her executing the commands, with Malcolm's calm direction, and walking at first tentatively, then gradually more confidently around the centre's training room. When they'd gone outside for a walk around the building, Ava had hung back, letting Carly and Malcolm work the dog together, but making mental notes as to what she might have to know herself, and how she could support Carly in this process.

At the end of the session, Malcolm had told Carly how well she and Luna had done. 'You get a gold star from me, Carly. And you too, Luna.' He'd ruffled the dog's head. 'A partnership made in heaven.' He'd nodded approvingly. 'Just remember not to combine the commands at this point, Carly. Keep them clear, simple, one at a time and well enunciated. Once you get to know each other better, you might develop a little shorthand here and there, but for now, it's best to stick to the book.' He'd looked over at Ava, who'd nodded her understanding. 'So, tomorrow, when I come to your house, we'll work on directional turning, stopping at the kerb, and identifying obstacles, OK?'

Carly's hand had gone down to Luna's head. 'Yep. Great.' She'd beamed, as Malcolm handed her back the harness. 'See you tomorrow.' She'd knelt and hugged the dog's neck, as Luna had begun another licking session of Carly's face. 'Ready to go home, girl?'

Tugging Ava back to the moment, Carly chimed, 'So, tomorrow we're going to work on her leading me around corners and stopping at hazards, and stuff. She's so clever, Mum. It's amazing.'

Ava glanced at the dashboard clock, calculating that by the time she got home, got Carly and Luna settled, then cooked them some dinner, it'd be quite late for her to turn around and go out to see Rick. Having been up since 4.30 a.m. was beginning to take its toll, and the idea of a hot bath and bed was glimmering in her subconscious. As soon as Carly stopped to take a breath, Ava took her chance. 'How would you feel if we stopped in and saw Dad on the way home? It'd save me coming back out after dinner.' Ava kept her eyes on the road as Carly dropped her chin and then turned to look out of the window. 'Carly love?'

'OK. But I'll wait in the car with Luna.' She shifted her body, turning to face the dog, who was panting softly.

'You wouldn't consider coming in?' Ava pulled her shoulders down, halting their progress towards her ears.

'Mmm.' Carly shook her head. 'Not yet.'

Ava shrugged, resignedly. 'OK. Just thought I'd ask.' She glanced over as Carly righted herself and faced front again, her hand on Luna's back. 'Don't you want to tell him about Luna?'

Carly stared ahead. 'You can tell him.'

Ava blinked to clear her vision. 'Well, just let me know when you want to come, all right?'

'I will.'

Ava ran her hand over Rick's chin, making a mental note to shave him the next day. She'd left his electric razor in the little bathroom off his room, and every other day would drape a towel over his chest, gently running the razor over his shadowy cheeks, then under his chin and over his throat, careful not to push too hard. It had become a ritual she almost enjoyed, and one the nurses now left for her to carry out. Such a small task, and yet something tangible she could do for him, other than simply hold his hand or talk through the mundane details of her day.

The room was cool but seemed less frigid than usual as she slung her bag over the back of the chair and shunted it closer to the bed. As she tried to block out the beeping of the monitors and the hiss of the ventilator, she leaned in and lifted his hand just as a waft of something cloying and meaty filtered into the room from the corridor, so she stood up and closed the door fully before returning to the bed.

'Hi, darling.' She stroked his stubbly cheek. 'It's me again.' She adjusted the gown that had wrinkled around his throat. 'We're just on our way home from the guide dog place. Carly met Luna today, and we're taking her home with us.' She sighed. 'Carly's so happy, Rick. If you could've seen her face.' She forced a swallow. 'The dog came up to her as if it knew her. They were cuddling and bonding right away. Like old friends.'

She nodded into the silence. 'You'd have been so proud of her. She was pretty nervous, and so excited, but she listened to Malcolm. He's the trainer. And then she did what he told her perfectly.' Ava ran a hand through her hair and, feeling the slight oiliness of the third day of not washing it, she sighed. 'I'm so happy for her, Rick. She really needed this.'

She sat back, letting her fingers linger on his wrist. 'Where are you, my love?' She stared at the closed doors of his eyes, as ever feeling shut out by their stillness. 'Can you hear me?' She tightened her grip on his hand, willing some sign of life to lift the blanket of weariness that had settled on her now that she'd let herself sit still for a few moments. 'I'm so tired. So incredibly tired. God, I miss you so much,' she whispered. Taking a shallow breath, she steeled herself. 'Rick, you need to help me. I have to ask you something.'

CHAPTER TWENTY-EIGHT

The next week flew by in a blur with continued early mornings for Ava, in order to get her work done and to get Carly up and moving before Malcolm arrived for their training sessions. As soon as he left, Ava would dash in to see Rick, grab some shopping, beetle home to clean, do laundry and cook an evening meal, before collapsing into bed and sleeping dreamlessly, for the first time in months.

Carly's training was going well, and they'd covered more commands, such as directing the dog to turn left and right, to stop at the kerb, halt at potential hazards, such as cars, drops in the pavement or other obstacles to Carly's safety, then to lay down, stay, come and heel. Luna was a dream, seeming to wait on tenterhooks for Carly to speak, then she'd snap to her instructions as if they were her life's work, which, of course, to Ava's unending gratitude, they were.

Malcolm was happy with Carly's progress, and with Ava shadowing much of the session each day, albeit at a distance, she felt confident that Carly was coping marvellously, and the critical trust that must exist between a dog and its handler was developing, day by day.

Today they were going into Dornoch on the bus so that Carly could become confident enough to go alone, and Malcolm was standing on the driveway waiting for her to come outside. Ava stood next to him, shielding her eyes from the bright morning light as a pair of seagulls swooped overhead, their calls like a conversation back and forth as the wind lifted them up, elevating them with its cool breath.

Malcolm subtly checked his watch.

'Welcome to my world. I spend a lot of time waiting.' Ava sighed. 'The concept of punctuality hasn't quite solidified with Carly.'

'Aye, well, she's female.' He grinned mischievously, revealing a row of white, slightly uneven teeth. 'She's doing really well, Mrs Guthrie. I'm feeling good about this partnership.'

Ava nodded. 'Me too. There is no way she'd have been confident enough to take a bus, before Luna. She's already turning Carly's world around, Malcolm.'

He smiled and gestured towards the door as Carly emerged with Luna at her side. 'Here they are.' He beckoned to Carly. 'Come on, let's walk down to the bus stop. You go ahead of us and your mum and I will follow.'

Carly pulled the door closed behind her and slipped her sunglasses on. 'Forward, Luna.' She spoke authoritatively and the dog's head came up and it walked forward, down the drive, heading for the road.

After successfully navigating their way onto and off the bus, and decanting at the Castle stop, Malcolm had suggested they circle the Square, Luna stopping beautifully at each kerb, crossing and corner. Seeing child and dog working together as a unit gave Ava a sense of calm, her own trust in Luna growing with each manoeuvre that kept her daughter out of harm's way.

Malcolm walked a little behind Carly, his arm hovering over her shoulder in case he needed to intervene, or stop her, should Luna miss something or react too slowly. Only once had he touched Carly, to remind her to let Luna guide her, when she'd stepped ahead of the dog at a crossing.

By the time they returned to the bus stop, Carly was beaming, and Malcolm was nodding approvingly. 'Excellent job, ladies,' he said. 'I'd say that was a pass, Mum. What do you think?' He eyed Ava.

'I'd say so.' Ava smiled. 'Very impressive.'

'Right, home then.' Malcolm gestured towards the bus stop, where two women were waiting, chatting to one another. One was tall and willowy with violet, curly hair under a clear plastic snood, and the other a rotund, pink-cheeked Babushka-type with a dark raincoat straining around her middle.

As Carly approached, the women stopped talking and watched her walk towards them. Carly seemed oblivious, her focus on the dog, but Ava saw the pity in their faces and the sight of it both angered and saddened her. While she appreciated that it came from a place of concern, she hated that that anyone should pity her marvellous, brave and accomplished daughter.

Seeming to sense her turmoil, Malcolm put a hand gently on her forearm. 'How's Mum doing?' He nodded at the women as they took their place behind them, close to the bus shelter.

Ava took a deep breath. 'Getting there. Day by day.'

Malcolm glanced at Carly. 'Yep. Slow and steady. Best way.'

Safely back home, they waved goodbye to Malcolm as he backed his Mini down the long drive. Luna sat at Carly's side, her ears flicking back and forth, her rosy tongue protruding slightly as she panted, while Carly stroked her ear. 'I think she's hungry.' She bent down and kissed the dog's head. 'Want some dinner, Luna?' The dog stood, its tail swinging wildly in response. 'Come on, girl. Inside.'

Luna turned and deftly led Carly back inside the house, as Ava followed a few paces behind. She closed the door and followed Carly into the kitchen, watching as she felt her way along the countertop to the cupboard where the dog food was kept in a giant plastic container. Carly opened the cupboard, pulled out the container and scooped some into the bowl at the back door. Then, as Malcolm had instructed her, she dipped her finger into the water bowl to check the level, and finding it close to empty, she set the food on the mat and lifted the bowl, sidestepped to the sink and filled it under the tap.

Luna sat, staring at the bowl of food, awaiting the all-clear to dive in, and as Carly lowered the water bowl to the mat, sloshing some over the side, Luna shifted to let Carly move safely past her.

'OK, Luna. Go on.' Carly pointed at the bowls, at which point Luna lunged forward and dove into the food, her buttery nose nudging the little morsels of meat and biscuit as she inhaled it at such speed that Carly laughed. 'Slow down, girl. You'll choke.'

'She's just like you, with my lasagne.' Ava nudged Carly, who stuck her tongue out playfully. 'Right, what do we humans want to eat?' Ava moved to the fridge, opened the door and scanned the contents. 'Speaking of lasagne, do you fancy some?' She watched Carly, transfixed by Luna and her demolition of the pile of food. 'Carly?'

'Oh, lasagne would be fab.' She turned to her mother, her face radiant.

'Great. Well, why don't you and Luna go and watch some telly or something while I get things going?' She reached for the minced beef and a twist of fresh basil that she'd picked from the garden that morning, the smell of which had filled the fridge with a tangy aroma that instantly made Ava hungry.

'OK.' Carly hovered behind Luna as she finished the food and meticulously licked the bowl, leaving it as clean as before it was full. 'Wow, she loves that stuff.' Carly grinned, flicking her hair over her shoulder as she lifted the empty bowl and put it in the sink. 'Come on, Luna. Let's go to my room for a bit.' She lifted the harness. 'Forward.' Luna's ears went back as she snapped into work mode, then she moved carefully towards the hall, Carly walking steadily beside her.

Ava made the meat sauce, the aroma of the fresh basil and oregano, simmering in the Roma tomatoes, prompting an overwhelming desire for a glass of wine. As she pulled out a bottle of Chianti and set it on the counter for later, she was transported back to the week she and Rick had spent in Tuscany, for their third anniversary. She'd found out she was pregnant the day before they'd left Aberdeen and had spent the entire week lusting after Rick's wine, as she sensibly stuck to sparkling water. He'd teased her as he'd poured himself generous glasses of the dark Barbera and ruby-coloured Sangiovese that she loved, saying, 'That'll teach you to get yourself up the duff.'

She'd feigned annoyance, all the while resting her palm on her washboard stomach, a deep sense of accomplishment warming her insides. 'Totally worth the sacrifice,' she'd quipped as he'd laughed, then reached across the table to touch her fingers, happiness simmering behind his eyes and a smile pulling at his mouth.

The significance of sacrifice had taken on a completely new meaning now, and as she watched the sauce bubble, the question that she'd been quashing eased back to the surface. Was there any sacrifice too great to make for one's child? As a mother, she could unequivocally say, no. There wasn't a single thing she could think of that she wouldn't gladly give to, or give up for, Carly, and the certainty of that was comforting. As for Rick, there was an identical, deep-rooted certainty inside Ava, that he would say the same, and as she stirred the simmering liquid so her mind spun forward to a life-altering moment in time, when she might have to make the ultimate sacrifice any wife could make.

Coaching her mind back from the shadowy place this train of thought took her to, Ava carefully assembled the layers of pasta, cheese and meat sauce, as an idea began to take root. There was so much lasagne, enough for at least six people, it would be a shame for it not to be enjoyed while it was fresh from the oven.

While she treasured her evenings with Carly, the need for some adult company was suddenly overwhelming.

As she slid the dish into the oven, she checked her watch. It was 5.35 p.m., and with the lasagne taking an hour to cook, she could safely go and see Rick and be back in time to take it out, then throw a green salad together before it was time to eat. Glancing over at the kitchen table, she pictured it laid for three rather than two, then blinked the painful vision away.

Reaching for her phone, she called Cameron, pacing around the kitchen as she waited for him to answer. He'd not been working in the barn the past few days, on her insistence, making the most of Adam's time at home, but she'd missed his company and their daily talks, so when he answered, she smiled.

'Hello there.' His voice was warm. 'How're things? Been missing me?' He chuckled.

'Not at all.' She gave a little snort. 'But I've made enough food for an army and wondered if you and Adam might want to come and help us eat it?' She sucked in her bottom lip, momentarily unsure whether her request was monumentally selfish, considering that Adam was only home for ten days. If she had not seen Rick for five weeks, she'd hold every moment precious and not want to share him with anyone. As she let the thought simmer, the realisation that she had not truly been *with* Rick for many more than five weeks drew her eyes closed, for a second.

'That sounds good. Hang on a minute.' Cameron covered the microphone and mumbled something, then his voice was clear in her ear. 'What time?'

'About seven.' She pushed away the swell of loss her thoughts of Rick had prompted. 'I'm popping in to see Rick, but I'll be back by six-thirty.' She tucked the phone under her ear and walked into the living room, opened the drawer in the sideboard and took out four tartan placemats, choosing the less faded of the set she'd been given as a wedding present by Flora. As she circled the dining table, placing them down, a tiny lilt of excitement warmed her face.

'Can we bring anything?' Cameron asked. 'Apart from wine.'

'Nothing at all. We've got everything we need.' She pulled four napkins out of the drawer and began folding them into triangles, as Flora had taught her. 'Just bring yourself and your lovely man. I can't wait to meet him.'

'All right then. We'll see you later, and Ava…' He paused. 'Thanks for asking us.'

She held the phone to her ear. 'My pleasure. It's purely selfish, of course.'

'Of course.' He chuckled. 'Goes without saying.'

'Oh, sod off,' she laughed. 'See you later.'

'Well, that's charming.'

Adam was exactly as Ava had imagined. Despite the nature of his job, he was smoother round the edges than Cameron, his Edinburgh accent lilting and cultured. His eyes were warm and his smile magnetic, and when he spoke, his tone was low and gentle, but he drew one's attention.

Cameron was putty around him, and it was amusing Ava to see her big, burly friend turn to mush when his partner complimented him, or let his hand linger on his shoulder.

Adam had been fascinated by the croft, and, after the main course, while Cameron talked with Carly, Ava had given Adam a tour, showing him all the improvements that Flora had made and the innovative way that Rick had designed the upper floor, utilising the roof space to create their master bedroom and bath.

'He's a talented architect.' Adam had nodded approvingly as he took in the skylights, and the wide windows that Rick had added to the back wall, overlooking the barn. 'It takes a special kind of eye to see a space's potential, imagine what it could be as opposed to what it is.' He'd looked pensive. 'I'm no good at that at all, but Cam's great at it. He saw through all the mess and pictured our place as it is now. I saw it as a weird semi-detached, with rotten floors and windows, and no walk-in shower.' He'd laughed. 'You'll need to come over and see what he's done.'

'That'd be lovely, thanks. It's really good to finally meet you, Adam.' Ava had smiled warmly.

Adam had looked at his feet, the shiny leather loafers in sharp contrast to Cameron's ubiquitous, dusty boots. 'I feel the same. Cam talks about you and Carly all the time. He's really enjoyed working on the barn conversion. He misses working with Rick.' He'd paused. 'I'm sorry that you're going through this, Ava. It can't be easy.'

His empathy had taken her by surprise, and yet she was not surprised that he had tackled the elephant in the room head-on. She could see already that that was his style, and she liked him all the more for it.

'Thanks, Adam. I appreciate you saying that.' She'd touched his arm, the smooth cotton of his shirt cool under her fingers. 'It's not easy, but we're managing. Carly's doing better now Luna's here, so that's the main thing.'

'Yes, that must be a huge boost for her confidence. These dogs are truly remarkable.'

'They are. I'm amazed.' Ava had pictured Carly sitting proudly on the bus, three rows ahead of her and Malcolm, patting Luna's head as she stared out of the window, her head tipping to the right and her profile showing her cheek lifted by a smile.

He'd pointed at the barn. 'Would you mind showing me what you've done up there?'

Pleased by his interest, Ava had agreed, and they'd gone downstairs, grabbed their wine glasses, and Cameron had joined them as they'd walked up the slope to the barn.

Now, Adam seemed impressed by the interior layout, the vaulted ceiling and the clever use of the space, taking time to inspect the cabinetry as Cameron stood back, shuffling his feet and looking mildly embarrassed.

'Gorgeous work, Cam.' Adam ran a hand over the surface of a door. 'No surprises there.' He looked proudly up at his partner. 'Ash or hickory?'

Cameron smiled bashfully. 'Hickory. Works great for the detail we needed.' He pointed at the panelling. 'Rick had great taste. He and Ava made some sound decisions in here.'

Despite her breath catching, Ava ignored his use of the past tense, not wanting anything to tarnish the evening ahead, and her enjoyment of the good company and lively conversation that it promised. 'It's all Rick. I just go along for the ride.' Her shoulders bounced as she righted the balance, bringing her slumbering husband back into the present. 'Come on. Let's go and have some pudding.'

A few minutes later, Ava was serving the apricot crumble she'd thrown together, as Cameron poured coffee for them all, while, next to him, Adam spoke to Carly. 'Luna is a beauty, Carly. Is it OK if I stroke her?'

Carly nodded. 'Malcolm says it's fine as long as I say so.'

Adam gently ran his palm over Luna's head as Carly looked on proudly.

'She's really clever, Adam. She knows exactly what I'm telling her, and I only have to say it once.'

Ava set a plate of crumble in front of Carly. 'Maybe I need Malcolm to come and work with *you*.' She laughed. 'Or me.' She locked eyes with Cameron, who was grinning.

'Might be a good idea.' He reached over and poked Carly's shoulder as she pulled a face.

'We always had dogs when I was growing up.' Adam took the plate Ava held out to him. 'There's nothing like it. You're lucky to have her, Carly. I miss having a furry pal around.'

Cameron poured cream on his crumble and passed the jug to Adam. 'That's what you've got me for.' He leaned his shoulder against Adam's and the two men's eyes met, and just for a split second, their love for one another was palpable.

Ava saw it and, suddenly overcome, she stood up. 'Excuse me for a sec.' She walked towards the kitchen, her vision blurring as she called over her shoulder, 'Please start. I won't be long.'

In the kitchen, she gripped the edge of the farm sink, the cool porcelain under her fingertips grounding her. That look. That connection that is so intrinsic that no one else gets it. She and Rick had that, and she missed it like a flower misses the sun. His eyes, warm and gentle, with the same glint of adoration she'd just seen in Cameron's, were her sustenance, and the lack of them felt as if she was starving, her flesh slowly melting from her bones as she waited for those eyelids to lift, to let her back in so she could find nourishment.

She blew out a slow breath, willing her heart to settle, as Cameron came into the kitchen, hesitating at the door. 'Are you OK?'

Shaking the hair from her eyes, she nodded. 'Yep. Just having a moment.' She turned to face him, seeing the concern on his face.

'Should we go?' He jabbed a thumb over his shoulder.

'Don't you dare.' She frowned. 'I'm expecting you to stay until at least midnight, to entertain me with sparkling wit and intelligent conversation that doesn't involve dog food or hospitals or…' She found a smile. 'I'm really enjoying having you both here.'

'Us too. Adam is quite taken with you, and Carly.'

'How could he not be?' She feigned surprise. 'Come on, let's go back in. The crumble will be getting cold.'

Cameron looped her arm over his. 'Um, no. I finished mine before I came in.' He nudged her. 'This is me we're talking about.'

'Did it even touch the sides?' She laughed, leaning against his bulky bicep. 'You're such a hog.'

As they walked into the living room, Adam was sitting on the fireside rug with Carly and Luna, as the dog sniffed his hair, ears, neck and closed eyelids.

'She's giving you the once-over.' Cameron lifted his coffee cup and sat in Rick's chair by the fire, as a tiny shot of pain made Ava look away. 'What do you think, Luna? Does he pass muster.'

The dog sat down and gave a single yap, sending them all into fits of laughter, the sound so spontaneous and uplifting that Ava let it soak into her pores.

An hour later, Carly stood up. 'I'm off to bed.' Ava made to get up, but Carly shook her head. 'I'm fine, Mum. Luna and I are cool.' She let her palm linger on the dog's head. 'Night, Cam, Adam.' Carly turned her head to the right, her eyes flicking downwards as she smiled. 'Don't stay up too late, Mum.' She grinned in Ava's direction. 'Early start tomorrow.'

Ava snorted. 'Oh really? You think?' She widened her eyes at Carly, who pulled a face and turned towards the hall. 'Goodnight, love. I'll pop my head in before I go up.'

Ava watched her daughter and her new best friend make their way steadily towards Carly's room, a lightness inside Ava that had been missing for months.

She lifted the brandy bottle from the sideboard and waggled it. 'Nightcap, anyone?'

Adam shook his head. 'No thanks. I'm driving.' He'd refused wine with dinner, sticking with water and coffee, so Ava turned to Cameron.

'How about you, trouble?'

Cameron looked over at Adam, who gave him a nod. 'Go on. I'm the DD anyway. Enjoy it for me.'

Cameron grinned. 'OK. I'll have a wee one.' He pinched his finger and thumb together. 'Wee, mind.'

An hour later, Ava had lit the fire, and the room was pleasantly warm, the fresh woodsmoke melding with the lingering smell of dinner. She held her brandy glass close to her middle as she lounged on the sofa, the men sitting opposite her, either side of the fire.

'This is such a gorgeous home, Ava.' Adam spread his hands over the arms of the chair. 'Do you miss Aberdeen, at all?'

'Not at all.' Ava shook her head, surprising herself at the speed of her response. 'Only the people.' She leaned forward and set her glass on the chest. 'It's a great city, and we were happy there, but it's so beautiful up here. There's so much more to see, and for Carly to paint, it wasn't a hard choice to make.' She paused, her heart once again cinched by the fact that the colours of Carly's world were fading, shades of grey and green her daily bread. Swirling the amber liquid around in her glass, Ava went on, 'My best friend, and Carly's, are down there so we miss them, for sure.'

Cameron's eyebrows lifted. 'I thought *I* was your best friend.' He pouted comically. 'That really stung.'

Adam laughed softly as Ava flapped her hand. 'You know what I mean. Jenna and I are like sisters. She's known me and Rick for years, since well before we were married. We've seen each other through so much...' Her voice trailed, shadows of more struggles to be got through flashing before her eyes. 'Anyway, they'll be coming back soon, for a weekend. We should all get together.'

Cameron nodded. 'You can come to us the next time. Adam will cook.' He stretched his leg out and tapped Adam's foot with his. 'As long as scrambled eggs on toast is OK.'

Adam feigned offence. 'Ha, OK. I know I'm rotten in the kitchen.' He huffed. 'Can't argue with you there.'

Cameron leaned forward, setting his glass on the hearth. 'Well, it's only fair that you're rotten at something.' He grinned. 'Otherwise you'd be a total pain in the backside.'

More laughter filled the room and Ava let her head fall back against the soft leather of the sofa as she breathed, slowly, deeply and contentedly, the woodsmoke filling her head and her insides still warm from the brandy. While Rick's absence surrounded her constantly, tonight, the gaping hole he left was a little less empty.

CHAPTER TWENTY-NINE

Three weeks later, life had taken on a rhythm that Ava and Carly had grown accustomed to. The autumn term had started, so their mornings were dedicated to schoolwork, and Ava would fit her own work in, in the afternoons, around household chores, shopping and her visits to see Rick.

Doctor Stewart was being respectful of Ava's position and had not pressed her too much about making any decisions on Rick's care. But, deep inside, Ava knew that as long as he remained suspended in this current half-life, it was only a matter of time before she could face a devastating choice that would affect them all profoundly, forever.

The subject of Carly going to school in Dornoch had come up again, and Ava had promised that she'd consider it, for the following term, once she felt totally confident in Luna, and their partnership. Carly had agreed, seemingly happy that it was at least a possibility, and the fact that Kelly attended the same school was added incentive.

At the weekends, they'd paint together or work in the garden, planting fragrant herbs and perennials in the beds near the drive, and installing pretty pots on the flagstone threshold of the barn, where Cameron had finally finished the kitchen cabinetry. They'd go on picnics to Golspie, to visit Dunrobin Castle, the gardens so beautifully tended and meticulously laid out they resembled a mini-Versailles. The peaceful fountains, and privet-lined beds crammed full of lavender, pale pink alyssum, and fragrant roses, were as artfully presented as in any Renaissance painting and provided Carly with such inspiration that she'd go home and try to interpret what she'd seen in watercolours, or creamy pastels, often to astonishing effect.

With Adam gone back to the rig, Cameron would sometimes join them on their outings, and for their walks along Dornoch Beach, or to investigate an accessible hiking trail in the nearby hills that Carly could safely navigate. They'd take a picnic, find a good spot to stop, then come home in time to watch the end-of-summer sunsets colouring the sky over the glistening firth.

Carly had grown fond of Cameron, often taking Luna up to the barn to sit and chat to him as he'd worked. He had endless patience with her, explaining what he was doing and letting her get up close enough to see the detail of the work he was producing. Even after he'd finished the work, Carly had asked if she could paint up there, so Ava had set up an easel for her, next to Rick's worktable, that still stood in place near the front window.

The table looked distinctly shabby now, next to the sleek new kitchen, and the shimmering wood floors, but Ava couldn't bring herself to take it down. She would dust it, replace the dog-eared plans exactly where they'd been, letting her fingers linger on the stub of a pencil, the half-empty packet of mints or the measuring tape Rick had left there, trying to divine something of his presence. Then, she'd pull herself up a little straighter, and return to the house.

Carly's eyesight seemed to have stabilised somewhat, and Doctor Anderson had extended the time until her next appointment to three months, unless there were any significant changes. Her counselling sessions were over, and Ava was relieved that Serena had helped Carly navigate some of the anger she'd been feeling, her daughter's sunny disposition reappearing more often now than it had in months. She'd been painting more again, sitting at the desk in her room, her new colour-correcting glasses on as she experimented with different mediums: oils, acrylic and watercolour paints, charcoal and even India ink. The results were astounding and every time she emerged with another piece of work, Ava would wrap it up and head back to the framers in Inverness. Each time she took in the growing gallery of Carly's beautiful work, Ava's heart swelled with pride.

Carly's confidence was blossoming with Luna's presence and her increasing trust in the dog, and she'd been enjoying horse-riding again. Luna would sit with Ava in the car, the dog's wet nose pressed to the window as Carly trotted around the paddock on Peek-a-boo, smiling and waving each time she passed them.

As she watched her daughter's renewed interest in her favourite things, Ava allowed herself to step back slightly from the ghastly dilemma she'd had playing on a loop in her mind, night after night. If Carly could function this well with Luna, the visual aids and special glasses, perhaps Ava could let the notion of letting Rick go fade a little? Would Carly even be open to accepting whatever help her father could give her, or would the idea be too disturbing? Ava had no idea and for now, she was avoiding asking the question.

To Ava's delight, Carly had asked if Kelly could come over, and she'd done so twice, once for lunch, and another time to watch a film and stay the night. Ava had been slightly anxious about the sleepover, wondering if the somewhat frail Kelly would feel comfortable being away from home, but rather than mention anything to Carly, she'd put away her concern.

Kelly's mother, a friendly woman called Diane, with fiery red hair like Jenna's, and a guttural laugh that could clear a room, had assured Ava that Kelly was champing at the bit for more freedom and would be totally fine to stay the night. The girls had developed an easy camaraderie, and the evening had inevitably resulted in a bout of lively giggling that had made Ava smile as she'd tiptoed past Carly's bedroom, on her way up to bed.

As Ava had curled up under the heavy duvet, she had turned away from Rick's empty pillow, closed her eyes and pictured Carly with Luna, and the sense of peace the vision brought had eased her troubled mind.

The bulk of Carly's training was complete, Malcolm being happy that she was proficient enough with Luna that she could venture out unsupervised, though he'd said he would still be coming out to accompany her on any new routes and experiences.

While nervous about Carly being out alone, Ava had checked herself once again, her promise to Rick surfacing whenever she felt she was crowding or fretting over Carly too much. Ava had resolved to take her lead from Malcolm, and so far, Carly had taken the bus into Dornoch, gone to the shops for some basic supplies Ava had asked for, and walked to the Lochans and back. Although she was delighted at her progress, each time Carly added another accomplishment to her list, Ava felt a tug of sadness that Rick wasn't around to witness those triumphs.

His condition remained unchanged, and each day Ava would hesitate, just for a second, right before she walked into his room, willing this to be the day when she'd see some sign of progress, but each day she'd leave her hopes behind, as she walked back across the car park.

As she'd drive the familiar route back and forth on autopilot, she'd force her mind to Carly, their routine, the day-to-day tasks that kept them both busy, and moving forward, however hard it was without her best friend, and partner to share the load.

Now, having left Rick just a couple of hours before, Ava pulled into the driveway. Leaving Carly alone was no longer as much of a concern, as even though Cameron was not working in the barn anymore, he dropped in almost daily, providing the additional comfort Ava needed to feel confident in popping out now and then, as necessary.

Disappointed that the old Land Rover wasn't in the drive, Ava flicked off her seat belt, got out and retrieved the bags of groceries from the boot. She elbowed it shut and walked up to the front door, and just as she slid both bags onto her one arm and started to pull her keys from her bag, her phone rang. 'Shoot.' She fumbled with the keys, trying to get the door open, then stepped inside and set the bags on the floor. Pushing the door closed with her shoulder, she found the phone and looked at the screen. The familiar number displayed had its usual effect, and taking a moment to gather herself, Ava nudged the bags away from the door with her toe and answered the call. 'Hello?'

'Mrs Guthrie?'

She recognised Doctor Stewart's voice, but his use of her full name was odd after all these months of calling her Ava. 'Doctor Stewart, is that you?' She frowned, scanning the room for any sign of Carly. Seeing that she was alone, she walked to the window, watching the trees down near the road bend in the wind, as her heart clawed its way up the back of her throat.

The seconds it took for the doctor to speak were each weighted, like thousands of iron filings gathering in her lungs as she sucked time in. *Why was he not speaking?*

'Ava, I have some difficult news.'

She leaned forward, her free hand forming a fist, her forehead touching the cool glass, and a patch of steam stretching under her open mouth as she exhaled.

'Are you alone?' He spoke quietly, but Ava sensed that what was coming was deafening, and catastrophic.

'Yes. What's wrong?' Her voice cracked the last word in two as she turned and leaned her thighs against the windowsill. She could hear the ticking of Flora's clock on the mantle and smell the remnants of the soup she'd made earlier, the heady scent of cumin hanging in the air as she bit her bottom lip, instantly tasting metal as her front tooth cut into the pulpy flesh.

'Is there someone other than Carly you can call, to come and be with you?' he asked.

'No.' She panted. 'Just tell me.'

After a few agonising moments, he spoke, his voice controlled and gentle. 'Just after you left, Richard suffered a massive brain bleed. We performed an emergency craniectomy, but unfortunately... I'm so sorry, Ava, but his brain stem was irreversibly damaged and now there's no clinical brain function, or respiratory drive.'

Ava could hear the crashing of waves, her pulse thumping so loudly in her ears that she shook her head to banish it. Her tongue was stuck to the roof of her mouth as a surge of nausea swept her legs from under her and she slid to the floor, her knees coming up to her chest as she wrapped her arm across her shins and hugged herself. 'What are you saying?' she croaked, knowing that what she was about to hear would change her life forever.

'It means that Richard is brain-dead, Ava. He's gone.'

Ava's breaths were coming faster and faster, and the room began to fade around her as she forced air in, and then out, trying to bring her surroundings back into focus. There were so many questions to ask and yet none came to her as she stared at Carly's painting of the sunset that she'd just hung over the sideboard the previous evening. The muted colours, the joyful abandon of the broad strokes, the image of Carly's smile when Ava had told her how marvellous the painting was, all faded to grey as tears flooded in and the outline of her world disintegrated.

'Ava, are you there?' He spoke gently.

'I'm here.' She choked the words out, as she tried to conjure Rick's face, his eyes bright and purposeful, his mouth wide and soft, his hands dwarfing hers as they mingled on top of the duvet, but all that came was an image of him lying still, lifeless, surrounded by machinery that was now doing his living for him.

'We're going to do a second brain death examination and determination in a couple of hours. I think you should have someone bring you in later, so we can talk. Please don't drive yourself, and I suggest you find someone to sit with Carly at home. There are things we need to discuss.'

Ava's eyes were skipping around the room, looking for something to land on that didn't hurt to look at, but, failing, she closed them. 'What things?' The seemingly vacuous question was all she could muster.

'About what you want to do with his organs…'

The rest of Doctor Stewart's words were lost as Ava dropped the phone with a clatter and stood up. Her nightmare, the one she'd been wrestling with for months now, was materialising and, this time, there would be no waking up. A barrage of thoughts scrambled through her mind, and as the two words *he's gone* reverberated in her ears, their devastating implications began to sink in.

Rick was gone and with him thousands of moments in time that would never be, myriad words she would never hear, sights she wouldn't see and sensations she would never feel. Countless memories would never be made, images that she could have tucked away in her heart and taken out and looked at later in life. Gone too would be the security of knowing that even when separated from him, she wasn't alone. By leaving her, he was taking so much with him that what was left looked empty and soulless.

Just as she felt herself begin to slip into a terrifying space in her head, an image of Carly's face flickered before her. She had to find her daughter, try to explain what had happened, figure out a way to impart this news that would inevitably tear her apart, just as Ava felt her own insides being shredded. As she stood frozen to the spot, she willed Carly's door to stay closed, just for a few more moments.

Ava focused all her energy into collecting herself so that she wouldn't scare her daughter with her tears, but as she stumbled across the room, bumping into the back of the sofa, her breathing ragged, Carly appeared in the bedroom doorway.

'I had my earphones on, and I didn't hear you come in.' She smiled, then, turning her head to the right and squinting, her face fell. 'Mum, what's wrong. Are you crying?' Carly lifted Luna's harness. 'Forward, Luna.'

The dog padded forward as Ava swiped at her face with her palms.

Reaching her mother, Carly halted the dog, dropped the harness and felt the air for Ava's hand. 'Mum?'

Ava wrapped her icy fingers around Carly's warm ones, suddenly sure of what she must do. 'Carly, love, I…' She swallowed. 'Something's happened with your dad and I have to go back to the hospital.' She cleared her throat. 'I'm going to call Cameron and see if he can come and sit with you, until I get back.' She glanced at the clock.

'What is it?' Carly's chin wobbled. 'Tell me.'

'Let's sit down, sweetheart.' Ava guided Carly to the sofa and sat beside her, as Luna settled onto the floor at Carly's feet. Taking a juddering breath, Ava began to speak. 'Doctor Stewart just called and told me that your dad started bleeding in his brain. They did everything they could, but there's been some damage.' The filtered truth tasted bitter after her promise to Carly, but Ava needed more time. She needed to be able to process the implications of the news she'd just been given, know what decisions she might be facing, before she told Carly anything more. If she could just have more time.

'What kind of damage?' Carly's chin was quivering. 'Is he going to be OK?'

Ava shook her head. 'I'll know more when I've spoken to Doctor Stewart, so let's get Cam on the phone and the sooner I go, the sooner I'll be home, and we can talk then.' She reached a trembling finger out and tucked a twist of hair behind Carly's ear. 'I promise I'll tell you everything I learn, when I get home, OK?'

Carly blinked several times, chewing the inside of her cheek, then whispered, 'Promise?'

'Promise.' Ava carved a cross on her chest and managed a smile as she pushed herself up from the sofa and scanned the floor by the window, looking for her phone.

Two hours later, after a stilted call to a somewhat confused Cameron, who'd mercifully stopped questioning her the minute she'd said, 'It's Rick,' Ava walked back into the hospital. The air inside was thick as she passed through A&E, ignoring the smiling nurses she would ordinarily have waved to, heading for Rick's room.

The tacky-floored corridors she'd walked almost daily for the past five months seemed newly grim to her, the walls scuffed with marks from the beds that were wheeled around, carrying faceless people struggling with the cruel hand life had dealt them. The yellow-tinged overhead lights seemed insipid rather than comforting now, and the smell of cleaning solution mixed with her own fear was rancid, as she tried to breathe without gagging.

Outside Rick's room, Doctor Stewart stood with his head bowed as a petite young nurse who Ava didn't recognise spoke quietly in his ear. Seeing her approach, he straightened up and the nurse filtered away, leaving the doctor hovering by the glass door.

Ava willed herself forward, knowing that however much she wanted to turn and run back down the chilly corridor, she had to face this, take in what he was going to say to her, each word torn straight from her nightmares, and the crippling fear she'd been keeping at bay for so many months, forming itself into a ghastly reality.

'Ava.' He held his hand out to her, but she couldn't raise her own to take it. 'Let's sit down for a while.' He gestured towards the waiting area behind him. 'Please.' Again, he held his hand out, but this time in more of a plea than an invitation. Sensing that, Ava slid her fingers into his and let him guide her to the spongy chair in the corner.

Doctor Stewart sat opposite her, an electronic tablet held close to his front. 'Did you bring anyone with you?' He glanced towards the corridor as Ava shook her head, silently. 'All right, well, as I told you on the phone, I'm sorry to say that the bleed caused so much damage to Richard's brain stem that his situation is irreversible. Richard has been pronounced clinically brain-dead, Ava. I'm sorry.'

Before she could stop herself, Ava snapped. 'Rick. His name is Rick.'

Taken aback, Stewart held his palm up in apology. 'Sorry, Rick. Rick is…'

'I know, I heard you the first time.' She cut him off, the sharpness of her tone and its potential to hurt him, even just a little, somehow easing the roiling pain inside her. Seeing him lean back, a look of resignation in his eyes, her gran's wise words, *Don't shoot the messenger*, filtered back to her. 'Sorry,' she whispered.

He assessed her for a few seconds, then leaned forward again. 'There are several things we need to discuss, the first of which is Rich— em, Rick being an organ donor. If you want to consider that, time is of the essence.' He eyed her. 'Ava, I'm so sorry. It is the hardest thing to bring up at a time like this, but we have to, and Rick obviously wanted this.'

Doctor Stewart moved to the chair next to her. 'I know how difficult this is.' He rubbed the side of his nose with his thumb. 'We have to ask now, while everything is still viable.' He dropped his gaze to the floor. 'We also need to talk about the timing of life-support cessation, and what arrangements you'll need to make.' He stood up and took a step towards the corridor. 'But, first, you'll want to see him.' He swept a hand out to his side. 'Take as long as you want, then please come and find me. I'll be in my office and I'll answer any questions you have. Are you sure there isn't someone we can call, to come and be with you?'

Unable to form a word, Ava simply shook her head, her insides quaking as she stood up and walked behind him, the floor spongy beneath her feet.

Rick looked just the same as when she'd left him, barring the heavy bandage around his head. His chest moved slightly under the sheet as the ventilator ticked and hissed, its work now a scam, a fruitless endeavour that made Ava want to scream as she shed her jacket and pulled a chair in next to the bed.

His hand was cold and papery as she slid hers underneath it, the cool breeze filtering in the window bringing the musk of faded roses and the peaty smell of earth, of living things, now somehow insulting inside the clinical space.

'Rick. I'm here.' She covered his hand with her other one and closed her eyes, sending all her strength through her fingers, picturing sparks of energy connecting them, a last attempt to reach him, before she released his hand, laying it gently back on the sheet. 'I need help. I need to know you're ready.' The words scalded her throat. 'I don't know if I can do this.' Tears tracked down her cheeks.

Earlier, knowing it was a bad idea, as soon as she'd called Doctor Stewart back, she'd taken her laptop upstairs and researched what would happen with the removal of life support. The imagery it had induced had been so impossible to digest, she'd slammed the laptop shut, peeled her clothes off and taken a long hot shower before coming downstairs to open the door to Cameron. He'd taken one look at her face, opened his arms wide and held her against his chest for a few moments, wordlessly giving her his support until she eased herself away, muttering about how long she might be, and thanking him for being there.

Now, as she scanned the room, the monitors and machines that had been a lifeline seemed like the enemy. She looked down at Rick, his dark hair, longer than he'd ever have left it, curling at his neck, a dark shadow on his cheeks and jaw where she'd have shaved him the next day. Seeing it, she stood up and walked to the bathroom, lifted his razor from the shelf and returned to the bed. Switching it on, she gently ran it over his face and neck, the buzzing a comforting, if fleeting, reminder of normality as the machine vibrated in her hand.

Satisfied that he would have approved of her work, she switched off the razor and ran her fingers over his cheek, letting them linger on his jaw. 'I can't let you go, my love. I just can't make this decision.' She leaned down, her brow resting on his forearm, as her tears trickled over his skin. 'I really need to know if you're ready, and if there's a chance for Carly, if you want me to...' Her voice failed her.

Sitting up, she lifted the razor and took it back to the bathroom, this time sliding it into the little drawstring bag that she'd found in the kitchen at Loch na brae, the day after the accident. His toothbrush hung in a metal holder, crisp and useless, and a deodorant and some toothpaste stood on the narrow shelf above the sink. The resident stone shifting in her chest, Ava lifted the items and added them to the bag, then hung it on the hook on the back of the door.

As she walked back into the room, a movement in the corner of her eye made her stop in her tracks. Catching her breath, she squinted at Rick's arm, where a beautiful scarlet butterfly sat on the thistle tattoo, its gossamer wings, with small, sky-blue circles at each tip, lifted in a V shape, vibrating ever so slightly. Afraid to move, Ava watched the little creature walk around the outline of the flower, the purple bloom yielding nothing that could sustain it.

Just as Ava took a tentative step forward, the butterfly lifted its wings, closing them like two palms coming together in prayer, then it opened them and rose into the air, fluttering in a small circle before heading to the open window.

'Don't go,' Ava whispered as she moved to Rick's bedside. 'Not yet.'

The butterfly settled on the windowsill, the powdery wings lifting and lowering as if in farewell, then it flew out of the narrow crack, leaving Ava bereft.

She sank onto the chair and put her head in her hands, cold resignation creeping up her back. 'OK, love. I heard you.' She choked out the words. 'I understand.'

The next half an hour slithered by, Ava numb, sitting in Doctor Stewart's office in a surreal haze, as he explained the process of removing life support, and the steps they would take. He told her that they'd remove the feeding tube, then stop the ventilator, and he warned her that at this stage it was possible that Rick's breathing might alter, momentarily speeding up or slowing down, and then may pause, the pauses getting longer until it was over. Then they'd turn off the monitor in the room and leave her alone with him, in order to say her goodbyes.

As she listened, trying not to give way to the scream that was clogging her throat, all she could think was that, finally, she could ask the question, the one that had haunted her for months now. Licking her lips and meeting his gaze, she spoke carefully. 'What about the organ donation? How, I mean when…?' The idea that Rick might help others, maybe even their precious daughter, began to glimmer under the ash of what lay ahead.

'We'd have you do some paperwork today, then as soon as life support is terminated, and you've given your consent, we'd harvest Rick's organs.' Doctor Stewart avoided her eyes. 'It needs to happen within twenty-four hours, Ava, so that they remain viable for transplant.'

As she looked at the face that had become as familiar to her as her own these past months, the agonising thought that had been whispering to her was now bellowing, surging up from the depths of her soul.

As she hesitated for a few seconds, Doctor Stewart eyed her. 'What is it, Ava? You can ask me anything.'

A dam giving way, Ava blurted, 'What about his eyes? Is there any way…'

Instantly grasping where she was going with this, Doctor Stewart shook his head. 'No. We'd only harvest the corneas, and that wouldn't help Carly, I'm afraid.' He gave her a sad smile.

Ava's heart somersaulted in her chest, the weight of the crippling burden she'd been carrying sliding away into the warmth of the room, as a single tear broke free and trickled down her cheek.

CHAPTER THIRTY

As Ava let his words sink in, so the past few months of self-imposed torture were exposed as pointless, a needless drip of painful *what ifs* that had come to nothing.

Her face warmed as, feeling ridiculous, she avoided Doctor Stewart's eyes. 'Sorry, I didn't know whether…'

'Don't apologise. Things change all the time in medicine, Ava, and in the future, who knows what might be possible.' He frowned. 'In fact, I was meaning to tell you about a new study I read about. Apparently, there are two universities in America carrying out clinical trials, on a stem cell treatment that can potentially regenerate photoreceptors in the retina where they're damaged, like with Stargardt's disease. They're fabricating retinal cell grafts from stem cells for transplants.'

For a second, another glimmer of hope brought her upright in the chair. 'Could Rick's stem cells… could you…?' She gulped, as Doctor Stewart slowly shook his head.

'Not in this case, Ava. I'm so sorry. But I'll send you the information on the trial, if it's helpful?'

Deflated, she nodded. 'Yes, please.'

As she turned and stared out of the window, her cheeks icy-cold and her mind's eye seared by the pictures Doctor Stewart's words were painting, he continued to talk about the order of events for the following day, each word now muffled, wrapped in layers of denial that she couldn't get through as he told her she could bring music, blankets, photos from home, anything that Rick might want to be surrounded by at the end.

When Doctor Stewart eventually stopped talking, Ava was trembling so badly, he walked around his desk, crouched down in front of her and took her hands in his. 'We'll do everything we can to make this is as painless as possible, Ava.' He paused. 'Whatever you need.'

She locked on his eyes, watery and kind as he assessed her, and she wondered what he was thinking. How many times had he done this thing that she couldn't even contemplate? How many people had he comforted in this way? Seeing the compassion in his face was more than she could bear, so she slid her hands back to her lap, took a shuddering breath and stood up. 'I need to go home. Talk to Carly.' She shoved her hair from her forehead as he stood up and returned to his chair. 'What time should we come in tomorrow?' Focusing on the practicalities of the unimaginable day that awaited her was the only thing that felt doable, every molecule of her being railing against the reality of what was to come.

'Nine o'clock. We'll have everything ready so you and Carly can spend some time with Rick, before…' He looked at the desktop, then back up at her. 'Ava, I'm so sorry.'

Numbness filling her, Ava nodded, unable to meet his gaze. At nine o'clock the next day, she had an appointment with death. 'Yes, I know.' She turned towards the door. 'I'll see you then.'

She walked out of the hospital, her mind in a fog, as outside, the early-evening light was gentle, the cool breeze making her shiver as she crossed the car park, suddenly unsure where she'd left the car. As she stood still, scanning the rows of vehicles, each looking much like the next, her hands curled into tight fists, and she rocked slightly on her numb legs. Where was the damn car?

Spotting the Audi, she stumbled over and slipped into the driver's seat, tugged the door closed and slumped forward, her forehead on the steering wheel, as tears trickled over her knuckles and landed softly on her thighs.

Carly's mouth fell open and her breath hitched, terror filling her eyes.

'Sweetheart, he's gone.' Hearing the words out loud was surreal, the manifestation of so many of Ava's recent nightmares, the ghastly ending that she'd always woken up right before, now sickeningly real. This time, there would be no sweats of relief as she sat up in bed, threw the covers off and walked to the window, seeing the moon, a pristine plate suspended in the midnight sky.

'What do you mean?' A tear oozed onto Carly's freckled cheekbone as she bit her lip.

Ava took a steadying breath, tightening her grip on Carly's fingers across the cushion that separated them, just as the fire gave a loud pop, making them both jump.

'Dad has no brain function, Carly. Since the bleed, his brain stem was damaged and the only reason he is still breathing is because of the life-support machines.' Ava halted, watching Carly's face contort as she took in the information.

'But he is still breathing?' Carly's eyes were questioning as she swiped at her tears.

Ava nodded. 'Only because the ventilator is doing it for him. His brain can no longer function, sweetheart. It will never work again. His other organs, like his heart and kidneys, are still working, but only for as long as they have oxygen. So, if the ventilator is on, they will still work for a while.' Ava fought to find words adequate to explain, without deepening the pain she could already see on her daughter's face.

As always happened in times of crisis, Ava's thoughts went to her gran. 'Remember we talked about this, when Gran Flora died? You asked me what happens, and I told you that I believe the soul of the person goes on, to a better place, and the body is just what's left behind? Well, Dad's gone on to that place. The doctors are keeping him breathing with the ventilator, but if the machine wasn't doing that…'

Carly shifted on the sofa, her narrow hips now facing Ava. 'So, he's brain-dead?' Her eyes flicked to the left as Ava caught her breath at the seemingly brutal statement.

Steeling herself, she nodded. 'Yes, he is.'

The next few moments became frozen, each breath, gesture and sound in the room weighted as if they were operating in slow motion. Carly rolled over and lay her head on Ava's knee, as Luna, softly whining, put her snout on Carly's arm. Ava ran her fingers through Carly's hair, teasing the long tresses into a golden shroud across her knees. The hands of Flora's mantel clock shifted in miniscule increments and a coil of woodsmoke spiralled from the fireplace as a large log shifted, the cracking sound splitting the silence that was keeping them suspended together, in a bubble of time.

Eventually, as her legs began to tingle, Ava shifted, and so Carly sat up, crossing her legs under her and facing the fire. Their momentary hiatus over, Ava braced herself, and turned to her daughter. 'I'm going back to the hospital tomorrow, and the ventilator will be turned off, so if you want to come with me to say goodbye...' She paused. 'I'm not going to pressure you either way, Carly, but I think it will be much harder for you later on if you don't see him.' She forced a swallow, all the while scanning Carly's profile, looking for signs of acknowledgement.

Carly sighed. 'I'd already decided I was going to ask if I could come with you tomorrow.' She swivelled around to face Ava, Carly's nose pink and her eyes swollen. 'I can still see your face when I get in close and use my left eye.' She tapped her temple. 'You're a bit blurry, but I know it's you. And I want to see Dad's face too, one last time, while I can.'

Ava's heart cracked a little more as she took Carly's hand in hers, the timing of this development adding another layer of heartbreak to the day. 'I think that's a really good decision, love. You know, you see with your whole being, and that's a rare gift. You'll be able to remember his face and keep him alive in there.' She lay her palm on Carly's chest, then stroked her hand, the youthful skin warm and supple beneath her thumb. 'I'm so proud of you.'

'Mum?' Carly leaned in, tilting her head to the right. 'Will we be OK?' Her eyes were wide, a sheen of unshed tears making them glow in the firelight.

'Yes, sweetheart. We'll be fine.' Ava nodded. 'It's going to be really hard, and we're going to miss him like hell, but you and I will help each other through it, and we'll get there. It might take us a while, but we *are* strong enough.' Rick's words of just five months earlier resonated, a sign that he was still here with them, inside Ava's every thought, word and action, still participating in the functioning of this family. 'We can do this, Carly.'

With Carly tucked up in bed, her crying having diminished into breathy snuffles, and Luna curled in a ball and snoring softly in her own bed, Ava backed out of the room and gently pulled the door closed. She walked across the living room and poured herself a large brandy, put another log on the fire and, grabbing her phone, sank onto the sofa and called Jenna, the need to hear her friend's mellow voice suddenly like that of oxygen to a drowning man.

'Hello, you. Where have you been? I've been calling all afternoon,' Jenna scolded. 'Out on the razzle again?'

Ava shook her head, the events of the day cascading through her mind then crashing headlong into what awaited her tomorrow, and without warning she burst into tears, the entire course of events tumbling out of her between gasps as her hands shook, brandy sloshing onto her jeans.

'Oh, Ava. Love. I don't know what to say,' Jenna gasped. 'I'm so, so sorry.'

Ava's breath hitched as she tried to compose herself, glancing nervously over her shoulder towards Carly's still closed door. 'I can't take it in. I mean, he's gone, Jenna.' She coughed. 'His heart is still beating, but he's not there.'

'I know. It must be impossible to accept.' Jenna sniffed. 'What can I do? Shall I come?'

Ava shook her head. 'No. Yes. I don't know.' She slumped back against the cushion and sipped some brandy, the amber fluid searing a track down her throat and into her aching chest. 'I'm not sure we are up to company, and tomorrow, well, that's going to be brutal.' She sniffed, rubbing her palm over her raw nose.

'You're not going into the hospital alone, are you?' Jenna sounded shocked. 'Ava, you'll need some support.'

Ava stared into the pinkish glow coming from the flames that were licking the sides of the logs, molten particles sprinkling down onto the brick hearth. 'I'll ask Cam to come with us. Carly wants to see Rick before…' She gulped. 'Thank God she wants to.'

'Oh, yes. That's crucial, so it is,' Jenna said. 'Are you sure you don't want us to come? It might be good for Carly, to have Mandy there.'

Ava swirled the remaining brandy around the wafer-thin glass, the ability to make a decision about anything evading her like shards of eggshell floating in a bowl of whites. 'I'll call you in the morning. I just don't know how we're going to feel.'

'OK, but just stay in touch with me. I'll be frantic about you both if you don't.'

Ava nodded, a chill creeping up her spine as she tipped her head back and finished the brandy. 'I will, I promise.'

'Ava?' Jenna's voice was so soft, Ava squinted and pressed the phone closer to her ear. 'He was an amazing man, and Mandy and I loved him so much.' She paused. 'You two had a phenomenal life, a love that everyone deserves.' Her voice cracked. 'Just remember that.'

Ava sniffed as fresh tears coursed down her cheeks. 'Love you.' She choked out the words.

'Love you too, girl. I'm here. Whatever. Whenever.'

'I know.' Ava nodded, swiping at her cheeks. 'I know.'

CHAPTER THIRTY-ONE

The following morning, Cameron arrived twenty minutes early, but, to Ava's relief, rather than come to the door, he stayed out in the Land Rover. The engine was idling as a smoky feather floated from the exhaust pipe, and the distant thump of a bass made Ava squint, the thought of listening to music, something so ordinary, unimaginable today.

Carly was still in her room, and Ava could hear her talking softly to Luna as she moved around, the scrape of a drawer and the clink of something metal against porcelain suggesting that Carly was choosing some earrings from the Spode dish that had once belonged to Flora, that sat on her dresser.

As Ava stood in the kitchen, a cup of tepid tea in her hand, her senses were on overdrive. Every sensation was turned up to maximum volume as she tried to keep her mind clear, willing her skin to hold tight, to keep her from melting into a puddle on the gleaming wood floor.

Cameron had been calm and collected the previous night, when she'd told him what was happening and asked if he could possibly drive them in to the hospital.

'You know I will, Ava. Whatever you need,' he'd said. 'What else can I do?'

'Nothing, honestly. I know this is a huge ask, but I just can't imagine driving home after…' She'd been unable to continue, and he'd stepped in, saving her from her own thoughts.

'You mustn't be alone. I'll take you both in and sit with Carly for as long as you need, then bring you home. I'll drop off some dinner that you can just warm up, and I'll only be ten minutes away if you need me to come back later. Or, I could sleep on the sofa, if you want company. Whatever you need.' He'd sighed. 'I wish I could do more.'

'That is more than enough, really. I don't know what I'd do if you weren't here, Cam. You've become such a part of our lives, these past months.' She'd stood at the window in the living room, watching the gruesome day fade to grey, as the rain pattered the glass, rivulets trickling down the panes in curly rows. 'I'm so grateful to have you.'

'I feel the same. You two are like family to me now,' he'd said.

'Good friends are the family we choose, right?' she'd whispered.

'Aye, too true. Try to get some sleep and I'll see you in the morning.'

Ava had taken a long bath, slipping down and letting the water fill her ears then cover her face momentarily, the silence surrounding her, blocking out everything except the thump of her heart. She'd soaked for almost an hour, topping up the water as it cooled, then she'd tiptoed past Carly's door, pausing briefly to listen for the steady breathing that indicated that her daughter had finally fallen asleep.

Upstairs, Ava had pulled on Rick's T-shirt and then wrapped his giant towelling robe around her, and just as she'd been about to get into bed, she'd stepped back, pulled a blanket from the cedar chest and gone downstairs.

Shoving two new logs onto the glowing embers, she'd lain on the sofa, covered herself with the blanket and watched the fire until the sun had risen, creeping into the room and illuminating the creamy walls with a watery light. She'd got up and made coffee, then snuck back upstairs, not wanting Carly to know she'd been downstairs all night, and now, with her hair still damp from her shower, wearing the soft blue woollen dress that was Rick's favourite, she poured the cold tea down the sink and waited for Carly to emerge.

There was a chill in the house, the beginnings of autumn leaching in through the stone walls, but not wanting to relight the fire when they were leaving soon, Ava turned up the central heating. Hearing the radiator under the living-room window start to tick, she caught Cameron's eye and waved. He waved back, pointing at his watch, and Ava nodded, turning towards the kitchen just as Carly walked out of her room with Luna, who had a tartan ribbon tied to the back of her harness.

Carly's hair was shining, loose around her shoulders, and she wore her pansy-covered butterfly-catcher shirt, and her denim skirt, over thick brown tights and her blue Ugg boots. While the colour combination was more restrained than usual, Ava focused on the shirt, a pop of purple that she knew Carly now saw as dark grey, the final, cruel fingerprint that Stargardt's disease had left on her young life. As Ava took in this image of her amazing, gifted, intelligent daughter, about to go and say goodbye to the father she adored, Ava's throat knotted.

'We're ready.' Carly smoothed her hair, her chin wobbling. 'Forward, Luna.'

The dog moved carefully towards her, as Ava, switching off the overhead light, slung the dove-grey pashmina that Rick had given her for their last anniversary around her shoulders, lifted her handbag from the sideboard and followed her daughter out the door.

They remained mostly quiet on the short drive to the hospital, Carly snuggling in the back seat with Luna and Ava, her face turned to the window, counting the trees that flashed past them, willing them to multiply and elongate the time between now and what was waiting for her.

Twenty short minutes later, they were sitting in the car park, and Cameron shut off the engine. 'Are you ready to go in?' He looked over at Ava, who took a moment to compose herself.

'Yes.' She watched Carly in the rear-view mirror, patting Luna's head, then fingering the glossy ribbon. 'Ready, Carly?'

Carly lifted her chin, her eyes flickering to the left as she slid on her sunglasses. 'Yes,' she whispered, her fingers winding around Luna's collar as, seeming to sense Carly's anxiety, the dog began to pant.

Cameron came around and opened Ava's door, helping her slide to the ground, apparently not noticing the tremble in her legs. He then waited for Carly to climb out of the back, carefully closing the door behind her, then he took both their hands and walked them across the tarmac towards the entrance, just as a gust of wind picked up behind them, chilly and insistent, seeming to usher them inside.

As they approached Rick's room, Ava was relieved that the corridor was empty, and Doctor Stewart was nowhere to be seen. She really wanted this time for Carly to see her father, after months of absence, and have it be untainted by white coats hovering around, drawing her focus.

'Cam, I'll take Carly in. You can wait over there, if you like.' She pointed to the seating area. 'I'll join you in a few minutes.'

Cameron leaned down and kissed Carly's cheek, then paced off towards the clutch of worn chairs grouped around a low, Formica coffee table.

Ava turned to Carly, who was chewing the cuticle around her thumb, her other hand gripping Luna's harness. 'Are you ready, love?'

Carly's glasses were shoved in her pocket and as she leant down to kiss Luna's head, they slipped out onto the floor. 'Hell's bells,' she hissed, bending over and patting the ground in search of the plastic frames.

'I'll get them.' Ava snatched up the glasses and tucked them into her bag. 'OK. Shall we?'

Carly hesitated for a second, then nodded, her eyes filling and her shoulders lifting as she took a deep breath. 'Ready.'

With Carly settled in a chair at the bedside, Ava moved to the far side of the room. Carly leaned in towards her father, her fingers resting on the bed covers as she twisted her head to the right and lowered her chin. 'Hi, Dad, it's me,' she whispered. 'Sorry I haven't been in to see you for a while.' She pursed her lips, shaking her head almost imperceptibly. 'I was scared to come.' Her chin began to quiver, making Ava want to rush over and hold her, but she stopped herself. This was Carly's time, and she needed space to spend it with her father, and Ava would respect that. 'Luna's here too. She's such a good girl, Dad. You'd love her.' Carly let her hand float down to Luna's head. 'She'd love you, too.' Her voice caught, then she turned to Ava, her chin circling. 'Can I please speak to him alone?'

Startled, Ava hesitated for a moment, then nodded. 'Of course, love. Take your time. I'll be right outside the door if you need me.'

'Thanks, Mum.'

Ava touched Carly's shoulder lightly as she passed, then walked out of the room, sliding the door almost closed.

Across the wide hall, Cameron sat in a chair, his long legs stretched straight out in front of him as he leaned back, his head touching the wall behind him and his eyes closed. Ava willed him to look at her, but he stayed still, and afraid to move too far from her daughter, she hovered outside the half-open door.

As Carly began to speak, Ava tried not to listen, to give Carly the privacy she'd asked for, but the gentle tone of her daughter's voice drew her closer to the door, until she was leaning against the glass, her ear near the opening.

'I can still see around the edges, and my left eye is still my best. But the smudgy bit in the middle is much bigger now, and a lot of the colours have gone, so I see mostly greys and greens. It's like a big grey fingerprint right in the middle of everything, but when I move my eyes, the fingerprint goes too.' She paused, and Ava held her breath, hoping Carly hadn't noticed her presence. 'I miss some things, like seeing my face properly in the mirror, and reading a normal book, not on the iPad or VMS. I mean that's helpful and everything, but I miss snuggling up with a book and falling asleep at night.'

Ava bit down on her lower lip, the image of Carly surrounded by her favourite paperbacks, a thing of the past.

'I love my phone, and all the cool apps that help me, though. There's one that identifies colours, and another that tells me what things are in front of me, like a can of soup, or a banana.' She laughed softly. 'Though I can still see the difference.'

Closing her eyes, Ava pressed her hand to the glass of the door, the cool surface feeling almost damp under her clammy palm.

'I want you to know that you've been the best dad in the world. You always took care of me and Mum, and I'm going to miss you so, so much. Forever.' She sniffed. 'But don't worry about us. Mum and I are going to be OK. We'll help each other, and now we have Luna too, and Cam, and Kelly. We're not alone anymore, Dad, so if you have to go, it's all right.'

Ava's throat clamped shut, her eyes blurring as she stepped back from the door. Startled by her daughter's words, but marvelling at the strength of this young person she'd had a hand in creating, she looked over at Cameron, who was now standing, his hands deep in his pockets as he stared at her. Seeing her look over, he mouthed 'OK?' Ava simply nodded, turning back to the door and peeking into the dimly lit room.

Carly had dropped Luna's harness and was holding Rick's hand between her small palms. 'Thanks for being so much fun. For always making me and Mum laugh, and for listening when I told you stuff about how I was feeling. You never made me feel silly or bad about anything, even if I was being a pain.' Her voice hitched, tugging at the invisible string that connected Ava's centre of being to her daughter's. 'I'm going to be all right, Dad. I'll be brave and strong, and all the things you said I was, even though I didn't believe you.'

Ava's skin was burning now, her every fibre soaked in the desire to rush in and grab her daughter, then shake her husband and scream that this wasn't going to happen to them, but she stood still, folding her arms across her chest to contain herself.

'I love you, Dad. I always will. And I'll keep a picture of your face locked in here, like a portrait.' She released his hand and tapped her chest. 'You can go to sleep now.' She dropped her head and kissed the back of his hand as Ava covered her eyes with her palms, the picture she was seeing too much like staring at a solar flare. 'Bye, Dad.' Carly sat up and wiped her eyes with her sleeve. 'I love you to the stars and back.'

Ava moved away from the door, wiping her eyes and blowing out a long breath as Carly walked out into the corridor, her face flushed, and her hair stuck to her tear-stained cheek on one side. She ordered Luna forward and, as she approached Ava, she lifted her chin.

'Where's Cam?' She twisted her head to the left as Ava gently turned her in the direction of the waiting area. 'He's over there, love. Straight ahead of you now,' Ava whispered.

Carly focused on Ava's face. 'Dad looks peaceful.' She hesitated. 'Like he's just asleep.'

'I know. That's how we'll think of him. Sleeping soundly.' She touched her fingertip to Carly's cheek. 'Go and sit with Cameron, and I'll see Dad for a bit, then I'll come and get you.'

Carly nodded, turned towards Cameron and said, 'Forward, Luna.'

As Ava hesitated at the half-open door, Doctor Stewart appeared at her side.

'Ava, hello.' He held her gaze. 'Are you ready?'

'No. Not yet.' Panic swelled up inside her as he stepped back.

'Of course. Take your time. I'll be at the nurses' station, so just come and get me. I'll be over there.' He pointed at the desk at the far end of the corridor. 'Whenever you're ready.' His last word was paralysing. She would never be ready for this.

Ava slid the door closed behind her and walked over to the window. She opened the outer curtains fully, letting the morning light flood through the sheer nets. From her bag, she pulled out her phone and searched for the Jack Johnson track that they'd danced to on the moonlit terrace of the villa they'd stayed in on their honeymoon, and when it started to play, she set the phone on the bedside cabinet. She took out the stub of the drafting pencil that she'd found on Rick's worktable and carefully put it in his hand, trying to wrap his unresponsive fingers around it, eventually just tucking it under his palm.

Then, she slipped his wedding ring back on his wasted finger, took out the bottle of Chanel he'd given her for her last birthday, scattered a few drops on a tissue and laid it next to his head. She dragged the pashmina from her shoulders and draped it over his chest, then carefully slid onto the bed next to him, laying her head on his shoulder.

She took his hand and wound her fingers through his and closed her eyes, seeing them both dancing, walking on the beach, sharing a glass of wine under the giant oak tree at the bottom of the garden in Aberdeen, as Carly, a toddler, ate a handful of mud.

She saw them on their wedding day, then in the labour and delivery room the day Carly was born, then at her fifth birthday party when she fell and bit through her lower lip. She'd screamed bloody murder while Rick iced it, and rocked her on his knee, until she calmed down and they'd taken her to A&E. The nurse had put a tiny butterfly plaster on it, which Carly had refused to take off for a week.

As Ava played the memories over in her mind, like a juddering video reel, she felt Rick's heart beating under her cheek, a gentle pat-pat, pat-pat, that forced her eyes open, its fraudulent message shaking her to her core.

As she lay still, breathing in the scent of perfume mixed with her own warm breath, she conjured Rick's voice, the gentle rumble that came from deep inside his chest, and she screwed her eyes up as she strained to hear what he was saying. Then, she remembered the gossamer wings of the butterfly, and deep within her, in that shadowy corner where she often found answers she wasn't looking for, she acknowledged the truth. Despite the depth of that certainty, she still didn't know if she had the strength to sit up, to tear herself from his side, this one last time, to walk out into that corridor and find Doctor Stewart, tell him she was ready to let go.

As she opened her eyes, blinking her vision clear, she heard Rick's voice inside her head, clear and calm. '*You are strong enough, Ava. You can do this.*'

She tipped her chin up and kissed his cheek, the fresh stubble sparking like a thousand tiny needles under her dry lips. She pulled in another breath and pushed herself up from the bed, smoothed the blanket around his hips and tucked a dark curl behind his neck, feeling the tiny hairs alive under her fingertips. Leaning in, she kissed his mouth, his lips cold and unyielding, and as she stood up, looking down on the love of her life, Ava whispered, 'Always and forever. You were the one.'

Outside, in the waiting area, Carly sat next to Cameron, her head on his shoulder as Luna lay at her feet. Ava walked slowly towards them, unsteady on her legs as she focused on her daughter's beautiful face, the features that she knew so well, and that resembled her father's more with every passing year.

Carly stood up. 'Mum?' She frowned as, next to her, Cameron shifted in the seat, his eyes on Ava's.

Ava nodded and held out a hand. 'Coming?'

Carly nodded. 'Forward, Luna.' The dog rose smoothly from the floor and took up her position at Carly's leg, then walked forward. Nodding at Cameron, Ava took Carly's free hand and they turned back towards Rick's room.

Inside, Ava moved both the chairs to the bedside, helping Carly sit on Rick's right. As Ava was about to settle in the other chair, Carly reached into her pocket and pulled out her phone. 'I want to show you something.' She twisted her head to the right, seeking Ava's face.

Unsure whether Carly was talking to her or Rick, Ava moved to the end of the bed.

'Mum, can you close the curtains and turn off the lights please, then sit next to Dad?' Carly felt for the bed, laying her palm flat on the blanket.

Momentarily confused but determined to give her daughter whatever comfort she could, Ava smoothed the net curtain out of the way and drew the heavy outer curtains together again, then crossed the room and put her finger on the light switch. 'Carly, I'm not sure…'

'Please, Mum.' Carly was insistent.

Ava sighed, then flipped the overhead light off, leaving the room in close to darkness. As she focused on her daughter's shape, adjusting to the murky light, Ava saw Carly hold her phone up to her left eye and stroke the screen several times.

'Come and sit with us.' Carly pointed at the bed, so Ava slipped behind the chair and perched on the edge of the mattress.

Carly twisted in the chair, aiming the phone up at the ceiling, then hit the screen with her thumb. As Ava looked up, still confused by this bizarre course of events, there on the ceiling was an image. Stunning rivers of green and blue floated ethereally across a deep-blue night sky, shards of pink and gold spearing down towards the ground, like ghostly fingers searching for something below. A scattering of stars sparkled behind the colours, pinpricks of light that gave the sky depth, and the entire image undulated as if a gentle wind was blowing from the west, easing the aurora borealis across the ceiling.

Ava's mouth sagged as she craned her neck back, taking in the spectacle, still unsure how this was happening. She dropped her chin and looked over at Carly, who was holding the phone steady, staring at the ceiling.

'Carly, how…? Ava whispered.

Carly blinked, not taking her eyes off the colour-streaked sky. 'It's a projector app.' She tipped the phone towards her, raising the image even higher so it was directly above Rick's head. 'We promised…' She fell silent as, in the light emanating from the phone, Ava saw tears trickling down her daughter's cheek.

Her throat tightly knotted, Ava reached over and squeezed Carly's shoulder. 'You are amazing. Absolutely amazing.' She swallowed her tears and shook her head, as Carly reached out with her free hand and found Rick's fingers.

'This is for you, Dad. Just like we said. We'd see it all together.'

Speechless, Ava tipped her head back again and took one more look at the spectacle above her, something she and Rick had talked about sharing with Carly ever since she'd been born. As the image flickered, so Ava's heart followed suit, momentarily halting altogether, then starting up again as she watched the spectacular colours shift and melt together in a palette of light and shade. As the image began to fade, the agonising symbolism made Ava press her eyes closed, just as one last ray of light speared down through the stars.

A few seconds went by until she could look over at Carly. 'That was spectacular.' Ava willed herself up from the bed and walked round the chair to Carly. 'Dad would have loved that.'

Carly slipped the phone away. 'Is it time?' She stared up at Ava, the look on her face one that Ava would never forget.

'Yes, love. It's time.' Ava took Carly's hand and helped her up, and they stood, side by side in the dark, mother and daughter, sister-warriors, looking down at Rick, husband, father and best friend, each of them locking his image away in their hearts, forever.

EPILOGUE

The year since Rick's passing had flown by, and this morning, as Ava stood and looked at the Guide Dogs for the Blind calendar that Carly had insisted they hang in the kitchen, the significance of the date had pulsed its presence into her heart, as she had taken a moment to let everything that had happened permeate.

Rick's absence still left a gaping hole in every day, but so much had changed that life had finally taken on a kind of calm. Now, when Ava woke in the mornings, walked across the bedroom and drew the curtains to let the light flood in the window, rather than want to hide from it all, she looked forward to her day.

She and Carly were enjoying the trips they'd take at the weekends, always talking about Rick and how he'd have loved this particular view, the smell of the rain in the woods, or the new espresso-flavoured ice cream at Alfie's, in The Square. As their lives moved on, they kept him with them, his presence as much a part of them and their family as it had ever been.

Today was a special day for more than just the significant date. The previous month, Ava had sent another email to the university in southern California that Doctor Stewart had told her about. This time, she'd attached all Carly's medical records, as requested, and ever since, had been crossing her fingers each morning as she checked her inbox, willing there to be a response. Just moments ago, in her tiny office, she'd opened an email that had sent her rushing into the hall. She'd tapped at Carly's door, but getting no response, she'd hitched her laptop up against her middle and walked briskly out the front door.

Carly was sitting on the front lawn, with Luna at her side. Her sight had stabilised somewhat, and her colour-correcting glasses had become a fixture whenever she painted. Today, she was sketching on a large pad balanced on her knee, then lifting it to her left eye as her chin did the characteristic circles Ava had grown used to seeing, as Carly sought a point of focus.

Ava made her way over, feeling the sharp stabs of the gravel through her socks, and wishing she'd taken a moment to slip on some shoes. 'Damn,' she hissed as a particularly evil stone stabbed her instep before she leapt onto the spongy grass.

Hearing her mother, Carly dropped the pad and turned. 'Mum? What's up?'

Ava paced over, sat down, crossing her legs under her, and balanced the laptop on her knees. 'I want you to read this. Hang on.' She maximised the size of the typeface on the screen and turned it towards Carly. 'Can you see it, love?'

Carly leaned in, turned her head and, using her left eye, squinted at the wording, her chin circling until she suddenly held still, her lips moving as she read. As Ava watched, the colour rose in Carly's cheeks and a smile tugged at her mouth. 'Did I read that right?' She looked at Ava, her face full of guarded excitement.

'I think so.' Ava re-read the brief email, a few lines that, while seeming innocuous, had the potential to change absolutely everything for Carly. 'So, how do you fancy a trip to America?' Ava's face tingled as Carly carefully reached for Luna's harness and stood up.

Her pulse picking up, and yet somewhat unsure what reaction she'd get to this news, Ava closed the laptop, left it in the grass and stood too, keeping her eyes on her daughter's face.

Just as Ava was about to ask the question again, Carly smiled so radiantly that Ava had to blink. 'Will I have to wear a cowboy hat?' Carly threw her head back and laughed, dancing from one foot to the other, a movement that Luna began to imitate.

'No, you wally. We're not going to Texas. We're going to California. The land of surfers, Disney and Hollywood.' Ava started bouncing on the spot, at first small lifts, her heels just leaving the warm grass, then gradually with more gusto, until she was jumping, lifting her feet high up behind her repeatedly, kicking blades of grass into confetti as she punched a fist towards the sky, until eventually Carly followed suit.

Exhausted, Ava flopped onto the grass, panting and laughing, as Carly sat down next to her.

'Am I really getting on the trial?' She sounded breathless. 'For real?'

Ava sat up, sweeping the hair away from her sweaty forehead. 'You are, my love. You are.'

Carly shook her head. 'I can't believe it. Mandy and I were reading the other day about stem cell therapy, and it's amazing what they can do.' Her mouth hung open. 'Imagine, Mum, if I can see properly again. Imagine how happy Dad would be.'

Ava smiled, unsurprised that Carly would default to Rick, and how he might react to something this momentous happening in her young life. Picturing him, the gentle eyes that had captured her heart, the warm smile, the capable hands always ready to take on her burdens, the man who was filled with such passion for his family that he'd have pulled down the stars for them if he could, Ava smiled. 'He'd be absolutely over the moon, love.'

'Perhaps this is happening because of him?' Carly turned to face Ava, her brow creasing.

'What do you mean, sweetheart?' Ava crossed her legs under her, the sweet smell of the approaching summer floating up the hill from the firth, on the gentle breeze that played with her hair.

'Well, he gave his organs to help lots of other sick people, didn't he? And he'd have given his stem cells too, if he could.' Carly focused on Ava's face, her chin circling. 'Maybe even to me.'

Ava's heart faltered, the depth of her daughter's understanding and compassion still enough to surprise her at times. 'Yes, of course he would.'

'So perhaps because Dad paid it forward like that, that's why I'm going to get this chance, this help from other people? It's like Dad made it happen.' She spread her arms wide, her eyes glinting behind a film of tears.

Fighting the prickle behind her eyes, Ava reached for her daughter, their fingers weaving together. She draped her free arm around Carly's shoulder and leaned in, their heads touching lightly at the temple. 'That is a perfect way to think about it, Carly. You know he'd have given you the world, if he could.'

Carly nodded. 'If this works, he kind of is.'

'Yes, my love. He is.' Ava pictured Rick smiling at her, nodding his approval, so she smiled back, sending him all the love she had in her heart, and soul, to keep him company on his next adventure.

A LETTER FROM ALISON

Dear reader,

Thanks a million for choosing to read *Her Last Chance*. I sincerely hope you enjoyed reading it as much as I did writing it. If you want to keep up to date with all my latest releases, just sign up at the following link. Your email address will never be shared, and you can unsubscribe at any time.

www.bookouture.com/alison-ragsdale

The idea for this book came about after reading an article on two brothers who have Stargardt's disease, and the way they overcame all obstacles to create a thriving business and lead rich and fulfilling lives. This sent my mind spinning about all the challenges, and possibilities, for people with the condition.

I love to write about mothers and daughters, and all the complex iterations of that relationship. Ava and Carly's bond was so fulfilling to develop, especially the way they came together, creating a united front in the face of heartbreaking adversity. Their story is one that will stay with me, as it reflects the strength of spirit and determination in certain, special people in my life, and maybe in yours, too.

The clinical trials that are underway on Stargardt's disease, using stem cell therapy, are incredibly exciting, and it felt important to include that potential for Carly, at the end of the story.

Thanks again for taking the time to read *Her Last Chance*. If you enjoyed it, it would mean the world to me if you would spare a moment to write a review. They are a great way to introduce new readers to my books, so it would be a huge favour to me if you did.

I love to hear from my readers, and you can get in touch with me via my Facebook author page, through Instagram, Twitter, Goodreads or my website. I look forward to it.

Thanks again for reading.
All the best,
Alison Ragsdale

authoralisonragsdale
www.alisonragsdale.com
AlisonRagsdale
alisonragsdalewrites
8529082.Alison_Ragsdale

ACKNOWLEDGEMENTS

My heartfelt thanks to the wonderful team at Bookouture, who dedicated their time, expertise and invaluable support in marshalling this story. Special thanks to my fabulous editor, Maisie, for connecting with my writing, bringing me into the fold, and for helping me sculpt this book from its rather basic beginnings. Also, thanks to Noelle, Lauren, Alba, Jade, Tom, and everyone who helped launch this story into the world. I am so fortunate to be working with a group of such talented professionals.

Heartfelt thanks to Lesley and Carly, my best friends, first readers, and most creative brainstorming partners. Everyone deserves sisters like you.

My sincere thanks to Lisa, of GuideDogs.org.uk, who patiently answered my numerous questions and educated me about the invaluable work these incredible dogs, and their dedicated trainers do to open the world up to so many.

Thanks to my friend and fellow author Peggy, who puts up with my frequent wobbly moments and always has sound advice. Thanks also to all the friends, readers, reviewers, book bloggers, and my Highlanders Club members who support my endeavours. I will never be able to express how much that means to me. Every one of you makes this writing life a gilded place for me to spend time.

Finally, and most importantly, to my wonderful husband. I thank my lucky stars every day that we found each other, and for your endless and unwavering support. I love the bones of you.

Made in the USA
Middletown, DE
01 August 2021